WICKED RIVALS

LAUREN SMITH

LAUREN SMITH

Copyright © 2016 by Lauren Smith

Edited by Noah Chinn

Excerpt from *Wicked Designs* by Lauren Smith

Cover art by Erin Dameron Hill

Illustrations by Joanne Renaud

Romance Art by Theresa Sprekelmeyer

The League of Rogues (R) is an officially registered Federal Trademark owned by Lauren Smith.

ISBN: 978-0-9962079-8-0 (e-book edition)

ISBN: 978-0-9962079-9-7 (print edition)

ISBN: 978-0-9962079-8-0

❀ Created with Vellum

For my mother, who inspired me to be a strong, independent woman and make my own destiny.

CHAPTER 1

League Rule Number 8:
As a man's independence is inextricably tied to his wealth, it is vital that no woman should be allowed to meddle with it, no matter how fine her eyes might be.

EXCERPT from the *Quizzing Glass Gazette*, May 29, 1821, the Lady Society column:

LADY SOCIETY IS ISSUING a challenge to Lord Lennox. She can't help but think he is afraid of a certain lady who is in direct competition with him.

Come now, Lord Lennox, what holds you in such fear and trepidation that you cannot be seen with her in public? At Lady Jacintha's ball you turned tail and fled when the cunning lady stepped out onto the dance floor.

You cannot hide forever behind your fleet of ships, nor can you call upon your friends for support. The League of Rogues are fast succumbing to the charms of Eros and taking wives. Perhaps they know something you choose to remain ignorant of? For a man of such intellect and acumen, surely you cannot let that stand.

I challenge you, my cool, collected baron, to spend one night with the lady and be on your best behavior. Wedding bells, dare I say, shall ring shortly thereafter.

"YOU WANT me to do what, my lord?"

Ashton Lennox stared at the gray-haired banker sitting across from him in the offices of Drummond's Bank. He knew what he was asking of the other man was daring—and quite possibly illegal. Nonetheless, retaliation was required against certain players in his field of business. That didn't mean his demands wouldn't frighten any banker with good sense.

"It's as simple as I said, Mr. Reed. I want you to deny Lady Melbourne gold credit if she should come to you seeking a loan." As he spoke, he let his words come out in that cold, smooth voice that brooked no argument, and he finished by brushing his fingertips over his trousers, smoothing them out. By the age of thirty-three, Ashton had learned how to make men do his bidding with a cool stare and an imperious tone. Those who crossed him or dared to go against his wishes often ended up suffering a blow to their financial positions.

"But, my lord," Mr. Reed said, his eyes as wide as teacup saucers, "she's always been a valued client here—"

"I've no doubt of it, but you and I have an understanding, do we not?" Despite his tone, it was not a question. Ashton met Reed's now frightened gaze. "It was I, as you'll recall, who assisted you in selecting the consols to invest in last year. You were able to buy a country house in Sussex with the profits you made, were you not? I would think you'd like to keep my counsel on future matters."

The old banker's throat worked, and he managed a shaky nod.

"I am grateful, of course, but with regard to the lady in question, she is…" He struggled for words.

"Troublesome?" Ashton supplied, the word escaping on a growl as his cool demeanor threatened to unravel whenever he thought of *her*.

Lady Rosalind Melbourne was more than just troublesome. As owner of Melbourne, Shelly & Company, she'd spent the last several months stealing bids on shipping lines and purchasing other companies by underbidding him.

The woman was a menace. He'd done everything a reasonable man could do by offering to buy out her shares and attempting to go about his own business, but she'd undermined his every effort —or more to the point, every *legal* effort. Had she been a man, he would have admired her tactics, the way she outflanked him, outmaneuvered him at every turn.

But she wasn't a man, she was a woman—an intoxicating, beautiful, *infuriating* menace of a woman, with a fiery Scottish temper that pushed him out of his own control.

The situation was not acceptable. Control was his foremost weapon and his first line of defense. Where other men lost their bodies to passions, their minds to obsessions and their hearts to love, he always stayed in control of himself.

Except when it came to Rosalind. If she hadn't been a woman, he would have called her out long ago and settled their differences on a field at dawn. It took a moment for him to regain his focus on the matter at hand.

"Are we in agreement, Mr. Reed? You will do as I've asked?"

Ashton rose from his chair and towered over the banker.

Swallowing hard, the older man nodded. "We will, Lord Lennox. Lady Melbourne will find her requests for credit denied until you direct me to do otherwise."

Ashton inclined his head in approval and left Reed's office. He straightened his cravat and retrieved his hat from the rack in the corner outside the office. Once at the front entrance of Drummond's, he hailed a hackney.

"Where to, my lord?" the driver asked.

"Berkley's Club." Ashton climbed inside the coach and leaned back with a sigh.

"Very good, my lord."

After this morning, an afternoon at Berkley's was exactly what was needed. He didn't enjoy using such drastic measures, but there was more at stake here than professional pride. Lady Melbourne's companies were being used by the only man in England who worried Ashton enough to make him lose sleep at night.

Sir Hugo Waverly had been seen visiting with the captains of Lady Melbourne's ships, and his men, or men whom Ashton suspected worked for Waverly, had been on her passenger lists more and more frequently. He suspected Waverly was using Rosalind's companies somehow. It was unclear what Waverly was up to, but Ashton believed it wasn't good.

There was a secret war going on, one fought not with guns or swords but with eyes and words, and not on open plains but in the shadows. Hugo had declared this war some time ago, and Ashton had been mustering a defense in his own silent way. It was in the best interest of the League to take control of the situation, which at the moment meant taking control of Lady Melbourne's companies so that he could analyze her business activities and see how Waverly might be linked to them.

Ashton had visited five banks in the city this morning and had secured promises from each that Lady Melbourne would not be able to obtain credit. That way, when his friends called in their notes at each bank, she would not have the means to pay for their notes in gold.

It would crush her. At least temporarily. The woman would not be down for long; Ashton wasn't foolish enough to believe he could ruin her. But a temporary blow to her income and self-sufficiency would be enough to bring her to heel.

Lady Melbourne brought to heel. A delicious thought indeed. *I will own you, Rosalind.*

Unable to stop himself, he thought back to the night when he'd caught her alone in an alcove of a theater. The intention had been to talk with her, convince her to leave his companies alone, but then he'd touched her and that plan had vanished, and something more primal had emerged.

He'd tried to use her body's response to his against her by bringing her to the brink of passion, only to let her suffer without relief as a reprimand for her unorthodox business tactics. It had been a foolish indulgence, yet in that moment he had been unable to help himself.

It also hadn't worked.

Instead, she'd turned the tables on him, and he'd come undone with the tight stroke of her hands. The memory of seeing her drop one dainty white glove at his feet, in a manner befitting a challenge to a duel, still made him hard. A duel of wits fought with seductive means... It was just how he liked to play his games. And now he'd met a woman who played as wickedly as he did.

Moves and countermoves, like a game of chess. Grudging admiration for her was impossible to deny, but he was determined not to let her win.

The coach rattled to a stop in front of the elegant townhouse that had been the home of Berkley's Club for more than fifty years. Berkley's had not been the only gentlemen's club Ashton had gained an invitation to, though it had been the only one he'd accepted. It had appealed to him, for those moments when he wanted to escape business discussions, political issues, and other things most clubs were famous for. Berkley's was strictly a club for men who wished to escape the whirlwind of life in London.

The club was also the only place where he and his closest friends—the League of Rogues, as the papers had dubbed them—

could settle in comfortably, away from the scandal rags and the gossip of that damned Lady Society. Her articles in the *Quizzing Glass Gazette* seemed determined to out their secrets for the amusement of London's elite. She'd been the one to make their nickname so famous over the last few years.

Ashton would readily admit that the League's title had always been an apt description of the original five members: Godric, Lucien, Cedric, Charles and himself. With the addition of Godric's recently discovered younger brother, Jonathan, they were now six.

Over the years, some of their activities had been ruthless, callous and even dangerous. But things were changing. The dark memories of the past were being buried by new ones, better ones. At least in some ways. They were settling down—a thing Ashton had never thought possible.

It had all started when Godric had abducted a young woman for revenge only to fall in love with her. Now, like ivory domino tiles, they were all falling one by one for women they could not live without. Lucien, one of the more scandalous rogues, had fallen for Cedric's sister, Horatia. And just last month Cedric had surprised everyone by proposing to Anne Chessley, the heiress.

Ashton had realized with some alarm that the League now stood equally divided between free men and those leg-shackled in matrimony. Their afternoon club discussions had changed from topics of seductions and conquests to the upcoming births of babes.

If we aren't careful, the League will change from a force to be reckoned with to a laughingstock. The power we've collected could be squandered, and our enemies will close ranks and try again to destroy us.

The thought made his blood freeze in his veins. The past year had been spent dodging one deadly event or another. The more the League let itself become divided by wives and children, the easier it would be for Waverly to harm the people the League loved the most.

It wasn't that he didn't wish well for his friends. They were happily, madly in love with their wives. But the power they'd all worked hard to attain since leaving university could crumble. New giants would arise from the dust of their fall and new enemies as well. Ashton could not rest until he was certain they were all safe.

Until then he slept with one eye open, and such a duty weighed upon him more and more each day. As the oldest of the members, he felt obligated to be the League's protector.

The cab halted at the entrance to the club. "Berkley's Club," the driver announced.

"Thank you." Ashton stepped out of the cab and paid the driver before walking up the steps. A young lad finely dressed in a Berkley's uniform opened the door for him. Ashton handed the lad his coat and hat.

"Looking for anyone in particular, my lord?"

Ashton tugged on his waistcoat. "Essex, Rochester or Sheridan." He waited to see if any of the titles registered with the boy.

The footman's face lit up into an almost reverent expression. "Of course. They are having drinks in the Bombay Room. Do you know the way, my lord?"

"Yes, thank you." He wandered through the club, passing tables and chairs of men drinking, talking and quietly enjoying a respite from the demands of society. The warm armchairs were welcoming by the fires burning in the hearths, and the smell of food and brandy teased his nose. Berkley's was like a second home.

The Bombay Room had Indian-themed décor and was located on an upper floor. The door was already ajar, and the sound of familiar voices inside filled him with warmth. He allowed few things to matter deeply to him, but the League, aside from his family, was the most important thing in his life.

The first thing Ashton heard as he pushed open the door was Cedric Sheridan's chortling.

"Ash will be furious. Lady Society is calling him out." The viscount was leaning back in his chair, holding a copy of the *Quizzing Glass*, grinning.

"Again?" the others asked.

"It's a good thing whoever writes that column remains anonymous. Ash would destroy her."

"Nothing ruffles Ash. He's far too clearheaded." Godric St. Laurent, the Duke of Essex, reached for the paper and scanned it. "Wait until Emily reads this. She is convinced that Ash and Lady Melbourne need to meet in a proper setting where they are forced to be civil."

Lucien Russell, the Marquess of Rochester, stood by the window and turned at Godric's words. "That's all Horatia has been talking about for the last month. She said Anne invited them to tea with Lady Melbourne this afternoon."

Ashton stood in the doorway, listening to the three married members of the League discuss their wives with lighthearted amusement. He burst out laughing, startling his friends, who hadn't been aware of his presence. "Good Lord, you let your wives meet for tea?"

Lucien was the first to respond. "You know how much trouble it is to try to stop them. If I ever said no, Horatia would throw an embroidered pillow at my head. Followed by a vase."

"They are as bonded to one another as we are, I'm afraid," said Godric. "Even gave themselves that blasted name. The Society of..." He trailed off, forgetting.

Lucien moved his hands in the air, as though displaying the name in the air. "*The Society of Rebellious Ladies.*"

"Quite." Cedric chuckled and put his booted feet up on the nearest table. "So long as Audrey isn't among them, they can't get into too much trouble."

Ashton wasn't entirely certain he agreed with that. Audrey Sheridan was Cedric's youngest sister, and while she was trouble enough, Ashton knew the other ladies were almost as talented at getting into mischief.

"Ash, have a look." Godric handed the *Gazette* to him as Ashton took a chair next to him.

He glanced down at the article they'd been discussing when he arrived. His temper soon flared.

"*Hiding* behind my fleet of ships, am I?" The growl that escaped him was completely unexpected. Struggling for calm, Ashton closed his eyes and counted to ten in Latin as he'd done all his life when quelling his temper. When he opened his eyes again, he was smiling. It mattered naught. His plan was set in motion, and soon Rosalind would be dealt with.

"Well, she does have it right about you three." He checked the article again to recite the exact words. "'Succumbing to the charms of Eros and taking wives.'"

Godric plucked the paper from Ashton's hands. "I wish I knew who wrote this drivel. Probably some old bat on Upper Wimpole Street who can't find a proper way into the *ton*, exercising her vengeance for not being among the elite few." His slightly sarcastic tone hinted at his dislike of his own class.

Lucien swirled his glass of brandy and left his position by the window to take an empty chair by Cedric. Inspiration seemed to strike him.

"Why don't we put our darling wives on it? It would certainly keep them busy and out of our affairs for a change if they were off solving a mystery."

Cedric laughed. "I dare say they might even learn who she is, but there is no way Emily, Anne or Horatia would betray one of their own. And as hard as we try, there's no stopping them when it comes to our affairs."

Ashton nodded his agreement. But the problem that lay heavy upon his heart was the danger that one part of the League's past presented to the women in their lives.

As if echoing Ashton's trepidation, Godric crossed his arms, a grim look in his green eyes. "That reminds me, where do we stand on the Waverly matter?"

Ashton was seized with tension, every muscle knotting. Waverly always drew out dark memories and old fears, along with a tide of guilt.

There was a time that Hugo was merely an annoying privileged sod they'd met at Cambridge. But due to an old family vendetta, Waverly had attempted to kill their friend Charles, but another student had died that night instead. One who had been blameless and only trying to make peace. It was a moment that had changed all their lives.

Ashton's palms twitched, as though he could feel the taint of that innocent man's blood still coating his hands.

"He's been seen at the docks where my fleet is, but I haven't been able to ascertain what his intentions are at present. I suggest we all watch one another until Waverly's next scheme reveals itself."

Godric tried to hold back a scowl but failed. Patience had never been one of his virtues when he felt action could be taken.

Ashton reached into his waistcoat and pulled out a small pocket watch on a slender silver chain. It had been one hour since he'd given his instructions to the last of the banks regarding Rosalind's credit. In less than half an hour, the men he'd met with would be sending in notices to Rosalind's bank to demand their notes be cashed in for gold. The little Scottish hellion would pay for embarrassing him at the theater last month.

If only I could see her face the moment she realizes she's ruined.

Of course, he wasn't so cruel as to send her to debtors' prison. The woman would get her fortune back in time, after he learned what secrets Hugo held within her business, after she learned he was not to be trifled with. Lady Melbourne deserved such a lesson for challenging him.

"Good God, Ash is grinning. That's never a good sign," Lucien muttered.

Ashton broke out of the almost gleeful thoughts he'd been having.

"Ash." Godric's tone was full of warning. "Care to share with us what is going on in that head of yours?"

Cedric, Lucien and Godric all leaned forward, as though afraid to be overheard despite the privacy of the club's Bombay Room. The grandfather clock in the corner chimed the hour, but it did not distract his friends' rapt attention.

Ashton slipped his watch back into his coat pocket and met their stares.

"As of one hour ago, I set a plan in motion that will financially break Lady Melbourne. It will allow me to put a stop to her activities and therefore hurt Waverly."

"She's in league with him?" asked Cedric.

"All I know for certain is that he's been using her ships to his own ends, and I want to stop him. He's partnered with her in several companies, and I wish to gain access to her books as well as shipping manifests. But the only way I can review her companies is to have a claim on them myself. Therefore, I've bought up most of her debts—not that she had many. I will own her in all but name."

A low whistle escaped Cedric's lips. "Ash, our wives have invited her to tea this afternoon."

For the first time in a long while, Ashton felt gleeful. "If only I were there to see her face when she learns the truth." To see her beautiful gray eyes wide with shock, her lips parted as she sucked in a surprised breath... It would be almost as beautiful as having claimed her body in his bed. But since he could not have her body —one did not sleep with one's enemies, after all—this would have to suffice.

It was several moments later when his friends finally broke the silence.

"It's not because of the incident at the theater is it?" Lucien queried. "You're wanting revenge because she got the upper hand in that alcove?" Cedric snickered, and Godric cursed under his breath. It was not the response Ashton had been expecting. In the past, this would have been normal for the League. They would have been congratulating him for such a victory.

"What?" Ash demanded hotly when the others remained silent.

Godric rubbed a hand through his dark hair. "What if Lady Melbourne takes this too personally and brings those wild brothers of hers down from Scotland? I still have nightmares about the last time I tangled with them. One of them broke a bloody chair over my back. I was left to pay for the damages to the tavern we fought in."

"Three wild Scotsmen do not scare me." Ashton had never lost a boxing match, and he had never lost a tavern brawl either. While Charles was the group's true pugilist, Ashton's skill was on par with his, though he fought only when necessary.

"No, *one* should scare you," grumbled Godric. "Three should terrify you."

"Isn't anyone else worried that right now our wives are entertaining the victim of Ash's scheme?" Cedric asked. "If they discover we knew about this, I'm liable to be spending the next month sleeping in my study rather than in bed with my wife."

The murmurs of agreement from Godric and Lucien made Ashton scowl at the lot of them.

"I'm starting to believe Charles was right. You are all getting soft."

Charles had once said that love and marriage were tearing the League apart, destroying its strength. At the time Ashton hadn't been inclined to believe him, but of late...

A rap on the door made them all turn to the entrance of the Bombay Room. A young lad opened the door, his eyes wide and hands shaking a little with the letter he carried. Their reputation still held some in awe, at least.

"Excuse the intrusion, my lords. I have an urgent letter for Lord Lennox." The boy's face darted between them. He sensed he'd interrupted something and no doubt felt the invisible tension present in the room.

Ashton waved at the lad. "Bring it here."

The boy practically threw it at Ashton and fled.

"At least someone still has the good sense to be afraid of us," Godric sniggered.

The thin paper contained a short message from his youngest sister, Joanna.

ASHTON,

You must come home at once. Our two tenant farms caught fire last night and are completely destroyed. Thankfully no one was hurt. The families are safe but without shelter. Please come home. The farmhouses will need to be rebuilt at once.

Yours,

Joanna

ASHTON CALMLY FOLDED the letter and tucked it into the inner pocket of his coat.

"Bad news?" Lucien inquired.

"It's from my sister. She says my two tenant farmers' houses burned down. I must go home at once." He rose from his chair.

"What about Lady Melbourne?" Cedric asked.

"What about her?"

Cedric raised a brow. "You set her up for financial ruin and now you're leaving London?"

A slow smile spread across his face. "If she decides to come grovel at my feet, please feel free to send her to my estate. I'll be happy to entertain her apologies there."

He swept his coat on and left the Bombay Room, leaving his friends behind.

If only it would come to that—Lady Melbourne on her knees,

begging him for forgiveness, her gray eyes bright with pretty tears and her long dark hair swept back in a Grecian fashion. Those long curls caressing her neck...

Yes, Ashton had imagined the scene too often in the last week. How he'd tell Lady Melbourne that if she really wanted to appease him she could think of a few creative ways to make amends, behind closed doors. Not that he could trust her even in bed, and he'd certainly never coerce a woman to bed him, but such fantasies were worth exploring in his head.

Ashton departed Berkley's and hailed a hackney. He would have his valet pack light so they could reach his estate quickly. Joanna's note was troubling. While fires were common enough, the fact that both his tenants were miles apart was troubling.

I do not believe in such coincidences.

Once again he imagined a chessboard in his mind. A game was in play, the League versus Waverly, and the clock was ticking down to each move and countermove.

CHAPTER 2

*H*ands *sliding up her outer thighs, raising her gown, warm breaths soft against her cheek, bright blue eyes aflame with wicked desires and the fall of pale-blond hair...*

"Lady Melbourne?"

Rosalind Melbourne came back to herself. She was sitting in a cozy armchair in a sunny parlor with blue walls. Three sets of feminine eyes were focused on her, all a little concerned. A moment ago, she'd been listening to her hostesses talk about the latest scandals and political intrigues when the conversation had turned to marriages and the men in their lives. It was only natural for her thoughts to turn to Ashton when his friends had been mentioned. And that had led to memories from the last time she'd seen him...at the opera...when they'd both lost control.

I should never have allowed that man to kiss me, nor should I have touched him. It was a mistake.

She reached for the cup of tea nearest her on the table. "I'm sorry. I was woolgathering."

"It's quite all right," Lady Sheridan said, smiling again. "We're so happy you've had a moment to meet with us."

Rosalind smiled back at her. Anne was one of the few women

in the *ton* she tolerated. Most of the simpering fools did not particularly like her either. As a Scottish lady having come from a crumbling castle with three wild brothers, bless them all, she'd had no chance of ever fitting in with normal London society, even when she'd married Lord Melbourne, God rest his soul. The man had been in his sixties when he'd asked for her hand.

That day was never far from her mind. Whenever her brothers hadn't been around, she'd caught her father's attention, and he'd taken his anger out on her. On that last night she'd run from Castle Kincade, almost blind with pain. She'd walked nearly two miles barefoot to the nearest village. Her father's blows still burned her face and back.

She'd stumbled into a tavern in the village and fell into Lord Melbourne's lap when she'd tripped over a loose floorboard. He'd taken one look at her face and with a scowl had said, "No one should treat a lady thus."

He'd insisted on buying her dinner at the tavern. After he'd seen that she was warm and fed and wearing a new pair of boots he'd bought from a barmaid, he'd taken her straight to a black-smith and married her that night.

Poor Henry. Such a sweet man.

After her marriage to Henry, she'd moved into her new London home, and he had died in his sleep only a year later. It had been a long time coming, but now she was the mistress of her own destiny. The dear man had tutored her in the ways of business strategies and banking. She'd always had a natural knack for it, but he had helped foster in her a confidence and knowledge that left her strong and able to stand on her own after his death. His companies had become her empire and would remain hers unless she remarried. Under English law, it would then transfer to her new husband, and she would become property herself.

My life wouldn't be mine ever again.

She had no intention of letting that happen. Being a powerful widow was preferable to being a married slave.

"Lady Melbourne, I understand you have a number of shipping companies?" the Duchess of Essex queried before sipping her tea.

The duchess, who had insisted on being called Emily, was a lovely creature with violet eyes, auburn hair and a smile full of mischief and cunning.

"Yes, that is correct," Rosalind replied. "I took over my late husband's company and have been growing it by acquiring other shipping lines as they go on the market. Sea trade can be a risky endeavor, but it has proved fruitful so far." She smiled a little, happy to be talking about business. It was one of her joys in life, the pursuit of companies, the acquisitions, the shipping. The mental challenges of running the companies that formed her fortune had always been vastly rewarding.

The other two ladies, Anne, Viscountess Sheridan, and Lady Rochester, who insisted on being called Horatia, exchanged glances. Rosalind wasn't daft. The three women had been doing this from the moment she'd come inside the Sheridan household for tea. She suspected they'd invited her to Curzon Street for some purpose, and she wished they would simply come out and ask her whatever it was they were interested in.

"Do you do any business with Lord Lennox?" Horatia asked. Her cheeks had gone pink, betraying the direction Rosalind had feared the conversation was headed. Given their husbands' close friendships with Lennox, she had been expecting this.

Rosalind sighed. "Lord Lennox..." The infernal baron had an uncanny way of coming up. It was he who had been on her mind moments ago. The man who'd ruthlessly kissed her in a theater alcove. He'd been out to punish her for her interference with his business, but that chastisement had turned to an attempt at passion, no doubt with the intent of leaving her alone and longing for him.

She had to fight hard to contain the little smile at that particular memory. She'd seen through his ploy and turned it against him, and he'd been defenseless against her. She remembered dropping her glove at his feet, a parting challenge before she'd left him to handle the problem of his stained trousers.

Lennox would no doubt be planning something to obtain his revenge; his ego would not allow otherwise. But these ladies were married to friends of his, so she would need to answer carefully.

"Well, our business interests, while shared, tend to put us in direct competition." She hesitated to say more. It was possible that anything she told these three women would make its way back to him through their husbands. The secret behind her success came from the subtle balance of obtaining information from others and keeping it away from indiscreet ears.

On more than one occasion, she'd come across the jilted lovers left in Ashton's wake—widows, daughters or unhappy wives of those he was in competition with. They had provided him with information over the course of an evening, often in bed, and he had used it to his advantage.

But he had also left a fair number of women who were willing to talk about *him* and his tactics as well. Rosalind had used that information to her own advantage and had been able to track his movements and strategies, even anticipate his business goals and outsmart him on more than one occasion.

Emily nudged Horatia's elbow. Horatia spoke up.

"I'm sure you must think we are spies on behalf of our husbands, but I assure you that is not the case." Horatia set her teacup down. "The reason we are asking is to protect you, if we can."

"Protect me?" Rosalind set her own cup down, a flicker of unease darting through her like a startled rabbit in the under-brush. "Whatever from?"

Emily cleared her throat. "What we mean to say is that we know Lord Lennox. We know what he's capable of when he's in a mood, that is. All of us admire your courage and your ability to compete among the men. And we don't want Ashton, that is, Lord

Lennox, to upset you simply because he has his trousers twisted. I adore the man, but like the rest, he can become harsh in his business matters where his pride is pricked. We only wish to protect you, Lady Melbourne. We ladies must stick together."

"Well..." What did one say to that? Rosalind plucked at her rose-colored day gown and glanced away, feeling a tad awkward.

"Have you any way to know if your finances are protected?" Anne asked quietly. "Cedric, that is to say, my husband, once said Ashton will challenge a man by dealing a blow to his banking abilities, such as his credit and his debts."

Rosalind felt her stomach drop out. These ladies were serious about Lennox. And she'd certainly pricked the man's pride. She'd bought three companies out from under him in the last month and had wooed old trading partners of his to her lines. But surely he wouldn't do something so drastic. But she had taken out credit lines to buy the last few companies, and her own bank was light in gold if any of her notes came due at this moment.

"But surely he wouldn't..." She went over the numbers and scenarios in her head. She saw it. A vulnerability. What if...?

Suddenly the room was too hot, too closed. She needed air.

"Quick, Anne, open a window!" Horatia gasped.

Rosalind rushed from her seat following Anne, who opened a window facing the back gardens. She leaned against the sill, her hands digging into the wood as she sucked in the fresh spring air.

"There, there," Anne soothed. "Breathe and you'll be fine."

Rosalind wished it were so simple. But if Lennox was setting that plan in motion, she would have little chance of stopping him, unless she could get to the banks and ask for more credit to cover the gold cash-outs. But that wouldn't solve her debt problem if he bought the debts. She would then still owe him everything.

"What can we do to help?" Horatia asked.

It took several long moments for Rosalind to recover. Her stays were too tight, and dizziness swamped her.

"I'm afraid I must go—" If she could get out in front of this, she might survive.

"Of course," Emily replied. "Would you like someone to go with you?"

"No!" Rosalind gasped, then recovered herself. "I mean, no thank you, Your Grace. I'm afraid it would not do to have you walk into a bank with me. They act poorly enough when I go in— I should not like to see how they react to a duchess."

Emily grinned, her violet eyes twinkling. "Nonsense. I have no qualms about scandals. You forget who I am married to. Scandal is nothing new to me."

Rosalind debated her options. She wasn't all that fond of accepting help, but something about Emily was reassuring. Neither she nor Horatia nor Anne seemed to be the sort of women who allowed men to control them, not even their husbands.

"Well, if you wouldn't mind." She finally sighed and rubbed her temples.

"Not at all." Emily shared another of those secretive glances with Anne and Horatia.

"Might I ask, why are you helping me, Your Grace?" Rosalind closed the window facing the garden and focused on the three women. "I cannot help but notice you keep looking at each other."

Horatia blushed. "We've all had to put up with men in the past when they've caused trouble. We wish to help you, and we know Ashton can do great harm to your business."

"I'll ring for my coach." Emily rose from her chair and pulled a slender cord on the door.

~

Half an hour later the coach bearing the Essex coat of arms rattled to a stop outside Drummond's Bank. It was the bank where Rosalind kept the majority of her lines of credit.

Rosalind and Emily climbed out of the coach and proceeded toward the bank, ignoring the stares of men and women on the street. It had amazed Rosalind to learn on the ride over that Emily was a skilled businesswoman herself. She'd handled her uncle's accounts, then taken over her husband's once she married. Through the course of the conversation, Emily had told her a fantastical tale of abduction, intrigue and eventually love, which had resulted in her marriage to the Duke of Essex. The local papers had certainly not given any of *those* details.

As they reached the door to the bank, Rosalind drew them up short. "Are you positive you wish to go in with me? There will be talk—more than talk—if you do."

With a chuckle, Emily replied, "It's been quite some time since I've been considered scandalous, so it's time to dive back into the gossip, I think."

If Rosalind's nerves hadn't been so raw, she would have laughed with her.

The inside of the bank was filled with men of business and members of the peerage, talking, perusing papers and making business deals. A collective hush filled the room when she and the duchess entered. Women were not supposed to enter such a realm without a gentleman escorting them. It was something she'd gotten used to, the quelling gazes of men who wished to intimidate her into leaving. But she never gave in. There was nothing any of them could do to her. After living most of her life at the hands of an abusive father, she was done letting men dictate her life.

"Is it always like this?" Emily leaned in to whisper. "The way they stare at you?"

Rosalind answered with a faint nod.

Suddenly a tall, dark-haired man with honey-brown eyes stepped out of the crowd and approached them. Rosalind recognized the gentleman. She had half feared that Emily's husband or one of the other so-called Rogues would be here to intercept her, but this man was not one of their number, though he was an acquaintance of theirs.

"Your Grace." His smile dispelled some of the tension around them. There were still a few grumblings, but the majority of the men returned to their previous conversations.

"Lord Pembroke! How lovely to see you," Emily greeted the man and turned to Rosalind. "Lord Pembroke, this is Lady Melbourne."

Pembroke bowed over her hand and pressed his lips to her knuckles. "A pleasure. What brings you ladies to Drummond's?" Pembroke's eyes darted around them, but he did not seem entirely surprised at their being in such a bastion of masculine activity.

"We're resolving an issue," Emily said. "Rosalind, who is it we need to see?"

"Mr. Reed."

"Very well." Pembroke offered an arm to Emily and she took it, winking at Rosalind while he escorted them to Mr. Reed's office.

The banker was settled at his writing table, poring over several letters. He glanced up and froze when he saw Rosalind, Emily and the Earl of Pembroke in his doorway.

"Lady Melbourne?" Her name escaped the banker in a stutter.

"Mr. Reed." She took a seat in front of him and studied the older man closely. His skin had taken on a white pallor, and he began to shuffle all manner of papers and items on his table. This did not bode well.

"What may I do for you?" Mr. Reed asked as he slid a finger beneath his neckcloth and tugged on it.

"I wanted to see about extending my line of credit."

"Your credit…" Mr. Reed swallowed and smiled a little, but the expression was forced.

"Yes, I have several notes out, and I am afraid they may be called in." She hesitated when Mr. Reed's glance darted away and then back.

"Lady Melbourne, I do regret to tell you this, but I cannot extend any further lines of credit."

Knots formed in Rosalind's stomach. She leaned forward in her seat. "Why not? Do you need more collateral?"

Mr. Reed shook his head. "I cannot extend your credit under any circumstances."

"Why is that?" Lord Pembroke demanded.

Rosalind saw he had remained with her and Emily. He was now scowling as he leaned against the door frame to Mr. Reed's office.

"Well, it's bank policy to make decisions that protect our stability and—"

"Mr. Reed," Emily cut in gently, though Rosalind caught a hard glint in the young woman's eyes. "You have a daughter coming out this year, do you not?"

"Why, yes. Amelia. My youngest." Mr. Reed sighed and dropped his head a few inches.

"She's a lovely girl, I recall," Emily continued. "And she could make a good match if she had help, say if a *duchess* sponsored her?"

Rosalind blinked. Was Emily actually offering herself as a sponsor to the banker's daughter?

Mr. Reed's face lit up. "Why, that would be wonderful."

Emily raised a gloved hand. "It would be an honor to sponsor her, but I'm afraid that I simply could not do it unless I trusted you, Mr. Reed, in *all* things."

The banker stared at Emily for a long moment. "You would help Amelia find a good man, with say ten thousand pounds a year?"

Emily's smile grew. "I have quite a few suitable candidates in mind already."

When Mr. Reed spoke again, his voice was low and he leaned close. "You must not tell him that I betrayed his confidence."

"We shall not. Now, *who* has told you not to allow any credit extensions? I assume someone ordered that, correct?"

"Lord Lennox."

It was the name Rosalind had dreaded to hear. Hearing her worries confirmed sent spirals of panic through her. So Lennox was finally making his play, after a month of letting her believe she was safe following that night in the theater.

"Thank you, Mr. Reed." Emily glanced toward Rosalind.

Pembroke looked horrified. "Wait a minute. Lennox is trying to stop you from obtaining credit? Whatever for? I know him. He's a ruthless man of business, but not to ladies."

With a mirthless laugh, Rosalind fisted her hands in her skirts. "It seems I am to be the exception." *How fortunate am I?* Her inner voice was a tad impolite, but who could blame her? Lennox had her back against a wall, and she wasn't handling it very well.

"Lady Melbourne, I was advised *not* to give you details. However," Reed said, glancing at Emily again, "I've been informed he also bought the debts you have and will be sending demand payments through proxies this afternoon."

Rosalind sank in her seat. That was far worse than the gold demands she'd been expecting, but it was oh so clever as well. A personal touch, to let her know exactly who had bested her.

"Why that pompous, bloody bastard!" The curse did not come from Rosalind, but Emily. "Just *wait* until I get my hands on him. He's supposed to be the most gentlemanly of the League. *Ooh!*" Emily's hands were curled into fists, and anger sparked in her eyes.

Pembroke growled and looked at the two ladies. "That is indeed a very low thing to do. If you give me the nod, I'll have half the *ton* give him the cut direct by this evening, and he'll be tossed out of his club."

"Thank you, James, but that won't be necessary. I've a better plan in mind to deal with our misbehaving friend."

Rosalind laid a hand on the duchess. "Please, Emily, you need not get involved—"

"Nonsense. That is *precisely* what I must do. But first, we have to get you home, Rosalind."

"But I need to handle the notes—"

Emily smoothed out her skirts. "Let me see to that. You must handle Ashton."

"How on earth do you suggest I do that?" She had her own ideas, of course. Strangulation being at the top of her list. But she was also curious as to what Emily might say.

"You are rivals, correct?" Emily asked.

"Yes." Lord help her if they were rivals in anything besides business.

"And how would you handle a business rival?"

Finally Rosalind felt like smiling. "By finding his weakness. Breaking him down from the inside."

"And do you know any weakness you might exploit?"

Her thoughts went back to the theater. One heated encounter in that alcove and he'd lost his control, but she'd kept hers. She'd won.

And I can win again.

Emily clapped her hands at the sight of Rosalind's cunning smile. "See, you have the right of it. I'm certain you can use that to your advantage. Now let's get you home so you can change into something more suitable for seduction."

The banker sputtered in shock, and Pembroke covered a laugh with a polite cough. "Allow me to escort you ladies to your coach." Pembroke nodded his goodbye to Reed.

"Thank you, Lord Pembroke," Rosalind said, but her mind was still reeling.

Seduction? She hadn't necessarily thought of that sort of plan, but there was logic to it. If it could get her back what was hers, her life, her independence, then she would play him like a fiddle if she must. But she'd only ever been with one man before, her late husband. Sweet and gentle in bed he had been, but his touch had never *burned* the way Ashton's had, nor had her entire body felt as though it was on the edge of something dark and wild when they had kissed.

But she detested Lennox. He knew just how to prod her until her barely leashed temper snapped. How was a woman to enjoy herself in bed when she wanted to strangle the man with his own bedsheets? Was he even *capable* of being seduced? She doubted he ever let himself be free enough to fall completely for a seduction, but what else could she try?

By the time she finally parted ways with Emily and Lord Pembroke, she had become thoroughly agitated. No, that was not nearly a strong enough word, but the words that came to mind were most unladylike.

As she reached the front door of her townhouse, her butler was there, anxiously holding out a letter.

"What is it, Pevensly?" She took the letter from his shaking hands.

"A man under the employ of Lord Lennox delivered this. He told me you must read it immediately and that he would be back within the hour to see that the letter's instructions are followed."

With trepidation, Rosalind peeled off her gloves and broke the seal on the letter as she entered the hall. Pevensly close the door behind her.

The letter was written elegantly, and yet as she began to read, it felt more mocking with each stroke of the quill.

My dearest Lady Melbourne,

As I'm sure you are now aware, Drummond's Bank as well as every other bank within your immediate traveling distance has been given strict orders not to extend or offer you any additional credit. All of your notes will be cashed in by my proxies if I hear of you trying to buy them back.

Additionally, I have purchased all of your debts. At this moment, my accountants and solicitors are taking a full account of your affairs at your offices in London and Brighton. Your entire fate lies in my hands. The house you stand in at this very moment? Mine. The clothes upon your back? Also mine. I own you, Lady Melbourne, in all but name.

What does this mean? I am putting you on the street. Your servants may remain at the house and I will see to their continued employment, but you, my cunning rival, must seek home and hearth elsewhere until I decide what to do with you.

I own you.

CHAPTER 3

I own you.

The words from Ashton's letter blurred as Rosalind struggled to breathe. No, he couldn't do this to her. Shock paralyzed her body, her muscles tensing painfully.

The past came rushing up from the depths where she had buried it, swallowing her in its icy waters, unable to stop the memories as they enveloped her.

The cold castle corridors, wind whistling through the faded, tattered tapestries. The booming shout of an angry father.

"You think you can tell me what to do? You little wretch! I own you, and you aren't worth the breath in your lungs!"

A cup of mead exploded against the wall where Rosalind, only sixteen, hid behind a half-opened door. The aching sorrow of her mother's recent death hung in the halls like an invisible cloud. It had sent her father over the edge.

"Rosalind," a deep voice chided from behind the hall. Rosalind jumped, but her older brother Brock steadied her. "Leave Father alone—he's been drinking."

The door crashed open as their father, Lord Kincade, launched himself at Rosalind.

He swung a balled fist at her, but Brock knocked the hand away.

"Oh! Think you're a man to take me on? No son of mine would dare!" He moved fast, too fast. The punch knocked Brock onto the floor. Rosalind too was hit, spiraling wildly as she bounced off the wall and fell beside Brock.

"Pieces of shite, the both of you! Not worth the clothes on your backs! I should sell you both for the uselessness you are to me." Their father snarled like a wild boar and stalked down the hallway, leaving them alone.

Tears leaked from her eyes as she reached for her aching jaw. It felt like it was broken. She knew it wasn't, but it hurt like the very devil.

A hand settled on her shoulder, causing her to flinch. "'Tis only me," Brock said gruffly, but there was a gentleness to his tone. It wasn't proper for a young lass to cry, but she couldn't stop. Living in fear of her father every day was chipping away at her soul.

"I can't do this anymore," she whispered. "He's going to kill me."

Her older brother was still no match for their father, but she knew he would keep taking blows for her. All of her brothers would.

"Rosalind, what are you talking about?" Brock cupped her chin, but she whimpered at the flash of pain and pulled away.

"I'm not staying. I have to get out of this house. Ever since Mother died, this hasn't been my home."

Her brother brushed the tears away from her cheeks, and his gray eyes, so like her own, were as silver as a waning moon up on the moors.

"Rosalind, this is your home. It will always be your home. And we shall protect you."

Rosalind believed him, but she was no fool. As the exact likeness of her mother, she could not stay here and continue to risk her father's wrath. She would have to leave one day. But she would need a way out, a place to land.

If only there was a man who could find in his heart to marry her, she might be able to escape. But who would want the broken daughter of the cruel Lord Kincade?

The past faded, leaving a bitter taste upon her lips and tiny thorns embedded in her heart.

This home was the one she'd made for herself, the one her late husband had let her run. It was her world, and that damned fool Lennox thought he had the right to take it all away from her? To cast her out?

She stared at the note and realized she hadn't finished reading it.

I AM NOT A CRUEL MAN. If you wish to discuss the situation, you may join me at my estate. However, you may not take your coach as that too falls under my control now. I'm sure if you were to come to me, we could come to some arrangement that would benefit us both.

Lennox

"AN ARRANGEMENT that would benefit us both?" she muttered. Anger and panic rippled through her, dueling for dominance. That damned bloody Englishman. She wanted to strangle him, but the truth of her situation was dire. He had full control over her and was toying with her the way a cat would a mouse. Something had to be done. Perhaps Emily's suggestion to seduce the man was indeed a good idea. Rosalind sensed an opportunity here. If Lennox desired her and believed she'd come to heel, she would prove just who was the one in control when she brought *him* under her command.

But she was taking her own coach, Lennox be damned!

I have to face him. Perhaps the duchess's advice about seduction wasn't so unreasonable after all.

"What is it, Your Ladyship?" Pevensly asked. His dark brows knit together in concern.

Rosalind stared at the address on the parchment, frowning, then handed it to him.

"You may read it, but please do not inform the rest of the staff —I don't wish them to worry. Would you please have my coach pulled around in an hour? I am going to sort this out. Rest assured I will come back. Please do not let the servants grow overly concerned." She left Pevensly gaping after her in the hall as she rushed up the stairs, calling for her lady's maid.

"Yes, Your Ladyship?" A woman not much older than her appeared through an open doorway at the top of the stairs.

"Pack my valise at once. The best clothes you can find. Don't bother with hats. I won't have space for the boxes."

Claire met her as they walked toward her room. "Is this about that man who came by earlier? Pevensly was near frantic when the man left. Seems he suggested you would not be happy when you returned from your errands this morning."

There was no point in hiding the truth from her. The woman's observations missed nothing; it was why she made an excellent maid.

"Lord Lennox has just tried to buy my life away through my debts. He's ordered me out of this house."

Claire raised a hand to her lips, but just as quickly that hand curled into a fist. "Surely you won't let that stand."

"I will not. I plan to travel to his estate at once to remedy this error."

Claire nodded. "Ah. Then I shall be accompanying you, of course."

"No, that won't be—"

"It will be," Claire insisted. "You're a *lady*. You must have a maid accompany you, and none of the other girls know you as well as I do. I'll not lose my head in a time of panic."

That much was true. Claire was a mother hen who watched over the household, but the woman had a backbone of iron too.

"Very well, you alone may come. But be warned, the means I intend to use to regain my life are best kept private." She trusted her staff, but secrets were always easier when one did not have too many keepers. "Thank you, Claire. Pack as much as you can. We leave in an hour."

She left her maid to pack while she went to her study to write a few hasty letters. She had a number of business partners who would need to be apprised of the situation immediately. Rosalind could only pray that they would be forgiving given the dire situation. She knew Sir Hugo Waverly would be most understanding. He, more than anyone, was aware of her competitive history with Lennox. Indeed, he had fostered many ideas that had led her to triumph over Lennox in battles of bidding and company purchases.

She sorted through the letters on her desk and paused when she found a palm-sized package addressed to her. The ink on the return address was blurred from rainwater, but it seemed to be from Scotland. Her heart began to pound as she unfastened the twine and opened the parcel.

An object wrapped in a handkerchief fell into her hands. She unbound the handkerchief and studied the object.

It was a pocket watch. Turning her attention to the handkerchief, she noticed an all-too-familiar letter K stitched into the corner. Kincade. Her father carried these. A lump grew in her throat at the thought. Had he finally discovered where she was? Had he known all along? Would he come for her and demand she return to Scotland with him?

She blinked back tears as she unfolded the cloth further, finding a single sheet of parchment tucked inside. A letter. She read it with shaking hands.

ROSALIND,

Keep this safe, keep it close. Take it home to Scotland. I've entrusted your brothers with a secret that even they do not understand. You may yet have the chance to undo the evils I have created in my life.

Montgomery

. . .

THE POCKET WATCH was a heavy gold piece with no remarkable engravings upon it. She opened it to see a simple clock face, and it appeared to be broken. What sort of game was her father playing? Whatever it was, she had no desire to go along with it. She folded the watch up in the handkerchief and set it back in the parcel next to the letters. There wasn't time to worry about it now.

She hastily finished the letters to her business partners, and with a final curious glance at the package she left her study. She found Claire busy packing in her chambers.

"Would you see that the stack of letters in my study is also packed? I shall need to read them and respond as necessary while we are at Lord Lennox's estate."

"I'll see to it at once." Claire departed, and Rosalind sat down on her bed, her mind still racing as she decided what she was to do about Lennox. She would have to worry about her father and his enigmatic gift later.

～

JONATHAN ST. LAURENT stood at the entryway of a fashionable townhouse on Half Moon Street. The keys to the door felt heavy in his palm, and his heart gave a quick thump. The residence had once belonged to a baron, Lord Chessley, who had passed away in early April. His daughter, Anne, had married Jonathan's friend Cedric three weeks later.

"Scandal be damned," as Cedric had said. Since Cedric and Anne both resided in his London townhouse on Curzon Street, they'd had no use for a second house and had chosen to sell it.

Now Chessley House was his. He'd met with the butler and housekeeper, and it seemed the entire staff except for Anne's lady's maid, who had agreed to stay on with him. Yet he felt strangely off balance being the one in charge of a household.

He'd spent his whole life as a servant of the Duke of Essex, only to discover that Godric was his half brother. After the late duchess had passed, Godric's father had secretly remarried his wife's lady's maid, and Jonathan had been the result of that union. The secret, but legitimate, son of a duke.

After that revelation his life had been turned upon its head. He was thrust into Godric's world and was even considered one of the League of Rogues. But now he was contemplating marriage and settling down.

He snorted. Perhaps not the settling down. The woman he was interested in was not at all tame, and she'd likely never settle down. But he'd wanted to at least have a home to offer her when he proposed.

"Sir." The butler emerged from the servants' quarters. "I did not know you'd be here today. Please come in and let me take your hat."

"Thank you." Jonathan handed his hat to the man. It was still strange to be a gentleman. He'd been a footman, a gardener, and a valet for the last ten years, and it was difficult to curb old habits, such as wanting to see to his own hat or shutting the door behind himself.

"How is the house? Do you and the rest of the staff have everything you need?" Jonathan asked.

"We're quite fine, sir. You received this note an hour ago. I was just about to have it delivered to Lord Essex's townhouse."

A sealed letter was handed over, and Jonathan unfolded it. A familiar hand had scrawled a few lines.

Jon,

Meet me at the Fives Court at two this afternoon. I'm of a mind to bloody a few noses in the ring. Should be good fun.

Charles

. . .

JONATHAN SNORTED. Charles. The Earl of Lonsdale was always up to something. Not that Jonathan was surprised. He'd grown up living on the fringes of the League's world and was well aware of the antics they got into. Now he was one of them.

He grinned. *Duty calls, I suppose.* It would be no hardship to join Charles to watch him box.

"Is there anything you need from me, sir?" the butler asked.

"Er…no, I'm going out again. I'm not sure if I'll be back for dinner, so don't let the cook worry about preparing anything. Cold cuts and a bit of wine will be fine when I return."

"Very good, sir."

Jonathan glanced at the clock by the base of the stairs. Half past one. He needed to leave immediately. He waved off his hat when the butler held it out.

"No need for that where I'm going." He turned right back around and headed outside, relieved to see the hackney hadn't yet left.

"Are you still available?" he asked the driver.

"I am." The driver jerked the reins up, and the black mare stomped and chomped her bit in irritation.

Jonathan climbed up into the cab beside the driver, and the vehicle rocked precariously.

"Where to?"

"Fives Court on St. Martin's Lane in Leister Fields. You know it?"

The driver flashed him a grin and smacked the ribbons on his mare's flanks. "I do."

Jonathan then slipped into the hackney and it jolted forward.

By the time they'd reached Fives Court, the sounds of a wild crowd could be heard outside the old brick building that housed the boxing events. Nearly a thousand men could press into the building and surround the square sparring ring.

Jonathan hopped out of the cab and paid the driver before turning to face Fives Court.

"Three shillings!" a lad cried out at the entrance. "Just three shillings to watch the pets of fancy fight in the ring!"

Pets of fancy. Jonathan chuckled. Charles was no one's pet and likely hated the nickname for the pugilists who fought there.

The little lad held out a grubby hand to him as Jonathan approached.

"There you are." He tossed the boy his three shillings.

"Thank you, sir. The fight just started."

"Oh? Who's up now?"

"Some blond-haired bloke. Lonsdale, I think, and another man who I don't know. He's a bit of the home-brewed if you ask me." The cheeky lad grinned.

"Lonsdale's fighting someone with little training?" That was unexpected. Fives Court matches were supposed to be between men trained and approved by Gentleman Jackson, London's finest boxer.

"He's a milling cove all right, Jackson approved, but he cheats if you ask me," the lad whispered conspiratorially.

"Well this should prove interesting indeed." Jonathan slipped through the doorway and glanced around the interior of the high-ceilinged building. Dozens of men near him were hollering wildly as two men on a raised platform circled each other, gloved fists raised.

Charles stood bare-chested facing a man equal his height. Charles was well-toned, strong, and muscled, but his opponent was a massive beast, a real bruiser. There was a fair bit of blood on the other man's chin, and Charles was dancing lightly on his feet and grinning like the devil himself. That wasn't a good sign, at least for the other fellow.

"Knock his block off!" a high-pitched voice cried out ahead of him. It stuck out over the low-voiced shouts of the men around him. Jonathan began weaving through the crowds, shouldering his way to the front of the platform. At the edge of the ring two lads were waving and cheering Charles on.

"Draw his cork, my lord!" the second lad cried as Jonathan drew even with them at the edge of the ring.

The profile of the first young man was one he recognized instantly. Tom Linley, Charles's servant and man-about-town, though barely old enough to be called a man. Jonathan had always felt something was off about him. He couldn't quite put a finger on what it was. The lad was…shifty, or perhaps simply secretive.

Secrets. The flashes of fear and defiance he had seen in the lad's eyes in the past had been a warning Jonathan couldn't ignore. There was something going on with Linley that puzzled Jonathan. But his loyalty to his master was equally evident now in the prideful expression he wore as he whooped and hollered.

"Give it to him, Charles!" The second lad's voice was…higher. Too high. Jonathan leaned forward to peer around Linley's face, and his heart pounded against his ribs. That darker-haired lad was no lad at all. The breeches he wore fit snugly around his…no…*her* full, feminine buttocks.

"Audrey?"

The dark-haired boy froze and slowly turned his way.

It was Audrey. Audrey Sheridan, Cedric's little sister and a notorious hellion. She was also the woman he was considering courting. There was certainly no taming that wild creature.

His possible future wife was wearing trousers, standing in a crowd of men who smelled like alcohol and was watching a boxing match at Fives Court.

Audrey's mouth parted as she wet her lips. She hastily reached up to check her costume and tuck a few stray wisps of her hair back under her cap.

"*Audrey,*" he growled, stalking over to her. Linley finally noticed him.

"Hello, Mr. St. Laurent. Have you come to see the match?"

Jonathan barely spared Linley a glance. "Audrey, what in blazes are you doing here?" His fingers curled around her upper arm.

Audrey struggled in his hold. "Let go of me!"

"Not until you tell me what you're doing!"

Her eyes narrowed. "I'm practicing disguises." Her little pink, all-too-kissable lips formed a delicate pout.

"Disguise?" Did she have no sense of the danger she was in? If one of the men around her realized she was a woman, she could be hurt, she could be... He shuddered and shook his head. No. That would not happen because he was taking her out of this place at once.

"If you don't unhand me this instant—"

"You'll what?" he challenged. "I've half a mind to redden that little bottom of yours so that you cannot sit down for the next week!" His threatening tone attracted more than one glance from the men around him.

Audrey's warm brown eyes were filling with flames from her temper.

"Everyone is staring. You had better let go of me."

"She's right, Mr. St. Laurent," Linley leaned in to whisper.

Jonathan hated to admit they were correct. Several men were losing interest in Charles, and the other man in the ring. They had instead turned to watch him and Audrey.

"Hellfire and damnation!" he cursed and dropped his hold on her arm.

With a far too dainty huff, Audrey plucked at her little blue waistcoat and checked to make sure the cap on her head was still concealing what he knew was a coiling of silken dark-brown hair. He'd gotten addicted to the way her skin tasted and the honeysuckle sweetness that clung to her tresses. From the moment he'd met her, Audrey had tied him into knots.

Sighing, he forced his attention back to Charles. In the short time he'd been distracted by Audrey's ruse, it seemed Charles had suffered. One of his eyes was a dark red, and blood trickled down the side of his chin from a split lip.

"What's the matter with Charles?" Jonathan asked Linley.

The lad shrugged, but his blue eyes were narrowed as he focused on the two men in the ring.

"My lord is fighting fair, but the other fellow is set on fibbing him."

"Fib?" Jonathan hadn't had much experience with boxing.

"Fibbing is a beating," Linley explained.

"Poor Charles," Audrey murmured. The initial excitement in her eyes from the first part of the fight had faded. The bigger boxer swung a gloved fist and Charles ducked, but he was panting hard. That wouldn't do at all. Charles was not allowed to lose a match, not if Jonathan could lend some support.

Jonathan rested his palms on the edge of the platform. "Finish him, Charles!"

Charles's gaze drifted across the crowd as he danced away from his opponent. When he caught sight of Jonathan, he started grinning again. "Wondered when you'd show up!"

Jonathan almost chuckled. "Here we go."

Charles dodged back, then forward, then to the side, his blows coming swift and hard. The other boxer didn't see it coming. Charles was finally displaying himself to advantage. The crowd cheered, and the men were shouting wagers on the quickly changing odds.

A masterful uppercut caught Charles's opponent off guard, and then he stumbled back and fell like a stone. His body hit the platform with a loud smack, and every man with odds on the bruiser winced. Chest heaving, Charles whooped in triumph and peeled off his gloves, tossing them to a man just off the edge of the ring. Then he slipped under the ropes and hopped off the platform.

"Jon," Charles greeted, his gray eyes sparkling with delight. "Just stalling for time until you showed up." He reached for a cloth a man passing by held out, and he wiped sweat and blood off his face.

Audrey beamed at him, sidling closer. "Well done, Charles."

Jonathan tracked the movement, a strange prickling sensation under his skin. He did not like the way Charles was standing there bare-chested and not at all aware that he was flaunting that chest in front of a virginal woman who was barely past her debut season.

"What did you think, lad?" Charles asked Linley.

The boy pressed his lips together in thought before replying.

"You missed an opportunity to gouge his eyes when he had you on the ropes."

Charles burst out laughing. "That's not how pugilism works, lad. This isn't a street match, but of two men with honor."

"Humph." Linley grunted in clear dissent. "If he wasn't fighting fair, why should you?"

But Charles was focused on Jonathan again. "Glad you got my note. We need to talk."

Shooting a glance at Audrey, Jonathan nodded grimly. "That we do." He planned to give Charles another black eye if he didn't have a good reason for bringing Audrey to a match like this.

"Don't you think we ought to send the lady home?" He jerked his head at Audrey.

Her eyes narrowed again, and she crossed her arms. "Oh no. I am staying here."

"Absolutely not." Jonathan eyed Audrey reproachfully and then looked to Charles. "Perhaps we ought to meet later?"

"I had a letter this afternoon that Ashton is in need of help at his estate. We ought to meet there this evening," Charles suggested.

"Very good, I'll see you tonight." He turned to Audrey. "Now, you're to come with me. I am going to escort you straight home, and you'd better pray your brother isn't there so I don't have to explain where you've been." He grabbed her arm again.

"Charles! You can't let him drag me out of here," Audrey protested.

Jonathan shared an intense gaze with Charles, who smiled. "Well, you remember my advice."

"I do."

"Advice? What advice?" Audrey snapped.

"That I carry you out of here and put my hand to your backside if you raise another word of protest."

Audrey bit her lip and tugged her arm, but Jonathan was adamant. She was not going to stay here where it was dangerous. Without letting her speak another word, he scooped her up and threw her over his shoulder. Ignoring the pounding of her fists against his back, he carried her out of Fives Court. She screeched like a little hellcat, spitting and clawing and drawing all manner of bad attention to the both of them.

"I'll get you for this!" she vowed.

"I'm sure you'll try, darling." He smacked her bottom in playful punishment as he headed for a waiting coach.

"Curzon Street, please," Jonathan told the driver and then opened the coach door and tossed Audrey inside. It was going to be a long ride, and he'd have to guard his loins from her little booted feet.

CHAPTER 4

⁂

*A*shes drifted across the fields like snow. The sight was eerie in the middle of a sunny English afternoon. The ruins of his tenant farmer's home were nothing more than blackened cinders and smoldering beams. It cast a strange contrast to the bright flowers in the field nearby and the contented bleating of sheep that dotted the roadside. A watchful sheepdog sat with them, his tail wagging in the dust. Several village children peered over the top of a waist-high stone fence along one side of the road, staring bleakly at the place that had once been someone's home.

Ashton rolled up the sleeves of his shirt and loosened his cravat as he studied the ruins.

"How did the fire start, Mr. Higgins?"

The farmer stared in bleak anguish at the destroyed remains of his home.

"I don't rightly know, my lord." The man scrubbed at his eyes as though to hide any evidence of fresh tears. The Higgins family had lived on this land and in that house for seventy-five years. And now it was gone. Mr. Maple and his family on the neighboring farm had suffered an eerily similar fate. Ashton knew what the man must be feeling. A sense of loss and shame at not being able to provide a roof for his children and wife. There was only one thing to do be done.

Ashton clapped a hand on Higgins's shoulder. "You and your family will be settled into quarters at Lennox House until we have new homes built for you and the Maple family."

The farmer paled. "No, my lord! We couldn't possibly—"

"Nonsense. I won't hear a word against it." Caring for his tenants was a matter he took seriously, and his prosperous financial situation would have a good purpose in rebuilding the homes. He would not allow them to go without shelter. It was a gentleman's duty to see to the well-being of his lands and his tenants.

"Thank you, my lord," Higgins said, glancing down as he did so.

"Let's return to the manor house, and I'll see that your family is settled in."

He and Higgins mounted their horses and followed the dirt road home. Behind them came a wagon with the children, pulled by two plow horses. A young woman stood on the front steps of the grand old Lennox House. A breeze tugged at the skirts of her pale-blue day gown. Long blond hair that matched his own was coiled on the top of her head in the fashion of the day. No bonnet, of course. His little sister Joanna detested the things.

"Ashton!" She rushed down the steps as he slid off his gelding and handed the reins to a waiting groom.

"Joanna." He smiled and opened his arms. She hastened to embrace him. It never failed to puzzle him that not one man in England had tried to court her since her come-out. She was lovely, if a bit shy, but exceedingly intelligent and formidable at conversation. He'd settled a large dowry on her, hoping to tempt some of the braver bucks to come calling, but none had. Perhaps what he saw as virtues in her were not considered desirable traits by other men. They were fools if that was the case.

"Thank you for your coming home so quickly. Mother and I

have been frantic for the tenants. We've assumed you might wish to bring them here until the new homes could be built." Joanna saw Higgins and his passel of children standing hesitantly a few yards away. "Mr. Higgins, please come in. Your wife and children will be settled as well, and we've prepared new rooms for everyone."

Ashton watched his sister with pride as she escorted the weary and stressed farmer along with his excited brood into their home. Following them at a distance, he paused at the grand stairs. Joanna would make a fine head of a household someday, if only he could find a man to marry her. If Jonathan St. Laurent hadn't already taken an interest in Audrey, Ashton would have been tempted to turn the younger man's attentions to his sister. He wanted a man he could trust to love and care for Joanna, not some buck fresh from university who was looking to run wild in London.

A cool voice interrupted his thoughts. "So, you've returned."

His mother, Regina Lennox, stood at the top of the stairs. Still lovely for a woman her age, she made an impressive sight in a cranberry-red gown.

"I was summoned. Therefore, I returned." He smacked his hands against his thighs, sending a cloud of dust in the air before coming up the stairs to join her.

"At least you care enough about the farmers to return." Judgment lay heavy in Regina's tone. It pricked his heart, but he shut down any emotions before they could show on his face.

"Don't start, Mother. I am not in the mood."

"As you wish."

As a boy he had adored his mother, and she had doted on him and his siblings. Yet after he was sent away to Eton, their father had burned through their fortune at the gaming tables. His mother had suffered from their fall from society when her friends turned their backs on her and she was invited to fewer and fewer dinners and balls. For a woman like his mother, who thrived on human company, she felt increasingly trapped and alone. And all of this had worsened when their father was run over by a carriage while leaving a gambling hell. He'd died and left their lives in utter shambles.

Ashton had come home and done everything in his power to put the family back into a good position. But his mother hadn't responded to his actions with joy. Rather, she'd told him that his need for money and power had made him just like his father.

The words had cut deep, and the coldness he'd felt from her since that day had left him wounded and angry. Even the memory left a bitter taste in his mouth. Needless to say, family dinners at Lennox House were damned awkward—when he bothered to come home for them.

Regina continued as if their previous exchange hadn't happened. "We are having guests tonight for dinner. The Mertons will be here at seven. It would be good for you to attend."

Ashton paused at the top of the stairs, meeting his mother's eyes. For a long moment neither of them moved, the silent challenge hanging in the air.

"Merton still has an unmarried daughter, does he not?"

Regina's eyes narrowed. "He does."

"Ah, therein lies the problem. I have no intention of dining with a family you seek to ally with by marriage." Ashton tugged his cravat free of his neck as he waited for his mother's inevitable outburst.

"Not everything is about alliances, child. Sometimes it's about love and affection. Heavens, I knew you had too much of Edmund in you, but I had hoped there might be a bit of me in you somewhere as well." Hurt and anger flashed in her eyes, surprising Ashton. But he'd spent too many years suffering her callous remarks about his cold heart and ruthless soul to be affected by her now.

"I'm a coldhearted bastard, Mother. Isn't that what you called me? That isn't about to change," he replied, his tone frosty. "Now, if you'll excuse me, I need to wash off this ash and see to some matters in my study. Charles and Jonathan will arrive tonight, so please have the housekeeper prepare two rooms in the south wing."

His mother said nothing, but he knew she would do as he asked. She may have disliked her eldest son, but she was always a warm and gracious hostess, even to the League.

Ashton strode to his chamber and started stripping off his clothes. His shoulder, the one that had taken a bullet last Christmas, still twinged with the occasional phantom pain. The muscles protested as he stretched the arm a few times. He stared into the mirror, startled by his face, which was still dusted with ash from the fire. Lines bracketed his mouth, and a weariness shadowed his eyes. He looked…like his father, with a pale, ghostly cast to his cheeks and a haunted expression in his eyes. The dark thought made him splash cold water on his face, wiping away the remnants of his personal nightmare. The last thing he ever wished was to be like the man who'd destroyed his family's world.

He didn't turn away as his valet slipped into the room.

"A hot bath is ready for you in your dressing room, my lord."

"Thank you, Lowell. How are the Higgins and Maple families settling in?"

Lowell, a young man of his midtwenties, grinned. "Well, my lord. The children are running about the kitchens, and Mrs. Gibbs can't make plum tarts fast enough to keep them fed."

A smile curved Ashton's lips as he headed for the dressing room to bathe. "I'm glad to hear it."

Mrs. Gibbs adored children, and the two tenant families would keep her happily occupied for some time. Lennox House rarely entertained guests. Their nearest neighbors, the Mertons, were the only guests to attend the infrequent house parties for dinner. Ashton spent all of his time in London or at the estates of his friends, preferring to avoid his mother except when business necessitated his return.

Sometimes he stayed at the bachelor residence of his younger brother, Rafe, or the estate of his older sister, Thomasina, who was married to Lord Reddington. Reddington was a good man, and Thomasina was utterly in love with him. They already had three children who were quite delightful whenever they visited.

Ashton hadn't ever given much thought to having a child, but if they were anything like Thomasina's brood, he'd be a proud father someday.

Ashton stepped into the hot water and sank into it chest deep, sighing. His head dropped back to rest on the lip of the tub, and he tried not to think of the future, marriage or babies. If he never married, the estate would pass on to Rafe, but Rafe had no head for business. He preferred living life to excess and was not particularly gifted at learning how to earn what he lost at the gambling hells. Their mother had no delusions about Rafe or his behavior, which put all the more pressure on Ashton to be the one to settle down and have the required heir and a spare.

Lord... Godric, Lucien and Cedric had found it easy enough to manage their wives. But Ashton couldn't imagine being leg-shackled to a woman he couldn't completely trust to do as he told her. It wasn't that he wanted a woman he could control, but more that he needed someone who would trust him without question in difficult times.

And he wanted someone sweet to take to bed each night, a woman who would purr and sigh as he made love to her, even if they were a bit rough at times. He wanted a strong but gentle woman who enjoyed passion. He'd slept with plenty of women, sometimes in the conquest of his business affairs, but none had satisfied him. There had always been something lacking.

He raised one hand out of the hot water, letting the drops splash back into the tub, rippling outward as he thought about what he truly desired. He wanted a certain fire in a kiss that burned him like an all-consuming blaze. Ashton wanted to be with a woman and completely lose himself inside her. Truth be told, there had only been one woman who had affected him in that way, and she was the last woman on earth he could ever trust.

The Scottish hellion he couldn't seem to stay away from, not since the moment he realized she was to be his competition.

Rosalind Melbourne was too cunning, too untrustworthy, far too much his equal in ruthless business tactics for him to ever trust her, in his bed or out. Yet when he had kissed her, he'd nearly lost his mind and his control. Something about her, the mutual struggle for power and pleasure, drove him insane with lust. If he ever bedded her, neither of them would be able to walk for days afterward. They'd most likely break a bed in the process, the thought of which he enjoyed immensely.

A slow smile twisted his lips as he thought of what it would be like to call that wild lass his.

She'd likely smother me after I fell asleep and flee to Scotland by dawn.

But not before he bedded Rosalind properly...many times and in many ways.

Yes, that would be a bloody good night.

∼

SIR HUGO WAVERLY reclined in a seat at the back of the card room in Boodle's Club, watching the evening unfold with little real interest. His mind was on more important matters. A cloud of cigar smoke hung at the base of the chandeliers like dark clouds, casting shifting shadows among the lights from the candles. Men threw cards upon the tables, gathering and losing fortunes over hasty gambles. But Hugo was not a betting man.

If I cannot secure my odds, I will not play.

The door to the card room opened, and a man Hugo knew entered. It was one of his most trusted men, Daniel Sheffield. With Daniel's help, Hugo ran the most efficient and effective spy ring in the country, which, sadly, was not saying much. Spycraft as a whole in England was woefully amateurish, and it left his country vulnerable. It also made those who took the game seriously, such as Sheffield and himself, indispensible. They'd saved the Crown from more than one foreign war, and yet they would never be given credit for their actions.

But there was more to life than accolades. He was well compensated, both financially and through the power and influence his position afforded. He could blackmail just about anyone to do anything he required. If a man couldn't be bought, he could be threatened, and that was enough for Hugo.

One step below the Crown. It was the closest a non-royal such as himself could ever be to ruling England.

Hugo made no sign that he noticed Daniel's entrance. Daniel toyed with his pocket watch, lingered by a table where men were playing faro, and with a discreet glance, waited for Hugo to nod slightly before he approached.

Daniel took a full minute to make his way through the room. He paused to collect a drink from a passing waiter, then meandered over to Hugo's table and chose a chair not close but not too far either. Tucked under one arm was the *Quizzing Glass Gazette*, and he slowly lifted it up to peruse the articles.

Lady Society's gossip column was clearly visible from where Hugo sat, and he scowled at the name. What drivel! If he could be bothered to find out who the woman was, she would have an accident that rendered her incapable of writing ever again. He was tired of her endless parade of articles that painted the League of Rogues as heroes. They weren't men to be admired or feared; they were fools. Dangerous fools. Fools he would destroy in good time.

The creak of wood told him that Sheffield had shifted his chair an inch closer. When Hugo ever so discreetly peeled his own paper aside, he saw Sheffield's hand gently rolling a glass of brandy.

"Fair weather today, but I saw a chance of clouds," Sheffield observed.

Hugo stiffened. That meant a situation he was having monitored was not going according to plan.

"What sort of clouds?" he asked.

Sheffield set his glass down on the table, and beneath it was a carefully folded note. "Black." Hugo laid his paper down and let it cover the surface by Sheffield's glass. Then he carefully nudged Sheffield's drink aside and covered the note.

"The lady I've recently become interested in," Sheffield added quietly, "has decided to visit friends in the country."

That would be Rosalind Melbourne. So, the Scottish raven had taken flight to the country? That was worrisome. She preferred to stay in town, and he preferred that as well. It made it easier for him to keep an eye on her affairs. So far he'd been fortunate enough to manipulate her into taking him on as a business partner, then coaxing her into disrupting Ashton Lennox's shipping companies.

"Which friends is the lady visiting?"

"The baron's." Sheffield took his half-empty glass from the table and drank.

Lennox? That was not good. Hugo wanted her and Lennox to remain at odds. If they were ever to form an alliance, half of his current schemes could easily unravel. The logistics of altering those plans with reliable substitutions would be bothersome to say the least.

He would need to find a way to entice Lady Melbourne back to London where he could keep a close eye on her.

"Hmm. Well, we can deal with that soon. Did the baron suffer any losses today?"

"He did. Two tenant houses burned down last night. It will keep him occupied and away from London."

"Excellent." That was just as he intended. He and Sheffield were arranging the transport of some agents to France, but Lennox had been keeping a close eye on Waverly's actions of late. Too close. And Lennox and his men had a tendency to stumble into his missions and wreck them. It would be just like them to be responsible for a war because they refused to keep to themselves. So Sheffield had seen to a decent distraction to draw Lennox away from London for a time.

Sheffield cleared his throat. "One more matter to attend to," he whispered, with a slight nod at the paper he'd tucked under the glass. "Urgent."

Hugo slid his paper back toward his lip, deftly grasping the note Sheffield handed him. He noted the red wax seal—Scottish in design. The seal was one he recognized. Kincade. That conjured up some old memories.

Ten years ago he'd been a young man just entering the service of His Majesty. England had recently signed an act that united Scotland and England, but already there were separatist rumblings. Hugo's job had been to suss out the leaders of the movement before it could gain popularity. And he had, a loose alliance of Scottish landowners who called themselves the Anti-Unionists.

Over the span of a year, all but one of its nine leaders had been dealt with in a series of accidents. Only one man remained, Montgomery Kincade—Rosalind Melbourne's father.

The wily bastard had betrayed his compatriots for a hefty sum and to have his own life spared. It would have been prudent to take care of Kincade as well, but the man was cunning and had protected his interests well. He had warned Hugo that if he should die under accidental or suspicious circumstances, a collection of letters that Hugo had foolishly written would be exposed.

Such a thing would ruin Hugo. Beyond the damage to his reputation, the Scots would want him dead, and the Crown would disavow him to protect the tenuous relationship between itself and Scotland. They might go so far as to ensure he had an accident of his own.

He would not have made such a mistake now, but he'd been young then.

There were few things Hugo forgot, but this...this was one thing he wished he could. Ironically, it had been this very mission that had ensured his place among his peers and helped him to the position he was in today.

With a steadying breath, he broke the seal and read the letter. It was coded in the pattern of the old cipher he'd used ten years ago. It required a special device, one which Hugo had designed himself, to decode. He still carried it with him and occasionally used it for less important communications. He slipped it out of his pocket and set the symbols to match in the upper left corner of the letter, which then gave him the key to deciphering the rest of the message.

SIR HUGO,

It has been many years since we last spoke, but my memory is still sharp. I write to you from my deathbed. You cannot punish me any longer. That is up to the Lord now.

But do not think that you have won. I took money in exchange for silence when you murdered my fellow countrymen, and they call to me for revenge. I can ignore them no longer.

I still have every letter you wrote, with the code set out. Soon, the only person I trust will receive the device you once gave me, along with instructions to find where I've hidden the letters. They will expose you at last for what you are.

Soon your king and your country will know how many you murdered for the sake of your precious nation. A nation built on lies. A nation that kills its own people when they so much as suggest standing up for themselves.

I'm laughing at you, Waverly. Laughing from beyond the grave. I suspect I will be seeing you in hell soon enough.

Kincade

. . .

HUGO COULDN'T BREATHE. The cipher device and the letters...the letters that could condemn him and ruin his life. And they were being sent to...whom?

Hugo scanned the letter again, searching for a clue. *The only person I trust.* He trusted no one, because he had been willing to betray anyone.

Except perhaps his family. If there was someone he trusted, it would have to be family. He thought back to what he knew of the man. Four children. Three sons and a daughter.

But it made no sense. Exposing those letters would destroy the Kincade name as well as his own. He wouldn't trust his heirs to destroy their own futures.

Rosalind, however...

Her wealth and status were independent of the Kincade name. And from what he knew from their meetings, there had been no love between her and her father. Quite the opposite. For that very reason, the old bastard could assume she'd be more than willing to expose her father's sins.

And she was en route to see one of his greatest enemies, presumably with the cipher in her possession. But not the letters. He still had time to find those before she did.

"Bloody hell," he whispered.

"Anything to be concerned about?" Sheffield asked.

Hugo folded the letter and pocketed it. As soon as he was home he would burn it.

"A ghost is trying to haunt me. Reach out to our man inside Lennox's estate. Have him send reports to our agent in Lonsdale's employ. I want them to find a way to steal back a cipher device that may be in Lady Melbourne's possession. It looks like this." He raised his own for Sheffield to see before returning it to his pocket. "I want Lady Melbourne's residence searched in case she left it behind. If it is not found, find a reason for Lady

Melbourne to return to London. I will be able to handle her myself."

"I'll see to it." Sheffield rose, and with a casual glance about the room, he set his empty brandy glass on the table and left Boodle's card room.

Hugo felt the weight of Kincade's letter in his waistcoat pocket. Rosalind possessed a weapon that could destroy him, and she was about to go straight toward one of his enemies with it. But on its own it was nothing more than a trinket. A curiosity. He would find a way to stop her from finding the letters before he did.

His nerves began to steady. Having a plan of action always calmed him. But as if to betray him and remind him of his concerns, his hands shook as he set down his glass.

Damn the League of Rogues, damn them all.

⁓

BROCK KINCADE WAS SLUMPED over his escritoire in his small study at Castle Kincade. The last candle he could afford to spare was burning down to the end of its wick, the wax pooling at the base of the candleholder. Outside, the wind whistled through the tapestries and cracks in the stone and glass, filling every room with an inescapable biting wind, even in the spring.

The papers in front of him blurred together as exhaustion plagued him. But he had to stay awake in case he was needed. It seemed that the weight of the world crushed down upon him. Upstairs his father was dying, and the thought of it was leaving Brock's life in a state of upheaval.

The study door banged open and his younger brother Brodie stood there, chest heaving as though he'd run the entire way.

"You must come. It's time."

Brock licked his thumb and forefinger and snuffed out the candle. He rose from his chair and followed Brodie up the winding, narrow steps to the tower where their father's chambers were.

They came to a halt outside the room, and Brock opened the door. Their younger brother, Aiden, sat at the foot of the bed, his face ashen.

Aiden stared at the old man lying in the bed. "He's not going to last, Brock."

Montgomery Kincade, once a tall, broad-chested and hard man, had become frail, small, shriveled. It was an odd thing to stare at the nightmarish beast of a man who'd hurt him so many times before and see him completely helpless.

Their father could not strike them now or shout at them now. He was too weak to do more than murmur. But Brock could see the glittering malice behind the old man's eyes as he glared at him.

"Aiden, you don't have to stay. You can say your goodbyes now and go," Brock said softly.

Aiden continued to stare at the feeble old man. "No. I want to stay and…" He cleared his throat. "Make sure he's dead."

Brock shared a surprised glance with Brodie. Aiden was the sweetest of the three of them, assuming any could be called sweet. He'd also been the one to care most for their ailing father as his health declined in the last four months.

"Stay if you want." Brock sighed and walked over to stand beside the bed. His father's eyes drifted from Aiden to him, no less cold, no less cruel.

"You finally have to listen to us," Brock said. "After years of suffering pain at your hands, you cannot move, cannot speak. 'Tis fitting."

He then folded his arms over his chest. "Know this, Father. We love you as God expects, but we have never liked you. You drove Rosalind away by your cruelty, but now you'll never hurt her again." His tone was soft, like a blade wrapped in a tartan.

His father's eyes glinted with a red hue, but when he opened his mouth, only a soft hiss escaped him. The stroke he'd suffered two days before had robbed him of his ability to move except for one hand, which he tried to raise.

"Letters." The word escaped the old man's lips. "Must give...to Rosalind."

"Letters? What letters?" Brodie drifted a step closer to his father as though torn between curiosity and hesitancy.

"Under...me." Montgomery's gaze dropped down to his lower back. Brodie lifted up the feather mattress and dug around for a minute before his hand halted. Brock watched his younger brother pull out a stack of letters, yellowed with age and bound with twine. Brodie handed them to Brock and looked back to his father.

"Must save...for Rosalind. Give them to her by...your hand."

Brock had held back his anger for so many years, and yet seeing his father broken, but still so full of malice, infuriated him.

"What are they?" he demanded.

Montgomery shook his head, the movement so faint that Brock almost missed it in the dim light.

"For...her alone. She has the key."

Brock smacked the letters against one of his hands in rage. He was not about to ride all the way to London to deliver to his little sister a set of letters that were likely full of hate and insults from a bitter, dying old man.

His father's lips twitched in a cold smile, as though he wished to laugh at his eldest son. "If you wish revenge upon me...these are the way..." His eyes fixed on the letters in his son's hands and he coughed.

"I'm not going to play some bloody game with you, Father. When you've passed, I will be master of this castle and things will be different."

"Brock, don't," Brodie warned. None of them wanted to have any more time with their father, but it wasn't wise to provoke him to an early death. It would be unkind, even though their father deserved no kindness.

But Brock had no pity left. No mercy. Three decades had left him weary and his control frayed.

For the next half hour, he and his brothers stared at the wrinkled visage of their father's face in the dwindling candlelight. It was close to midnight when the old man suddenly jerked, all of his muscles contracting. Then his gaze drifted heavenward and he exhaled, a weak, shallow breath.

His last. Montgomery was dead. The weight of the letters in Brock's hands felt as heavy as a mountain of stones. He walked over to his father's bed and shoved the letters back under the mattress. He could burn them tomorrow if he wished, but he would not give them to Rosalind, not when he was certain whatever was inside would cause her harm.

Brodie leaned over the bed and brushed his fingertips over their father's eyes and closed them while Brock and Aiden watched.

"What…what do we do now?" Aiden asked.

Brock picked up the sputtering candle, and with one glance at his brothers he blew it out.

"Father is dead. We take back our lives."

"What of Rosalind?" Aiden asked. "Will she come home now?"

The last that they knew of their sister was that she'd married an Englishman, had been widowed, and was now living in London. They'd learned that much through occasional reports from friends who went to London every few months. But they'd not dared to contact her since she'd left. It hadn't been safe. They'd feared their father would have gone after her, dragged her back home and punished her, even though he'd never cared about her.

"I want her home," Aiden said. "I miss her."

Brock nodded. "I know." Brodie was thirty, but Aiden was a mere two years older than Rosalind, and they'd been close growing up. All three of them had mourned her leaving, even knowing she had to go for her safety, but Aiden had acted as though part of his heart had been ripped out. He had so much of their mother in him. Like Rosalind, he was all heart.

"We will bring her home. She's safe now. We all are."

∼

IT WAS the worst coach ride Rosalind ever had. When she'd made arrangements to leave that afternoon, the skies had been clear and the day fine and sunny. Yet as they'd climbed in the coach that evening to leave, she'd thought she'd smelled rain in the air. About an hour outside of London, storm clouds had gathered upon the horizon, and shortly after that, the skies opened up.

Rain lashed at the windows, and the driver cursed as the horses balked. It felt like her driver was aiming for every hole and ditch in the road.

"Heavens, this is a dreadful storm," Claire exclaimed, wrapping her cloak about her.

"It would rain," Rosalind muttered darkly. A wretched day could always turn worse.

"How long until we reach Lord Lennox's estate?"

"At least an hour or more."

The coach suddenly dipped. Rosalind and Claire crashed to the floor. Rosalind's arm stung sharply with pain as she landed awkwardly on it.

"Are you all right, Your Ladyship?" Claire asked.

"Yes. What's wrong? We've stopped." The coach was no longer moving. The fine hairs on the back of her neck prickled. If her driver was stopping in this storm, it wasn't for a good reason. She opened the door and blinked against the rain as she sought the driver. He stood beside the back wheel of the coach.

"Mr. Matthews! Why have we stopped?"

"The wheel's fractured, my lady. It cracked on that last dip. We won't make it far in this weather before it completely breaks."

"Oh, heavens." Rosalind groaned and looked about the rain-spattered road before her heart stopped. A shadow flickered on the edge of the road, drawing closer. Someone was coming toward them from the woods. She ducked back inside the coach.

"Claire, fetch my reticule. I have a small pistol inside." She hoped to God she wouldn't have to use it. She had heard these smaller country roads were prone to highwaymen and other thieves who would prey on travelers.

Her maid found the reticule and handed it to her. Rosalind dug around until her fingers closed around the pearl-inlaid handle.

"Stay back while I see who it is."

She opened the coach door and froze. The driver had started to climb back up to his perch, his hands in the air. A cloaked figure wearing a domino mask concealing his features had a pistol trained at the driver. A highwayman. They were to be robbed.

CHAPTER 5

O f all the trouble Rosalind had imagined getting into when trying to get her life back from Ashton's steel grip, she hadn't expected to be robbed by a highwayman.

"Who's inside?" the man demanded of the driver.

"Lady Melbourne and her lady's maid."

"Step away from the horses and go over by the road." The man flicked the end of his pistol to indicate where he wanted the driver to go.

"What is it?" Claire whispered.

This isn't bad. Not compared to what you've faced before. She prayed she could convince herself of that.

Without taking her eyes off the armed man, Rosalind whispered back, "I believe we're about to be robbed." Her heart pounded hard enough that she could barely hear herself think.

"What?" Claire gasped.

"Let me handle this. Stay behind me at all costs."

"But—"

Rosalind raised her hand with the pistol as the masked man strode purposefully toward the coach. Just as he reached the door,

Rosalind aimed her pistol at his chest. She had never shot a man before, and she prayed she wouldn't have to now.

The man halted, as though startled by her sheer audacity to point a pistol at him. Then he smiled at her hesitation.

"Don't even think of shooting me. I have men in the woods ready to take my place should I fall. The end result will be the same, though they are likely to be less kind than I." The highwayman's accent was refined and strangely familiar. She couldn't quite place where she'd heard his voice. Despite the storm, there was light enough to see those electric-blue eyes as the man stared at her. Eyes she recognized. The eyes of the very man she was desperate to find and throttle.

"Lord Lennox?" she gasped.

The man's eyes widened a second before they narrowed. The lightning illuminated his own pistol aimed at her chest.

"Be wise, madam, and put your weapon away. I want any money you possess and your jewelry."

Rain coated Rosalind's face as she leaned out of the coach a little, but she didn't blink, didn't back down. Still, she was hesitant to use the gun.

"We have no jewelry or money."

The man laughed. "And yet you wear such an expensive gown? I do not think so." He pressed the muzzle of his pistol right above her heart, the metal cold against her skin. "Your money. *Now.*"

Rosalind made no move to do as the highwayman demanded, but suddenly her purse was being handed over her shoulder by Claire.

"What are you doing?" she hissed at her lady's maid.

"Saving our lives," Claire whispered back.

The masked man flashed a cool smile as he plucked the purse from Claire's trembling gloved fingers.

"At least one of you has the good sense to do as you're told." He stepped back, pistol still raised, and waved the bag with all the money she had on her. "Have a lovely night, ladies." He ran for his horse, mounted up and kicked his boots into the horse's flanks.

It was too much for her to bear. Aside from the fact Rosalind couldn't imagine being in a worse possible position, stranded in the middle of nowhere with a broken carriage and no money, this monstrous personal violation was intolerable. It would not stand.

Rosalind leapt out of the coach, her pistol arm raised, and she fired. The man flinched and clutched his arm but kept riding away until he vanished beneath the heavy rain and darkness.

"Thank heavens you missed him!" Claire exclaimed.

"I was aiming for his black heart." Wiping the rain out of her eyes, she looked for the driver. Her hand with the pistol started to shake. She'd never shot a man before, and only now did the repercussions of that begin to set in.

The driver came forward, grim-faced.

"I assume we can't make it the rest of the way on that wheel?" Rosalind asked.

Mr. Matthews shook his head. "We won't make it more than a mile. I do know of an inn not far from here. The woman who runs it might allow us to stay the night, and I could see about bargaining for the wheel replacement or riding back to London at first light if the storm lets up."

Rosalind sighed, frustration pricking beneath her skin.

"I suppose that will have to do." She climbed back into the coach. Her gray bombazine gown was heavy with water, and it made her feel bone-weary dragging the skirts back up the steps. Once the coach started rolling again, her maid leaned close to her.

"You called the masked man Lord Lennox," Claire said quietly. "It couldn't have been him, could it, Your Ladyship?"

Rosalind hesitated. "I thought it was. The eyes were like his, but the way he talked... I don't know." She shook her head. "It's foolish. Lennox has no reason to rob anyone at gunpoint when he does it so well with solicitors and banks. I suppose that cad is simply foremost on my mind of late."

Claire said nothing as they drove onward.

"Well, it doesn't matter. Not tonight. For now, we must focus on food and shelter. I can't seduce Lord Lennox into giving me back what is mine unless I'm able to rest and get some food in me." Claire handed Rosalind her shawl to act as a towel to wipe herself dry as the coach jerked forward once again.

By the time they reached the little inn, Rosalind's dress was still heavy and damp and her skin was chilled. Mr. Matthews unloaded their bags and brought them to the common room before he left to find someone who might repair or replace the wheel. Her stomach grumbled at the aromas of soup and bread.

Peering around the dim room, Rosalind glimpsed too many people, too many faces. Most were men who stared at her in mild interest, unused to seeing a lady of quality stopping at such a small inn. They were on a single road with many travelers. What if the inn was full? She shook her head. What did it matter? She and Claire had no money to pay for a room.

"How can I help you ladies?" A stout woman with a cheery face ambled over to them.

Rosalind inhaled, then slowly blew out a breath at the plea she was about to make.

"We are hoping you might have a spare room for the night?"

The pleasant woman's smile faded. "'Fraid not. Just booked the last one."

With a sinking feeling in her chest, Rosalind's head dropped in defeat. "I feared as much, given the storm. What about some food?"

"Plenty of that, thank heavens." The innkeeper smiled at them. "What would you like?"

For a brief moment, Rosalind was relieved, but then she remembered they were still broke. She was not the sort of person to take anything without giving something back.

"Thank you, ma'am, but we've no money to pay," Claire interrupted. "Her Ladyship and I were accosted by a highwayman who took everything but the clothes in our trunks. Is there any way we could earn our supper? I can cook and wash dishes."

Rosalind stared at her maid. Such a simple solution hadn't occurred to her. When she got control of her own tongue, she hastily added, "I can help as well."

The innkeeper smiled. "We've been short-handed tonight on account of the storm." She nodded at Claire. "You can help in the kitchens. And you"—she looked to Rosalind—"can serve the tables. I'll have you get started, and in a few hours, the three of us can eat."

Rosalind removed her gloves and scarf, handing them to Claire before she followed the innkeeper to meet the bartender. Then she set to work, rushing back and forth from the dozen tables in the room to the bar and the kitchens.

Arms laden with trays of food or pints of ale, she had to concentrate on not spilling anything. Most of the men treated her with a decent amount of respect. Only one or two tried to pinch her inappropriately. It wasn't the first time she'd had men make a pass at her, and one steely gaze sent their way made their wandering hands drop.

By the time the inn had quieted for the evening, she collapsed on a nearby chair at a now vacant table. Her feet ached, and she knew she'd have blisters where her ankles had rubbed against her boots.

"Here we are, dear. You've earned it." The innkeeper set a steaming bowl of beef stew in front of her and then turned to wave at Claire, who was just leaving the kitchen, her dress covered in flour and stained with grease.

"Now, eat up you two." Their host went to fetch her own bowl. When she returned, Rosalind was licking her spoon clean and feeling a little drowsy.

"Where were you ladies headed before you were robbed?"

"We were headed to Lennox House. How far is that from here?"

The woman thought for a moment. "Lennox House? You're still a ways off. About an hour by coach. Three by foot."

So far? "I don't suppose anyone would allow us to ride in the back of a cart on their way past the house?"

The innkeeper looked disappointed. "If I hadn't sent my son off to the village, I would have had him take you. But he'll not be back for two days."

"Thank you. We appreciate all you've done for us." Rosalind meant it. This woman had done far more for them than she'd needed to.

"We women must help each other." The woman chuckled, but Rosalind sensed she had worked hard in life for a reason, and earned her little inn without help from anyone. As a fellow businesswoman, she admired the innkeeper for it.

"I have some sacks of grain in the storage room, and you can make pallets out of them for the night. If you need to, you can stay till my son gets back."

Rosalind glanced at her maid and then nodded. "That would be fine." Lord knows she'd slept on worse in her youth. They followed their hostess to the storage room and helped her lay the sacks of grain down before she and Claire crawled over on top of them. Claire puffed her sack once and then promptly fell asleep.

It was not nearly as easy for Rosalind. The sounds of the grain shifting in the bags, hissing in the dark, clawed at her nerves. The wood walls of the inn creaked, and the scuttle of rodent paws scratching away kept her restless. A cold draft slipped in through the cracks beneath the storeroom door. She punched at the grain beneath her, but she couldn't get comfortable.

Have I gotten so soft since I married Henry? Before then, she'd slept on the stony floors of the stable on more than one night, with naught but a bit of hay to keep warm. This was far better than those days had been.

Every time she closed her eyes, thoughts of the highwayman, his cold smirk and arrogant blue eyes, were all she could see. It made her heart slam hard against her chest all over again. But his voice—it wasn't Ashton's. An echo, perhaps, but not the same. Each leap in her pulse was not because of the robber himself but because of whom he'd reminded her of.

Am I being a silly peahen? To be imagining Lord Lennox as a masked robber? It was utter nonsense. The man had no need to rob ladies upon the road, and it didn't seem like the sort of activity he'd engage in for amusement. And knowing him, if he'd robbed her, he would have taken his mask off and lorded it over her.

Still…something about him reminded her of Ashton. Perhaps it was simply because she'd felt robbed by him already and was clearly determined to associate all villains with that bloody baron. She paused, her thoughts circling around something that startled her. Ashton's plan to take her businesses had been cunning, brilliant, and she had to admire the tactics he'd used.

Somewhere around midnight, Rosalind's shoulder was jostled and she rolled over, half-asleep, to stare at the innkeeper.

"The storm's let up, dear. One of my lads is willing to take you half the distance on his horse, but he can only carry one of you."

Rosalind blinked, looked at her sleeping maid and sighed. *I should let Claire sleep until the coach can come for her.* She couldn't afford to wait two days to confront Ashton.

"I'll go. Would you mind letting my maid stay here until I can send for her? Our coach should be repaired before your son returns. She'll work for room and board in the meantime, and I should be able to pay for any deficiencies once I reach Lennox House. Please let her know to wait for our driver."

The innkeeper nodded. "That'd be fine. I'd love some help in the kitchens. I'll tell her when she wakes. Now come on, the lad's waiting for you."

Wiping her hair back from her face, Rosalind brushed off the dirt from her carriage dress and followed the innkeeper through the quiet common room.

A restless young man waited by the door, and he bowed bashfully when he saw them walking his direction.

"Hello, Your Ladyship."

"Thank you for letting me ride with you." Rosalind meant it. When the lad opened the inn door, rain was still coming down, but it had softened to a drizzle. The young man offered her a foot up on the saddle, and she kept the horse steady as he mounted up behind her.

"What's your name?" she asked as he reached around her to take the reins.

"Rolfe, Your Ladyship."

"Thank you. I won't forget this, Rolfe." She'd find a way to repay him and the innkeeper. She may be ruthless against someone like Ashton but not these folk. They reminded her too much of home and the wonderful people in the villages near her family's castle.

As they rode for the next half hour, her hair fell loose and her barely dry dress was soon soaked again. By the time she reached Ashton's estate, she would look like a drowned cat, not a woman ready to seduce a man for revenge.

She still wasn't convinced that Emily's plan would work. Was Ashton even the type of man who *could* be seduced? He was so cool and dispassionate…yet that night at the opera she'd seen another side of him, one that had given her power over him in that moment of blind passion. Perhaps he could be seduced…

"Here we are." Rolfe tugged the reins to halt the horse at a pair of old stone columns marking the entrance to Ashton's lands. "You're lucky. Seems the storm barely touched here."

"How far is it to the house?" Rosalind's feet were sore just thinking about the trek in this weather in her black boots.

"About three miles." Rolfe slipped off his horse and lifted her to the ground with the grace of a gentleman. "I'm sorry I cannot take you farther. Will you be all right?" He waited for her to respond, eyes wide.

"Yes, thank you. I've managed longer walks."

"Stay on this road and you can't miss the house," Rolfe called out. He got back on his horse and rode away as fast as he'd come. "Safe journey!"

Rosalind squared her shoulders and began the long, agonizing march down the dirt road, hoping she'd see the house soon. The rain picked up, and the road turned thick as mud. The once beautiful skirts of her carriage gown were soon ripped, sodden and caked with mud. It dragged, heavier and heavier, weighing her down until she felt as though she were wading knee-high upstream through a river.

Her feet burned as the leather chafed against her thin stockings. Trees dotted the roadside ahead, forcing an endless line pointing to her goal. A sneeze caught her off guard and she stumbled, almost fell, but managed to catch herself.

I must keep going. No matter how much she wished she was curled up in front of a fire with a good book and a bowl of hot soup.

Ashton's face filled her mind. A driving force to push her onward, even if it killed her.

CHAPTER 6

*J*onathan leaned over a billiard table and prepared to take a shot. "It's a damned good thing Cedric wasn't home when I brought Audrey back from Fives Court."

Ashton idly rubbed the tip of his cue against his booted foot, not missing the way Jonathan's face was intense as he talked.

"You are planning to marry that woman, aren't you?" Ashton asked as he waited for his turn.

He'd been relieved to have his friends arrive this evening after dinner. He'd spent the entire meal trying not to give poor Miss Merton the impression she was to receive a marriage proposal. Between his friends' wives and his mother's schemes, it was getting damned hard to stay a bachelor these days.

"I intend to propose once I've had time to settle into the new townhouse and get everything prepared. No sense in rushing." Jonathan smacked a red ball into a corner pocket.

"Nicely done," Charles said. "But let's be honest, Jon. That little sprite is too much for any man to handle and still keep a grip on his sanity. I doubt you'd be able to keep up with her. She even had me on the run once, as you'll recall."

Ashton watched Jonathan's face redden. He had his older brother's jealous temperament, it seemed, but he kept it far better hidden than Godric.

"I swear," Charles continued, "I've never been chased by a woman before, and yet there she was, tackling me on a settee. What's a man to do, I ask you?"

"I still can't believe you let her kiss you like that," said Ashton. "She's a lady, not a lightskirt. I'm not at all surprised Cedric blackened your eye for it."

Charles gave an indignant huff. "You've never been accosted by her. You have no idea how strong her delicate little hands are, or how she can tackle a grown man right to the floor. She's a menace to every decent bachelor. I'm keeping my distance until you marry her." Charles lined his cue and took a shot, missing wide enough that he cursed.

"Distance? Then why on earth did you let her attend your match at Fives Court? That was dangerous and you know it! What if she'd been recognized? Or worse, what if a man had taken her while you were in the ring? Linley wouldn't have been able to protect her—that lad's too scrawny for that." Jonathan bristled.

"Tom's just young. He'll fill out. I was smaller than a lot of men until I turned twenty-three, wasn't I, Ash?"

"You were," Ashton agreed. Charles had indeed been slim as a young man; it was one of the reasons he'd needed help that night in the river. Waverly had needed no help in overpowering Charles. The dark thoughts and memories swirled close to the surface, and Ash buried them.

"I'm sure Tom's a capable lad, but Jonathan has a point about Audrey. It was not wise to let her come to Fives Court."

Charles sighed dramatically. "She's assisting Lucien's brother, Avery, in his...occupation, as you know. A clever lady is worth her weight in gold, but one who can also disguise herself is that much more valuable. Audrey was merely trying to see if she could fool a crowd. She was pulling it off."

"No, she wasn't. I recognized her," Jonathan insisted.

Charles snickered. "Because you stare at her little backside far too much *not* to recognize it."

"Have a care, man," Jonathan warned.

Ashton saw the younger man's temper building up and decided to intervene. "As soon as Jonathan marries Audrey, I'm sure we won't have to worry about her running off and getting into trouble. Problem solved."

"*Ha!*" Charles was clearly not convinced.

"Regardless, whose turn is it?"

"Hell if I know," Charles muttered and stalked over to the window facing the front of the house.

"I believe you're up, Ashton." Jonathan leaned against his cue, still scowling at Charles.

Charles leaned against the bay window, peering out in the darkness. "I say, do you get many beggars on this road, Ash?"

Ashton propped one hip on the edge of the billiard table. "Out here? Not particularly. Why?"

Charles pointed to the windows. "You seem to have one, and he's headed straight to your front door. Muddy little thing, it seems."

Ashton set his cue down and joined Charles at the window. It was nearly an hour past midnight, and only the light from the windows provided any illumination upon the poor figure trailing its way up to his house.

"It's a woman, I think," said Jonathan.

"I think you're right," said Charles. "Hard to tell with all that mud, however."

"Perhaps you ought to check on the poor creature?" Jonathan suggested.

Ashton nodded. "Yes. I'll only be a moment." He left his two friends and headed for the front door. When he reached it, he heard a faint scratching sound and then a heavy thump as though something heavy had hit the door. Or someone.

Ashton pulled the door open and stepped back as the entrance hall lamps colored the pathetic, crumpled form of a woman on his doorstep. He knelt down and reached for her shoulder and rolled her over. His mind went blank for a second as he stared down at the person at his feet.

Lady Melbourne was lying unconscious at his feet, soaked and chilled to the bone.

"Good God!" He recovered and dug around until he could get one arm under the woman's knees and his other arm under her back. What was she doing here? No, that he knew well enough, but why like this? How had she traveled in this weather on foot?

Charles appeared on one side and Jonathan on the other. "What's the matter?"

Ashton grunted as he rose and carried the heavy, water-logged, muddy woman inside.

Charles tried to peer over Ashton's shoulder. "Wait a minute. I know that face."

"I can't believe she's here," Ashton murmured to himself. He cradled the woman close, oddly protective of her. But of course he was. This was his fault. Whatever had driven her to this, he was ultimately responsible for it.

"Who is she?" Jonathan asked.

"Lady Rosalind Melbourne," said Charles.

Ashton ignored the men following at his heels. He headed straight to his bedchamber. Jonathan rushed ahead to open the door.

"Jon, fetch my sister and her lady's maid. I know it's late, but we have an emergency." Ashton called for Charles to lay out a blanket on the bed before he placed the wet, muddy woman on it. Her dark, heavy hair was thick and sticking to her face. Ashton brushed the locks back. Rosalind looked like a half-drowned kitten, and damned if the sight wasn't upsetting.

He had expected her arrival eventually, but in a coach, accompanied by solicitors. She was not supposed to endanger herself in a storm like this. It stirred within him two emotions he tried to avoid: pity and tenderness. And he knew this creature was generally strong enough to need neither.

"What on earth were you thinking?" he said to himself, taking in her features. The creamy pale skin that glowed like alabaster and the long lashes that fanned across her cheeks. Her heart-shaped face and soft rose-colored lips seemed ready-made for smiles and kisses.

"Ash?" Joanna's weary voice came from the doorway. She was clutching her dressing gown, her blond hair in waves about her face. He hastily sidestepped away from the bed.

"I'm sorry to wake you, Joanna, but we are in need of your assistance." He gestured to Rosalind's unconscious figure on the bed.

His sister rushed to the bed, her maid Julia behind her. Both women gaped at Rosalind.

"Who is she? What happened?" Joanna put the back of one hand over Rosalind's forehead.

"This is Rosalind Melbourne. As to what happened, I am not entirely sure. It seems she may have walked here through the storms."

Joanna put a hand on his chest and shoved him back. "Julia and I will take care of things from here. You must go outside at once. All of you."

Ashton realized Charles and Jonathan had been flanking him the whole time like silent sentinels.

With a nod he encouraged them to leave, but as he closed the door he remained in his chambers. Joanna and Julia didn't seem to notice at first.

"Ah, the poor dear's half-frozen," Julia said with her Irish lilt. "Soaked to the bone, too. I'll prepare a bath. You strip her out of those muddy clothes."

The carriage dress was a crumpled heap on the floor by the time the ladies noticed Ashton was still inside.

"Ashton, *leave*. You cannot be in here." Joanna shielded Rosalind's body with her own by standing in front of the bed, arms crossed.

"You'll need help getting her into the tub." He gently pushed his sister aside, her mouth agape as he picked up Rosalind and carried her to his large brass bathing tub. Julia just stared at him for a minute.

"Do you need help with the bath?" he asked the maid.

"No, my lord. You may set her inside. The water is hot."

"Thank you, Julia." He turned to his sister. "Please bring down a spare nightgown."

His sister looked scandalized. "And leave you two alone?"

"She's a widow, Joanna, not a debutante. Her reputation is not at stake the way yours would be. Now go, fetch me those clothes."

Joanna nodded and grabbed her maid's arm as they departed. Once he was alone, he turned his focus back to Rosalind.

Even though she still wore her chemise, Ashton knew his sister and her maid would protest that he'd gone too far by staying any longer. He bent over the tub and gingerly set Rosalind inside. Her cold, pale skin started to color as he knelt beside her. Her head rolled and her lashes fluttered. Ashton cupped her cheek and brushed the pad of his thumb over her left cheekbone.

"Claire," she murmured drowsily. "Did I fall asleep in the bath?"

Ashton had to swallow his chuckle. "Something like that, my little hellion. Wake up for me."

Rosalind's eyes flew open. "Lennox! You bloody bastard!"

Crack! Her palm connected with his cheek, catching him off guard, but he did not retaliate. Holding very still, he stared at her, watching the play of emotions that crossed her face. Shock, rage, embarrassment, and then to his displeasure, he saw fear overcome all of these.

His little Scottish hellion was finally awake.

CHAPTER 7

"How did I..." Rosalind glanced down at herself, and Ashton saw every one of her muscles tense.

He could almost hear her thoughts trying to catch up with her panic. She was all but naked and sitting in a tub of warm bathwater with Ashton just inches away. A hot blush flamed her face.

"I found you on my doorstep. Unconscious." He couldn't help that his tone sounded gruff. The image of her passed out at his feet was difficult to look back on.

"Oh." She ducked her head, but he could still see the wheels turning as she tried to piece together what series of events had led her to this tub.

"Did you walk all the way from London?" he asked, drawing her attention back to him.

Rosalind's shoulders dropped, and she covered her breasts with her arms, all too aware of where his focus was drifting. "What? No, of course not. Don't be foolish."

"Then how in blazes did you end up at my house in such a muddy mess?" Ashton sat on his backside by the tub and continued to regard her, now with amusement.

When she didn't answer, he reached into the tub with his long fingers and flicked droplets of water towards her in an offhanded way. He bit his lip when he noticed her eyes tracking the movement of his hand. *Skittish as a foal...*

Forcing herself to drag her eyes from his hand, she met his curious look and raised her chin, silently defying him to splash her again.

"I took my coach, even though you forbade it. My maid and I were halfway here when..." Her eyes narrowed and she suddenly lunged at him, punching him hard with a balled fist.

Despite the surprising strength behind the blow, Ashton did not flinch.

She stared at him as though searching for some type of reaction, and she seemed disappointed that she didn't find it. "Blast."

"The first blow I can understand. Dare I ask what *that* was for?" Ashton raised a brow. He wasn't going to let her escape without an explanation.

A red blush stained her cheeks.

"Come now, Rosalind, you've struck me twice now in my own home. You were expecting something. A reaction. What for?"

Her gray eyes flashed. "My maid and I were robbed by a highwayman this evening after a wheel fractured on my coach. The man was blond...and he had your eyes."

"*My* eyes? Don't tell me that you're seeing me as a phantom in the night."

"Don't be ridiculous!"

"Then you hit me because...?" He watched her closely, half amused and half concerned.

She raised her chin. "As that wretched man rode off with my purse, I fired a shot and hit his right shoulder. If it had been you, then I daresay you wouldn't have been able to hold back your pain."

A highwayman? There weren't any in these parts of Hampshire, at least none he'd heard of.

"So you were robbed and thought this fool was me?"

"I considered the possibility, yes." She closed her eyes, as though utterly humiliated.

He was infuriated at the thought of anyone aiming a pistol at Rosalind. And he was even more put out that she'd thought it was him.

Of course, after orchestrating her destitution, even if was only temporary, could he blame her? Suddenly his scheme was not the wonderful victory he'd hoped for. Greater good aside, it left him feeling hollow and petty, and there was a stirring of nervousness inside his chest.

"And then?" he prompted.

She didn't continue right away. She kept her eyes closed, her head resting on the back of the tub.

"Our driver went to see about repairing the coach. He dropped us off at an inn."

Ashton sensed she still wasn't telling him everything. "But you couldn't stay the night because you had no money?"

"We were able to obtain a place to sleep and a meal."

He snorted. "No doubt you assured her you would make me pay for everything once you'd visited me and demanded your assets back." It was exactly the sort of thing she would do.

Rosalind's eyes narrowed to angry slits. "I did nothing of the sort. My maid and I earned our food and place to sleep."

"Earned?" He couldn't picture Rosalind earning a meal. "How the devil did you do that?"

The look she shot him could have frozen a lake. "The innkeeper let my maid help in the kitchens while I waited on the tables. The rooms were full, but they allowed us to stay in the storeroom on sacks of grain."

She'd slept on sacks of grain in a storage room? Rather than make him laugh, the image cut him deep—sleeping on lumpy bags of grain, how it would knot her muscles and leave her sore the next morning. Enemy or not, a woman like her deserved to lie on a downy feather bed with a mountain of blankets to keep her warm.

"If you were supposed to be sleeping there, how did you end up here?"

"A boy gave me a ride halfway to your house before the storm started up again. I *walked* the rest of the way." She raised one delicate foot out of the water. Red and angry blisters dotted her ankles. She sighed and lowered her foot back beneath the surface.

This should have been his moment of triumph, the fall of his greatest rival. Yet finding her half-dead on his doorstep, the fear in her eyes upon waking, and now witnessing her blistered feet... it tore at his heart. His little Scottish hellion was a brave and worthy opponent. There was no pleasure to be had in her suffering, and he wanted her back on her feet.

Ashton stood abruptly; the sudden press of self-loathing for what his actions had caused had made him too uncomfortable to face her. He needed a minute to breathe, to remember that he was in control, and he wouldn't let his emotions get in the way.

"I'll send a messenger to the inn tomorrow to pay for your maid's stay and have your coach repaired and brought here as soon as it is ready. Please take your time in the bath. I'll have food sent up. My sister, Joanna, will have spare clothes to lend you. If you require anything, you need only ask."

She snorted. "Because you *own* me, correct?"

His words thrown back at him stung. His first impulse was to challenge her, declare she *did* belong to him. Then he remembered another young woman, one who'd taught him last year that a lady in distress was well within her rights to lash out. And when she did, she needed a gentleman to respond, not a possessive brute. Emily had taught him much in the last few months.

"You may not believe this, but once upon a time, I was a gentleman. You are in need of food, shelter and clothes. It is my duty to provide that, seeing as how my actions caused your situation." He left her to bathe and went back into his room.

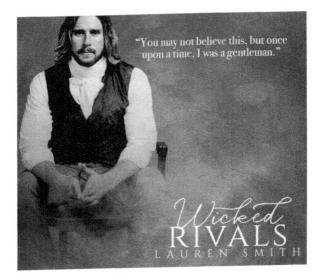

"You may not believe this, but once upon a time, I was a gentleman."

THE SOUNDS of her light splashing echoed through the partially closed door. He sighed and leaned one arm against the back of a chair and watched the fire make shadows across the floor.

Have I gone too far? I've robbed Rosalind just as much as that damned fool of a highwayman. It does nothing but mark me as a villain. No better than Waverly.

That sobering thought brought him up short. He had to find a way to still achieve his goals without causing her any more harm.

The sounds of water splashing increased, and he sensed Rosalind must be ready to get out. He reentered the dressing room and retrieved a towel. She sat huddled in the bath, arms covering her breasts and her legs tucked up. The sight of her looking so small and vulnerable made something in his chest ache. He spread the towel out and held it up for her.

"You'd best get out before the water chills. Remove your chemise. It will need a thorough washing."

Her eyes glinted dangerously, and for a moment he worried she'd remain in the water out of spite.

"Hold it a little higher," she ordered.

He raised the towel to the point where it would prevent him from seeing her body as she climbed out of the tub. He heard the splash of water and the slick sound of wet cloth upon skin, then the smack of the chemise upon the floor. He inched the towel down just enough to see the sloping of her shoulders before she hastily took it and wrapped it around her body. She had curves. He liked that, but her figure was leaner and smaller than he'd realized. When she stood to her full height she only came up to the top of his shoulder.

"You mentioned food, *my lord?*" She stressed the words with a mocking tone that had him wishing he'd stolen a few strips of red silk from his friend Lucien. Tying this woman to his bed sounded like a perfect punishment for her temper.

He shook himself. He shouldn't be thinking of her like that. Certainly not at this moment. He'd never let on how creative his tastes in bed ran. He saw himself as not unlike Lucien, loving a good restraint or two and mirrors perhaps to watch his sensual domination from every angle, but he trusted few women with those secret desires. The last thing he needed was talk in the *ton* about his appetites and to have them used against him.

"I did promise sustenance. I shall dine with you, of course."

She jolted. "I beg your pardon?"

"It would be remiss of me to let you take supper alone."

She wrinkled her little nose, an expression he found oddly endearing.

"Why would you torture us both by dining with me? Neither of us can stand each other."

He allowed a smile to curve his lips. "Why indeed? Perhaps it is because this is my bedchamber and I shall have to go to sleep at some point tonight."

Rosalind, who had been combing one hand through her wet

hair, froze. *"Your* room?"

"Naturally. What was it I said? Oh yes, I *own* you, Rosalind." He caressed her name, letting each decadent syllable roll off his tongue, delighting at the fire in her eyes. Now she was ready to do battle again.

"I demand another room. Take me to one at once." She started toward the door, intent on storming out.

"Demand?"

"Yes, demand." Watching the defiant sway of her hips in that towel was too much for any rogue to resist.

"Very well then." Before she could stop him, he'd lifted her up in his arms and tossed her over his shoulder.

"Put me down, you wretched oaf!" She shouted and kicked, nearly dislodging the towel about her body. He reached up and firmly held the towel against her backside, relishing the indecent hold far too much.

"I said put me *down* you—"

His chamber door swung open, and they both stilled at the sound of a voice.

"Ashton Malcolm Lennox, what in God's name are you doing?"

Regina, in her nightgown and robe, hair plaited to one side, was staring at him. Behind her were Joanna and Julia, holding clothes for Rosalind. Beyond them, Charles and Jonathan were leaning against the opposite wall, smirking. The bloody bastards.

Ashton sighed. "I was about to see to our guest's request regarding accommodation."

Regina stared at him. It had been nearly twenty years since she'd called him by his full name. That did not bode well.

"Did she request to be carried over your shoulder wearing only a towel?"

"No, Mother."

"Mother?" Rosalind gasped. "Heavens, put me down Lennox, *please!*"

Ashton backed up a few steps, turned around and walked over

to his bed. He dropped Rosalind down on top of it.

"Joanna informed me that we are entertaining an important guest. Lady Melbourne, I believe?" She stared pointedly around Ashton's shoulder at Rosalind.

When Ashton glanced her way, he saw she was now clutching the bed coverlet around her.

"I apologize, Lady Lennox, to meet you in this fashion." Her words were awkward and strangely shy, something he unexpectedly found charming.

"A simple misunderstanding, I'm sure. It's lovely to meet you, dear. I hope my son is...behaving himself." Regina glared at Ashton. "He should have brought you down from London earlier today so you could have dinner with the family and our neighbors." Now she was smiling again, and Ashton couldn't help but stare.

What on earth was his mother doing? Did she plan to take Rosalind to an afternoon tea? Lord...that thought gave him an upset stomach. He didn't want his mother anywhere near this woman. The two of them could plot a coup and overthrow him.

"Mother, why don't you go on to bed? I'm sure Rosalind would be much happier to meet you properly in the morning."

His mother raised a brow. "The morning? After she spends tonight in your bedchamber? How interesting." By her cool tone he realized she was being facetious.

"On the contrary, I..." Ashton paused, sensing an opportunity might be presenting itself. Perhaps it wouldn't hurt if his mother assumed a few things. "I'm sorry. You were saying?"

Lady Lennox continued. "You failed to mention to me this afternoon that you finally decided to settle down. I'm thrilled, of course. She's lovely. That will mean beautiful grandchildren."

Ashton was unsure of what shocked him more, that his mother seemed genuinely pleased to meet Rosalind, or that she was already talking about grandbabies. He did not want his mother planning *his* future.

An idea suddenly clicked into place. If his mother believed he was courting Rosalind with an intent to marry, she would cease her endless parade of eligible ladies through his front door. He'd be left in peace to handle matters on the estate, at least until he figured out what to do with Rosalind.

What if he could entice her to play along with him? She wouldn't agree to an actual relationship, he knew that much, but if he offered her control of her companies back once his mother successfully believed they were courting... Yes, that might work. And in the end, if things progressed, he might even end up with a wife.

Marrying Rosalind would solve a number of his problems. He'd have full control of her companies and could monitor Waverly's involvement and movements much more easily.

"Oh, we're not—" Rosalind started.

Ashton interrupted. "We haven't set a date yet, Mother. Rosalind is still debating whether she wants to marry me." He could feel the invisible daggers being thrown at his back. Too late, though—he'd made up his mind. He was going to convince his mother he was planning to marry his Scottish hellion. She need never know his real intention was to stop her from marrying him off to the neighbor's daughter.

"Debating? It's a wee bit hard to debate when ye've not even asked me!" Rosalind's brogue thickened in her anger.

Regina cleared her throat, silencing them both. "Well, that's certainly not what I expected from you, Ashton. Taking a woman to bed without a proposal. I'm not going to have this family's name blackened by scandal, not again."

His mother glared at him. The look of anger, hurt and determination hit him hard when she said those words. Already today she had thrown the past in his face, and now a second time. His hands curled into fists, and he bottled his anger as he'd always done.

"No more, Ashton. I cannot bear it." His mother's voice shook.

"No more scandal." The word was uttered softly, yet it threw him headlong into memories that carved deep gouges into his soul.

His father stumbling out of a brothel and Ashton, a boy of fifteen, chasing after him, crying out for him to stop and come home. The sound of hooves and men screaming.

Scandal. His father's drunken death and the mountains of debt that followed. Ashton had grown up very fast and saved his family by the skin of his teeth.

Years later he'd embraced scandal as part of the League, but it wasn't the sort his father had accomplished. He and his friends had pushed the boundaries of acceptable behavior for years. But their scandals were those of seductions and stolen hearts, and they had earned their fortunes rather than lost them. It was a different sort of scandal, one that teased the minds of society in ways they secretly wished for themselves, even if they would not admit it.

His mother's eyes narrowed as if she were reading his thoughts.

"Have you ever wondered why no man has offered for your sister?" Behind his mother, Joanna bit her lip and looked away. "You and Rafe are *completely* irresponsible with your lives. It's destroyed her chances because no one will take a woman whose brothers lack a basic sense of responsibility."

Joanna's face turned crimson. "Mama, it has nothing to do with Ashton or Rafe. Gentlemen simply aren't—"

"Nonsense, Joanna," Regina snapped. "I've seen a number of less lovely ladies married off this past year with dowries far smaller than yours. This is Ashton's fault, and he will see to it that he becomes respectable so as to provide you with a suitable match." With a determined set to her lips, she dared him to disagree.

"I plan to do that, Mother. But it seems my bride-to-be is the one who needs convincing."

A hand curled around his arm, and he looked down once again

at Rosalind. She was biting her lip hard enough that he feared she'd draw blood.

An hour ago he would not have said he planned to marry her, but the moment his mother had made the assumption, he'd decided that was exactly what he wanted to *pretend* he intended to do. If it happened to help Joanna's chances for marriage, all the better. She'd been on the shelf for two years now with no sign of a man taking any interest.

Cedric had faced the same issues with his sisters. League members tended to frighten off potential beaux. In Horatia's case, she hadn't sought out many suitors, but Cedric had purposely driven off a number of Audrey's gentlemen callers.

"Mother, I shall talk with you more on this matter in the morning. Rosalind and I need some time *alone*." He held out his hands to Joanna, who, red-faced, handed over the nightgown she was holding, and he promptly shut the door in his mother's face before he turned to his little Scottish hellion. It didn't stop him from hearing Jonathan and Charles chuckling just outside the room. He ignored them.

"Rosalind?" He let her name come out a gentle question.

She blinked, shook her head and uttered one word. "*No.*"

A strange pain in his chest caught him off guard, and he sucked in a breath.

"Wait a moment. Let's think this through, shall we? I know you don't wish to marry me, but consider this: I have a desire to put my mother off the scent of matrimony, and the best way to do that is to convince her I plan to marry you. She need never know we don't intend to go through with it."

She arched a brow. "I sense you're offering something to me to entice me to play along? It had better be worth it."

"Say the Southern Star shipping line to start. I would revert your ownership of that company to you and release parts of your debts in order for you to sustain that company on your own without fear of me claiming it back. In time, I would see fit to return the remaining companies and assets to you. Our solicitors could draw up the necessary paperwork first thing tomorrow."

There was a heavy pause, but she soon nodded. "I suppose that would be acceptable. But let me make it perfectly clear that I shall not and never will marry you, no matter what games we might play in public for your mother's sake."

It was an answer he'd expected, but the intensity of her resistance piqued his curiosity. He placed his hands behind his back and began to pace in a militaristic fashion. "What are your objections to marrying me?"

Rosalind shivered and glanced away. "Do you mind if I take that nightgown? I'm cold."

Without a word he handed it over. She walked closer to the fire, turning her back to him as she dropped the towel. He caught a full view of her naked backside, the sloping indentations of her waist and the flare of her full hips. A beautiful, addictive silhouette against the fire before she dropped the nightgown over her head and covered herself. It was impossible for his body not to respond to such a glorious sight, and he swallowed hard as he fought to quell his rising arousal.

"So what are your objections?" He waited, staring at her.

She walked over to his bed and picked up the dressing gown, sliding it over her body and tugging it closed.

"Simple. We cannot stand each other."

Ashton scrubbed a hand over his jaw. "That's not true, at least not for me. I find you rather fascinating when you aren't stealing my business. Do you truly dislike me?"

He took two slow, measured steps toward her. Perhaps a little reminder of how hot it could burn between them was called for. When he was done, she would be moaning his name and begging for him to do all the wicked things he'd been fantasizing about for months.

CHAPTER 8

*R*osalind couldn't believe the mess she was in. Marry Ashton? Was he serious? She wasn't repulsed at the thought of pretending—truth be told, a part of her secretly enjoyed it—but now he was asking her why she wouldn't *actually* marry him.

She shivered, even though the dressing gown she wore was warm against her. Her wet hair still lay thick and heavy on her shoulders. She felt vulnerable, too exposed physically and emotionally. Given the intense gleam in Ashton's eyes, she knew he was aware of this vulnerability, and no doubt planned to use it to his advantage.

Yet she sensed in him a practiced restraint that always amazed her. She'd never met a man with so much control. Any other man would be pressing his advantage to slake his lust, but not Ashton. If it hadn't been for that moment in the theater, she'd wonder if he even desired her. Was it all a game to him, even his passions?

"Is the thought of marrying me so dreadful to contemplate that it turns your stomach? What do you find distasteful about me?"

Rosalind's eyes narrowed.

"Business practices aside, of course." Ashton stepped closer.

Only a few inches separated them now, but she held her ground. She raised her head and met him stare for stare.

"Let me think..." She tapped her chin with a finger as she compiled her list. "You're too tall, for one thing. You're arrogant, more so than most men. You think you can possess anything or anyone, and your actions are always justified if it gets you what you want. And frankly, I do not care for the way you kiss."

She swore she saw a ghost of a smile. He raised one dark-gold brow and slowly lifted a hand to her cheek, brushing his knuckles over her skin. His touch felt wonderful, and she *hated* that it did.

"As to the first, it can't be helped. The second I would call confidence, not arrogance. I readily admit to the third, and I believe you're lying through your teeth about the last. Still, I see no reason why we shouldn't go forward with this scheme to deceive my mother. Not if you believe it is to our mutual advantage. Should we see to settling the matter with our solicitors?"

She bristled. "That is perhaps what I despise the most. Everything is business with you. Details, facts, figures. All of it so cold and emotionless," she growled in frustration.

"It *usually* is, but it certainly doesn't have to be. I am a masterful lover."

"There is that arrogance again."

"Confidence," Ashton corrected. His warm breath fanned across her face. She tried not to think about how good it felt to be so close to a large, warm, masculine body. She never asked anyone for help when she could avoid it, but sometimes she could still be tempted by the strength of a man like Ashton. Someone she could imagine would protect her, care for her.

It doesn't make me weak; it's simply that he's too hard to resist.

"I'm not interested in being your lover," she said. Yet she couldn't stop staring at his lips. Full, sensual, *kissable*...

"You don't have to be. But a few kisses at the right time would at least convince my mother we are courting. And it should seem to her as if we have kissed before."

"We *have* kissed before."

"Practice does make perfect..." His head dipped a few inches toward hers, but his lips did not touch hers. Her body was nearly exploding with tension at being so close to him. She was angry, yet full of desire and utterly confused, but she knew she did want to kiss him...because he was right about her lying before. She liked how he kissed far too much.

She wasn't sure who moved first. When their mouths met it was like setting a torch to a keg of gunpowder. All that she'd endured the last two days exploded out from her through her kiss, equal parts anger and passion.

She gripped Ashton's shirt by his neck, clinging to him, meshing her lips against his. Suddenly she was lifted up in the air, and she wrapped her legs around his waist.

Hard wood slammed against her back as he pressed her against the wall and kissed her ruthlessly.

Even in this we compete. The thought had her smiling, and then a chuckle escaped between their breathless kisses. When he paused to look at her, she couldn't help her silly grin.

"What?" he asked, his tone playful. "What is so amusing?" He nuzzled her cheek.

She almost didn't tell him, but the fire in the room and his hot body flush against hers felt divine. She couldn't think past the delightful haze sweeping through her.

"We compete, even in kissing."

His laughter at that was dark and delightful.

"We are rivals, darling. Perhaps we ought to compete in bed as well?"

"We are rivals, darling. Perhaps we ought to compete in bed as well?"

Wicked
RIVALS
LAUREN SMITH

His suggestion flooded her with images of their bodies entwined, fighting to be the best at pleasuring the other to the point where neither of them would recover for days.

"Don't you want to best me in that, future wife?" he asked huskily. "Put me in my place?"

Future wife. That brought her dire situation crashing back down upon her.

"This is only a game." It was as much to remind herself as it was him.

He pulled away, but only a few inches. "I know, but why are you so frightened of the idea?"

She wrinkled her nose. "Because I cannot give a husband what he would want." She could never let him know just how terrified she was to lose the sense of identity she'd managed to build for herself.

He kissed the corner of her mouth, gently fisting one hand in her hair. The gentle but possessive hold made her body burn with heat.

"Why...not?" Ashton asked again, licking the shell of her ear now.

"Because I don't..." Her mind was too fuzzy, her body too hot to think clearly.

One of his hands stroked up her outer thigh, his grip hard but not hurting. Just right...

"Come now, sweetheart, what has you so frightened?"

Damn, the man knew how to hold her, to touch her... "I cannot let *any* man control me ever again." Memories of long, cold, frightening nights in Scotland when her father's temper ran high had left scars on her heart.

He pulled back from her in order to stare at her. "Your husband was cruel to you?" Ashton guessed.

With a shake of her head, she pushed at his shoulder, but he didn't release her.

"No, not my husband. He rescued me from hell, but he also taught me strength and how to be my own woman. He was my white knight."

"He sounds like much more than that. Any knight who teaches a damsel to wield a sword and defend herself is a man I can respect. But if he wasn't the one who controlled you, then who was?" Ashton's eyes narrowed. "Your brothers?"

"They would never! They often took the beatings to spare me."

Clarity sharpened Ashton's eyes. "Ah. Your father."

She didn't respond. He could read her face and the pain she'd spent years trying to hide.

"It's a story I've heard far too often," Ashton continued. "The weak hurt those who are weaker so they can feel strong. No man should ever do that to a woman, let alone his own child."

He reached up and brushed a damp lock of hair back from her face. She ducked at the touch but didn't retreat. She felt less threatened than before. He'd echoed those words Lord Melbourne had said the night he'd met her, and she didn't think Ashton would lie about that. There was an earnestness in his voice that made her believe him.

Ashton brushed a hand through her hair, tucking it behind her ear. There was a myriad of questions she saw flash in his eyes before he finally spoke. "What if we played this charade for a week? If you find it not too disagreeable, we could continue on for a while longer to give me more time to assuage my mother's incessant need to see me settled down."

"A week? I suppose I could suffer that long, but I'm not sure I'll wish to continue this beyond that."

He dropped his hands from her hair. The loss of that soothing stroke surprised her, as did it when he let her down from where she'd been pinned against the wall. She hadn't noticed how relaxed his touch had made her feel until he stepped back away from her.

"Then it's settled. I'll have my solicitor contact yours to start returning the Southern Star company to you. I'll check on your supper. Please stay here. I can't have you running about my house half-naked. It's likely to give my mother a case of the vapors if I give her any more shocks tonight." He was the cool, collected baron once again.

He left her alone in his bedchamber. The chill that his kisses had melted minutes ago soon returned. She stayed put, leaning against the wall, her mind racing, her heart beating wildly. What was she going to do?

The door opened a few minutes after Ashton was gone, and Lady Lennox slipped inside.

"Lady Lennox, I am so sorry to have met you like this," she apologized.

Regina waved a hand. "I have no doubt that whatever brought you to our house like this is my son's fault and I'm the one who should be apologizing. My daughter explained to me you were discovered half-dead on our doorstep, covered in mud and water."

Blushing, Rosalind nodded. "I was forced to walk a few miles through the storm."

"Heavens, child! I'm almost afraid to ask what role my son played in all of this, but I must know." She led Rosalind over to one of the two chairs by the fire and ushered her into one before taking the other.

Rosalind fiddled with the lace of her borrowed nightgown. "I don't wish to upset you."

Regina pursed her lips before speaking. "Please, tell me. It cannot be as bad as what my fertile imagination has supplied."

Where to begin? Rosalind tried to ignore the sudden throb of a headache that built behind her eyes. She sensed Lady Lennox was far more observant than her son believed. She wouldn't simply fall for some ruse of his intent to marry out of the blue. It would be best if she stuck closer to the truth.

"Lord Lennox, in some Machiavellian attempt to punish me for competing with his business, has frozen my accounts, stalled my credits and bought my debts. He took possession of my town-house in London. I used the last of my money to come here, only to be robbed by a highwayman after my coach fractured a wheel. I was then forced to work for my supper at an inn before I walked here through the storm." There, she'd said it all, but the headache didn't go away.

Regina's face was ashen. "Then...but...you're not marrying my son after all that, are you?" she asked, a little worried. "If I'd just endured all that, I'd want to *kill* him, not marry him."

Despite her black mood, Rosalind chuckled. "Yes, that is *exactly* my sentiment towards Lennox, but the damned fool believes he'll marry me. He is quite used to getting his way in things, as you know."

"Of course," Regina murmured in agreement, her eyes still wide with concern. "Oh, my dear, what a mess this is. I suppose it is my duty to save you from him, seeing as how it is my fault he is the way he is."

"In what way, Lady Lennox?" Rosalind didn't have any idea what Ashton's mother was talking about.

The older woman sighed and leaned back in her chair, staring at the fire, or rather staring through the fire and seeing something beyond it that no one else could.

"My two sons have the two worst parts of their father in them. Rafe has all the love of vices, women, gambling, racing, and Ashton all the cold, power-hungry determination to control the world. Despite my efforts, I could not remove those qualities from them. Their failures are my own, I'm afraid." Ashton's mother wiped one of her eyes and blinked.

"I don't believe Lennox is the sort of man who would let anyone shape his future but himself. You mustn't blame yourself for his stubbornness." It was strange to feel herself allied with the mother of her sworn enemy.

Regina gave a watery chuckle. "Stubbornness? That's an awfully polite term for it. Let me guess, you have brothers?"

Rosalind grinned. "Three of them. All as stubborn as your son, perhaps even more so because of their Scottish blood, which I can attest is far worse."

Ashton's mother laughed. "We have Scots in the family, on my side. I know *exactly* what you mean."

They shared a quiet moment together, smiling at each other. Regina straightened her dressing gown. "So, we must decide what to do about this marriage business."

Sobering, Rosalind replied, "I told him I am afraid to marry again." She hesitated, but there was something sincere and honest in Regina's expression that Rosalind trusted. "I lived under the iron fist of a brutal father. My late husband was many years my senior, but he left me well off. If I were to marry, most of the fortune I've built since his death would transfer instantly to my next husband. I will not sacrifice that control over my life to another man."

Understanding lit Regina's blue eyes, eyes so like Ashton's it was almost eerie. "Ashton's father was a loose-handed spender. I came into our marriage with a large dowry, which he lost at the card tables. He had no control when it came to his vices. The fool I was, I still loved him, even when he brought shame and ruin to this house. I understand better than anyone how you must feel."

Rosalind had to admit that it seemed like Regina did have some understanding of being powerless, but marrying Ashton would only worsen her situation.

Regina played with the ends of her plaited hair. "May I ask a question, my dear?"

"Of course."

"My son has never shown an interest in marrying before, and I have tried to settle him down with countless suitable young ladies. Yet the night you arrived here, he seems intent on marrying you. I know my son. I know he would not let scandal force his hand on matrimony, not unless he was genuinely interested in a woman." Regina paused, letting her silent question float between them.

What makes me different? Rosalind shook her head, trying to erase the insane assumption that followed. Ashton's interest was logical, removing the pressure his mother still lay upon him regarding marriage.

"Have you considered that perhaps you have more power than you realize?" Regina asked.

Was Ashton's mother suggesting what Rosalind had intended to do since she'd left London? That she seduce Ashton to get her property and fortune back? "What do you mean, Lady Lennox?"

Regina leaned in to whisper, even though there was no one to overhear them. "What I mean is this—a woman who can seduce a man often gets her way whenever she pleases. If you were to marry him as he wishes, you might be the one with the control over your fortunes. If he's desperately in love with you, you could demand anything you wish of him, *including* control of your lands and property."

That was not unlike what Emily had suggested—seducing Ashton into getting her own way. But did it always have to come to this? She had built her business with cunning and intelligence, not her body. Still, when the male sex held the upper hand in so many parts of society, one fought with the weapons one was provided. At this moment, Ashton was convinced she would willingly play along in his marriage charade in exchange for what was rightfully hers, and his mother was suggesting Rosalind seduce Ashton to the same end.

But why limit herself to the games of others? She could have smiled at her own cunning.

I shall let Ashton woo me to please his mother, and then I shall seduce him in return to convince his mother that I am playing her game. In the end I shall get my companies and assets back on my own terms.

Regina rose from her chair. "I know he doesn't seem the type to fall in love. Two hours ago I would not have believed him capable of it, but there was something about the way he looked at you, my dear. Yes, I think love may not be out of his reach after all."

"But I am not the sort of woman to deceive a man," Rosalind said, hoping to hide that she was intending to do just that. "Honor is all I have left, and I won't use my body as a tool to deceive him."

It was a lie, since that was exactly what she intended, but for some reason she wanted to hold on to Regina's respect. It made little sense that she liked Lady Lennox so much while she despised Ashton, but Regina had proven herself an intelligent woman and seemed nothing like her infuriating son.

"That is why you would be such a wonderful wife for him. What a conundrum we're in." Her laugh was a little bittersweet. "Well, rest tonight, my dear, and don't fret. You are quite safe in this house. We shall see that you're well cared for. Ashton is a gentleman, and I will remind him of that as often as is needed. If you like, I shall have the servants find you a separate room."

"I suppose, except it would be better to stay here and tempt him, wouldn't it?" It would be akin to sleeping next to a hungry wolf, but she'd set her mind to this course of action and needed to stick to it.

Regina smiled. "You may be right. But if you change your mind, ring for me."

Rosalind had no intention of waking Lady Lennox should Ashton choose to take things too far. She was not above kneeing a man in the bullocks to escape him if she thought he meant to do anything against her will.

Yawning, Rosalind stood and followed Regina to the door, holding it open as Ashton's mother slipped into the hall.

"Thank you, Lady Lennox."

Regina patted her cheek. It had been too long since Rosalind had felt a mother's touch.

By the time Ashton had returned with a tray of food, she was almost asleep in a chair by the fire.

"I thought perhaps a light meal would be better, in case your stomach gives you fits." He set the tray down on the table between them. A bowl of hot soup and some bread with two glasses of wine were waiting for her.

He seated himself in the chair next to her and folded his hands in his lap. It was nerve-racking to be so keenly watched while she ate her dinner, but he would not look away.

"Your maid, she is still at the inn? Should I send for her?"

Swallowing a chunk of bread soaked in soup, Rosalind shook her head. "She's at the inn, but she's sleeping. Please do not send for her tonight. I'd hate to have her woken up. If my coach is repaired by tomorrow afternoon, she can return here with it."

Ashton steepled his fingers as he seemed to think things through. "I shall make sure all of that is taken care of tomorrow morning."

They ate in silence for a few minutes, which was surprisingly pleasant with the warmth of the fire and the soft pop and crack of the logs. She used to be afraid of silence after her mother died. It meant her father could be lurking around any corner, waiting to strike her. When she'd first left Scotland, she couldn't stand such silence and had trouble sleeping in a quiet room. But now, a truly pleasant, safe silence made her feel calm in ways she hadn't felt in years. She even felt safe enough to ask the question she knew he wouldn't want her to ask.

"Will we be able to return to London?" She didn't want to ask outright if he planned to let her go back to her home and remain there. The question of her debts was still a problem.

"Rosalind, I'm not letting you go. Not until we settle this situation between us, even if that takes longer than a week." He leaned forward, resting his elbows on his knees and staring deep into her eyes. She shivered, but it had little to do with the cold. From the moment she'd first met Ashton, she'd known he was dangerous. He was a man with quiet intensity, whose observant gaze missed nothing.

What frightened her more was the thought of him seeing through her, the English title and the fancy clothes, of him glimpsing the wounded lass who was afraid to let anyone close ever again.

"How did you come to marry your first husband?"

The firelight showed the hint of gold stubble on his jaw that, if left to grow into a beard, would make him even more attractive. She blinked, took a hasty sip of her wine and tried to smile.

"I never agreed to share the secrets of my past with you."

"Fair enough. What if I shared my secrets with you in return? Ask me anything. Personal only. There is no room for business here tonight."

Personal secrets? The offer was too tempting to resist. "Very well, but you must go first."

He flashed a crooked grin. "I shall hold you to that. Ask away."

This was a moment of importance. She could ask him anything, and she didn't want to waste her question. There was one burning issue she'd wanted to know for months.

"Your friends, the ones the papers call the League of Rogues. How did you come to be? I've heard rumors, but I doubt they're true."

"Rumors?" His eyes were frosted now with displeasure.

"Yes, that you are spies for the Crown, or that you have a club where you sacrifice the virginity of willing maidens on a bed altar while the others watch, or that—"

"Good Lord, did the *Quizzing Glass* say we do that?" He burst out laughing. It was clearly not the type of rumors he'd been expecting her to share.

"Oh, this was another paper, one less flattering than the *Glass*. I swear that author seems to sing your praises while also teasing us with your scandals. It seems everyone wishes to have a piece of your story."

"You mean wishes to invent. I can't say I care for the attention those rags give us."

"It's not true then?"

He waved a hand dismissively. "We avoid virgins when possible, at least I do." He leaned back in his chair and crossed his booted feet at the ankles.

"Then how did you come together?" She was nearly done with her supper, and except for her curiosity at hearing his response, she would have fallen asleep. Her head seemed to weigh too much for her shoulders.

"The story is long and complicated, but I shall explain as briefly as I can. Charles Lonsdale had a history with a man at our school. This man dragged him from his chamber in the middle of the night. They quarreled and fought. In the end, he intended to drown Charles in the river."

Rosalind covered her mouth in shock.

"Lucien and I were crossing the school grounds, returning from a night on the town, when we saw the struggle. Godric and Cedric came upon the river at the same time. The four of us worked together to get Charles safely out of the river. After that night, the five of us became inseparable."

There were shadows in his eyes now, and Rosalind, although fatigued, did not miss that. There was more to the tale, much more, but she had a feeling he would not reveal those last few details for any reason.

"Your turn. How did you come to marry your husband?"

"I fled my father's home. I came to a tavern, exhausted. Henry saw the state I was in and took me to the nearest blacksmith and we married over the anvil. Then he brought me to London so I did not have to return to Scotland ever again."

She didn't tell him everything, not about the home she'd left or the abuse she'd suffered before escaping her father. Those were not stories she would share with anyone unless she trusted the person completely.

"Do you miss it? Your home, I mean?"

She shrugged. The castle had never been a welcoming place, but the truth was she missed her brothers. But while her father still lived, she would not go back to see them.

"And your brothers? What of them?"

"I love them all, but as long as they remain in Scotland, I cannot see them." She pulled the dressing robe tight and sighed. "My lord, could I trouble you for a glass of water?"

"Of course." He rose from his chair and walked into the dressing room.

Rosalind rested her head against the back of the chair.

If I close my eyes for a brief moment, I won't fall asleep...

CHAPTER 9

*P*oor creature.

Ashton paused in the doorway between his bedchamber and the dressing room, a full jug of water in his hand. From where he stood, he could see Rosalind fast asleep in the chair by the fire.

After tonight's events, she was worn out. It was a miracle she'd held out as long as she had. He set the jug of water down on the dresser and walked over to her chair. She did not stir as he cradled her in his arms and carried her to his bed. He set her down long enough to pull back the covers on one side, then picked her up again and placed her under them.

When he tried to tuck her hands under to keep them warm, she grasped his fingers and wouldn't let go. The connection sent soft warmth through his chest. He didn't want to let go of her hand. He pulled off his boots, then scooted her over in the bed so he could lie down beside her, still holding her hand in his. He lay there, watching the firelight play across her face and the shadows under her eyes.

He had learned much about his darling rival tonight, things that made him respect her that much more. The idea that she'd lived under the heavy hand of an abusive father vexed him, however. Godric had also lived such a life. He'd learned that the people he loved could hurt him, a lesson he had carried with him for far too long. It had taken the words and wisdom of Emily Parr to break down the duke's defenses and prove to him that love could be gentle and kind, not full of pain.

Ashton brushed a lock of dark silky hair back from Rosalind's face and tucked it behind one of her ears. She had such dainty little ears, ones he'd fantasized about nibbling as he slid into her over and over again.

He stifled a groan. It had been months since he'd taken a lover. He'd been so caught up in the League's silent war with Hugo Waverly that he'd not bedded a woman in ages. He had too many people he cared about who needed his protection, and satisfying his own desires had taken secondary importance to his duty. Until this moment, finding measures to keep Waverly from destroying everything he held dear had been his main concern.

If only I knew what Waverly was dreaming up next...

Rosalind curled deeper into the pillows and released his hand so she could tuck it up against his chest, like a child. She had survived so much harshness. Ashton could let her have this sweet weakness here in bed, let her sleep deeply and without fear.

"I'll watch over you."

A soft knock on his bedchamber pulled away his attention. Jonathan and Charles both appeared in the doorway.

Ashton pressed a finger to his lips. They waited for him to carefully exit the bed without disrupting the sleeping Highland lass.

Once he was away from the bed, he joined his friends at the door.

"How is she?" Jonathan asked.

"Exhausted. She had quite an adventure trying to reach my house."

"I imagine so, given the way she looked when you found her."

Charles started to laugh, but Ashton shot him a disapproving scowl.

"What? I thought that was your grand plan. To make her come to heel."

Ashton gritted his teeth. "My plan was to remind her who was the better businessperson. I had no intention of her getting robbed, or having to spend the night waiting tables like a common bar wench, or sleeping on sacks of grain before walking here through a storm."

Charles and Jonathan looked toward the woman in shock.

Jonathan shook his head. "Good God. That would be a hard night for any of us."

"Remind me to place all my bets on that woman in *any* fight," said Charles.

"I think, given the late hour, that I shall retire and keep watch over her. You both should rest as well. We have our hands full tomorrow clearing away the burned farmhouses."

"Right." Jonathan paused, then turned at Ashton. "Ash, I meant to tell you, your brother came in from London after you went upstairs. It seems he took a nasty fall and hurt himself during the storms. Your mother sent for the doctor, but he won't be here until morning. If Lady Melbourne feels ill tomorrow, the doctor could look in on her as well."

As always, Jonathan surprised Ashton with his thoughtfulness. He had many of his older brother's wicked ways, but the same tenderness as well. He was a fine addition to the League.

"Thank you, Jon. I appreciate that. I'll see you both in a few hours." He bid them good night, but stopped them as they left. "Jonathan? What sort of injuries did he suffer? Is it serious?"

"Just his arm, I believe. He said he landed on his shoulder."

Ashton nodded and quietly closed the door. He was halfway back in his bed next to Rosalind when a thought struck him.

Rafe riding out in the storm…with an injured arm.

His gaze shot to Rosalind, and he recalled what she had said about a highwayman who'd looked like him. The one she'd shot in the arm.

Hellfire and damnation!

If Rafe had done something so daft and foolish to pad his pockets for the gambling hells...

I'll bloody kill him!

Ashton was temporarily lost in thoughts of getting his hands on his wayward brother until a soft little sound from her caught his attention. Strangling Rafe would have to wait until morning. He had more important matters to attend to.

He eased back onto his bed, lying close to Rosalind, but unable to justify taking her hand again, not when she was burrowed so deep beneath the warmth of the blankets.

"Sleep well, my wicked rival, so we might fight again tomorrow."

∼

ROSALIND HAD the most peculiar dream.

She was lying in bed with a man, held close against his long, lean muscled body, his warm breath stirring her hair as he breathed deep and slow. It was a strange and wondrous feeling to lie so close to a man she'd been battling in business for months and feel so protected.

Her husband had always kept a separate chamber for sleeping and only visited her bed once a week; then after a sweet kiss goodnight, he'd leave her to sleep alone. It was an older custom, one more suited to noble classes, but she understood that Henry wished to let her have her privacy when they weren't together. It had been sweet, but then again, Henry had been a wonderful man. A safe harbor from the storms of her past.

But this...this was a lovely dream. She'd heard Emily and her friends speak about the joys of sleeping so close to a man for the entire night.

I mustn't let such stories fill my mind before sleep.

Sure enough, when she opened her eyes, there was no man beside her. Morning light cut through the half-closed curtains. Just beyond the windowpanes she caught a glimpse of flowering trees with white blooms. She smiled. Springtime was always full of magic with the warm sun, the heady scent of flowers and green everywhere. It was as though the world could go on forever, with days that never ended and dreams that seemed tangible enough to touch.

Birds chattered in the leafy branches, wild and excited the way birds usually did following a harsh storm. Storm... The memory of the previous night jolted her awake, her heart pounding.

"Good heavens!"

This was not her bed. This was not her room.

She fell back against the pillows as she recalled the wild series of events that had left her in Ashton's bed wearing a borrowed nightgown.

The door to the dressing room opened a moment later, and Ashton strode in, fully dressed and looking far too pleased with himself. His valet trailed behind, carrying a recently pressed cravat.

"Save that for this evening, Lowell. I'll be out in the fields today." He shot a look her way. "Good, you're awake. I shall be working to clear away some burned farmhouses if you wish to join me."

"You want me to go with you?" That surprised her. She assumed that he wouldn't want to be near her. Not after last night. A wet, bedraggled creature who'd shared her weaknesses? It was not her finest moment and certainly not her most attractive one.

The smile that curved his lips pricked her pride. "What else would you do all day? Mope about? Rosalind, you aren't the sort of woman to remain idle during the day. So what's it to be?"

The idea of spending a day indoors with nothing to do wasn't at all appealing. But did she want to spend time with Ashton? She supposed she ought to given the ruse they'd agreed to play. And she supposed it would be interesting to see what he did most of the day.

Rosalind blinked. When had she become interested in Ashton's daily life? Yet she was—and far more than idly curious. It wouldn't hurt to indulge that curiosity while she played the part of a courted lady.

"I suppose I could accompany you…for appearances' sake."

The damnable man was still smiling. "Excellent. Your maid Claire just arrived with your coach. She's eaten and is ready to assist you. Have a quick breakfast, and then we shall ride out." He took the coat Lowell held out and strode to the door.

She called after him, "I'm still not agreeing to anything else beyond our arrangement!"

Ashton paused in the doorway. "And I'm still giving you a week to change your mind." Before she could reply, he was gone.

Lowell cleared his throat. "Do you wish me to leave, Your Ladyship? I usually tidy up now, but if you need to…" His face turned a ruddy color.

"Oh, I'm sorry…Mr. Lowell, is it? If you could bring Claire to me, I shall be out of your way shortly."

"Yes, Your Ladyship." Lowell hastily departed, and Rosalind climbed out of bed, wincing as a number of muscles twinged in protest. Her feet were still blistered and her back still sore from the grain sacks. Her arms ached from an evening of carrying dishes. Walking through the pain, she rushed to the dressing room to see to her needs before Lowell returned with her maid.

When she returned to the bedchamber, Claire had already placed Rosalind's valise on the bed and was muttering to herself as she shuffled through the clothes.

"Your Ladyship!" She rushed over to embrace Rosalind. The intimate gesture was not at all appropriate, but after what they'd been through, it came as a relief.

"Are you well? What happened? Why did you leave me at the inn?" The flurry of questions made Rosalind's head throb.

"I'm fine, Claire, truly. I'll explain everything."

As her maid ran a bath and began sorting through her travel case, Rosalind narrated the entirety of the night's events, though she left out the more intimate moments with Ashton. There was no need to have Claire thinking she was *actually* going to marry the man.

"So you are to remain here then? In His Lordship's chambers?" Claire's keen eyes took in the understated elegance of the room. Noting something off, she pointed suddenly. "What are those for?"

"What?" Rosalind looked to where her maid was gesturing, over the bed. They came closer. Over the headboard hung a rather curious drapery. Rosalind climbed onto the bed, giving the curtain a little tug. The fabric fell away to reveal a large, ornate gilt mirror. It hung out from the wall at an odd angle.

"That's strange. What do you suppose…?"

She covered it up, not wanting to pry, but still curious about what such a mirror could be used for. Then again, Ashton was full of mysteries. She'd have to add this to an ever growing list of things she wanted to know about him. But that would have to wait. She took a hasty bath, mindful that at any moment Ashton could return.

Her maid beckoned to a chair. "Come and sit. I'll see what I can manage with your hair."

Claire was putting on the finishing touches when Ashton returned. He halted mid-step, and she watched him in the reflection of the tall mirror. For a moment she swore there had been warmth in those eyes.

Perhaps I'm only imagining what I wish to see.

"Rose is a fetching color on you." He came over, walking a half circle around her, his eyes sweeping over her from head to toe. "Yes, that color is magnificent."

Rosalind frowned. She didn't like how he behaved, as though her appearance required his approval. As though he *owned* her.

"Claire, find my green gown," Rosalind said. "I shall change—"

"No!" Ashton cut her off, not sharply, but firmly. "Don't be silly, Rosalind. Claire has better things to do than change your clothes simply because you wish to be contrary to me."

She arched a brow. "It is not my goal to please you. If I wish to change, I may change."

His eyes twinkled. "I agree. You have every right to change clothes. However, a woman of your intellect has far better uses for her time than figuring out how to rebel against me with petty wardrobe changes. I'd much rather put your mind to a better task. I have architectural plans for my new tenant farmhouses, and I should like to consult you on them."

"Consult with me?"

Ashton tugged on his waistcoat. "Shipbuilding is a bit like house building, and we've both had a fair amount of experience with that. I'd like your opinion on whether the proposed layouts are suitable. Besides, Mother would be delighted to see us interacting on something like this. It would help convince her I'm serious about you."

"What's wrong with the houses?" she asked, eager to divert her attention to something else.

"They were burned to the ground two days ago. I am eager to rebuild them because the families who lived there are out of house and home."

"Oh no. Where are they staying?"

"They are currently in my spare servants' quarters until I can see to the new houses."

"The families are here?" She couldn't picture Ashton opening his home to simple farm folk. It was too...*kind* of him, and in her dealings with him she knew Ashton was not a kind man. Cunning, calculating, respectful of his obligations, perhaps, but not kind.

"Of course. They are my responsibility."

She bit her lip. "Both houses burned down the same night? Were they next to each other?"

"Different properties, but nearby."

"That sounds like it was not a coincidence."

His eyes narrowed, and his gaze turned distant. "Yes, I suspect someone orchestrated the event."

"Does this have anything to do with what led to you being shot last Christmas?"

That was something she would not soon forget. When she'd first met him, one of his arms had been in a sling. She'd gotten him to admit that he'd been shot at a brothel. To her surprise it had not been while sampling the pleasures of the ladies, but rather investigating rumors of an assassination attempt on his friend's life.

"I'm not sure, but I shan't let my guard down. So, will you consult with me on the house plans?"

She bit her bottom lip as she thought it over. "I suppose I could."

"Excellent. Are you ready for breakfast? I'm famished after last night." He gave her a roguish wink. Before she could stop herself, she was smiling, but she hastily forced her lips into a scowl.

"You're trying to embarrass me in front of Claire," she hissed in accusation as she joined him at the door.

He was still grinning as he offered her his arm. "I do admit to a sense of exhilaration in the art of provoking you."

This side of him caught her off guard. Never in her wildest dreams would she have imagined the cool, collected man to be so...playful.

She let him escort her downstairs to the dining room. Just because he wasn't always acting the gentleman did not mean she would stop acting like a lady.

The dining room was a lovely space with walnut-paneled walls and a host of family portraits. Two long sets of windows overlooked a garden full of roses, forsythia and a dozen other colorful plants. The sunlight bathed the room in a cheery haze of soft light that made Rosalind feel at home. The castle she'd grown up in did not have such luxuries. It was dank and dreary by comparison, a holdover of long-forgotten glories.

"Do you like it?" Ashton asked.

"Yes, very much. I was thinking of how different this is from my childhood home. My late husband's townhouse is lovely, but I've always preferred the country. It reminds me of Scotland."

Ashton escorted her to a chair and seated her, then began to prepare her a plate without even asking. Rather than be upset, she enjoyed the thought of him doing something so polite. It should have seemed out of character for him, given her experiences with him, but it didn't.

He'd only just set his plate down when two other men burst into the room, laughing and talking. She recognized the golden-haired, rakish and handsome Earl of Lonsdale immediately. The *Quizzing Glass Gazette* had once claimed that he'd bedded thirty women in one night during a lavish party in Covent Garden. It had to be a rumor because she'd heard that men tended to fall asleep after just one encounter. There was no way he could have survived thirty.

She eyed Charles as he flashed a winning smile. He had a muscled physique much like Ashton's. Perhaps some men *could* go all night...

"Good morning, Lady Melbourne. I don't believe we've been properly introduced. Ash, come over and see to the introductions." Charles nudged the second man as he beamed at Rosalind.

Ashton came to stand beside her. "Rosalind, this is Charles Humphrey, the Earl of Lonsdale, and this," he said as he nodded at the second man, "is Jonathan St. Laurent, brother to the Duke of Essex."

"It's a pleasure to meet you." Jonathan bent in a courtly manner over her hand and kissed it. Charles did the same, but with a glint in his eyes that made Rosalind nervous.

"I have heard of you both," she said, challenging Charles with a smirk of her own.

"Only wicked things, I hope," Charles said with a chuckle. "Sadly, only half the stories I hear about myself of late are true. Except the one about the swans—that's most definitely true."

Rosalind had no idea what he was talking about. "Swans?"

Ashton cut Charles off with a cough.

"Right," Jonathan covered smoothly. "How are you feeling, Lady Melbourne? You suffered a great ordeal last night. I trust you have had some rest?"

"Yes, thank you, Mr. St. Laurent."

"Please, call me Jonathan or Jon." His smile was more warm and friendly than Rosalind had expected of someone who was friends with Ashton. He was so calm and cool, and she expected his friends to be equally so.

"I am well, thank you, Jonathan. I believe I'm mostly recovered from my adventure." She would not admit her feet still hurt or that her body ached.

"I imagine so, walking so far in a soaked dress. You must have been carrying your own weight in rain and mud." Charles took a seat.

"She's a strong lady," Ashton informed Charles. A frown twisted his lips.

"Er…indeed," Charles agreed, and then he stared at Jonathan's plate. "For God's sake, man, eat some fruit. You can't survive on eggs and biscuits alone."

Rosalind nearly missed it, but she saw Ashton's lips twitch as he watched Charles order the younger man about. There was something about this moment that held significance. She was glimpsing a moment of Ashton's private life, a time when his guard was down and his heart was open.

He'd hinted last night at how he was bonded to his friends, but seeing it was another thing entirely. Something about these men made her feel homesick for Scotland and her brothers. Brock, Brodie and Aiden had taken care of her and each other just like these men did. It was what family was for, to love and care for one another. The League was Ashton's family.

When she'd sat down for tea with Emily, Horatia and Anne, she'd sensed a similar connection. Those women were friends just as their husbands were. Loyal, true, honest. Thinking of them reminded her how she wished she could share some of that closeness. She felt even more alone here watching Ashton with his friends.

Would it be that way if she ever remarried? Would she find herself in a circle of friendship such as this, or were the League of Rogues and their wives an anomaly in the city of London?

"Here." Ashton refilled Rosalind's plate and poured more tea for her.

"Thank you," she said, feeling strangely shy. It still shocked her that this was all happening. Two days ago they were ready to kill each other, and now it was feigned courtship and real kisses?

"Will you be joining us to assess the tenant farms?" Jonathan asked.

She looked in Ashton's direction, expecting him to answer for her, but when he didn't, she almost sighed in relief.

"I believe I shall."

"Excellent." Jonathan smiled, and they enjoyed the remainder of their breakfast. Jonathan and Charles insisted on sharing a number of stories about Ashton, and she could tell by the rising color on his face that these were stories he didn't wish for her to hear.

"Did you know he was the only one among the League to get top marks at university?" Jonathan told her.

"The only one who did it without charming any of the professors' daughters," Ashton corrected.

"Oh?" She laughed at the disgruntled expression on Charles's face.

"What's wrong with bedding a lady simply because her father is a professor? Doesn't mean a man cheats, you know."

"It is when you forget to hide the parchment with the examination answers." Ashton chortled.

Charles threw his head back as though searching the heavens for an intervention. "Take Pepper Plumsby to bed *one* time..."

"Pepper?" Rosalind giggled. "Oh dear, was that really her name? Did she have a sister named Salt?"

Ashton's rich laugh startled her, but then the other two men started laughing too.

Jonathan smacked his thigh. "She has a point, Charles. You ought to pick bed partners with better names."

"You of all people should know appearances can be deceiving," Charles cut in. "Pepper was a lovely little chit and quite good in the blankets. She had this way of using her—"

"Charles," Ashton warned, nodding towards Rosalind.

"Oh, right. Well, should we go? The tenants will be anxious to get started on clearing away the debris, see if there is anything worth salvaging. I know you don't mind hosting them here, but pride can sting, and they'll be wanting to be settled in their new houses soon."

Ashton and the others rose from the table, and Rosalind followed. They saw Lady Lennox in the hall as she was rounding up a group of children with Joanna.

"Mother, there you are. Do you wish to look over the designs for the new houses with Rosalind and me?"

Regina shook her head. "No, thank you, Ashton. I'm quite busy with the children. We're taking them in one of the wagons to play in the fields. I'm sure Rosalind will have many wonderful ideas for you. Won't you, Rosalind?" Regina sent her a knowing look, and Rosalind smiled back in understanding. It was a both a cue and a blessing to begin her seduction.

This merry game she was playing with mother and son was more amusing than she'd thought. Neither one had a clue what the other did or did not know.

Ashton nodded to Charles and Jonathan. "Why don't you two head out? Rosalind is going to look over the new designs in my study, and then we shall join you."

Rosalind shivered as they left, but not from fear. Pretending to be attracted to someone was entirely different when one actually *was* attracted to the person, even if she wished she wasn't. Whenever she and Ashton were alone, things between them intensified, and she was worried about where things would lead if he continued to stare at her the way he was right now. As though he wished to take a bite out of her, then kiss her.

CHAPTER 10

ord, I can't let him kiss me again. I seem to lose all good sense when I do.

Rosalind stepped back from Ashton and attempted to start a conversation.

"It is kind of you to let the tenants stay here." She hadn't told him that before, but she'd wanted to.

He stared at her intently. "I'm not a brute, Rosalind." She had the impression he was attempting to convey something about how he intended to deal with her.

"Are you a mind reader as well?" She kept her tone light, doing her best to tease him back. Outside of her brothers, teasing remarks had always gotten her ears soundly boxed.

His lips twitched again. "A mind reader?"

Rosalind had the sudden desire to see him smile more fully. "Ashton, you are far too serious. Why don't you smile more often?"

He curled an arm around her waist and guided her into a room on the right of the hall. She peered around curiously at the room, taking in walnut wood bookshelves brimming with everything from books containing folded maps of the world to lurid gothic novels.

"I might be smiling in a few minutes. Now, come take a look at the plans." His hand dropped from her waist as he rifled through the stacks of paper covering his writing table. She looked back to the filled bookshelves. She adored reading. Her mother used to say that a person's library revealed much of who they were.

She read the spines and paused, stifling a giggle. "*Lady Mabel and the Brooding Baron?*"

Ashton leaned over his desk and glanced up. The sun lit his pale-blond hair, burnishing the strands with gold. He looked angelic, but he certainly didn't act like an angel. Or kiss like one, for that matter. As with all things, the man was more a sinner than a saint, she was quite sure.

"I blame Lucien. He's been reading those stories by that awful L. R. Gloucester. I wouldn't touch them, but Lucien wagered I couldn't finish one. And then I admit I was rather sucked in. I am ashamed to admit I've devoured every book she's written."

"She?" Rosalind stared the initials on the book. "How do you know it's a woman?"

Ashton came around the table and joined her at the shelf, pulling the volume out.

"Two things lead me to that conclusion. Using initials is a well-known way of hiding one's gender, but more importantly, the phrasing and the characters are telling. They seem, well, far too accurate in depicting the feminine mind. No man could ever possess that much insight. It would surprise me very much if it weren't a woman. Here, you must give it a try."

He handed her the book, and she didn't refuse it. If she was to remain here a week, she would enjoy something to read.

"Now, come see these plans." He put an arm around her waist and tugged her closer to the writing table. "I had these drawn up a few months ago for additional houses on other parts of my estate.

It was fortunate because these same designs should work for rebuilding Maple's and Higgins's houses."

He spread out a set of drawings and weighed them down with glass paperweights that glinted in the sun. Rosalind stared at the drawings, assessing the number of rooms, the placement of them, and the way the house was constructed.

"Should the kitchens be a little larger? These are families and will need more space than you have allotted. A woman needs plenty of counters and cupboards in her kitchen. I'm not sure what you had intended for the other houses, but a house should engender itself to the creation of a family, which provides your lands with more hands to work once the children are older."

He eyed the plans critically, and to her surprise he conceded. "You're quite right. What else?"

For the next half hour, they discussed the houses at length, with Rosalind adding space to the rooms, explaining that the children would need enough room to separate the boys from the girls for privacy and the need for the addition of proper barns and a stable for domestic animals. When Ashton was satisfied with the changes, he wrote down some notes and summoned a footman to take the old plans back to his architect in London and have a new set drawn up with the changes.

As he escorted her out of the office, he was grinning like a lad. "See? I'm smiling."

"Dare I ask why?" Nerves fluttered her belly, but she was excited too.

He gently tucked her arm in his and bent his head to whisper in her ear. "Because that is one of the two conversations in the last day where we have not quarreled. Imagine how it would be if we were *actually* married."

She stopped short. "Why are you so interested in marrying me? You have control of everything of mine already."

Ashton shook his head. "I admit that my initial interest was taking control of your property. But I've given it a great deal of thought. You have a keen mind. With our forces combined, we could own all of London. Think of it!"

She had, but she didn't trust him. Once he had her property and her money, there would be nothing she could do to reclaim herself. With the stroke of a pen on a marriage license, he'd strip her of her security and her identity.

It would be like living with her father all over again, only this man would have even more power over her. He would be her husband. She couldn't flee in the middle of the night; he would have her life caught in an iron fist. Wives were no better than a man's livestock, and it was well within his rights to beat, starve or do anything he wished to his wife. What sort of torture would Ashton visit upon her if she ever displeased him? Henry had always left her enough control that she'd never felt helpless, but she knew Ashton was a different sort of man. She would choose death over such a fate.

"What's the matter? You're shaking." Ashton was peering down at her. Rosalind was mortified to realize she *was* shaking.

"I'm sorry." She wasn't sure why she apologized but she did.

Ashton curled his arms around her back and cocooned her. She was shaking too hard to fight the warm embrace and buried her head against his chest. He smelled like pine forests and a hint of sandalwood. It was an addictive sort of smell, one she could get used to and even crave when she was without it.

"Talk to me, Rosalind. I don't have any desire to frighten you."

It took a long while for her to find her breath again. She wiped at her eyes. "Please, I don't wish to discuss this. May we go?"

Ashton cupped her chin, forcing her eyes to meet his. "You can't run away every time. Someday you will have to talk to me."

Not when I finally escape this madness. The thought tasted bitter, but it was the truth. She was trapped here for a week, putting on a show for his mother's benefit. But once the week was up, she would return to London whether he wished her to or not.

He sighed, and his look of disappointment cut her in unexpected ways.

"Very well. I trust you can ride in that gown?"

"Yes, if I go astride."

His half smile returned. "And allow me to glimpse your legs? Then I have yet one more reason to smile."

They left for the stables, and inside she found the comforting scents of horses, hay and leather—just the sort of thing to make all her worries evaporate. It was going to be a lovely day, and she would not let any emotional storm clouds dampen her spirits.

"Let's see, perhaps you should take my favorite mare? She's a lovely creature." Ashton led her to a stall where a strong but beautiful white and gray dappled horse was nudging her oats bucket and huffing.

"She's lovely." Rosalind meant it. She adored horses. "What's her name?"

Ashton stroked his palm down the horse's nose, smiling indulgently as he fed her a few chestnuts from his pocket.

"Milady. Nothing else seemed to fit her. Even when she was a foal, she pranced about the paddock like a proper lady." He rested his forehead against Milady and patted her face.

"And who will you ride?"

Ashton pointed to an inquisitive-looking gelding that was entirely black except for his white socks. "Prince."

Ashton had a groom prepare the two horses. While they waited she had a chance to admire the fine stables. She was lulled into a sense of peace at the scent of fresh hay, the whicker and snorts of the other horses who peered curiously out of their stalls at her and Ashton.

"Your stables are beautiful," she said, stroking a fingertip along a gleaming blue painted stall door.

"Thank you. I take great pride in my horses and want them to have only the best."

"The horses are ready, my lord," the groom announced as he led both beasts, one on either side, out into the stable yard.

"Thank you. Rosalind?" Ashton took her arm and led her toward the horses.

Then he lifted Rosalind up onto the saddle. She lifted her skirts and settled onto Milady's back. Ashton mounted Prince and then turned his horse toward hers.

"Up for a race across the field?" he asked.

"Perhaps. I assume you have terms in mind for the winner?"

"Naturally."

She kicked her heels to urge Milady closer to Prince.

"What are they?" She was almost afraid to ask him. He'd likely take whatever else she still possessed that he had not yet ripped from her. Still…she couldn't resist a challenge when it came from him.

With an arrogant grin, he tossed his hair out of his eyes. "A kiss if I win."

"And if I win?" She arched a brow.

"You don't want to kiss me?" he teased, wriggling his eyebrows.

Rosalind's eyes narrowed at such a transparent ploy. "I do not think so. If I win, you must apologize to me for the last few days."

He sobered. "I'm willing to do that now."

His sincerity shocked her, but she was hardly going to make it easy for him. "Then perhaps I'll only require you to apologize on your knees if you lose, instead of on your belly." She stroked Milady's neck.

Ashton studied her, and then with a wicked gleam in his eyes, he kicked his horse and shot off across the field.

"Why, you cheating cur!" she hollered and slapped the loose ends of the reins against her horse's flanks, jolting Milady into a gallop. The gold grass of the field rippled in a breeze as she and Milady raced after the speeding gelding.

She was laughing as she started to gain on Ashton. He did not look back until they were a few feet from being neck and neck. He leaned down over his horse and started to stretch Prince's stride, regaining his lead.

"No!" She kicked her horse harder, but it was no use. The gelding had more speed.

Ashton raced across the small dirt road where a crumbling burned ruin of a house stood. In an effortless move, he slid off his horse and caught her reins as she pulled back to stop Milady.

"You..." she panted. "Cheated."

"Not true. I allowed you to catch up, after all. But I had a faster horse. I admit that readily."

"Oh!" She leapt off her horse to tackle him. He caught her, and she slammed her balled fists against his chest.

"Easy, my little hellion, let me have my kiss..."

"If you think I'll honor a wager that you—"

Her dozens of planned curses were silenced by Ashton's lips. He captured her wrists, holding them behind her back with one of his hands. She struggled a moment, but only a moment. Being held prisoner in his arms sent a wild thrill through her. Her skin burned as his lips plundered hers. It was easy to lose herself in this man's kiss.

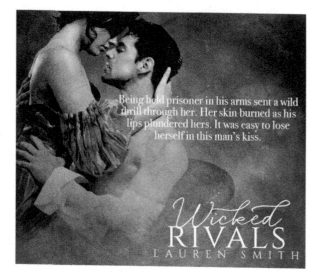

Being held prisoner in his arms sent a wild thrill through her. Her skin burned as his lips plundered hers. It was easy to lose herself in this man's kiss.

Wicked
RIVALS
LAUREN SMITH

HE NIPPED her bottom lip and she gasped, strangely flushed with primal heat at the sting of his bite. She struggled in his hold again, but he only laughed huskily.

"Steady on, darling. This is not something you are in control of. Not this time."

She relented and let him take over. Hidden in his words was a promise of a next time in which *she* would be in control.

Ashton kissed like a dream. She'd never taken lovers after Henry died, and yet she knew if she'd had them to compare to this, this baron would still come out on top. It was the way he kissed, as if he had all day to explore her. There was not a hint of haste. Just slow, deliberate passion, potent and drugging. She fell harder against his chest. Suddenly her hands were free and she curled her arms around his neck, dragging him closer to her.

"Do you want me to stop?" he whispered in her ear before he kissed a path from her ear to her throat.

The feel of his lips, hot and soft on her sensitive skin, sent shivers rippling through her.

"Stop?" she echoed through the rising haze of hunger.

"Yes," he answered with a throaty chuckle. "Shall I keep kissing you or not?"

"Keep..." She dug her hands into the long strands of his hair. "Kissing me."

Rosalind gasped as they toppled to the ground. She fell on a sea of gilded grass, with Ashton on top of her. She instinctively tried to part her thighs, but her skirts were in the way.

"My skirts." She moaned as he kissed her collarbone and nuzzled the swell of her breasts.

"Right." He dug at her thick skirts and petticoats, pushing them up to her thighs. She threw her head back as his palms slid up her legs and between her underpinnings. He stroked her with a fingertip before slipping it inside her. She jolted and clutched his shoulders.

The blue sky above her seemed to stretch on forever as she stared at the cloudless expanse. Ashton rose above her, blocking out the sun as he continued to slide his finger in and out of her. The invasion was gentle but insistent, and she trembled at the building tension. Only he had ever made her feel so wild and reckless, as though all her worries and fears had faded when he touched her.

"You belong to me, Rosalind. Do you understand?" He moved his hand faster and his thumb found the sensitive bud on her mound that made her cry out sharply when he pressed on it.

"No," she panted. She did not belong to any man—her life was her own.

Ashton's blue eyes were so like the sky above, but intensified with an inner fire.

"You *are* mine. And I care for what's mine. I *pleasure* what's mine." He relented in his tender seduction only a moment, and she wriggled in frustration, wanting him to keep touching her, yet fighting what accepting it would mean.

"Not yours." Still she resisted, but his lips curved into an irresistible grin.

"Deny it all you like, but I own you, *Lady Melbourne*." He emphasized her title, and she clawed at his back.

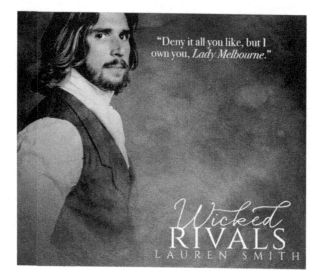

"PLEASE..." She needed him to finish what he'd started, but not like this. Not on these terms.

"Say it or I walk away." His hair fell across his eyes, and the shadow of a faint beard made him more of a rakish pirate than the business-minded gentleman he showed the *ton* back in London. It was as though she could see back into time a few hundred years and see Ashton's ancestors raiding the English coast. Tall, blond-headed warriors who took whatever they wished at any cost. It was both frightening and exciting. Her skin heated and her nipples hardened beneath her gown at the thought of him taking her right there in the grass. There would be no one to stop them from getting carried away.

Do I yield or resist?

He pursed his lips and sat back on his heels, pulling her skirts back down.

"But—" She needed him to keep touching her. He couldn't just stop…

"Until you can answer yes without hesitation, I won't be rewarding you." He stood and brushed off the grass from his clothes, then caught her waist and lifted her to her feet. His eyes were fierce with a determination to deny her what she wanted most in that moment. To be back in the grass with him. But no, he was paying her back for when she had left him spent in the opera house from her own gentle ministrations. He'd caught her fairly in a trap she'd walked right into. Damned *Sassenach*!

"You are no gentleman!" She huffed, her body still humming with need and frustration.

His booming laugh set her teeth on edge. "My dear, I just stopped myself from tupping you right here in a field. I believe that actually proves me a gentleman. If I had no control, your dress would be ruined with grass stains because I would have taken you as hard and as savagely as we both wanted. But *you* stopped me. Remember that. You wouldn't say what I wished to hear."

"What you wish to hear I cannot give. To you it's just a game, but not to me."

He plucked at the ends of his shirtsleeves, fixing his appearance, and Rosalind hissed beneath her breath like an angry cat.

"I've got work to do. Would you take the horses somewhere close by and tether them?" He turned his back on her, and she had the sense she'd disappointed him, which infuriated her because she didn't need to please him. She did *not* belong to him.

Still, a little place deep inside her kept asking that simple, dangerous question.

What if?

CHAPTER 11

"You're serious about this marriage business?" Charles asked as he, Jonathan and Ashton lifted yet another charred beam away from the foundations where the Higgins farmhouse had once been. They set the beam in the back of a large cart. Several other men from the village and surrounding lands were busy assisting in the clearing away of the destroyed houses.

"Yes, I am." Ashton paused to wipe his sleeve across his brow. It was too damned hot for this sort of work. If anything, he should be supervising the others. It was not fitting for a man of his station to perform manual labor, but he could not sit idly by, not when he was flooded with frustrated sexual energy. If he couldn't take Rosalind to bed, he needed to use that pent-up passion for something productive.

"But *why?*" Charles repeated. "I thought you swore off marriage."

"It's complicated, Charles. Mother is pushing me to marry for Joanna's sake, and I am tired of fighting her. If she believes Rosalind and I are courting, it will buy me some time."

"But pretending to court is different than actually courting her. I thought you said this would be a ruse and nothing more." Charles was frowning at this point.

"Well, that had been my original desire, but the more I think of it, if I could marry her it would be profitable in more ways than one."

"Marrying for profit? But is that…" Jonathan let his words die as he too frowned.

"*Mercenary* is the word you're looking for," Charles added.

Ashton didn't deny it. It was indeed mercenary in nature, but given how the last day had gone, he'd begun to feel that things could get better, perhaps even pleasurable if they ended up marrying. Of course, she couldn't learn his real intention was to take this ruse and turn it into reality.

"I need to hold control over Rosalind's companies until I can learn to what ends Hugo has been using her. Furthermore, if I control her assets, nothing can happen without my knowledge."

"Yes, but you've been doing all that without throwing in this marriage nonsense," said Charles.

"I have been considering marriage to her for a few days now, and after last night, I feel obligated to do so, and not just because I want to control her property. The poor creature needs looking after."

No matter how strong a woman like Rosalind was, she needed to be protected, cared for. And given her tragic past, she deserved a bit of spoiling, too. Once she stopped being so bloody resistant to his romantic overtures, he could give her the world and anything else she might wish.

Jonathan laughed. "Needs looking after? You make it sound like pity. The woman I met doesn't seem to need that."

Charles seemed to agree. "She was doing well enough on her own, even besting you at your own game, until you decided to overreact and try to ruin her."

Growling under his breath, Ashton shot a glower at his

friends. "You've never complained of my methods before when it's a man involved."

"But she's not a man," Jonathan pointed out. "And as far as I know you've never taken such extreme measures with your other competitors."

Ashton realized the truth in Jonathan's words. "Yes, well, it's my damned fault I went too far. I'm doing my best to remedy the situation and make amends in what way I can."

Charles frowned. "You send a woman flowers and jewels when you run afoul of a lady—you don't marry her. I don't like it."

"You don't have to. *I'm* the one marrying her, not you."

"But—"

Jonathan cut in. "Has she even agreed to the marriage?" He brushed his sooty hands on a cloth rag hanging off the back of the wagon.

"Not yet, but she will."

The distant sound of children laughing had the three of them turning.

Rosalind and Joanna were chasing a dozen or so children about the meadow, those belonging to the Maple and Higgins families. Joanna's actions did not surprise Ashton; she had an open heart for everyone, and children seemed to gravitate to her. But Rosalind? He could not believe she had joined in.

Her hair was coming loose from its pins, and her rose-colored gown was wrinkled and dirty, yet she didn't seem to notice. She captured a boy who couldn't have been more than two and swung him around, causing the lad to squeal in delight. The older children clapped and laughed.

The rosy hue to Rosalind's cheeks filled him with warmth. She was feeling better it seemed, and that in turn made him happy. It was clear she enjoyed the adventures of business, but she was also a free-thinking woman with ideas of her own, something which made his conversations with her fascinating rather than tedious. He'd spent many a dinner or ball engaging with young ladies who were only too quick to agree with anything he said or laugh at any comment they thought might be a joke.

It would be quite a stimulating experience to be married to Rosalind and share his life with her. They could ride, plan business decisions, even take long walks in a pleasant silence together. And by the looks of it, she enjoyed children. That gave him a strange light feeling deep in his chest. After everything she'd endured, Rosalind deserved some sort of happiness. Money alone would never achieve that, as he well knew.

I could make her happy. If there was one thing Godric, Lucien and Cedric had taught him, it was that the happiness found when one combined a well-matched husband and wife was not a matter of addition—it was multiplication.

Joanna called out, waving to him and his friends. "Ash, come and have some lemonade."

"Shall we, gentlemen?" Ashton nodded at the area by the road where two blankets were spread out and refreshments were waiting for them.

His mother was in her element, marshalling the children and Joanna while the men worked. They had decided to make a picnic of it while the local men aided in the removal of the debris. It hadn't gone unnoticed that his mother was watching Rosalind with an intensity that was beginning to concern him.

Regina knew better than to meddle in his business affairs, but he didn't doubt for one moment she'd meddle in his romantic ones. All the more reason for his and Rosalind's game of pretend courtship. He needed to remember to do something today in front of his mother to show his interest in Rosalind.

"Ashton, a word if you please." Regina was seated on a corner of one of the blankets, a glass of lemonade in one hand and a lacy fan in the other.

"What is it, Mother?" He crouched down beside her on the blanket. She folded up her fan and patted a spot beside her, then held out a glass to him. He took the glass and settled on the ground.

"I thought you were jesting when you said you planned to marry that woman, but I'm starting to see something in her I rather like. I simply wished to let you know you have my approval and blessing."

"I don't need either of those things," he replied coldly, but instantly regretted it. "I'm sorry, Mother."

"As you should be. For once, we agree upon something, and you act beastly about it."

For a moment neither of them spoke, each of them looking pointedly in different directions. The light breeze that drifted across the blanket and ruffled the grass cooled his body and his temper enough that he gave in to the curiosity of what his mother had just admitted.

They rarely agreed on anything, especially in ladies. She was constantly throwing women at his feet, and he would turn up his nose and walk off, having no interest in whatever young miss she was convinced he should marry that week.

"You truly like her?" he asked.

His mother resumed fanning herself. "I do. There's something about her, a strength I see in her that reminds me of myself."

"She is strong." He certainly agreed with her on that.

"But she's guarded, and for a reason. You must take care, my boy. She's been hurt before, that much is clear. It would do neither of you any good to push her too far too fast. Do you understand?"

"I will be careful with her," he assured his mother.

Regina smiled. "That's good, because she deserves to be properly wooed. You may start tonight at the Mertons' ball. I had to turn down our invitations, but when Mrs. Merton learned it was because we had guests, she sent invitations this morning for Charles, Jonathan and Lady Melbourne."

"A ball?" He stifled a groan. Courting Rosalind was supposed to put a stop to his mother sending him off to these blasted balls. But it seemed there was no way to avoid this one.

"Yes, and you will attend. There's a nice young man I want Joanna to meet. If you come and show off your new fiancée, it would look well for Joanna. And a decent, respectable country ball will keep your friends out of trouble."

How bloody thoughtful of Mrs. Merton to think of adding a few more guests to her list.

"I ought to ask Rosalind. She may not wish—"

Regina laughed. "Don't be ridiculous. Every woman loves a ball. Dancing is the best way to a woman's heart."

Ashton scoffed. "Dancing? I doubt that." While it was one of his many talents, dancing was not something he particularly enjoyed.

His mother's fan smacked him in the chest with a resounding *whack*.

"Of course it is. How do you think I fell in love with your father?" Regina's face softened as distant memories resurfaced. She sighed and dabbed at eyes, which were suddenly bright. "He was a wonderful dancer." It had been so long since his mother had spoken of his father in a positive light.

Ashton held his breath, wondering if his mother would keep speaking about his father or if the past would be too painful. His mother's eyes glistened as she looked at him. He'd never wanted to think about how hard it had to be to love someone who hurt you. Regina had loved his father, despite the womanizing and the gambling. She *still* loved him.

She looked up at the sky. Sunshine covered her face, and for a moment he could imagine how she had looked as a young woman Rosalind's age. *Lovely.*

"When a woman dances with a man, she feels safe. It's a special sort of intimacy, one that promises love. So tonight, my dear boy, you will take her out onto the dance floor and stare deep into her eyes as you waltz. Seduction is not always about what happens between the sheets. Do you understand? Seduce her *heart.*"

Love. He hadn't thought of Rosalind in such a way before. Protection, advantage, mutual pleasure, certainly. But love? If he was honest with himself, the thought of love scared the hell out of him. Ever since he'd witnessed Godric and Emily fall in love a secret part of him had yearned for that, but he was a man who dealt in realistic notions and practical behavior. The need to control his life, to protect everything fiercely—it didn't bode well for any woman who dared to love him.

"Ashton." His mother's voice cut through his thoughts.

"Yes?"

"Promise me you'll consider it." She was looking right at him.

"Consider what?"

"*Love*, you silly boy. Winning her heart."

Ashton could not believe he was having such a frank discussion with his mother, especially on such a subject. He shifted on the blanket, trying to feel settled, but it couldn't be helped when a man was discussing love with his mother. Was this how Lucien felt when his mother had tricked him into seducing Horatia last Christmas?

Lord, save us all from meddling mothers.

"I'll consider it." Ashton turned his gaze back to Rosalind. She was wearing a makeshift blindfold now, searching for the giggling children around her. Their little bodies danced out of reach as she called for help to find them. Joanna was laughing and shouting directions to avoid being captured.

With a grin, Ashton left his mother to finish her lemonade, and he crept up behind Rosalind. Before Joanna could speak, Ashton raised a finger to his lips. She smiled back and kept quiet.

"Oh! Where are you?" Rosalind muttered, half giggling as she spun and ran straight into Ashton.

He captured her by the waist, pressing her body flat to his. Her body fit to his with a startling perfection. Her features were animated and lively beneath the spring sunlight, and it filled him with a quiet joy that made his heart race.

She could be mine...if I can woo her.

"Well, it seems like I've captured a pretty prize," he said. "What is my reward?"

Her lips formed a little O in surprise, and she tore the blindfold from her eyes. There was no better time than now to kiss her, in full sight of his mother.

He cupped her face and slanted his mouth down over hers. The taste upon his tongue reminded him of just how much he had restrained himself before. Her mouth opened beneath his, and he encouraged her with his tongue to be bold and not focus on the fact that they could be seen. He wanted her full attention upon him and this single decadent kiss.

When their mouths finally parted, he rested his forehead against hers, their eyes meeting. A blush stained her cheeks as she sought to regain her breath, and that only made him wish they were entirely alone so he could keep on kissing her.

"We don't have to stop," he said softly against her lips.

"But the children—"

"Are tired and should settle down to have a bit of lunch. As should you." With a sigh he stepped back from his tempting Highland lass and nodded toward one of the empty blankets. He was relieved she did not fight his attempt to escort her there. He wanted to show her he could treat her the way a woman ought to be treated, as though she was precious. Even as his business rival, she was still a lady, and he wasn't about to let her go uncared for.

"It does feel good to rest. I suppose I'm still not feeling as strong as I ought to."

He had to agree. She appeared far too flushed from the game. He handed her a small plate of finger sandwiches and a glass of lemonade.

"Thank you." She accepted the food and drink. They enjoyed a moment of companionable silence.

"I see you and Joanna have been taking advantage of this fine day." He chuckled as he watched the children on a distant picnic blanket squirming around Joanna like restless puppies as she handed out sandwiches.

Rosalind laughed. "Yes, it has been wonderful. The children are sweet. I suspect their mothers will be grateful we wore them out in the fields so they will sleep well tonight. Thank you for asking me to come out here with you. I did not believe I'd enjoy it as much as I have." She sipped her lemonade and nibbled on her sandwich.

Was now his chance? Ask her about the ball while she was happy and with a full stomach? Surely she'd agree—it was part of their arrangement, after all. A dance would be public, and his mother would have little chance to question his motives if he brought Rosalind to it.

"Rosalind, there is a country ball tonight. One of our neighboring families is hosting it. When they found out we could not attend due to the presence of guests in our home, they extended invitations this morning to all of you. Would you like to join me there? Joanna is coming as well as my mother."

"A ball?" She turned and stared anywhere but at him. "Are you asking me simply because of our agreement?"

He stared at his plate of food and considered how best to respond. "I won't deny that is my primary goal." He sipped at his lemonade and then set it aside before he captured her chin and forced her to face him. Sparks lit her gaze, dark flashes of defiance mixing with glints of light from excitement when she battled with him.

She looked at him slyly. "And by doing so in such a public setting, you aren't trying to pressure me into some kind of actual agreement of marriage?"

Ashton huffed. "Of course not."

"Good." Her blunt tone held a challenge in it, one that Ashton was quick to take up.

"But would it be so terrible? As my wife, you would be powerful, twice as wealthy, and safe. I would protect you with my life, and my friends would as well."

How could she refuse such an offer? The world at her fingertips. What woman wouldn't want that? It was madness.

And it wasn't just what he could give her, but also what he wanted. He *wanted* her to be his, to call this feisty little hellion his own so that no other man would have the right to her.

The smile on her lips began to fall, and a flash of pain in her eyes stung him. "Yet you fail to offer me the two things I value above all else."

"What are those?" he asked, leaning closer. He didn't want her to retreat from him. If she told him, he could give them to her, no questions asked.

"Love and freedom."

Love and freedom? He could not speak with certainty to the first, but the second was not something he understood. How would she not be free? For the first time in his life, a woman had left him baffled.

"You would be free to do as you please," he argued.

Her laugh was as harsh as a slap. "Really? If I choose to move investments, sell or acquire a company or do anything with my property, would you let me?"

His hesitation in answering cost him. He couldn't say yes, but not for the reason she expected. If Hugo was using her, he could not let her do anything that would aid the League's greatest enemy. It was not because he wished her to cease being the woman he respected.

She set her plate of food down and reached past the edge of the blanket to pluck a long stem of green grass. Rosalind raised it to her cheek, letting the green strand run along her skin before she sighed and let the breeze steal it from her open palm.

"I thought as much. As a widow, I have full control over my destiny. I am not merely the asset of a man. I *exist* in society, albeit grudgingly. Marriage destroys all of that. I would lose myself and become part of you. Everything I am would vanish in an instant. You cannot understand that. It is the folly of men. You believe you understand our feminine minds and hearts, that we're simple creatures who crave new gowns and attending balls and that we have no thoughts or opinions or desires that match or exceed your own." There was a hardness to her face now, a frustration that he'd seen glimpses of in other women throughout his life.

Lucien's younger sister was a brilliant scholar but could not attend university. Audrey Sheridan was one of the most politically minded women he'd ever met, yet she covered her interests with talk of fashion to avoid ridicule. She would never have a voice in the House of Lords. And then there was Rosalind. She was the most cunning and intelligent business rival he'd ever faced, and he'd been bested by her clever strategies more than once. He suddenly realized that Emily's Society of Rebellious Ladies might have more of a purpose behind them than to simply distract their husbands.

She gazed into the distance, her eyes full of that sadness that ate away at his resolve to talk her into marrying him.

"I would not give any of that up. Not unless I knew I would be loved and that I would be free. The first you cannot promise, and the second you cannot give."

He reached out and stole one of her hands, closing his fingers around hers and raising them to his lips for his slow kiss.

"Consider this. I have my reasons for wishing to control your business, but they are not what you believe them to be. I would return control of them to you in time." It was the most he could reveal without telling her about Hugo Waverly. None of the League had ever divulged the depth of their worries when it came to Waverly. He was far too dangerous, and the less involved their families and friends were, the safer they were. At least, that was what Ashton believed.

"Assuming you could even find a way to legally protect my

property as my own after marriage, when would you give me control back?" A hint of hope in her eyes made him feel wretched since he couldn't say for sure when it would be safe to do so.

"I don't know the exact time—"

She jerked her hand free of his and turned her face away. "Because there is no such time. My answer will always be no. I shall not marry you. We shall play our charade for your mother's sake, and that is all."

He attempted to ignore the sting of that refusal, but he failed.

"That does not solve your problem, Rosalind. I own your entire life still—do not forget that," he warned her.

Her eyes glittered like sharp silver pieces of a broken mirror. "Oh, I haven't forgotten. I suppose trusting you to hold to our agreement was foolish of me. You will return one company to me, but now it sounds as though you'll hold the rest hostage unless I marry you? Forgive me for not being pleased with the situation." She paused, and with a sharp look she added, "If necessary, I shall marry another man, and then you may *own him* while I shall be free of you."

"Bloody hell, woman!" He lunged for her, but she moved fast for a woman burdened by skirts. She was up and dashing back towards the children in the field.

"Ashton!" Joanna's voice interrupted the stream of wild thoughts he was currently entertaining.

"What is it?" he snapped.

"Don't be a fool." Joanna was standing over him, arms crossed and glowering.

"My apologies." He only half meant it. Rosalind's stubbornness was putting him in a foul mood.

"Mama is right. You are a wretched seducer. I am beginning to wonder if the rumors about you from London are in fact *only* rumors."

Ashton got to his feet and frowned at his sister.

"You aren't supposed to hear such things." She wasn't allowed to go unchaperoned to any events and even then only to events he and his mother deemed appropriate. Rumors about his seductions should not have spread to any such places.

Joanna frowned. "Rosalind is right—you don't understand women, and you clearly underestimate them. Stop being a pompous idiot and court her properly. I'll see if I can convince her to go to the Mertons' ball tonight."

Joanna twirled her bonnet on one finger and walked away.

Fuming, Ashton stalked toward Charles and Jonathan, who were both sniggering and not even attempting to hide it.

"Trouble with your lady love?" Charles asked.

"Laugh again if you wish to have a bloody nose."

Charles threw up his hands in mock surrender. "Touchy, eh? Jonathan, you owe me a pound. I do believe a certain lady will not be attending the ball tonight."

Jonathan dug around in his pockets, but Ashton caught his arm.

"Don't pay just yet, Jon. Double your wager. I will see that she attends tonight." And then he left in search of his horse. He needed to go on a long ride to cool his heels. If he was to play the courtly gentleman tonight, it would take all of his focus and control. Or else he'd do what he'd been threatening to and take Rosalind to bed because she needed a release as much as he did.

Courting her is going to be the bloody death of me.

CHAPTER 12

r. Pevensly took pride in being Lady Melbourne's butler and seeing to the duties which helped him care for Her Ladyship's residence. Holding his head high, he descended the stairs, white gloves running the length of the banister. When he reached the bottom stair he lifted his gloved fingers, examining them for dust. They came away clean. With a satisfied smile, he proceeded through the rest of the house, checking on each room. The last door he came to before he was to join the staff downstairs for supper was Her Ladyship's study.

Pevensly opened the door and glanced inside, assuming all would be in order. But before he closed the door a breeze drifted through the room from an open window facing the mew below. Papers on the desk rustled, and the curtains slowly lifted and fell.

Frowning, Pevensly walked over to the window and slid it shut. A maid must have left it open, for what purpose he could not fathom, but he would speak to the maids and remind them not to leave open windows in an empty room. He then tidied the papers on the desk and left.

By now his stomach was rumbling, and he was interested to know what the cook had prepared. It might be a while until Her

Ladyship returned, and she always insisted that the staff dine on the best food while she was away so it would not have to be thrown out. It was one of many reasons why Pevensly appreciated his mistress. With a pat on his stomach, he proceeded to the door that would take him downstairs to the staff kitchens.

~

ROSALIND GLARED AT JOANNA. "How on earth did I let you talk me into this?"

Ashton's sister was almost a feminine version of her older brother, with bright blue eyes, pale blond hair and stunning features. Unlike Ashton, however, Joanna was a creature made of pure sweetness. She was always full of smiles, even if she did have a mischievous gleam in her eyes.

"If I remember correctly, it's because I told you how many wonderful gentlemen will be attending tonight, which will give you many chances to make Ashton *very* jealous. He won't be able to do anything because he will be forced to behave himself." Joanna nudged Rosalind in front of a tall mirror and grinned.

Rosalind couldn't help but smile. She'd brought a lovely round dress of white figured lace over a white satin slip. Her maid had packed it because it worked equally well as an evening dress or for balls, not that she'd planned on dancing when she'd prepared for this journey. No, she'd been contemplating seduction, and this dress brought out her dark hair and accented her figure to advantage. The sleeves were alternately puffed with pink *gros de Naples* and white lace.

She hadn't really let Joanna talk her into the ball—it was part of her bargain with Ashton to keep up appearances, and she intended to do her part. She had given their argument in the fields some thought and felt she had to trust him to return her companies to her if she played her part. But seducing him back might just help ensure that he did keep his word, and a ball might help that along.

"This is beautiful," Joanna said with a sigh. "I love it when gowns have wreaths of field flowers on the hem. You have exquisite taste."

Rosalind examined Joanna's gown. It was a similar white lace round dress with a bodice strewn with rosebuds, and the sleeves were interspersed with pearls and flounced with bluebells and roses. A lovely gown, but it did not do much for Joanna's pale hair and creamy skin.

"It's a good thing white is in season. I have plenty of white gowns." Joanna plucked at her skirts and sighed.

"But with your fair complexion you should try other colors. Rose or dark blue," Rosalind suggested.

"Do you think so?" Joanna studied herself in the mirror, as if picturing herself in such a gown.

"Oh yes. Men notice color more than you think. Try something striking—don't let any matrons' gossip bother you. I know many believe pastels are the only suitable colors, but if it washes out your coloring, it fails to serve its true purpose, which is to aid you in hunting for a husband."

Ashton's sister laughed. "It's silly, but I haven't found a man who is interesting enough to tempt me into matrimony. But there is always so much pressure to find a match." Joanna sobered. "Every time I attend dinners and balls in London during the season, I watch my friends find husbands, and every year the married ladies ask me when I shall find a match, as though that was all I was created for. It's maddening to think that I only draw breath to serve as a vessel for bearing children. I want to find a man who will love me for me, a man who will be a partner in my life, someone who is wild and adventurous and not concerned with the cut of his coat or the style of his cravat." Joanna blushed when she glanced at Rosalind. "I'm sorry. I should have not said that."

Pity and understanding filled Rosalind, and she clasped Joanna's hands in hers. "We are of the same mind, you and I. Never think you cannot speak your heart to me." She smiled. "What you need is a husband who will move heaven and earth for you, yet still sees you as an equal."

Joanna frowned. "Assuming such a man exists. How am I supposed to know if a man sees me in such a way?"

It was a good question. Men so often seemed to speak of women as prized possessions in public circles. It was hard sometimes to tell how they thought of them as people.

"If a man professes his love for you, look close at how he speaks about you and ask yourself—does he love *who* I am, or *what* I offer? Let the answer guide you. After seeing how Lady Essex, Lady Rochester and Lady Sheridan's husbands are with their wives, I see now it is possible. If you can make a match like that, you'll escape the sense of being trapped. I promise you." She gave Joanna's hands a gentle squeeze before letting go.

"Thank you. I'm too afraid to talk to Mama of such things. Not that she'd be angry with me, but I think she feels she plays a part in my failure to find a husband. It has been a strain on her."

Rosalind nodded. "I imagine so, but you mustn't let it bother you. You must look happy and relaxed for a man to be interested."

Ashton's sister beamed, hope making her eyes bright and excitement putting a blush in her cheeks.

It was nice to help Joanna and offer her advice. Her own mother had died before they could have talks like this, and it had left a deep empty well inside her. Inside everyone in her family. There had been no balls, no suitors, no giggling over dresses or discussions on how best to catch a husband. All the things that mothers and daughters would have shared, she had not been able to do. Rather than a come-out, she'd been trapped in an aging castle, coping with every vicious blow her father dealt and hiding every minute she could manage.

"Well, it's too late to change my dress now." Joanna gazed at her reflection again, a tad wistful.

"Next time then," Rosalind assured her. "Are you ready?"

Joanna nodded. "We're taking a coach. The men will ride."

"Thank heavens for that," Rosalind muttered. If she had to share a coach with Ashton, she'd likely stomp on his foot on purpose…more than once. Not that it would do much good. He'd be wearing sturdy leather shoes, and she would be in white satin slippers.

"Here." Joanna handed her a pair of elbow-length evening gloves before tugging on her own. It had been a relief to not have to change in Ashton's bedchamber tonight. She was still furious with him after what had happened in the field, and if she'd had to be alone with him again so soon, she might have thrown something at that stubborn, pragmatic head of his.

As they came down the main stairs, Regina was waiting for them.

"The men have just left, even Rafe, though he wanted to take the coach with us because of his injured arm. Ashton insisted he ride."

The older woman's words bought Rosalind up short.

"Mr. Lennox hurt his arm?" She had not yet made the acquaintance of Ashton's younger brother.

"Yes, he fell and badly injured his shoulder. We had to have Dr. Finchley come and see to him. It was bloody, far more so than I would have expected from a fall. I would have fainted had I been allowed to see it, but Rafe wouldn't let anyone but the doctor in. Stubborn boy."

Rosalind thought over how a man might injure himself in a fall. It was possible, she supposed, if he'd landed on a broken branch or a sharp stone. But still, she thought back to those eyes from the night she was robbed. His hesitation when she'd called him Lord Lennox. What if it was an entirely different wound he suffered…such as a gunshot?

Could Rafe be the highwayman who'd robbed her?

"I'm afraid I haven't had the pleasure of meeting your brother before," Rosalind said. "What is he like?"

Joanna leaned close to Rosalind as Ashton's mother walked ahead to see if the coach was ready. "Rafe is...well, he's quite the opposite of Ashton. Rafe never looks before he leaps. I daresay he is never without a mistress, and he loves gambling. He always says life is about taking risks."

"That does sound like the opposite of Ashton, except perhaps for the mistress part."

"That's brothers for you. Do you have brothers, Rosalind?"

Rosalind couldn't help but smile as she and Joanna climbed into the carriage. "I have three."

"Three? Lord, I can barely tolerate having two. What are yours like? Surely they are better behaved than mine."

"Brothers?" Regina caught up on the conversation.

Normally Rosalind would not have divulged so much of her past to strangers, but she rather liked and trusted Ashton's mother and sister.

"Brock is my eldest brother. Then there's Brodie and Aiden. They're all older than me. And lovable, though more than a wee bit stubborn. I am not quite sure any of them qualify as gentlemen."

Regina chuckled. "Scotsmen are something entirely different. They will drive you mad, but they have many irresistibly charming qualities." Regina laughed outright when she glanced at Rosalind. "I mean that as a compliment. We have a few Scots in our family."

"Ashton did mention that. He even knew a bit of Gaelic."

"Yes, that boy loves languages. He excelled at his schooling, and he and his friends are all fluent in half a dozen of them."

Joanna giggled. "One night they were talking about something and didn't want me to overhear, so they spoke German for the next half hour. I was more impressed than upset by the end of their discussion."

Envy filled Rosalind. She wanted to learn more languages but hadn't had the time. After her husband passed, she'd become caught up in the running of her businesses and had little time to study.

"Do you know many languages, Joanna?"

"No. I'm afraid I don't have the head for it. I am far better at mathematics, like Ashton."

"Did you study much?"

Joanna nodded. "Ashton made sure both Thomasina and I were as well educated as any man."

"Thomasina?" That was a new name to her.

Regina brimmed with pride. "My eldest. She's married and living in London with her husband and two children."

The rest of the coach ride was filled with stories from Regina and Joanna about Ashton's childhood. Apparently he hadn't always been a cool, calculating man. He'd once been a veritable scamp.

Rosalind assumed both ladies were doing their best to show Ashton in a favorable light since they believed she and Ashton were courting, but the stories were told with smiles and genuine warmth. Once he'd been a sweet, trouble-seeking boy with frogs in his pockets and a talent for pranks. She couldn't help but wonder what had happened along the way to change him.

"Ah, here we are," Regina announced as the coach rolled to a stop before a grand house lit by moonlight. Lamps illuminated the windows, and the large oak front door was open as grooms took charge of coach horses and a butler came out to collect their shawls. The sound of music and laughter inside lifted Rosalind's spirits. She had been to so few balls in the last few years.

A footman offered her a hand down, and she lifted her skirts before placing her palm in his. This was her first country ball, a private one, but since she had received a formal invitation from the Mertons, she felt comfortable in attending. Even she knew that one could not attend a private country ball unless invited.

"Welcome!" A middle-aged man with graying temples dressed in a fine blue coat was just inside the door, greeting the guests.

Regina made the introductions. "Mr. Merton! Thank you so much for inviting my family and my guests. I would like to introduce you to Lady Melbourne."

Merton bowed. "Charmed, simply charmed to have you here, Lady Melbourne. Please come in. We are letting gentlemen sign the ladies' dance cards." He handed her a small card on a string, and she slipped it around her wrist. The use of dance cards meant there had to be a number of people in attendance.

"What a crush this will be! Come with me." Joanna tucked her arm in Rosalind's, and they proceeded to the location where all of the gaiety was occurring.

The ballroom was full of people laughing and talking with delighted animation. It was more informal than the balls she'd attended in London. It was clear that this was an occasion to be celebrated among friends, not a place for political or business alliances and gossiping matrons with social agendas.

Against her own wishes, Rosalind sought Ashton out, trying to find him in the throng of people.

Mr. Merton followed them into the ballroom. "I shall be the master of ceremonies tonight. Let me take you through the room and make the necessary introductions. Then you will be free to accept dance invitations."

Rosalind met a series of polite and charming bachelors, all strangers to her except one. And his presence came as quite a surprise.

"Lady Melbourne! This is famous! How glad I am to see you again." The Earl of Pembroke kissed her hand. "How is…everything?" He nodded discreetly in the direction of Ashton, who was standing close to the far wall, scowling with his arms crossed.

Jonathan and Charles were talking next to him, but Ashton was staring at her and ignoring them.

So he'd been hiding against the wall. The baron was a wallflower? She nearly laughed at the thought.

"It has not been easy," Rosalind admitted. "At this moment he controls everything, my lord. I'm not sure how to escape him."

Lord Pembroke shot Ashton a furious look. "What's he demanding? Perhaps I could buy your debts up and—"

"No, thank you, my lord. I must deal with him on my own. He intends to marry me, and nothing will dissuade him."

"Lennox wants to *marry* you?" Pembroke's shock was a little upsetting. Surely she couldn't be that much of a poor prospect as to shock the man.

"Well, I know I'm not an ideal match as a widow, but—"

Pembroke held up a hand. "You mistake my surprise, Lady Melbourne. Lennox has always been so mercenary in his interest in the fairer sex. I simply cannot fathom a romantic side to him. Then again, you are a tempting prospect." Pembroke's smile was warm and genuine.

Rosalind nudged him with her fan. "You mustn't tease me, my lord." It was so easy to see why Emily Parr liked and trusted this man. He was a true gentleman.

"I would marry you, Lady Melbourne, if you wish it. I am a loyal man and have been told I'm a good lover." He winked roguishly. "I must confess, I'm rather fascinated by you."

Two offers of marriage in less than two days? She had to hide her surprise at Pembroke's unexpected offer. It was incredibly chivalrous of him.

"No, that's not necessary, my lord, although I am honored by your offer."

"I mean it, Lady Melbourne. I would be *happy* to marry you."

"I see why Lady Essex values your friendship, my lord."

Pembroke sighed, taking the subtle refusal as well as he could. "I will admit I am disappointed, but I see you're determined to fight this battle on your own. Very well. However, might I suggest a plan that would make Lennox jealous?"

Rosalind beamed at him. "What a wonderful idea! He's far too possessive, and I'd very much like to remind him I am a free woman."

"Then allow me to sign your dance card." He searched her arm and then penned his name to the first two dances. "I wouldn't want to cause too much of a scandal by taking more than two, but any more than one is bound to be noticed by Lord Lennox."

"Thank you, my lord."

With a smile, Pembroke kissed her hand once more. Then Rosalind watched him move on to another young lady.

A tall, blond-haired, blue-eyed man approached her. He was so like Ashton that he startled her at first.

"So, you are my brother's latest paramour." His lips twitched as he captured her hand, kissing her gloved fingertips. She noticed he used his left hand, not his right.

"And you must be Mr. Lennox, Ashton's wayward brother."

He chuckled. "Wayward? Steady on, Lady Melbourne, I should like to prepare myself for your sharp tongue. I was warned by Lonsdale, you see."

Rosalind huffed. "My tongue is not so sharp. The earl is exaggerating because he enjoys trouble."

"And *are* you trouble, Lady Melbourne?"

Rosalind stared deep into his eyes. "Not as much as you, I suspect." And then she let him sign her dance card. It would be the best way to see if Rafe was in fact the highwayman she'd shot in the storm. If he was, she was going to demand her money back, and she wanted to make sure he never stopped another carriage like that ever again.

Her card was nearly full by the time the festivities began. She peeked at Ashton from behind a row of couples set to dance and saw he hadn't moved from his place against the wall. He was still staring at her.

"Ready?" Pembroke returned to her, claiming her for the first dance, and they joined the others. "I promise you shall have an excellent partner." He then leaned in to whisper, "I *rarely* step on toes."

Rosalind took her position across from him as the dance started. He was certainly a wonderful gentleman, but each time the dance let her spin to face the wall where Ashton stood, she was momentarily lost in the intensity of his gaze. It pulled her in, promised dark, delicious things. If only she could bed the man and walk away like many other widows seemed to do, but he was marriage-minded and intent on controlling her life.

"He looks very upset, your wicked oppressor." Pembroke chuckled as the dance ended, and they clapped for the musicians who finished the lively tune.

"Yes, he does," Rosalind replied, pleased by Ashton's obvious displeasure.

"This next is a waltz." Pembroke brushed his dark hair out of his brown eyes before bringing her closer to him. "Shall we make him furious?"

Rosalind placed her hand in his and smiled when he curled an arm around her waist, holding her too close for propriety. But given Pembroke's motives, she allowed it. She grinned wickedly.

"Let's make him *very* furious."

CHAPTER 13

*L*ord Pembroke was as good as his word. By the time the waltz had ended, with Pembroke pressing himself as close to Rosalind as he could for every turn, Ashton had pushed away from his wall and was stalking toward her, eyes blazing. But before he could speak to her, Rafe slipped in between them.

"Sorry, brother, but I am next." Rafe flashed a wolfish smile at his brother.

Ashton attempted to take Rosalind's other hand to pull her away. "Surely you should not be dancing after your fall."

"Nonsense," Rafe replied. "I've been resting too long. Some activity will do me good."

Rosalind bit her lip to hide a smug smile as she walked past Ashton to follow Rafe out onto the dance floor. "I'm sorry you shan't have what you desire, Lord Lennox."

Ashton visibly clenched his fists.

Rafe glanced at his brother with a chuckle. "So, Lady Melbourne, tell me, are you going to marry my brother? The talk of the house is that you will, which makes little sense to me. I noticed a tension between you two that isn't at all bouquets of flowers or kisses in the dark."

There was little point in hiding the truth. In fact, given his and Ashton's opposing natures, Rafe might be the sort to enjoy defying his brother and offer her advice on how to escape him. She hadn't yet given up hope that there could be some way to win her life back without resorting to devil's bargains and seduction.

"He's put me in a position of financial ruin in order to obtain me in marriage."

Rafe's eyes widened. "Devil take it—that's low even for my brother."

"Yes, well, you know what sort of man he is as well as I do. I've agreed to marry him, but in truth, I would love to find a way to secure my property and remain my own woman."

They spun around another couple in the dance and had to briefly separate before they could come back together.

"Lady Melbourne, would you take my advice if I offered it?"

"I may, if your intentions are honorable."

"Lady Melbourne, you strike my heart with such a remark. Of course my intentions are honorable. I don't like to see my brother push anyone into doing something they don't willingly agree to, and I freely admit that I should love to see him punished for his scheming."

He seemed honest enough with that answer. "Very well. What is your advice?" She had to wait another moment as they stepped back to let two couples dance between them.

Rafe gave a conspiratorial grin as they came together. "Are you any good at games of skill, such as cards, or perhaps chess?"

"I'm awful at cards but quite good at chess." Being alone in a castle with only her brothers, she'd learned that game very well.

The dance ended, and Rafe curled her arm through his to lead her off the dance floor to an alcove where he leaned in close to speak to her.

"Then I suggest this: wager him your marital and financial freedom. My brother is useless at chess. He understands the fundamentals only and none of the finesse. You could beat him if you make it a matter of honor."

Surely Ashton would not allow her such an easy way out. He'd promised to return her property in time, but then again, he'd also threatened to keep it if she didn't consider marriage to him. And she feared that threat would become more pronounced the longer she refused. Perhaps something like this would make it a matter of honor he couldn't ignore.

"I don't think he—"

"Play into his vanity. Challenge him to a game of skill, one where you start on equal footing." Rafe glanced around. "Blast, he's coming this way, and he looks ready to throttle me."

Sure enough, Ashton was making his way toward them. On the surface he seemed as calm as ever, but the way he pushed past those in his way made Rosalind see why his brother sounded concerned.

"Rafe, why don't you fetch Lady Melbourne a glass of arrack punch?" Ashton suggested with a precision that could cut through bone.

"Of course." Rafe winked at Rosalind and left for the refreshment tables.

Ashton captured Rosalind's wrist and tugged the little card up close so he could inspect it. "I don't suppose you have any dances left open?"

"The last dance," she said, watching him, trying not to smile as he continued to glare at the names. He might think he was maintaining his composure, but he would be lying to himself if he did. He used a slender pencil to inscribe his name at the bottom and then let go of her.

"Good. You're mine for the last dance then." He sounded far too smug about that.

"You should dance with someone else before me, my lord. It's inappropriate for you to dance with one lady only. People will talk."

His blue eyes blazed as he leaned down close to her. "Does it look as though I care?"

Rosalind tried to retreat, but not because she felt overwhelmed by him. Several couples were watching now, and she didn't wish for Mr. Merton's ball to become a scene of scandal and gossip.

"My lord, please step back. People are staring."

He reached up and brushed a loose curl of her hair away from her neck. "Let them." The touch sent heated tingles through her. It was torturously sweet and sensual as his fingers lingered against her neck a moment too long.

Was this what it felt like? To be loved and cherished as a woman? She knew Ashton did not love her, that his overtures were always focused on the practical and advantageous, but there was affection in that touch. Some part of this ruthless baron cared about her. It should not have mattered to her, but it did. She wanted someone to care about her, even if it had to be her business rival.

"I look forward to our dance." He let his hand drop from her neck and walked away.

"Heavens," she muttered, fanning herself.

The last dance was to be a waltz. Something so intimate was not a good idea. Not that she had control over what the orchestra played. Perhaps fate would be on her side for once.

～

THIS NIGHT WAS hell on Ashton's control.

Watching Rosalind, *his* Rosalind, going around the dance floor from one man to the next…it was going to kill him. Every time someone touched her hand or made her smile, he flinched.

"Two more dances. That's all I have to endure." He forced his attention to the rest of the room. His mother was laughing as she huddled in a corner with the other married ladies. A dozen or so ostrich plumes bounced as the ladies bent their heads to gossip. It was his mother's element: the social scene.

She was the daughter of an earl, one with a vast fortune, and despite having had her pick of eligible bachelors had married his father out of foolish notions of love. His father's decline had hurt his mother by association. It was only in the last few years that she had entered back into society.

He'd helped arrange that, of course, using the fortune he'd built for their family to buy their way back in with wealth and influence. Not that his mother had any notion of the lengths he'd gone to in order to secure her happiness and Joanna's future. No, she thought he was a heartless bastard, no better than his father.

But he'd always looked after his family, seeing to Rafe's education as well as Joanna's and assuring that his family had every comfort they could need.

When the League had formed at university, it had been forged in the aftermath of tragedy. But it had also forged bonds of friendship that were unbreakable. Those bonds had saved him from himself. He had not been able to let go of that part of him that obsessed over money and power, trying to rebuild his family's wealth and status after his father's ruination. But the League had reminded him that life was about more than those things. It was about friendship and loyalty.

Love was not part of his equation, but it did not change these yearnings he had that left an ache in his heart when he watched his three married friends with their wives.

"You are in my debt, dear brother," Rafe announced as he sidled up beside him. He removed a slender hip flask out of his coat and took a quick swig.

"What's that?" Ashton asked, nodding at the drink.

Rafe tapped the flask. "Courage in a bottle. You should try it." He pressed it into Ashton's hands.

Out of the corner of his eye, he watched Rosalind dancing with another man, laughing at something her partner said. His blood burned beneath his skin, and he raised the flask to his lips, only to gag. It tasted like sour brandy.

"What in blazes is in this?" He wiped his mouth on his gloved hand.

"It's not important. You'll thank me when I tell you how I've just secured you your future wife."

Ashton took a long drink of the dreadful swill before handing it back to Rafe. "What are you on about?"

"When I was dancing with that lovely Scottish lady, I convinced her she would be able to win her freedom from your notorious clutches."

He grabbed Rafe and forced him against the wall. "What?"

Rafe muttered a curse, and the color drained from his face.

"What's the matter? I didn't shove you that hard."

"Have a care, brother. It's my shoulder."

Ashton pressed a hand into his brother's shoulder. "Ah yes, your wound. A wound from your fall, or a *bullet*, perhaps?"

"What?"

"Rosalind was robbed by a highwayman on the way to Lennox House. She thought at first that this man was me. Admit the truth to me now and I will decide how to deal with your foolishness another time."

"I…" Ash pressed harder on the shoulder when he hesitated too long. Rafe sent a venomous glare toward Rosalind. "Hell of a shot it was too, through the dark and rain. I don't know how she managed to hit me."

Ashton groaned. His fool of a brother was really playing the part of a highwayman? What was next? Would levelheaded Joanna run off to Gretna Green with a stranger?

"Do you want to end up on the *gallows*, you fool?"

The sudden silence surrounding them made him and Rafe look around. To Ashton's dismay, quite a few people had stopped in their conversations and had turned to stare at them. He'd lost sense of where he was in the midst of this argument.

"We shall discuss this tomorrow. Now, what were you saying about Rosalind?"

Rafe's smile was cold. "If she asks you to play chess tonight, I'd take her up on it. Lie about how proficient you are."

"I don't follow you."

"Must I explain everything? You'll figure it out." Rafe shoved away from the wall and stalked off into the crowds.

"What was all that about?" Jonathan walked over to him, his face flushed.

"Nothing. Rafe is being irritating as usual. You've been dancing?"

A flicker of guilt passed over the young man's features. "It's my first real ball as a guest rather than an attendant. I find I rather like them."

Ashton felt like a selfish fool. The last few months had been a seemingly endless whirlwind of dangerous threats thanks to Hugo, and in the midst of it all, Jonathan, as a newly recognized member of the *ton,* had only now attended his first ball at the age of twenty-five. He should have been providing the young man with advice—Lord help him if he had asked Charles instead—but he seemed to be doing well enough on his own.

"Is it the dancing or the ladies you fancy?" Ashton asked.

"The dancing," Jonathan replied without hesitation. His gaze sharpened. "Why?"

Ashton waved a hand to dismiss Jonathan's suspicious look. "You don't have to marry Audrey, you know. Simply because she took an interest in you does not mean you must return it. She takes interest in many things, then moves on to something else just as quickly. I wanted to make sure someone told you. None of the other League members would think to tell you because they assumed you knew. But you have a right to choose your wife."

Jonathan was silent a long while, his focus on the whirling couples on the dance floor. There was a prickle of annoyance in his features.

"I'm no green lad. I have had my share of lovers. But the last few months, when I've had the opportunity to bed a woman, I've let the moment pass because none of them is *her*. I do not know if it's mere lust and fascination or a strange inescapable pull, but for now, I cannot see myself with anyone but Audrey. She's young and so..."

Ashton chuckled. "I'm sure there aren't enough adjectives in the English language to describe the girl."

"No, there aren't."

"Just have a care. With that one, if there is a heart that ends up being broken, it might not be hers."

Jonathan ran a hand through his sandy hair as the music died down and prepared to start up again. He turned to face Ashton. "Last dance. Are you finally going to take your woman for a waltz?" He nodded at Rosalind, who was fanning her face.

She looked positively radiant. Dancing suited her. If there was one thing Ashton knew, a woman who loved to dance often equally enjoyed lovemaking. Rosalind curtseyed to her partner and then raised her dance card, still smiling.

He waited, watching her face as she realized there was only one dance left. One name left. Her face flushed and she glanced around, then found him and froze. Her breasts rose and fell slightly with her breaths, but everything else about her was still. He approached her.

"Rosalind."

He held out his hand and lost himself in the silver pools of her eyes. Such lovely eyes, so full of emotions. Not the blank, sweet eyes of a young woman who'd never lived, but the eyes of one who had fought for everything she had.

A fellow warrior.

When she placed her hand in his, with anticipation. He led her back onto the floor as the musicians started to play a waltz. If he was to dance, he preferred a slow, measured one designed to seduce a woman. He was in no mood to hop about like a silly fool.

Ashton slid one hand around her waist. "I've been watching you. You are an excellent dancer."

"But you haven't danced with me yet." Rosalind's lips curved into a smile. "What if I tread upon your toes?"

"You won't," he assured her. "Because I dance even better."

"A bit full of oneself, are we?"

"Not at all. It's merely a fact." He tugged her a little closer to him, and they began.

For the first time in his life, he was captivated by a simple waltz with a lovely partner. He had not been bragging about his dancing skills. Dance was math and motion combined. It was something that could be studied and perfected. It was an art, but one he was able to execute with an academic's precision.

But this was different. Rosalind moved with him as though they'd danced together for years. She made the steps effortlessly and followed his lead without any urging. The chandelier light illuminated her alabaster skin, making it glow.

Too damned lovely.

"Have you enjoyed the ball, my lord?" she asked. Her tone was light, but her lips were a thin line as she waited for his answer.

"It has been fairly agreeable." *Aside from watching you dance with every man but me.*

"My lord, I—" She stopped short, and he saw her raise her chin and square her shoulders.

"What is it? Please speak. I should hate to think I frighten you into silence."

A fire sparked in her eyes. "I'm not frightened of you."

"Then what's the matter?"

"We need to resolve this...matter between us. Mere discussions have led nowhere, and I grow impatient. What if we instead made a wager? A win would be definitive. We could make a binding contract, of course, to keep it fair."

"A wager on whether you'll marry me?" For some reason, his heart beat against his ribs hard enough to make his breath catch.

Had this been Rafe's idea? Could he win Rosalind's submission this easily?

"Yes. We would both be bound by our mutual sense of honor. If I lose, I marry you. If I win, you return my property as promised by the end of the week, sell my debts to parties of my choosing and allow me to return to London."

It could not have been any clearer unless she'd said, *"And then I'll be free of you."*

"It would not be true to my intentions if I readily agreed to this." He held his breath just as the waltz came to an end, but he did not let her go.

"Please," Rosalind begged. "We can have a witness to our agreement."

Feigning resignation, he glanced up at the ceiling. "Very well, but we need an impartial party to choose the game."

Biting her lip, she shook her head. "I was thinking the same thing. What about your brother?" She nodded at Rafe, who was scanning the crowds with a bored expression. When he noticed them watching him, Ashton waved him over.

"What is it?" Rafe asked.

"Rosalind and I intend to make a friendly wager, and we need an impartial party to choose the game we play. Pick something fair, a game of skill."

"What about chess?" Rafe suggested. "You're not terribly good at it, nor are you that poor."

Rosalind's heart jumped. Rafe was helping her even more than she'd thought he could. She had to remember to act as though she was merely passable at chess.

"I suppose we could play that. I consider myself a fair player." She focused on not fidgeting.

Ashton stared hard at her. "Very well. Chess it is. But we will discuss how to even the odds when you and I return home."

"But—"

Ashton pressed a finger to her lips. "You do not want me to

elaborate here. We're in danger of being overheard." He nodded discreetly at a trio of young ladies who were avidly observing them but attempting to carry on a conversation behind their fans.

"Yes, of course," Rosalind muttered and tried to pull away from him.

He did not allow it. Instead, he captured her hand and tucked it into his arm to lead her away.

"Where are we going?" she demanded, her eyes darting around at the other guests.

"Home. I have a very important game of chess to win."

CHAPTER 14

*R*osalind clutched her shawl tightly about her shoulders as Ashton offered to lift her down from the coach.

"Come on, darling," he teased. "Don't be frightened."

"*I'm not.*" She held out her hand, but he stepped closer and caught her waist, lifting her down. Beyond him the lights of the house bathed the front lawn in a soft golden hue, a lovely contrast to the heavy darkness of the midnight hour.

"I'll have a footman bring us a bottle of wine. By the looks of it, we'll need it." He was chuckling as he helped her up the steps. The butler opened the door for them, and Ashton took him aside to speak to him while a footman collected her shawl.

"Ready?" Ashton asked as he returned to her.

"With you I doubt I'll ever be truly ready," she said as Ashton led her up the grand stairs. Risking her future on a game of chess? It was madness, but it was a risk worth taking if she could free herself from Lennox's manipulative agenda, and it was not much of a risk at that, if Rafe was to be believed.

"Wait. Why are we playing in your bedroom? Surely there's a more suitable location." Rosalind jerked to a halt, balking as he attempted to drag her inside.

"As chess is not my forte, I require some advantage in my favor. Please come inside and I will explain how I intend to even the odds." Ashton pushed the door open farther and stepped back, allowing her to make the decision of whether to enter.

There was that fiery intensity in his eyes that she couldn't turn away from, even though it frightened her. He would do her no harm, not physically, but there was something about Ashton Lennox that warned her that if she got too close, he'd burn her up all the same.

Her feet moved before she could stop them as she walked past Ashton into his bedchamber.

Please don't let this be a mistake.

She turned to face him, giving him her most imperious look. "I'm here. Now talk, Lennox." A silly part of her thought she could keep things businesslike between them if she used his surname. The last thing she wanted right now was to speak his given name in such an intimate environment.

"I was thinking that—"

A rap of knuckles on the open door announced a footman with a bottle of wine.

"My lord." The footman held the bottle out to Ashton, who gripped it by the neck.

"Thank you, William. Fetch me a chessboard from the drawing room, would you?"

He closed the door and gestured for Rosalind to sit in a chair by the fire. He joined her and set the bottle of wine on the table between them.

"The terms, as I understand them, are thus. If I win, you will marry me straightaway. I'll obtain a special license in London. If you win, I will transfer your debts to the party of your choosing and tell the banks to open your lines of credit again by the end of the week."

Rosalind's hands curled into fists. "*If* we marry, I suppose you will let me live where I choose and we need not bother each other except a few times a year for appearances?"

Ashton leaned back in his chair, crossing one leg over his knee. "Absolutely not. If we marry, we live together, share a bed, share a *life*. If there is one thing I don't wish to be scandalous about, it is my marriage. My wife living apart from me would be a scandal. I've done my poor sister enough harm with my lifestyle to date. For my family's sake, I wish this one thing not to be tainted."

Share a life with Ashton? Strangely that thought didn't frighten her, not as much as she thought it would. The only thing she didn't want was a man who controlled her. She wanted a partner, not a gaoler. But how could she trust that he wouldn't be the thing she feared most—a man just like her father?

"Ashton, you must promise me that you don't...you won't..." She held her words inside until they threatened to choke her.

"Won't what?" He leaned forward. "Tell me, Rosalind. There should be no secrets between us. I want you to always feel free to talk."

She could see the sincerity in his eyes.

"I could not survive in a marriage where I was merely a pawn to be moved about without a thought. I need you to promise me that we would be *true* partners in our shared life." She prayed he would understand. He had to.

Ashton uncrossed his legs and then very slowly reached across the small table and cupped her chin.

"The only place I would dominate you would be in bed...to our mutual pleasure. In all else, you will be my equal. You have my word." His thumb caressed her bottom lip, the sensual touch also tender as though he wished to reassure her.

Dominate her in bed? Rather than be frightened by the thought, she was entranced. It was not a threat, but a promise of ecstasy, of things she had never experienced with her first husband.

With a shaky breath, she nodded. "Then I agree to your terms."

Ashton did not release her chin even when the footman returned with the chessboard and pieces.

"Bring it here, William." Ashton finally let her go and tapped the table with his fingers. The young footman set the board down, and Ashton began to arrange the pieces, then paused as he made a mistake in the placement of the king and queen and fixed it. The mistake made Rosalind relax.

"Why don't you finish setting it up? I'll pour us some wine." He stood and went over to his dresser, where two glasses sat next to the bottle of wine. He picked up the glasses and set them on the table beside the board. Rosalind finished placing the last few pawns on the board. As Ashton poured their drinks, the crimson liquid splashed against the glasses. The wine bouquet was sweet, with a hint of cherry and oak.

"Now, drink up. We've one more thing to discuss." He sipped his wine and walked over to his bedchamber door and slid the lock into place.

"I've already agreed to your terms."

He held up a hand. "This isn't about terms—it's about rules. It's simple enough. To even the odds, we will play the game as follows. After each of us makes a move, whoever loses a piece to the other must also sacrifice an article of clothing."

Her pulse hummed and her face flushed. "What?"

"Each of us must strip down as we lose. It will distract us both."

"How is this an advantage for you?" she demanded. "I could have you naked in a dozen moves."

The wicked little grin made her shiver. "That would be far more of a distraction for *you*, I assure you. I'm more comfortable in my skin than you know. I doubt you would be as confident in nothing but yours." He raised the glass in salute and took another sip.

"I refuse. This is beyond inappropriate."

"I'm afraid I must insist. Come now, Rosalind. We are behind closed doors, and everyone we know is still at the ball. Don't tell me you wouldn't find some satisfaction in embarrassing me by stripping me bare? Assuming you can, of course."

Rosalind's eyes narrowed. She didn't say a word, but in her glare she accepted his challenge.

He rotated the board so the black pieces faced her. "Ready to play?"

"I prefer white," she cut in.

"And so do I."

Gritting her teeth she glowered at him. "Of course you do. Very well. You make the first move."

Ashton casually flipped a pawn forward. Rosalind immediately moved her pawn to counter in the square directly opposite it. When they looked up at each other, his lips curved and he hid the rest of his smile behind his wine glass. Then he moved his knight and she moved one of hers. The next two moves brought their bishops face to face. Each move was mirrored as Rosalind waited for Ashton to leave an opening. Ashton nudged a pawn forward, and Rosalind seized her chance, using her bishop to claim it.

"I believe that means you must remove a piece of clothing." She was smiling despite herself as she tipped her wine glass back. The subtle flavors were sweet upon her tongue. He had excellent taste in wine. Not too bitter, but a soft, velvety, full-bodied red.

"Correct. Well, Rosalind. You choose what I shall remove." He rose from his chair and came toward her.

She stood as well, needing to feel a little taller as she faced him. Her eyes ran over his clothes. He'd removed his coat before they'd even started their game, and she didn't want to remove his breeches. He'd been right about her being distracted by the state of his dishabille. His waistcoat, though, would be fine. She ran a fingertip down the front of the embroidered gold silk.

"This will do."

"Then by all means." He waved his hands at the row of pearly buttons.

He wanted her to undress him? With unsteady fingers, she plucked the row of buttons from their slits and then slid her hands underneath the silk to peel it off his body. He was warm and his enticing scent teased her as she tugged the cloth off his shoulders and let it drop to the floor. He cleared his throat and they both stepped back, but the tension between them was thick enough that already it muddled her thinking.

He took his seat and moved a pawn, and then she moved a bishop away from his. Another white pawn moved, and Rosalind claimed it with her own black pawn.

"Lucky me," Ashton muttered and stood again. "Name your price, Rosalind. And the cravat counts as part of my shirt, I'm afraid." He'd cut her off before she'd had the chance to think of something that clever.

"What about shoes and stockings?" she asked.

"Shoes and stockings together as a pair."

"Then remove those." She pointed at his shoes. He slipped out of his leather shoes and stockings before standing there in his bare feet. After a moment of silence, they sat and resumed the game.

He switched his rook with his queen. Then Rosalind advanced one of her knights. In the next turn they both moved their bishops, and then their pawns. With a satisfied smile, Ashton used his pawn to claim hers.

"Thank heavens for that. Now..." He crooked a finger at her.

Rosalind stood and approached him, heart pounding as he studied her.

"The dress, I think. Turn around." The soft but firm command in his tone made her shiver, but not with dread. She turned away from him and closed her eyes as she listened to the creak of the chair as he rose up behind her. His hands settled on her shoulders, making her tense.

"Relax, my dear," he murmured. "It is *only* your dress."

CHAPTER 15

*H*er dress...

Rosalind suppressed a shiver as Ashton stood behind her, his warm breath fanning across her neck. Once she removed her dress, they would both be completely indecent.

Exposed.

Ashton's hands moved to the laces of her gown, and he began to pull the threads out. His touch made her jump.

"What about my slippers?"

His lips twitched and a devilish gleam settled in his eyes. "I don't want your slippers."

"This is entirely unfair."

"Steady on, darling." His chuckle was bedroom soft and deliciously dark.

"Just take it off," she muttered, her temper sparking.

His fingertips stroked her bare shoulders, teasing patterns over her all-too-sensitive skin.

"And ruin the delight of the moment? Not a chance." The heat from his body enveloped her from behind, and she fought the part of her that *wanted* this infuriating, seductive man.

The movements of his hands were slow and methodical. The

fabric gaped slightly when he'd undone all the laces. She clutched her hands at her sides as he began to pull the gown down her body until it collapsed onto the floor in a puddle of fabric.

So little was between them now. It would be so easy to toss caution and good sense to the wind and go to bed with this man. As a widow she enjoyed certain freedoms other women did not. Society permitted widows to carry on affairs discreetly, but until now she had never been tempted. If only the past between them wasn't tainted by their struggles for power. If only her future wasn't at stake. *If only...*

He lifted her by the waist and set her down away from the gown and closer to him. Her bottom rubbed against the front of his thighs, and he briefly pressed against her. A wave of heat flooded through her as she struggled for air.

She now wore only her chemise, petticoats and stays. It was exciting but all too frightening. She'd been close to naked with him before, but this was different. Not only was her future at stake, but she had willingly agreed to it. Still, she reminded herself she was the better player, and she must win.

"I believe it's my turn." He pushed her a few inches away, and she stumbled back to her seat on shaky legs but managed to keep her wits about her. Ashton moved his rook, and she hastily moved a bishop.

Ashton stared at the board. When he met her gaze, he slid his white pawn forward and claimed her black bishop. He'd fallen for it. In search of an easy prize, he'd left himself exposed. She used her knight to claim his queen.

"A victory to each of us. Me first." Ashton stroked his chin thoughtfully. "The petticoats. Remove them." Rosalind slipped out of them and let them drop onto the pile of her gown.

"Your shirt, if you please," she countered.

Ashton tugged the white lawn shirt from his breeches, then used one finger to loosen his cravat. He pulled the neckcloth off, and then pulled his shirt over his head and tossed it to the floor.

Ashton's bare chest was...glorious. Golden, as though kissed by hours in the sun. How could a gentleman be so tan? It required him to be shirtless for lengths of time. But then, perhaps it wasn't so unusual for him. He'd spent time working at the farmhouse alongside the villagers. That was a day she would never forget. The sight of him toiling, muscles straining, his powerful body lifting up wooden beams...

"See something that interests you?"

Damned if his eyes didn't twinkle when he asked her that. She wanted to strangle the bloody arrogant fool. Rosalind shook her head, but the way her cheeks heated, she knew he'd see through the lie.

"My turn then." Ashton deftly moved a white pawn and claimed a black pawn. "Make your move, and then I shall collect another piece of your clothing."

Rosalind tried to clear her head. After analyzing the board, she moved her king forward. No piece to claim, but she had to look to the long game.

"I believe I shall take your stays." He waited for her to present herself to him, then unfastened her laces and let it drop to the floor. He kicked the garment away and took hold of her shoulders. The action was possessive, though not rough, and it sent waves of heat through her body and deep into her womb.

He spun her around to face him. It should have appalled her that the thought of him taking control of her body was so tempting, but it didn't. Instead it seemed a sinful, wonderful idea, one that she had to banish lest she lose focus on the game.

"Such a lovely figure." His husky words sent shivers through her. "Soft and yet strong in all the right places."

Trying to regain some control, she raised her chin. "I would return the compliment, but I doubt a man would like to be called soft."

Ashton's lips curved as he captured one of her hands and placed it on his groin.

"Most certainly *not* soft, my dear."

Swallowing, she jerked her hand free of his. "Enough. Let us finish the game."

Sighing, Ashton resumed his seat and moved his bishop directly beside the black knight. Rosalind rushed to move her king forward. Ashton responded by sliding his knight forward, and Rosalind mimicked him.

I will win. She was close. If he played wrong, she'd have him soon.

A white knight retreated, and she advanced her king again.

"This is why chess is a game of skill." He put his bishop diagonal to her king, but she could not take it because it was guarded on two fronts.

"Indeed." She stared hard at the board. Something wasn't right. The possible moves were few and none of them good. How had this happened? Did he realize he'd stumbled into such a favorable position, or had it been his plan all along? Had she been tricked?

Ashton's eyes, usually such a bright blue, had darkened now to a rich Prussian blue and threatened to ensnare her. For a moment she couldn't think, couldn't see anything outside those eyes.

"Go on, make your move." His gaze was burning straight through her as she realized what her final move had to be.

She reached out and set her king next to his white bishop. She couldn't take it, but she could use it defensively from this position. Blood began to pound in her ears, and her heart beat hard and fast against her ribs.

He leaned forward, resting his elbows on his knees as he met her panicked gaze squarely.

"I want you to remember this moment, Rosalind. The moment I won you." His pawn captured her knight, which opened up the rook behind it, placing her under threat from all sides.

"Checkmate."

The pieces on the board blurred. A thousand protests perched on the tip of her tongue, scrambling to get free. He had won.

Fairly. There was no way she could protest. They'd set out the terms, and she had agreed. It was a matter of honor.

"You have won," she echoed. "How? I thought chess wasn't your game!"

"I'm sure I pale in comparison to the masters, but I do play quite well, especially when motivated." He leaned back in his chair, a smirk on his full lips.

She got to her feet, her anger returning, momentarily burying the shock of losing. "You cheated?"

His eyes narrowed. "In what way did I cheat? We played a well-matched, fair game. Given the stakes, it was only fair. Now stop playing the damsel in distress, Rosalind. We both know you're above such nonsense."

Damsel in distress? Oh, she was going to strangle him, all right.

"And you also owe me one last bit of clothing."

"But—"

"The rules must be honored. Wouldn't you agree?" Ashton's smug grin made her want to slap him. *Hard.*

"Damn you," she growled. New anger sparked to life inside her. He may have won, but that did not mean she had to be complacent about it.

"I'm not above tying you down to get what is owed me."

"Tie me down?" she hissed. "I'd like to see you try, you—"

Ashton pounced, catching her wrists and pulling her toward him. He made a soft *tsking* noise as he tugged her to the bed and shoved her down upon the soft coverlet.

"Let me go!" Rosalind clawed at the bedding to get free, but he kept her pinned while he leaned over her to the table beside the bed. She kicked out when she heard him opening a drawer.

"These should work." He wound something silky around her wrists, then tightened it, trapping her hands together above her head. She tried to flip onto her back and pull her arms back down, but by the time she could try, she found her wrists bound with a white silk neckcloth. Ashton stood at the side of the bed, arms folded as he watched her.

"You can sit there and behave while we have a rational discussion, or I can tie you down completely."

The silk was not tight, but it gave her no room to free her hands. Shooting daggers at him, she replied, "I shall sit here, but if you think I'll consent to anything else—"

"Despite your impressions of me, I am not that much of a black-hearted bastard."

"Oh yes, your actions here are those of a perfect saint!"

"Well, I never claimed that, either." He chuckled and knelt by the bed and picked up one of her feet.

"What do you think you're doing?"

"I'm removing your slippers, what is owed to me. Surely you don't plan to go to sleep in them." He gently slid her shoes off. The heat of his palms singed her skin through her thin stockings. It felt nice. She didn't want it to feel nice. She wanted to hate him and hate how she desired him even while he infuriated her. He set her slippers on the floor and then rose up over her, his fingers toying with the loose ends of the white silk around her wrists.

"I usually don't bother with things like this, but on you, I find bound wrists rather intoxicating. To know I'm finally your master, at least in bed." His lips curled in a slow, delighted smile.

"We are *in bed* only in the most literal way. When I get free, I'm going to wring your bloody English neck." She wanted to sound furious, but her blood was heating in a different way at the thought of him doing anything he wanted to her while she was bound. It sounded so wicked...and divine.

Blond hair fell into his eyes as he leaned close. "I adore your fire, my dear. I never want it to leave." Ashton breathed slowly as he played with a loose lock of her hair.

Her eyes closed as she relished the sensual little caress. If only he hadn't won the wager, then she could be free to say yes to him without this fear of the future.

"Aren't you the least bit curious?" he asked.

"Curious?"

"About what it could be like between us." He reached up and trailed his fingertips down her cheek, and then to her neck. The touch set fire to her blood. "Just once. Trust me to show you how good it could be. Forget the wager and think only about this." He tilted her head back and leaned down to kiss her. The simple press of his lips sent her stomach into wild spirals. When he pulled back from her, she tried to keep kissing him, but he spoke against her searching lips.

"Let me take you to bed, Rosalind. Let me make love to you. I know such things that will make you weep with pleasure. I want to show you what you have to look forward to as my wife."

Would it be so bad to say yes? She wanted to feel that fulfillment of what his hands and mouth had promised her so often.

"Say yes," he urged, his voice rougher now.

She peeped up at him through her lashes. His fingers still touched her neck, the hold firm but gentle. His eyes were dark and hot, and power emanated from his body as he waited.

The silence between them was charged with unspoken challenges and seductive promises. Finally, she uttered the word that would change her life forever.

"Yes."

The fire in his eyes intensified. He freed her hands of the silk and slid his hands up her calves and thighs as he rolled her stockings off one by one and let them fall to the floor. Her breasts felt full and aching, nipples rasping against the white cloth of her chemise. She waited for him to shove her onto her back and mount her, but he didn't.

"Move back, darling." While she did as he instructed, he stepped back and unfastened the front of his breeches but did not remove them.

"Now, lie back and part those pretty thighs for me."

Her heart raced. Slowly, she lay back, parting her legs. He

crawled up the bed and knelt between them. The muscles of his chest rippled as he moved, and she stared at the light dusting of pale-gold hair along his pectorals. She ran one palm along his chest, feeling the silkiness of the hair before she trailed her hand down his abdomen. His muscles twitched at her exploring touch. She scraped her nails lightly across him, eliciting a groan from him and delighting in the fact that she would mark him as hers.

And here she was, tempted to explore every inch of this body. He was beautiful, masculine. His skin soft, but his body hard all over. A small knotted scar on his shoulder caught her attention, the old bullet wound. She'd once teased him about it. As she leaned over, she pressed a kiss to the spot, wishing she could make the pain it still caused him vanish.

Ashton kissed her forehead, then her cheeks, then her mouth. The sweet slide of his tongue against the seam of her lips entreated them to open. The man knew just how to kiss, sweet and seductive one moment, dominating the next. It kept her guessing, kept her riding on an ever building wave of unexpected thrills.

When he sat back on his heels, she ached for his warm hard body to cover hers again. He slid her chemise up to her waist and then farther up until she had to lift up for him to slide it off her. She folded her arms over her chest, covering her bare breasts.

"Don't lose that fire and bravery now," he said.

Terrified yet excited, she lowered her hands and lay back against the pillows.

"You are a goddess." His reverent whisper stirred emotions inside her, ones that scared her, because they held hope for something she believed she couldn't have.

"Does that make you a god as well?" she teased, smiling a little.

"In the presence of such beauty, I am a mere mortal."

"And you wish to dominate me? Things never turn out well for mortals who compete with gods and goddesses."

"Yet they continue to try, because the rewards are so tempting."

He leaned over her again, kissing a sensual path down to her collarbone before nuzzling the swell of her breasts. He braced himself on one forearm and cupped one breast with his free hand as he explored their sensitive peaks.

He sucked one nipple between his lips and her hips jerked. It was so intimate, too much to bear. A frightening, exciting, unquenchable fire raged throughout her body.

She moaned his name and he growled in answer, the vibrations running along her skin and heightening every sensation even more.

"Please," she panted. "I can't stand it."

He released her nipple long enough to chuckle before he teased and taunted her other breast with flicks of his tongue. She threaded her hands through his hair, tugging on the soft, silken strands.

"Harder!" he urged. "Tug harder." And she did. The bite of pain was echoed when he nipped her breast. Sparks shot through her, straight to her womb.

Ashton kept moving down along her body, pressing kisses to her abdomen and hips, nibbling at her, making her laugh at the tickling sensations. It felt so good to laugh, to enjoy herself like this. But he didn't stop. He placed his palms on her inner thighs and pushed them farther apart.

She wriggled to get free, startled by this turn of events. "What are you doing?"

"Ah no, my lovely Scottish hellion, I'm afraid this one pleasure you must endure." He lifted his gaze to hers, and then he bent his head and licked her...*down there*.

If he hadn't been holding her thighs down, she would have spasmed at this foreign pleasure. He kept licking, kissing, torturing her aching flesh. It was more than she could take. Just when she thought it would kill her, he lifted his head, and with a wicked grin, he sat up and tugged his breeches down enough to free himself. Then with one hand he guided himself into her. He was large and thick as he thrust in. Rosalind hissed at the tightness.

"Breathe, darling."

She gritted her teeth. "I am."

He laughed and then leaned over her, pressing her down into the bed as he captured her mouth. The kiss, added to the weight of his body on hers, made her relax. She felt safe. He was controlling the kiss, their bodies—he would not hurt her, and he would give her the satisfaction she craved. It was a promise he made with every press of his lips.

Ashton gripped her wrists and pinned them on either side of her head, his fingers curled around her arms, trapping them. She was truly owned by him now, and yet she knew if she asked him to stop, he would.

"How do you feel?" He rocked his hips, pushing in deeper.

Rosalind lifted her hips, then kissed him back before replying.

"Wonderful." She blushed at the admission. "You?"

"You grip me like a fist."

She was about to object, since he was the one gripping her wrists, until a tight thrust explained his meaning.

He circled his hips. "Are you ready?"

Ready? What did he mean?

Ashton withdrew and began to pump his hips hard, keeping her wrists pinned as he took her. She didn't know that a man could move like that, that fast, that hard.

But Ashton seemed to be able to keep up this wild pace all night. She knew she wouldn't survive that—it felt too good to hold on to her control. Not when her body demanded the release that was building inside her like a summer storm. The pressure in her lower belly mixed with the delicious heat of her arousal…she was so close…

"Hold on," he growled.

She struggled against him, needing to find the right rhythm of friction, harder, faster. He somehow learned what she craved through whatever moans and cues she gave him and began to thrust into her even harder. Their bodies were slick with sweat. The sounds of their lovemaking were primal, animalistic. Simply thinking of that proved too much for Rosalind.

She careened off the ledge of sanity and fell into a realm of sheer bliss. Every muscle in her body went limp. An instant later Ashton shouted and collapsed on top of her. He buried his face into the pillow beside her, and his lips feathered a delicate kiss on her ear. That sent rippling aftershocks through her. Her inner muscles clenched around his shaft and he groaned.

"Bloody hell, woman. You are..." He didn't finish, but his face turned to hers and she caught a glimpse of his roguish smile.

"I'm what?" she panted.

"Perfect." The smile turned boyishly charming. It melted her in places she thought she'd never feel again. It was scary for her to realize she felt the same about him.

"How do I compare to the others?" he asked.

"The others?" She stared at him, confused.

He shifted his body, not fully rolling off her, but easing most of his weight to the side so as not to crush her.

"Yes, your other lovers."

Other lovers? Had he not guessed she'd had no other lovers save her first husband?

That amused her for some reason. He believed she'd had paramours? It was a common assumption, she supposed, since a number of notable young widows had collected lovers by the dozens, but she hadn't.

"There aren't any. I have only ever been with Henry." Despite his assumption, she was oddly shy in admitting that she hadn't had more experience. Ashton's brows rose.

"Well, I must admit, I like the idea of having you all to myself. I'm rather a selfish creature, you see."

"Really? I had no idea." She prodded his chest with a finger, making him laugh again. It was a rich, deep sound that made her think of melted honey.

Ashton moved off her, withdrawing from her body. The sense of emptiness that followed angered her just a little. She didn't want to miss his warmth, the feel of him deep inside her. The feel of them connected.

He slipped out of bed completely bare and padded over to the fireplace, put a few more logs on the fire, then extinguished the candles by the bed and joined her under the covers. When he settled in, Rosalind cuddled up to him, placing a hand on his chest. He covered it with one of his, squeezing her fingers.

"I'll leave for London first thing tomorrow. What do you say about a wedding in the little parish church a few miles away?"

Rosalind tensed. The wedding.

He tensed beside her. "You promised, remember? The terms—"

"Yes. Whatever you wish—I do not care." She pulled away from him and rolled onto her side facing the opposite wall. "Why couldn't you be satisfied with being just lovers?"

The bed dipped as he moved, but he didn't try to touch her again. "I enjoy being complicated. Now I suppose you'll be cross with me."

"I'm not cross with you," she snapped.

His chuckle made her bristle. "Goodnight, Rosalind."

She didn't respond except to reach behind her and sock him in the hip with a balled fist.

It was going to be a long night.

CHAPTER 16

$\mathcal{A}$shton stood on the steps of the Sheridan townhouse on Curzon Street and tried to quell the sudden bout of nerves in his stomach. He'd risen well before dawn at his estate and slipped out of bed, pressing a light kiss to Rosalind's lips before leaving. It had taken two hours of hard riding to reach London, and his horse was lathered and exhausted. But it was important that he arrive in time to catch Cedric before he left his house for the day. He and Anne were likely to be selecting new mares at Tattersall's this afternoon.

For the mission he had this morning, he only trusted Cedric. Today he was acquiring a special license to marry Rosalind. In the past, he'd always been the one to accompany the others to the Doctors' Commons, but it was strange to think today was *his* turn.

He couldn't ask Godric or Lucien. They had married for love alone and would challenge him for marrying Rosalind for mercenary reasons. He could, perhaps, admit that he was marrying her because he wanted to, because he found her fascinating and enticing. But to do so would only prompt further interrogation from his friends, and he didn't wish to deal with that until he had time to fully understand his own feelings about her.

Cedric, however, would understand. He and Anne had married to save her from fortune hunters after her father had passed. They'd married as strangers but had found love along the way. Ashton hoped Cedric would understand where Ashton's decision came from. Not everyone was lucky enough to fall in love.

His heart gave a strange little hop inside his chest.

I just want a small measure of happiness. Despite the pleasure he had given her, he was under no illusions about what Rosalind truly thought of him, and given his treatment of her in the past, he had no reason to assume that would change simply because of one night of passion. He would likely never have a great love like his friends, but he hoped Rosalind would someday learn to love him in some small way.

He removed his hat, brushing the dust of the road off of it before tucking it under one arm. Then he raised the heavy brass knocker and let it drop against the door twice. Shifting restlessly, he waited for the butler to answer.

"My lord," the butler said with a smile. "The master and the lady are in the parlor. I'll take you to them."

"Thank you." Ashton followed him, amused that after so many years of friendship, the League never stood upon ceremony. In most households he would have had to wait upon the steps while the butler ascertained whether anyone wished to receive him.

The butler stopped in front of a closed door and opened it, slipping inside. Ashton listened to him announce Ashton's arrival.

"Show him in," Cedric said from the other side.

The butler reappeared and allowed Ashton to enter the parlor. He ground to a halt at the sight of four other people he had not expected to see there. Godric, Emily, Lucien and Horatia were all present.

Good God, he could not do this, not with everyone there to mock him.

"Ash!" Cedric stood and came to shake his hand. "Thought you'd be in Hampshire dealing with the tenant farms."

"I was." Ashton glanced at each of his friends' faces, sensing he'd stumbled into the middle of something. It might prove to be a good excuse for him to depart without admitting his reasons for coming. "If I am interrupting, I could—"

"You aren't." Anne assured him as she stood up, a warm smile on her lips. "Would you like some tea?" She gestured to the tray on a nearby table and a footman who hovered next to the doorway. "Nelson just brought us some fresh pekoe, and it smells divine." The domestic scene, the three of his friends and all of their wives meeting for tea—Ashton didn't know whether to laugh or to turn tail and run.

"Tea?" He choked on the word.

"Yes, *tea*," Emily replied. "It's what friends do when they visit each other, have a cup of tea." The glint in her eyes warned him she had sensed his rising unease. The little duchess was far too observant. It was one of the things he admired about her, except when that keen gaze was directed his way.

This was a dreadful mistake. He couldn't ask Cedric for a favor, not when everyone was there staring at him. He could not let them know what he was up to until he had his license in hand and Rosalind on the way to the altar. Anything else might disrupt his plans. Emily might even attempt to sabotage his plans if she felt he was taking advantage of the woman.

"My apologies, but I should go. I forgot I had an appointment this morning."

Lucien was soon on his feet, blocking Ashton from retreating through the door.

"Ho there, Ash, what's the hurry? Surely a cup of tea with friends isn't something to run from?" Lucien's smirk filled Ashton with a sense of rage. If it wasn't for the fact that the man would be a father in a few short months, he would have knocked him on his arse.

Emily rose from the settee she'd been sharing with Godric and walked toward him. "Ashton, are you *blushing*?"

Godric laughed. "Em, darling, men do not blush."

"I don't know about that," Horatia chimed in, one hand resting on her slightly swollen belly. She hadn't stood when he entered, and he wouldn't have wished her to. She was due in October and needed to rest. "He is certainly turning a tad ruddy-cheeked."

The focus of all eyes on him only made the flush on his face that much stronger.

"I'm *not* blushing," he growled. "I have just ridden in, and I am nearly as exhausted as my horse. Cedric, I'd like a word with you—outside, if you please." He knew he'd have to get his question out sooner or later, so he might as well get it done with now.

Cedric's grin faded as he shared looks with Lucien, who still blocked the doorway, and Godric, who rose automatically and came over to join them.

"I said *Cedric*, not you lot."

The men laughed. "If you think there's anything he won't tell us the moment you're gone, you're mistaken," said Godric.

Ashton sighed dramatically. He was right, of course.

The three of them followed him into the corridor, and Ashton shut the parlor door to prevent the ladies from overhearing him.

"What is it, Ash?" Cedric asked. "Is it Waverly again?"

"No, nothing like that." Taking a deep breath, he readied for the humiliation he expected to follow. "I was hoping you would accompany me to the Doctors' Commons to obtain a special license."

"The Doctors' Commons? Who's getting married?" Cedric asked.

Ashton let out a slow sigh. "I am."

Godric gasped and Lucien made the sign of the cross, muttering half a prayer. Their overreactions made Ashton scowl.

"It's not as though the four horsemen are riding down Curzon Street," he snapped.

"Tell me you're joking. Who the devil would you marry? You

broke it off with your last mistress months ago." Lucien crossed his arms, studying Ashton critically.

Godric snapped his finger. "Wait! I have it! You made a bet with Charles and lost. I say, though, awfully bad high stakes. Who are you marrying? Freddy Poncenby's little sister? She's a sweet gal, but that family...imagine the Christmas dinners. Lord, you don't want that, do you?"

"Miss Poncenby? You know I'd never—"

"Then who?" Cedric prompted. "I can't believe you'd marry, Ash—it's not exactly your cup of *tea*." At the mention of tea his friends sniggered.

"This isn't a joke, and I don't want any bloody tea. Christ, you all are enough to drive a man to the bottle. I require someone to come with me to the Doctors' Commons. That is all. I was hoping, Cedric, that you would be the *least* likely to make this matter difficult."

Godric sobered a little. "I think he's telling the truth. The question now is *why* would you marry? Have you fallen in love?"

Cedric shook his head. "It's an alliance, I'll wager."

Lucien's eyes suddenly lit up. "It wouldn't happen to be a certain Scottish lady, would it?"

"This isn't about love, but yes, I am marrying Rosalind even if it kills us both."

Without warning, Emily burst through the parlor doorway and hugged him. "Oh, Ashton! You and Rosalind have sorted out your differences. How wonderful!" She beamed at him, and in that moment his heart sank. He was about to disappoint her. Emily, the woman who believed everyone deserved to be loved.

Godric gently pried his wife off Ashton. "Let the man breathe, darling."

"How did it happen?" Horatia asked. She and Anne had joined them, forming a large group in the hall. "When we last saw Lady Melbourne, she was furious with you and determined to save herself from the financial ruin you put her in."

Emily suddenly narrowed her eyes. "Ashton, were you inconsiderate to her? She is a friend, and I shouldn't like to discover you bullied her into something. I won't allow it."

She thought she could control him? How sweet. How utterly misguided. "I did not bully her." *Not exactly,* he silently amended. "She lost a game of chess, and the stakes were marriage if I won."

Lucien frowned. "That doesn't seem like you, leaving an outcome to chance."

"Hardly chance. There's a reason none of us play against him anymore," said Godric. "But how the devil did she make the mistake of playing chess with you?"

Ashton grinned. "Rafe had convinced her my skills were... below average."

Lucien snorted. "There's the Ash I know."

"Why would Rafe say that? He's not usually in the habit of helping you," Cedric added.

"Indeed," Ashton agreed. "But he was foolish enough to rob Rosalind's coach, and—"

Godric cut in, waving a hand. "What?"

"Rob?" echoed Lucien.

Emily held a hand to her mouth in shock before Godric continued. "What in blazes was Rafe doing robbing a coach?"

"It seems he's added highwayman to his ever growing list of questionable talents," said Ashton.

"Good God," Lucien muttered. "That man is going to hang someday."

"Yes, I'll have to deal with him later, once I've married Rosalind."

"Oh, no you will not!" Emily jabbed a finger in his chest hard enough to make him stumble back a step.

"Emily..." Ashton felt exasperated. He was not in the least bit interested in receiving another lecture about how he should treat Rosalind with kid gloves.

"Don't you 'Emily' me, Ashton. I'll not have you mistreating

Rosalind. She's a wonderful creature, and I won't let you break her spirit out of some misguided notion of pride. What, it was not enough to simply ruin her finances, you now must *possess* her as well?"

She honestly thought he had it in him to break a woman? God's teeth, he'd never do that. He loved the fairer sex far too much to be that cavalier in his interests.

"She *is* wonderful, and I have no intention of breaking her," he countered. "This is to our mutual advantage."

Emily halted her military-style advancement. Her violet eyes grew wide and searching.

"You think she's wonderful too?"

He nodded. "Of course." How could he not? She was intelligent, beautiful and stubborn.

"Yet you don't love her?" Emily asked, her violet eyes full of curiosity.

"I am fond of her and wish her no harm, but you are correct."

Emily looked briefly at Anne and Horatia before she spoke again. "Then off you go to the Doctors' Commons. We ladies have some dresses to shop for if we're to be ready for the wedding."

It took a moment for Ashton to absorb what had been said. "Pardon?"

"Yes," Anne agreed. "It's important we are all there. Weddings are family affairs. And you are family in all ways but blood."

"She is right, you know," Cedric said. "We all ought to be there. When's the special day?"

"I thought tomorrow."

All three women gasped in alarm as if he'd threatened to do something so scandalous that even his reputation could not be salvaged.

"Tomorrow? Oh no, Ashton, that's far too soon," Horatia protested. "We need a few days to pack and arrange travel to Hampshire."

Ashton knew these three ladies well enough to know that he

could not fight them on this. Well, not fight them and expect any form of victory.

"You have two days," he informed them. "I'm not risking anything longer than that in case my fiancée should try to back out of our bargain."

"Would she?" Lucien asked, half smiling.

Ashton shrugged. "I honestly don't know, and I certainly don't want to give her the chance."

His friends laughed. Godric glanced at Ashton. "Well, should we be off?"

"You don't have to come."

"Nonsense." Godric pressed a kiss to Emily's lips before he faced the others. "We wouldn't miss this for the world. Em, darling, you'd best have the servants see to packing, and notify our solicitors where to reach us should any business matters arise while we are out of town."

"Have fun making Ashton blush. He's still red." Horatia giggled and kissed Lucien.

It was all the public displays of affection that were making him blush, not the idea of obtaining a marriage license. It was business and nothing more. Even if Rosalind was equal parts wonderful, infuriating and fascinating.

Ashton waited on the front steps while his friends collected their hats and coats.

"We ought to take the coach. I'll have it brought around." Cedric disappeared inside, leaving Ashton with Lucien and Godric.

"Are you sure about this?" Godric asked with true seriousness.

"I am," Ashton replied. He now understood more clearly the irritation Cedric must have felt when he first announced his engagement to Anne. The League hadn't embraced the idea at first. Not having the support of one's friends was off-putting and filled one's head with doubt. After a decade of being in complete agreement with them on nearly everything, it felt strange to disagree with them on the matter of whether he should marry, and do so without hesitation as to whether they would agree with him or not.

"There's more to my reasons than my male pride, as Emily puts it," he added quietly, "For three weeks now I've been monitoring Lady Melbourne's shipping company activities. Hugo Waverly has been using her ships to transport men and supplies to and from England for purposes I cannot yet explain. I don't know what he is up to, but I'd certainly sleep better at night if I had access to the manifests and passenger lists."

"But you already own her debts, and the companies are as good as yours," Lucien said. "I thought you had accountants and solicitors going over her accounts."

"I do. But I want there to be no question as to the ownership. When I marry her, it will be easier for me to manage all the companies and look deeper into her records." He turned at the rattle of wheels upon the cobblestones and saw the Sheridan coach pull up the steps.

"Right-o, lads." Cedric bounded down the steps to meet them as they all prepared to climb inside.

"I feel like we ought to be getting Ashton foxed tonight to prepare him for marriage," Godric said with a laugh.

"Or a final trip to the Midnight Garden," Lucien suggested.

"Absolutely not." Ashton laughed. "The last time I set foot there I was shot. I have no desire to repeat the experience."

"Touché." Cedric closed the coach door and slammed a hand outside the window to signal the driver to go.

As the coach jerked forward, Ashton settled back in the seat, smiling as his friends teased him, but he didn't mind. Rosalind was going to be his, and that was all that mattered.

CHAPTER 17

*N*elson Lewis, a footman in the Sheridan household, lingered in the doorway to the servants' quarters, straining to pick up any bits of conversation from the three ladies still standing in the hall.

"Emily, why did you stop pestering once he admitted Rosalind was wonderful?" Lady Sheridan asked.

The Duchess of Essex played with the pearls around her neck. "I don't believe Ashton has ever said that about any woman. I believe he has stronger feelings for her than he admits, even to himself."

Nelson nudged the door an inch further, studying the well-bred ladies as they walked back into the parlor. But before they disappeared inside he heard Lady Rochester speak.

"A wedding in Hampshire. It will be lovely."

Lennox was to be married? He shut the door and came down the stairs to find the butler, careful to appear as though he was about his normal duties. The older man was standing in the servants' corridor, speaking to the housekeeper.

"Ah, Nelson, there you are. We have a few errands for you to run." The butler held out a strip of parchment.

Nelson glanced at the parchment and tucked it into his vest pocket. "Of course." He had become accustomed to the patterns of the household and knew he'd most likely be sent off about now. He bid the butler a hasty farewell and left the Sheridan house.

He walked for some time before he deemed himself sufficiently out of sight and allowed himself to wave down a hackney.

"Where to?" the driver asked.

"The Strand." He handed the man a few coins and leapt into the cab.

The cab rattled past Covent Garden, and Nelson watched the streets as they passed. During the day the Strand was fairly reputable, with shops open and decent folk exploring the stands and peering into the shop windows. At night, however, the street took on a more ominous character. Not that Nelson was afraid to travel then. He had been well trained in ungentlemanly combat. It was those who might interfere with him who should be afraid.

The cab stopped at the edge of the Strand, and Nelson hopped out. He dodged the fine ladies in their walking dresses and the men escorting them from shop to shop. Nelson ventured farther until he saw the Coal Hole Tavern's sign creaking in the light breeze.

The door burst open, and several men and two women stumbled out laughing. Their faces were familiar, actors he'd seen at recent plays. That was of no surprise, though. The Coal Hole was a gathering place for many actors and had even been a private theater at one time. Nelson let the men and women pass by before he caught the open door and slipped inside.

The taproom was rowdy but not as unseemly as a tavern would be in other parts of London. But by nightfall the lightskirts and pickpockets would be out, much to the respective delight and despair of men brave enough to venture here after hours.

A barman stood near the back stairs that led to the upper rooms. Nelson made his way over.

"What do you need?" the barman grunted.

"Have you ever seen a White Lion?" he asked.

"I believe we have a painting of one. Last door on the left." The barman moved his considerable bulk aside and let Nelson pass.

The sounds from the rooms he passed showed that more than one soul was out enjoying their pleasures early.

As he reached the last door on the left, he rapped his knuckles in a specific pattern.

"Enter."

Twisting the handle, Lewis opened the door. The two men inside stared at him, one seated at a writing table and the other leaning against the wall by the window. The man by the window was in his late twenties, and the other man was in his late thirties; Lewis reported to the latter.

Hugo Waverly waved a hand at Nelson. "Ah, Lewis. Report." He dropped his gaze back to his papers, his dark hair falling into his eyes as he shuffled pages, looking for something. The man by the window, Daniel Sheffield, Hugo's right-hand man, encouraged Lewis with a nod.

"I completed a search of the Melbourne residence for the item you were seeking. I'm afraid I could not find it."

Hugo scowled. "Damn. She must have taken it with her when she left London. Anything else?"

Nelson nodded. "Lennox is off to the Doctors' Commons for a special license. He plans to be married in two days' time in Hampshire."

Hugo's quill ceased scratching on the parchment. He slowly raised his head.

"Married to whom?" He gave each word such weight that even Lewis, who'd been raised in a thieves' den, got chills.

"Lady Melbourne."

The quill tip snapped, spilling ink across the page. Sheffield came around the side of Hugo's writing table.

"Do you have any other details?" Sheffield asked.

Lewis stood straighter, recognizing the seriousness with

which they took this news. "Essex, Rochester, Sheridan and their wives will be traveling to Hampshire to stay with Lennox and will be there for the ceremony."

With a vicious growl, Hugo crumpled up the stained report and tossed it into the fireplace.

"Sheffield, we must ride for Scotland immediately. We may not be able to delay the wedding, but we *can* disrupt the League long enough to finish our West Indies operation if we can buy ourselves more time. The necessity of obtaining those items we discussed is even more paramount." He folded his hands pensively. "Blast. I was a blind fool. When Lady Melbourne left London, her letter indicated that it was to fight to get her property back. But if he's somehow wooed her and won her, then those properties will be exposed to his scrutiny."

Hugo dragged his hands through his hair, his eyes a bit wild and his face a mask of ferocity, causing Nelson to take a small step back. "We cannot delay. If she has the cipher, our efforts should be focused on getting to the letters before her. Kincade would not have sent those letters to London in case they were lost en route. No, he's too cautious for that. I would bet my life he has them somewhere in his castle tucked under a floorboard or behind some loose stone. I will find them and retrieve them and then collect the cipher from Lady Melbourne as time allows."

Sheffield nodded. "Suppose we approach the lady's brothers? You mentioned a falling out with her and their father. They might be willing to do our work for us and retrieve Lady Melbourne from Lennox's clutches and bring her home to Scotland, especially if they thought she was in some sort of danger."

"Excellent idea. Better to have them tangle with the League than us. Kidnapping can be a messy endeavor." Hugo began rifling through the papers on his desk. He and Sheffield were seemingly unaware that Lewis was still watching them as they made plans.

Without raising his head, Hugo said, "You may go, Lewis. Send reports here if there's any change. Sheffield will have a man waiting to see you. You will know him as the Black Boar."

"Understood, sir." Lewis turned and fled the room. Waverly paid well, but there was something dark in that room that disturbed Lewis. Better to be back at the Sheridan house where he was out of sight and out of mind until he received his next orders.

~

LIPS BURNED WITH DESIRE, *whispered words, the imprisonment of her hands, those blazing blue eyes...*

Rosalind woke from the hazy dream that replayed last night. The other side of the bed was cold. Ashton was long gone. She sat up and hugged the sheet around her. Last night she and Ashton had made love, passionately, wildly, and then tenderly. It had been unexpected and wonderful, yet now regret weighed heavily upon her.

What have I agreed to?

There was no way to escape this. She was going to marry Ashton, and he'd own her. She'd cease to be, all over again.

Breathe, just breathe.

She covered her face with her hands and drew slow breaths to steady her heart. It would have been easier to hate the man if he hadn't been such a wonderful, giving lover the night before. He always seemed to find a way to draw her in, seduce her into trusting him.

But he couldn't be trusted. His motives for marrying her had nothing to do with love and everything to do with giving him control of her properties. It did not matter that he claimed he would restore them to her later. Once he had her, he would be under no obligation to honor those words. She hadn't worked so hard the last few years to build her business up just to hand it over to her biggest rival. How would she puzzle her way out of this?

A servant knocked on the door.

She flopped back onto the bed, pulling the coverlet over her head to hide herself. "Enter."

"Your Ladyship, you should get up. I've drawn a hot bath and laid out a gown for you." Claire's voice came from somewhere above her.

Rosalind pulled the covers back down. "Fine."

Claire stood beside the bed, a blue dressing gown held up for her. Her maid's eyes critically assessed her, as though to check for damage.

"I must say, you look well, Your Ladyship. No harm done?" Claire's question was carefully worded.

"No. No harm done." What had occurred last night had been entirely consensual, and she wouldn't play as though she hadn't wanted or agreed to bedding Ashton. Rosalind slipped out of the bed and donned the dressing gown. After a long night, she was unprepared for what she knew would be a long day.

"His Lordship will be back this afternoon to tour the church with you. Lady Lennox will take you to town with Miss Lennox to select a wedding trousseau." Claire was smiling, pleased as punch.

"Claire, I've sworn to despise Lennox, and you're grinning like a cat who has fed on too much cream. You're *my* servant, not his."

"Oh, but I am, Your Ladyship. I know how clever you are, and it's only a matter of time before you have him eating out of your hand. That is what you want, isn't it? To take control back from him?"

Rosalind didn't reply as she approached Ashton's copper tub. Steam curled up from the hot water, warming her skin as she slipped out of the dressing gown and laid it over Claire's outstretched arm.

"Is everyone else up?" She squinted at the pale light through the window.

"Aye. You've slept 'til close to noon. You were fast asleep the last few times I checked on you." Claire bustled around the table by the bath, setting out a hairbrush and some pins.

Rosalind groaned. "Noon?" How had she slept so late? She had always been a light sleeper, waking at dawn—if not before then—to start her day. She rarely slept all the way through the night. Those nights she did, demons from her past tended to emerge in nightmares that haunted her through to morning. Yet she'd slept like a babe last night in Ashton's bed.

"If it's not too forward of me to say, sometimes a man in your bed can help a lady sleep." Claire had her back turned as she folded a towel, but Rosalind knew her maid was smiling. She could hear it in her voice.

"I don't see how. The bloody oaf took up most of the bed and left little room for me." And she'd been forced to curl into his body, which meant he'd wrapped an arm around her all night. *Damned infuriating...wonderful man...* With an angry little growl, she scrubbed a bar of soap over her skin.

"I suppose it goes back to the old days," Claire mused as she hung up the dressing robe on a peg by the door.

Rosalind rubbed the lather of the soap over her body. "What do you mean?" The scent hit her, the masculine aroma. Ashton's. Fresh memories from last night swept through her and she dropped the soap, splashing water out of the tub. She slicked her hair back and then dug around the bottom of the tub to find the slippery thing.

"A woman likes to know she will be safe, that someone will protect her. Hate him or love him, Lord Lennox is very much a man to protect what is his. Last night you became his, and deep down, you know he will care for you, Your Ladyship. That is why you slept so well."

"How did you know about what happened last night? The marriage, I mean."

Claire shrugged. "Servants always learn about these things first. Whispers are like wildfires in the corridors of any great house."

"So the entire *house* knows we are to be married." The thought of everyone knowing her shameful situation gave her a dull throb behind her eyes.

"Yes, but…" Claire paused. "The staff seem fascinated by the thought of their master marrying. They say he's never shown lasting interest in a lady before, at least not with a mind to marriage, and according to the upstairs maids, he has never had a woman visit Lennox House."

"I wasn't exactly invited," Rosalind reminded her. She washed her hair and glanced around for a towel. Her maid held one out.

"Well?" Claire asked.

"Well what?" Her response came out a tad harsher than she intended, but the idea of everyone knowing the intimate details of her private life had proved upsetting.

"Is it true that he is showing you favor?"

A derisive snort escaped Rosalind. "If by favor you mean to blackmail me, cause me to wager my future on a game of chess, deceive me about his skill at the game, and seduce me into bed with bloody good kisses, then yes, I'm a favorite of his."

Claire was biting her lip to keep from laughing.

"What?" Rosalind snapped.

"Bloody good kisses? Oh dear, Your Ladyship, we mustn't let *that* happen again." Amusement honeyed Claire's sarcastic tone.

"It's not funny!"

"Of course it is, Your Ladyship. He sounds like quite a man, and you're fighting the fact that you like him." Claire giggled.

"I do not!" Rosalind started to laugh, despite her best attempts not to. She was fighting the fact that Claire was right.

Claire smiled. "You'll win him over. I would guess he'll be eating out of the palm of your hand in a fortnight."

Calming down, Rosalind finished drying her hair with a cloth and went back into Ashton's bedchamber. She found the light rose Jaconet muslin gown her maid had selected draped over one of the chairs, along with white stockings embroidered at the ankles with spring buds. A sky-blue shawl, white gloves and half boots in the same color finished her outfit. It would be elegant, yet show her figure to advantage. Claire had chosen well. If she was to suffer through this marriage business, she might as well look pretty.

"No bonnet?" Rosalind sat in a chair to pull the stockings on.

"Heavens no. It would be a shame to hide your face away on a day like today."

Rosalind dressed quickly and let Claire style her hair in loose ringlets with a threading of blue silk in a band around her head in Grecian fashion.

"They'll be dining at a late luncheon, if you're ready," Claire added as Rosalind headed for the door.

The dining room was empty save for two people, Charles and Rafe. When Rosalind saw them, she halted in the doorway.

"I hear congratulations are in order." Rafe raised a glass of juice in her direction, then winced, touching his arm. The arm she knew she'd shot when he'd robbed her coach.

Quelling the rush of her temper, she walked over to take a chair beside him and then, without any warning, punched his concealed wound.

Rafe howled, leaning away from her, his blue eyes flashing with ice. "Bloody Christ!"

"You assured me he was a subpar chess player. You *lied*."

Charles made a grand show of settling in to watch the scene across from him, sipping his tea.

"Of course I lied. You shot me!" Rafe growled.

"You *robbed* me, you blackguard. Did you think I wouldn't figure out it was you that night on the road? I demand you return my money to me at once!"

"I most certainly will not! Consider it a country toll, you damned hellion!"

"Don't call me that!" she shot back.

"Ash calls you that," Charles noted. Both Rosalind and Rafe shot venomous glares his way.

"Well, he's to be my husband, and I let him because he means it sweetly. Unlike you, you thieving cur!"

Rafe attempted to rise from his chair, but Rosalind struck his wounded arm again. Rafe cried out as his chair toppled over and he flew backwards onto the floor.

Charles clapped, even when Rosalind turned an icy glare at him. "I'm a pugilist. I cannot help but admire a good punch. Please, continue."

Rafe got to his feet, cradling his bad arm and throwing daggers at her with his eyes. "I hope you drive Ashton mad. He deserves a harpy like you." And he stalked off, leaving her and Charles alone.

"Don't let him bother you. Rafe has always been a bit of an arse. He and Ashton are very different and rarely see eye to eye."

Rosalind calmed and brushed a few wisps of hair back from her face.

"Did you not hear what I said before? That man *robbed* me. He was the reason I had to walk here in the rain and mud."

Charles frowned, though he still seemed somewhat amused. "Yes, Ash had warned me that might be the case. I'll be curious to see how he deals with the man when he returns. I suspect he saw the event as some sort of lark. You're lucky he had no intention of hurting you."

"He's lucky the storm blinded me, or my shot would have struck his chest, not his arm.

"Rather bloodthirsty of you. Not surprising for a lady of Scotland. Your lot are still warriors at heart. Your brothers especially."

"My brothers? You know them?" Rosalind stilled, a little afraid. The thought of her past colliding with her present at such a point in her life sent chills through her.

Charles licked a dab of honey from his fingers before setting a piece of toast down on his plate.

"Oh yes. Godric and I had a tussle with them a year or so ago. Never saw a trio like them before in my life. Heads like boulders and fists like anvils. It didn't matter how many times I got a punch in, didn't seem to do anything to them."

Rosalind's heart leapt into her throat. "You fought them? Whatever for?"

Charles blushed. "Godric and I may have been enticing a few of the sweet little bar wenches at a tavern in Edinburgh. I believe the chits had initially promised to go home with your brothers. That was before they met us, of course. They decided we might be more fun instead. Your brothers took offense." He grinned. "It was one of the few fights I've ever run from. Scary blokes, your brothers."

"Scary indeed," she muttered, but they weren't the true terrors of the family. Charles had no idea what sort of monster her father was. Her brothers were good men, and for as long as she'd known them they'd never done any harm to those undeserving. But they did enjoy the fairer sex, and like her, they did have tempers. She was not too surprised to learn they'd fought Ashton's friends over women.

"I must admit, I can't believe you thought Ash would be a poor chess player. Whatever gave you that idea, other than foolishly trusting Rafe? It's a game of logic. It seems natural he would excel at it." Charles leaned back in his chair and steepled his fingers, watching her.

Meeting his stare, Rosalind shrugged. "When someone is desperate, they are likely to believe in things they otherwise would not. I overestimated Rafe's dislike of his own brother, and I underestimated his dislike of *me*."

"Well, you did *shoot* the man. It would make any decent fellow a bit vengeful." Charles finished off his slice of toast.

"How many times must I say this? He *robbed* me!" She slammed her teacup down on the table, making it rattle.

"Hmm, yes, so you've said." Charles hummed thoughtfully. "And now you must marry Ashton."

"Yes." Rosalind finally ate a bit of lunch and helped herself to some marmalade.

Joanna burst into the room, a vision of loveliness in a light-blue muslin gown, her face beaming. "Rosalind! What do you think?" She performed a little twirl, and halted when she saw Charles, her cheeks turning a cherry red.

"It's perfect," said Rosalind.

"You look lovely, Joanna," Charles added.

"Thank you, Charles." She ducked her head a little as she took a seat next to Rosalind. "Is it true? You and Ashton are officially affianced? Mother was worried it would not happen, but Ashton told her this morning before he left that he was setting a date!" The hope in her voice surprised Rosalind. She'd only known Joanna a few days, but she acted as if this was news she desperately hoped was true.

"Yes, it's true."

"That's wonderful! Oh, Rosalind... Wait, may I call you that?"

"Please."

"I'm so happy for you! For us!" Joanna's grin was nothing if not infectious. "I've always wanted a sister."

"Joanna, you have one. Or are you forgetting Thomasina?" Charles asked.

"She was married when I was still a child. It will be wonderful to have you here. With Rafe and Ashton around, I'm always outnumbered."

Rosalind patted her hand. "But won't you be married soon, and with your own children?"

Joanna paled. "My seasons have not gone well. Not one card, not one call at the house. I don't know what's wrong with me that no man should—"

"Now see here, Joanna," Charles growled. "Don't put the blame on yourself. It's your brother who's scaring men off, even though he doesn't mean to. It's the same with my sister Ella. She can't find a soul to court her, because all the sensible men believe I'd test them in the ring at Fives Court."

"Would you?" Rosalind asked.

"Of course. Anyone who couldn't best me wouldn't be allowed in my drawing room."

"That hardly seems fair to your sister."

Charles shrugged. "It is what it is."

This declaration made matters worse by the way the color drained from Joanna's face. "Then I'll never have a chance."

"No, don't say that. I can help you. Ashton and I both will." If she was to be part of this family and Joanna wanted to marry, the least Rosalind could do was help her with that.

"Thank you." Joanna's eyes brightened again. "I heard we're going shopping today for your trousseau?"

"Apparently." Rosalind chuckled. "I look forward to it."

"Shopping? Lord, what a bore." Charles pushed his chair back and rose from the table. "I'm off to do a bit of riding."

Rosalind and Joanna finished their meal before leaving the dining room.

A footman came forward. "The coach is ready. Lady Lennox is already waiting."

"Thank you." Joanna took Rosalind's arm as they walked toward the carriage. "Can you believe it? We're actually getting my brother married."

Rosalind sighed. Yes, and in doing so she was sealing her fate.

CHAPTER 18

"*I*f I ever have to look at another bonnet again, I'll die." Rosalind laughed as she exited the milliner's shop.

Joanna yawned. "Agreed. I didn't know there would be so many to try on."

After spending two hours at various clothing establishments searching for gowns and other assortments of items needed for a trousseau, the Lennox House footman was laden with boxes piled so high he could barely see. Rosalind and Joanna couldn't stop giggling each time the poor fellow bumped into something while they walked along the street.

Regina joined them, pulling on her gloves. "I believe we must have bought half the shops out." She nodded to the footman. "Thank you, Jacob. We're done for the day. I believe it's time to return home."

"Yes, I'm famished." Joanna laid a hand on her stomach. "I missed luncheon because...well, Charles was there, and that man always makes me so nervous. Besides, Ashton will be home soon."

Rosalind's heart gave a wild thump. *I should not be so excited to see him.* She reminded herself that he had tricked her into that chess match. There needed to be a reckoning for that deception.

But then he'd taken her to bed and changed everything she'd understood about lovemaking. She'd never known a man and woman could come together with such passion. And she'd slept soundly afterward, feeling the safest she'd ever felt in her life.

Now for the first time, she'd gone shopping with two other ladies and enjoyed herself—even if she had tried on far too many bonnets. It had been a day of frivolous pleasantries instead of hard business and dealing with men who consistently dismissed her talents. Rosalind was afraid to trust that life would grant her such a luxury for long. But that treacherous little emotion of hope made her want that more than she should.

They climbed into the waiting coach as the footman loaded the boxes.

Regina and Joanna were smiling as they watched Rosalind remove her gloves and tuck them into her reticule.

Rosalind noticed and stared back at them in some concern. "What?" Was something on her clothing amiss? Was her hair coming undone?

"You look *happy*, my dear," Regina noted. "For the first time since meeting you, you seem at ease."

"Do I?" Rosalind hadn't given much thought to the idea, but she did feel relaxed.

"I know Ashton can be positively overbearing at times," Joanna added, "but I think he's happy to be marrying you. He hasn't smiled this much in years."

That shouldn't have mattered, but the moment Joanna said it, Rosalind couldn't help the flutter of nerves at the thought of Ashton and his smiles. They could be so lovely, when he wasn't acting so distant.

Rosalind glanced out the coach window as it pulled away, lost in daydreams and trying to hide the little fear inside of what would happen when her dreams were shattered. Soon they were riding past Kingsley Stream, the water high from the recent storms.

Suddenly a woman was running alongside the bank, waving at the coach. Rosalind jerked up in her seat as the coach halted. The ladies were nearly unseated by the quick stop.

"What is it?" Regina asked, her voice high.

"There's a woman. She looks upset," Rosalind said, opening the coach door and hopping out.

The woman's face was strained with fear as she saw them climb out. Her clothes were wet and her white linen cap was askew.

"Your Ladyship, please forgive me." She stopped and curtsied in front of Regina.

"Mrs. Stadley, what's the matter?"

The woman wiped tears from her eyes. "It's my husband. He was attempting to fix the wheel on the mill. He was holding on to a side of the wheel when it broke loose from whatever had stopped it, and I fear it's pulled him under! I'm afraid he's going to…" The woman was shaking hard now and didn't say the word, but everyone knew what she was thinking. *Drown.*

"How long has he been under?" Regina asked.

"He fought to keep above water, but he went under just as I saw your coach coming up the road."

The women rushed out of the coach and to the riverbank.

The giant wooden wheel was turning, water dripping from the panels.

Rosalind stepped forward. "I need someone to help me out of my dress."

Ashton's mother gaped at her. "You can't go in after him. It's too dangerous."

"I assure you, I can swim quite well, and it seems there's no one else around who can help the man in time. Joanna, please help me." Rosalind turned her back as Joanna hastily undid the laces of the gown, and then Rosalind slipped off her stockings and hurried to the river.

"Please, miss, you don't—" Mrs. Stadley began, but Rosalind dove into the water, missing whatever else she said.

The cold water swallowed her whole. Using the roots against the riverbank, she held still as she peered through the gloom of the murky depths. She could just make out the dark, looming shape of the wheel as it slowly turned, and there she saw it, a shape toward the bottom of the river. A man was struggling to get loose from an underwater branch that had caught the back of his trousers. He must have been pulled down once the blockage was freed and snagged at the bottom.

It had been years since she'd had to swim like this. Kicking her feet hard, she managed to reach him. He jerked in surprise when she gripped one of his arms. His cheeks were puffed out as though he was fighting to contain his last bit of air. Rosalind gripped the hem of his trousers near his lower back and dug her nails into the threading. The man grew still as she fought to rip the fabric away from the branch. He suddenly jerked violently and went limp, air escaping his mouth just as she got him free of the branch.

Lungs burning, Rosalind wrapped one arm around the man and clawed through the churning waters to the surface.

The light seemed so far away, and Mr. Stadley's body was weighing her down.

Must...keep...going...

~

ASHTON RACED along the road that would take him home to Lennox House—and Rosalind. His heart thumped a little too fast at the thought of seeing her again. Heavy hooves beat a staccato rhythm into the dirt road, but he barely felt it. The ride was a blur as he was lost in thoughts of Rosalind and how she made him feel.

No. I can't let her affect me like this. It's lust. Nothing more.

After what they had shared the previous night, it had to be lust that had him desperate to be near her again. It had been months since he'd found such pleasure with a woman, and last night had reminded him just how much he missed physical intimacy.

Soon he would have that intimacy at his fingertips again, to be called upon whenever he desired. The folded papers of the special license that were tucked in his coat were an assurance of that.

The scent in the breeze was heady with spring flowers. Kingsley Stream, a small river, was just around the bend where the trees thinned. He hoped Rosalind would love the Lennox lands as much as he did and would want to stay here with him when they weren't working in London. With his mother in high spirits after he'd told her of his plans, he was convinced they would stop quarreling so much. If that was the case, he would be free to come home more often. He was lost in dreams and plans as he reined in his horse to a slower trot as he came closer to the river.

A coach was pulled up ahead just off the road, and several ladies were standing by the bank, their skirts blowing in the breeze against their legs. They were gazing at the river where Stadley Mill was. A fourth woman jumped into the water and disappeared. An odd sort of spectacle, to say the least.

As he got closer his heart leapt into his throat as he recognized his mother and sister were two of the three women at the edge of the bank. The third was the miller's wife.

Ashton took in the scene quickly, noting the miller's wife's clothes were soaked and a beautiful walking dress lay abandoned on the riverbank. Everyone on the bank was staring at the water by the mill. The footman and the coach driver were soaking wet as though they'd been in the water too. Suddenly he couldn't breathe. Where was Rosalind? Hadn't she gone with them to... The fourth woman jumping into the water...

He kicked his horse hard, making it gallop the rest of the way to the bank. Once he drew up beside them, he leapt off his mount.

"Mother?"

"Oh, Ashton! Quick, go after her!" Regina pointed to the river, her face pale.

"Where is Rosalind?" Even as he uttered the words, a dreadful pit formed in his stomach. "What happened?"

"She is trying to rescue Mr. Stadley, but she's been under too long." Regina was wringing her hands, her eyes wide with terror. He knew his mother couldn't swim well, nor his sister, or one of them would have tried to find Rosalind.

Ashton ripped his coat off and his boots, shoving them and the special license papers at his mother's driver.

"Keep those dry!" he shouted before he dove in.

He couldn't lose Rosalind, not when she was about to finally be his.

Ashton hit the water close to the wheel, the icy depths sending him momentarily into shock. He couldn't make out much in the murk. Too much of the bed soil had been disturbed by the rushing waters and those within it.

Where was she? The fear billowing up inside him was as smothering as the water itself. What if he couldn't find her in time? What if he lost her?

A flash of white in the dark, a quicksilver movement, caught his attention just as his lungs began to burn. He couldn't stay under, not without breathing in the river.

With an inner curse, he kicked up to the surface and sucked in a lungful of air.

"Did you see her?" Joanna's frantic voice bounced over the rushing water around him, cutting through the ringing in his ears.

He shook his head, inhaling deeply, even though his chest was burning and his body was shaking.

Just as he was preparing to dive again, Rosalind sprang up nearby, sputtering as she gasped. One of her arms was secured around Mr. Stadley's chest. The miller seemed to be unconscious.

"Thank God!" he bellowed and seized hold of the woman, almost crushing her.

"Lennox, let go! I can't stay above water! Take him!" Dutifully, he gripped Stadley's body and hauled the man ashore.

"We have to revive him." Rosalind gasped as she collapsed to her knees beside the unconscious man. "He has water in his lungs."

Ashton rolled Stadley onto his back and pressed his hands down on the man's chest, pumping several times.

The miller suddenly coughed as he expelled river water from his lungs. Ashton helped him shift onto one side and he continued to cough violently. Mrs. Stadley, weeping, rushed over to them and embraced her husband.

Ashton looked over the heads of the reunited couple to see Rosalind, her face pale as she coughed a little herself. He stood and came over to her, lifting her gently to her feet.

"Are you hurt?" he asked, studying her face for signs of distress. He could barely think, barely breathe after the fear and panic he'd endured the last few seconds when he thought he wouldn't find her in time.

She shook her head. "No."

Anger swept through him. She could have died. What the blazes had she been thinking to go in after a man when she might drown herself?

"Good. Because when we get home I have a mind to put my hand to your backside. How could you scare my mother and sister like that?" He'd almost admitted that he'd been the one most terrified. The thought of her lost in the river—it was too close to the past. He shut his eyes, trying to hold the memories at bay.

Icy water, the screams of young men, a struggling body bound in ropes, shouts of rage fighting with shouts of reason. Three men had gone under that night, and one had never come back up. Charles and Hugo had resurfaced, and all of them had searched for a young man who would never be seen again. Hugo had crawled onto the opposite bank on his hands and knees, his voice filled with anguish and then rage as he cursed Charles and all those who had stood with him to hell.

Ashton opened his eyes. "It was a brave thing you did, saving Stadley. But swear to me you will never do something so foolish again. I cannot lose you, do you understand?"

A strange emotion filled her eyes, but she did not speak right away. She must have seen something of his pain and fear because she slowly nodded.

"I'm sorry," Rosalind whispered.

"Come, we must get back to the coach."

Relief began to overwhelm his anger, and Ashton was feeling closer to his usual self. Rosalind was halfway up the riverbank when he noticed she was in her underthings. Her gown and petticoats lay clumped in a pile by the coach. He'd forgotten that in his panic, and so had she apparently, because she would have been scrambling for her dress had she remembered.

"Rosalind, wait." He caught up with her and placed a hand on her back. "You're painting far too tempting a picture for the men, sweetheart. Stay here." He waved for her to remain ducked down behind the sloping bank while he called to the driver.

"Fetch my coat, but remove the papers from the inside pocket." He waited for the man to do as he asked, and then he carried it back down the bank.

"Put this on. It will cover you enough to keep you warm."

Shivering, she let him slide the coat over her body. A sudden flash of a memory from last year almost made him smile. He'd helped Godric protect Emily when Godric had fallen off his horse into a lake and she'd chased in after him. *Now it is my woman I'm protecting.*

"Ashton, are you well, my boy?" His mother and Joanna were staring at him.

"I'm fine. We're all fine. Just had a bit of a fright." They had no idea how true that was.

"Have the driver tie Ashton's horse to the back of the coach," his mother told Joanna. Then she ushered him and Rosalind into the vehicle.

His mother patted his shoulder and touched Rosalind's cheek. "You'll both need hot baths and soup. I want you to stay by the fire in your room until dinner. We do not need anyone taking ill due to the chill."

Ashton sat beside Rosalind, and before she could protest, he lifted her onto his lap and tucked her body close to his, not caring if his mother considered it scandalous.

His fiancée struggled, but he held fast and put his lips to her ear. "Rest and take my body heat. Fight me later once you're warm and dry."

After a moment, her body relaxed and all of the tension seemed to flow out of her at last. Ashton ignored the worried glances of his mother and sister.

"That was a very brave thing you did, my dear." His mother leaned over and patted Rosalind's hand. "Very brave." As she said this her voice had a slight tremor to it.

Ashton bit back a snarl. "She risked her bloody neck!"

"And saved Mr. Stadley's life," Joanna cut in.

He waited, expecting Rosalind to come to her own defense, but she said nothing. Instead she remained still in his arms, and every now and then a little shiver rippled from her. It only made him hold her tighter.

She sat on his lap, a determined set to her chin.

"I'll not let you lay a hand on me," she warned quietly.

"What?" He didn't follow her remark.

Fire flashed in her eyes. "You said you'd take a hand to my backside before. I won't let you. Not for any reason. Certainly not for doing what was right."

Ashton studied her, the wide eyes, the firm line of her lips and the clenched fists at her sides. And then it all settled into place. She'd been hit before by her father. She didn't understand a bit of sensual bed play and teasing threats compared to actual harm.

"I was angry, and I should not have said that. I was frightened more than anything else." He hoped this admission would win some trust from her. He had to make her understand how scared he'd been when he thought she was gone.

"Because you'd lose your property?" She didn't spit in his face, but the way she'd cast those words in a soft, spiteful tone she might as well have.

"No, because I…" He rubbed his temples with his palms, swallowing the words that would expose him. She could never know he was coming to care for her, not as much as he was. She wouldn't hesitate to use that against him.

"Because what?"

Ashton took a long moment to respond, weighing his words carefully and remembering his mother and sister were there as well. "When I realized you were under the water, it terrified me. I once told you that Charles almost drowned in a river. What I didn't tell you was that one of my other friends did drown that night. It was one of the worst nights of my life. I could not lose you like that."

If he lost her, it would kill him. He was going to do everything within his power to keep her safe.

CHAPTER 19

*T*he weight of three feminine stares made Ashton's stomach clench. His mother and sister knew nothing of what had transpired all those years ago. Aside from academics, they knew he'd formed deep bonds with his friends and that was all. And he hadn't planned on telling Rosalind more unless he had to. She pulled away from his hold to stare up at him, those gray eyes soft as dove feathers.

When he'd first gone to Cambridge, he'd had no friends. His father's death and his subsequent debts had destroyed their societal connections. A year later he'd made true friends, whom he had brought home to meet his family. But he had never shared how he had met the rest of the League.

"Ashton, I never knew that," his mother said, eyes as wide as saucers from the Lennox family china.

"It is a bad memory. I never wished to share that burden with anyone else."

"I'm so sorry," Rosalind whispered again.

He rested his forehead against Rosalind's and stroked her back. She could be furious with him as much as she wanted, but he would not take back his anger and fear at the thought of her being harmed.

When the coach stopped in front of Lennox House, he let his mother and sister out first, followed by Rosalind. Their wet clothes squelched as they marched to the front door. The butler opened the door for them, brows raised as he took in their appearance.

"We had a quick swim in the river," Ashton said curtly.

"I see." The butler's lips twitched, but he knew better than to laugh.

"Send a footman to run a bath, and send for Lady Melbourne's maid," he added.

Rosalind hurried up the stairs, anxious to remove her wet apparel, and he rushed to catch up with her, catching her by the hand just as she reached the top step.

"Rosalind, wait." Her face was pale and her body was trembling. She raised her head, silently daring him. To do what, he wasn't sure.

Frustrated by her continued resistance, he scooped her up in his arms and carried her the rest of the way.

"I have legs," she reminded him.

"You do. Lovely ones. But I am carrying you the rest of the way because I bloody well want to."

She bit her lip at first, then nodded imperiously, permitting him to proceed.

Lowell, the valet, was in the process of folding shirts and froze when Ashton entered the room with his fierce little woman in his arms.

"That's enough. Put me *down*! You're embarrassing me in front of Lowell!" Rosalind hissed, pink flushing her cheeks.

"Excuse us." Ashton carried Rosalind to the bed and dropped her onto it. His valet blushed and fled the room.

The quiet in the room soon filled with tension. Ashton stared down at his fiery future bride, wondering if she was going to be worth all the unending aggravation. Then, before he could think it through, he cupped her face and slanted his mouth over hers. He had to kiss her, to hold her in his arms and reassure himself that she was all right. Her sweet taste pushed away any doubts he might have had. The woman, once she stopped being surprised, returned the kiss like a dream. She climbed onto her knees to get closer to his height and curled her arms around his neck.

With a stumble, he fell onto the bed, her body beneath his as he continued to kiss her. He craved the way she moved beneath him, her hands grasping his hair just the way he liked it. The beast inside him that had raged and panicked at the thought of losing her ceased its restless pacing. He relaxed, slowing his kisses, and her responses slowed in kind. Then they were simply staring at each other.

"Please don't ever frighten me like that again." His voice was rough with emotions he couldn't reconcile.

Her gray eyes had a dreamy expression, softening the usually hard silver pools. She caressed her fingers along his jaw from chin to ear. "I'm sorry, my lord."

"Please, call me Ashton. You only seem to do it some of the time."

"Ashton," she breathed and leaned up to press a kiss to his lips again. Her body shivered.

"We should get you in the bath. I can't keep getting you wet, not like this."

Her lips twitched as though she understood the little joke he'd made.

"You've made me plenty wet," she said with a chuckle. His body responded with a wave of arousal that startled him. There was something about Rosalind that made him half-mad with desire in a way no other woman had, and he couldn't imagine why that was. He'd been with enough women to know the difference, but he simply couldn't understand it. Yet it was undeniable fact— Rosalind was special.

"Now you're tempting me." He bent again, ready to kiss her, but a footman entered the room, disturbing them.

"Pardon, my lord. I've come to run a bath and start a fire." The servant averted his gaze, but the disruption had pulled Ashton back into a clearer frame of mind.

"Right, well, see to it then." He refused to take his eyes off Rosalind. One of these days he was going to lock his door and have this woman all to himself without any interruptions.

He rolled off Rosalind, got to his feet and walked into his dressing room. He raked his hands through his hair, trying to gather his control again. His clothes were damp and clung to his skin. If he hadn't been so hot with need for his little hellion, he would have been chilled to the bone. He reached up to unbutton his waistcoat.

"Need some help with those?"

He turned to find Rosalind there, barefoot in her chemise, his coat still wrapped around her. She was so small, so delicate looking, like a fairy from a stone circle. Her dark hair hung completely free, still wet around her shoulders, a few errant curls touching the tops of her breasts above the stays.

To hell with his control. "If you're offering to assist me, then I certainly do."

She crossed the space between them and reached up to unbutton his vest. Then she removed the neckcloth and dropped it to the floor. When she got to his shirt, he helped raise it over his head. She ran her palms up along his bare chest, and a soft sigh escaped her.

He chuckled and caught her hands, bringing her palms up to his lips.

"You're so warm," she said, leaning into him.

"And you're freezing. Again. I swear as your husband I'll find a way to keep you warm." Her happy grin faded, and she stiffened in his arms.

Ashton lifted her chin. "You cannot keep flinching every time I mention our marriage."

Her eyes were soft and sad, tugging at his heart. "It's not *you* I object to. Can't you see that?"

He couldn't. It wasn't as though she would vanish once they were married. She would still be the woman he cared about, the fiery, battle-ready Scottish lass. She would simply be his wife in addition to everything else.

"Surely you'll settle in. Emily, Anne and Horatia have all taken to married life well," he argued.

"Ach!" She scoffed and shoved him away. "You truly are blind, aren't you? I'm not like those ladies and never have been. They drink their tea, discuss fashion and the latest gossip."

Ashton laughed harshly. "Is that what you think of them? That they are silly ladies without substance?"

Rosalind looked away. He doubted she truly felt that way, but something in his words had hit the mark.

"Rosalind, perhaps it is you who are blind. Emily handled her uncle's business books and has been the one to straighten out Godric's investments these last few months—to a healthy profit, I might add."

He continued to undress as he spoke. "Anne is hardly idle. She is a champion horse breeder, a skill developed long before she married Cedric, and they are now working to breed some of the finest racers England will ever see. And Horatia? She's a voracious scholar and a member of the Lady's Astronomy Society in London. None of them lost who they were to their husbands." He stripped out of his trousers and shirt and climbed into the hot bath. "And if you think I'd ever *want* you to vanish, then you are a fool, and I will not marry a fool."

The hot water felt good on his skin, and he tilted his head back to rest it against the back of the copper tub.

"You swear to me?" Rosalind asked, kneeling beside the tub. He raised his head and met her gaze.

"Rosalind, you have a brilliant mind for business. For me not to allow it to flourish would make me more the fool than you. I swear to you. I like the way you are and would hate it if anything changed." He patted the water teasingly. "Now, would you like to join me? The tub is large enough for two, and the water is hot."

One of her hands idly played in the water close to his hip, and then she flicked her flingers, splashing him.

"Would you scrub my back?" she teased, her lips curving into a sultry smile.

"God yes, and I'd certainly do a lot more than that."

"Good." She stood and removed his coat, then knelt by the tub and offered her back to him. "My stays," she said.

He scrambled to get his clumsy wet fingers though the laces. Once he was done, she let her loose chemise drop to the floor before she climbed into the tub. Her body was an ever present temptation with its gentle curves and enticing softness as he reached up to grip her hips.

"Lie back on me," he said, pulling her shoulders against his chest. The water level rose with their two bodies, sloshing close to the top of the tub, but Ashton didn't care. It felt good to have her lie on top of him. He massaged her shoulders, resisting the urge to slide his hands down and cup her breasts. This was about trust, not satisfying his urges.

She shifted against him, and he bit back a groan as his lower body stirred to life.

"That feels lovely."

"I thought tomorrow we could tour the local chapel, if you wish." He held his breath, waiting to see if she would react poorly again to the mention of the dreaded wedding.

"I suppose. If I do not like it, could we marry somewhere else?" she asked. He sensed in her renewed tension that she was testing him.

"Of course. If you do not care for it, then we shall find another place. One of your choosing."

Rosalind sat up, and before he could react she was turning around and straddling him in the bath. He had the glorious view of her glistening bare body. Her full breasts were too tempting to resist. He trailed his fingers down from her neck to her breasts, cupping the soft flesh, kneading it. Rosalind rubbed against him, her lips feathering kisses against his throat.

"Perhaps we ought to do something else to keep warm?" she suggested, then bit her lip in an attempt to hide her charming smile.

"Hmm?" He played with one erect nipple, making her hiss when he lightly pinched it.

Rosalind lifted her hips, took his erect length and placed it at her entrance.

"Ah, that...something." His laugh changed to a moan of pleasure as her body enveloped his shaft. She was hotter than the water and felt too good to be real.

"Am I dreaming?" he asked, his head feeling a little fuzzy at the waves of delight moving through him.

"Perhaps." She grinned and leaned forward to nibble his bottom lip while her breasts rubbed against his chest. He'd never made love with a woman in a tub before. It seemed too intimate a thing, and he'd never wanted that kind of intimacy before. Now he craved it with a woman who was torn between lust and hate for him, all because he'd tricked her into a pledge of matrimony.

"Stop thinking, *my lord*. I can almost hear your thoughts." Rosalind kissed a path up to his ear and licked the shell. His cock jerked as a sharp bolt of arousal shot through him.

"Hellion," he growled.

"*Sassenach*," she replied saucily. "I suspect you like that about me." She purred as she raised her hips and sank back down, taking him completely inside her.

"I suspect you're right." He gripped her hips, digging his fingers into her flesh as he jerked her back down on his shaft, *hard*. The soft splashes of their wet bodies accompanied their little sighs and moans as they made love in the large tub. It felt as though they were weightless as they moved together in the bath, their mouths hungrily devouring each other.

Neither of them could talk after that. Ashton took her hard, making her cry out in pleasure in a way she would not be able to deny later when she was angry with him.

The bathwater sloshed over the sides of the tub as Rosalind clung to his shoulders, and he watched the inner storms of her gray eyes as she climaxed. Her sweet, delectable lips parted as she tried to breathe. Everything about that moment was burned into his memory. She was the loveliest thing he'd ever seen. His body went rigid as he unleashed his last ounce of control, and he came inside her with a shout that made Rosalind jolt.

Rosalind settled on top of him, exhausted, their bodies still connected. He circled his arms around her, holding her close to him as he stroked her back.

"I fear we left more water on the floor than in the tub," he murmured with a drowsy chuckle, and she smiled.

"May I ask a question?" He drew patterns between her shoulder blades, and her muscles twitched at his touch.

She pressed her cheek against his chest. "You may."

"How did you become involved in business? I understand that your husband left you his, but most women do not get involved in business affairs."

Rosalind did not pull away; rather, she pressed against him even closer.

"From the moment I married Henry, he insisted that I learn how to run his businesses. He often said he saw my keen mind in our morning discussions over breakfast and wanted to foster it. I believe he feared he would die early into our union, and he wished to make sure I could handle things after he was gone."

Her cheeks flushed. "He loved me, so much more than I expected, since he had not been looking for a bride that day he found me. I will always treasure his kindness and compassion."

Jealousy and understanding of what she'd said mixed inside Ashton. He'd once believed he was in love with Emily Parr, for a brief few moments before Godric had stolen her heart completely. But in truth he had treasured her love and affection in the way that she taught him to crave love for himself and not stand alone. He loved her for it, but in a different way, perhaps the way Rosalind loved her late husband for showing her how to trust in herself after he was gone.

"If more men were like him, England would be a merrier place for it," he replied softly.

"I agree." Her words warmed him. They were finally agreeing on something. He decided to see if he could continue to get her to talk. There was so much about her he still wanted to know. "Why shipping companies? You have all your primary business interests in sea trade. I am curious as to what drew you to that. Your husband never invested in those."

"Henry had interests in several businesses. I sold all of those except for the country bank he owned. I focused on ships because..." She paused. "Because I liked the idea of being able to get on any of those ships and sail away." Her voice was so soft, almost a whisper, as if she was embarrassed to admit it.

"Why?" He lifted one of her hands and brought it up to his lips, kissing little places along her inner wrist and palm. It was so easy to enjoy this woman. He'd loved bed play in the past, but this... this was infinitely more. These small touches and tender kisses were built upon more than mutual desire; there was a growing affection and understanding that ever deepened what he felt for her.

"Please, talk to me."

"I'm not good at sharing things, especially the things that hurt."

Her pain wounded him, but he knew that sharing these secret parts of herself would only help to connect them.

I want to connect with her, at any cost. He wondered how it had been for his friends when they'd fallen for their wives. Had it been this frightening? This exciting? To bare their souls like this, not knowing if their dreams would somehow be dashed?

"I cannot say I am the most gifted at sharing myself, but we can try together. You talk, and then I will. Ask me whatever you wish." He stroked his fingertips between her shoulder blades, waiting patiently for her to answer him. It was her choice, and he would not insist on it if she wasn't ready.

"After growing up with a brute of a father, escape was my only dream. I imagined myself sailing away to shores unknown, where I could forget the years of cruelty I'd suffered under him. And I promised myself I would someday. Each of my ships is a promise I keep for my younger self."

Ashton's breath caught, and he struggled to find the right words, to say something that would soothe the hurt she was clearly suffering, but he was tongue-tied.

She raised her head and met him with a bold stare. "Tell me about Charles and the river. All of it."

He knew she would ask that. It was one of the darkest moments in his life. But she'd shared her darkest moments with him, and he owed her the same openness.

"Someone tried to kill him. They tied him up and put him in the river by our college. Lucien and I were late back to our chambers, and we heard the shouting and splashes. We went in after him and…" His throat closed momentarily, and he swallowed hard before continuing. "It took four of us to save him, but we couldn't save Peter."

"Peter?"

He tightened his arms around her. "He was the first to try to save Charles, but he was under too long and the current was too fast. Peter was a friend." That was all he could say. The words made fresh cuts in the old wounds of his memories.

They stayed together in the tub, watching the late-afternoon sun burst through the window, forming longer and longer shadows across the floor. They remained together until the water began to cool and the sounds of servants in the corridors echoed through to them.

"I believe we ought to get out. Dinner won't be long now, and I should not like to be wrinkled for it." He played with a damp lock of her hair, and she traced the scar on his shoulder. It was an almost perfect moment that Ashton couldn't resist stretching out, despite what he'd just said. He would never want to give this up, or her, for anything in the world.

She gave him a disappointed but clearly teasing frown. "Very well, if we must." Then she leaned in and kissed him before she climbed out of the bath in all her naked glory. With an impish grin, she held out her hand to him and he stood, water rushing down his body as he stepped out of the tub onto the wet floor, where they retrieved a pair of towels. He wrapped one around his hips and then shielded her with one, holding her close as he used his body to warm hers.

"This was lovely," Rosalind said as she nuzzled him.

"It was, wasn't it?" he replied, a little surprised himself at how wonderful it had been to bathe with her.

For the first time in as long as he could remember, Ashton was filled with hope.

CHAPTER 20

*T*om Linley lingered in the shadows of the servants' stairs, his heart hammering wildly. A footman came down the steps and froze at the sight of him.

"You will know my servants by the silver star pin on their neckcloths."

His master's instructions were not something he would forget anytime soon. He stared hard at the footman and saw a silver star glinting near his throat.

"Lovely afternoon for a stroll," he said.

The footman looked to Tom. "Indeed, but rain can always come from cloudless skies."

"And a black sky sometimes doesn't rain at all," Linley agreed.

"Why don't you give me a hand with polishing the silver?" The footman gestured to the silver cabinet, holding a set of keys.

Linley followed the man and waited for him to open the cabinet door. The footman glanced about, searching the hall for other servants, then leaned close to Linley.

"I've sent word about the wedding between Lennox and Lady Melbourne."

"Good. I've not yet had a chance to." Linley slipped a piece of paper into the other man's hand. "Could you see this gets posted for me?"

The footman tucked the letter away. "I'll see it done."

"Thank you." Linley feigned interest in the silver spoons a moment longer before he spoke. "I should return to Lord Lonsdale."

He left the footman and headed back up the stairs into the main hall. Now that he'd delivered his report he could pursue his next objective.

Linley came to the room where Lady Melbourne was residing with Lennox. The chamber would be empty, he hoped. Just before he touched the knob, the door opened and a little girl scrambled out, her face red and her little giggles undeniably sweet.

"Shoo! You shouldn't be in there!" Linley chastised, but he couldn't help but laugh as he watched the giggling child race down the corridor. Once Linley was assured that no one else was in the hall, he turned the latch and slipped inside. Lennox's bedroom was large and masculine, yet the tastes were clearly refined, like Lonsdale's.

A small dresser drew Linley's attention. He rifled through the drawers, finding dresses, undergarments and other items which belonged to Lady Melbourne, but no evidence of what he'd been charged to find—an object that could decode messages. It had been so important that Daniel Sheffield had broken the code of silence to contact him, albeit indirectly.

Tom had been told they'd searched Lady Melbourne's residence and turned up nothing. Therefore, it stood to reason that she had brought it with her, and Tom was in the best position to find out.

As he searched the last drawer of a small table beside the bed, his fingers brushed something cool and circular. He clutched it and raised it up in the light. A pocket watch. Sheffield had said the cipher would resemble a watch, but inside it would have symbols and letters rather than a watch face. He popped the lid open.

Linley's heart sank. No decoder, just a common pocket watch. He dropped it back into the drawer and faced the room, trying to decide what else to search.

Digging around the bedding and through Lennox's clothes, Linley huffed in disappointment. He checked every place he could think of but found nothing. *Curses!* Waverly would be furious. The thought made him feel faint. A sound outside the door made him jump.

Darting behind the door, which had started to open, he held his breath. A chambermaid entered, carrying a bucket and a cloth sling with firewood logs. While her back was to him, Linley ducked around the open door and out into the corridor again. He would have to try again tomorrow.

He trotted up the main stairs and headed for his master's chambers. Lonsdale was inside, facing the fire in his room, elbows resting on his knees as he stared at the flames. He rolled a glass of brandy between his palms and didn't turn around as Linley approached.

"There you are, lad. I'm having the worst fit of the blue devils. I don't suppose you'd care to go a round or two with me in Ashton's leisure room?"

"Boxing?" Linley clarified.

"Yes, what do you think? I've been idle for too long and need to be occupied." Charles turned around in his seat, hope shining in his eyes.

Linley found himself nodding. He always preferred to have Charles happy and smiling when he could manage it. It kept him from asking questions.

"Excellent. Let me show you the way." Charles finished his brandy and set it on the mantle before heading to the door. He seemed as comfortable in Lennox's townhouse as in his own.

"Do you know where it is, my lord?" Linley asked.

"Oh, I've been coming here since I was eighteen. Often we in the League would gather at one member's house while on holiday. Saved us from having dreadful relations trying to marry us off over and over. But those days seem to be coming to an end."

Charles led Linley on a tour through the elegant, sunny halls. Linley was so rarely able to appreciate beauty. Even when he seemed to be relaxed, his mind was on his mission, wary of potential threats. But now he could steal glimpses of how the rich and titled lived.

An ache formed deep in his chest as he thought back to his life before his master, when he'd been a child in a happy household, his mother a lady's maid to a beloved countess. Life had been full of joy then. Every room was filled with light and laughter. And then it was gone.

Lennox House reminded him of those happier times. The servants were welcoming, and with the tenant farm children running about, it was full of the sounds of love and family. It was nice to have the little scamps underfoot.

The ache in his chest grew for little Katherine, his baby sister he'd left back in London at Charles's home. It was hard to leave her for so long, even if she was well cared for. In some ways, Katherine was all he had left of his life before.

Charles stopped in front of an open room. There was a space for fencing and equipment hanging on the wall. There was also a boxing ring on the floor outlined in white paint on the wood. Charles stopped by the ring and removed his waistcoat and hung it on a peg by the fencing foils. He rolled up his sleeves, exposing his tanned, muscled forearms.

"Well, come on, lad. Take that cap off and let's go."

Linley held the cap tight to his head. "I'll keep it on if it's the same to you, my lord." Then he rolled up his sleeves and stepped into the ring.

"I'll only end up knocking it off."

"I'm hoping you'll go easy on me, my lord."

Charles raised his bare fists. "Put up your paws and let me see your form."

Linley curled his fingers into fists and lifted them up awkwardly.

Charles dropped his hands and walked up to Linley with a critical eye. Linley held his breath as the other man raised his hands higher.

"Like this." Charles seemed to be satisfied, and then he walked backward, putting distance between them before he raised his own hands.

"Should I throw a punch?" Linley offered.

With a nod, Charles waited for him to move.

Studying his master's body, Linley looked for points of weakness. He'd spent more than a year learning how to fight from a master. He could see Charles's brandy had weakened his stance, and one elbow hung lower than the other. With just a shift to the right he could cut through Charles's guard without his master even being aware of it before Linley had him on the ground and pinned.

It was not the way a gentleman would fight, of course, but he hadn't been trained to fight like a gentleman. He'd been trained to survive.

"Don't dawdle, lad. Show me your moves." Charles danced a step closer, gently feigning a throw with one hand.

Linley analyzed the way he moved, graceful as a waltz. Linley would not get past Charles's defenses by fighting fair. Knowing this, Linley sidestepped, and the instant his opponent mirrored him, he shot forward and landed a blow to Charles's shoulder. It was a glancing blow, not intended to hurt.

Charles's gray eyes lit up with delight. "Well done. Again."

It was a ritual. Charles was banishing the demons that so often tried to drown him. The nightmares he suffered were beginning to haunt Linley too. More than once, he'd woken to the sound of half-strangled screams, and he'd find his master thrashing about in the sheets, unable to wake.

The memories of those long nights spurred Linley to move faster, strike harder. Whatever was causing Charles grief built a fury inside Linley that he could not understand.

He was meant to betray this good man someday, lead him like a lamb to slaughter the day his master commanded it. He'd made peace with that fact. And yet he hated that this man was hurting in such a silent and lonely way. He deserved better than the fate that would someday come to him.

A light punch to Linley's chest sent him stumbling back.

The blow had caught him off guard, and though it only stung a little, he reacted with instinct. He swept Charles's leg, knocking the man off his feet. He hit the floor with a thud and a groan.

Ha! Linley grinned, then winced. That had been foolish. He should never have used such a move. The art of combat could be as distinctive as a signature, he'd been told, and if Charles suspected that this had been more than just luck…

"What the devil?" Charles growled as he got up and lunged for Linley. He had no choice but to take the blow to avoid suspicion. Suddenly the world was spinning and he landed on his back with a crash. Charles rolled on top of him, pinning him down.

The shock of the impact sent a hundred buried memories through Linley.

Pain. So much pain. Hands on his throat. His true master taking everything from him. His world destroyed, but a new one offered. At a price. A guttural scream ripped from his throat and stars dotted his vision.

"Tom! Shake it off, lad, you're fine!" Charles's voice barely cut through Linley's terror, but at least he could breathe now.

Sweet, blessed air.

He sucked it greedily into his lungs, and his vision cleared. He was back in the leisure room with Charles.

"Are you all right? You scared the bloody hell out of me, Tom."

Charles's face was carved with lines of worry, and he crouched beside Linley.

"I'm sorry...my lord," he whispered. His voice was too hoarse for anything else.

Charles placed one hand on Linley's shoulder. "I thought you were ready for some more of the rough tactics when you took out my leg like that."

"Just something I saw once. Never tried it before."

"I'm sorry. It was my fault for assuming. I keep forgetting that your last master had a rough hand. I am sorry, Tom."

"I promise to do better, my lord."

Charles simply stared at him for a long moment. "Don't get so serious on me, lad. It's just a bit of sport. Never apologize or make such a vow again. Whatever that man did to you was wrong. You didn't deserve it, and you must never believe that ever again. Do you understand?"

Linley's throat tightened and his eyes burned with treacherous tears.

"Ah, don't cry, lad."

Linley scrambled to his feet and raced out of the leisure room. He was relieved when Charles did not come after him. He ducked into a darkened room down the hall and shut the door, leaning back against it as he regained his breath and his wits.

He missed Charles's townhouse and he missed Katherine. Katherine was in good hands, but it didn't make Linley miss her any less.

She was why he was doing all this. His master would take her away if Linley didn't do as he was told. For now it was information. But someday, when the time was right, he would have to deliver Charles to him. To Hugo.

God save me for my treachery...

～

CLAIRE FUSSED over Rosalind's hair before dinner and laid out a dark purple silk gown with a plunging neckline that would no doubt draw Ashton's attention. Rosalind tugged the bodice up and raised a brow at Claire.

"You did tell me to pack lightly, Your Ladyship."

"I did, but I did not mean to pack the gowns with the least amount of cloth to them. It will attract the eyes of every man in the room."

Her maid chuckled. "There's nothing wrong with displaying a lady's bosom in a fine gown."

"I quite agree." Ashton's voice made Rosalind and Claire both jump.

He stood in the doorway, those blue eyes more alive than she'd ever seen them before. Rosalind looked away, still embarrassed by how much of herself she'd revealed this afternoon in the bath. He'd used intimacy to break down her walls and make her share the darker parts of her heart. She felt...perhaps not betrayed, but *exposed* at the very least.

"Claire, would you mind giving us a minute?" Her maid bowed, backing away as Ashton walked over to Rosalind by the dressing table. He reached out for a loose curl of her hair and wound it around his finger. Rosalind's breath caught as she looked up into his face.

"I thought, given how the last few days have been, that things between us deserved some..." He continued to play with the lock of her hair, but the expression on his face had become oddly bashful.

"Some what?"

A red tint suffused Ashton's cheeks. Rosalind's lips curved into a smile. What could possibly make the baron bashful?

"I swear, if you laugh, I shan't mention it again."

She bit her lip and nodded.

He let go of her hair and slipped his hand into the pocket of his waistcoat. What he retrieved surprised her. Dangling from his fingers on a fine gold chain was a trio of amethysts spaced a few inches apart and set in gold.

"I thought, although it feels strange to do so, that I should make a romantic gesture of sorts. Show you my committed interest in our match." He held the necklace out for her to get a closer look.

It was the most beautiful thing she'd ever seen. The necklace reminded her of one her mother once had long ago, one that she used to wear to balls. The gesture was impossibly sweet, and as a sign of commitment it sent her heart skittering. The delighted whirl of her thoughts came to a crashing halt, however. Was he trying to buy her affection?

Rosalind stared at the gift, then him. The earnestness on his face fed the well of hope that had begun to grow within her. She would not have thought him capable of a romantic gesture like that, ever. Yet here he was, holding out a part of his life to her, with hope in those bewitching eyes of his. It was such a beautiful necklace, and it would look exquisite on any woman.

He cleared his throat. "The stones represent the past, present and future. Very few valuables survived the year my father destroyed our family fortunes. This was one of them. We hid it away, saving it for Joanna, but tonight she told me she'd much rather have it go to you. I wanted to give you something that was part of *me*, not part of our business dealings."

She wasn't sure what to say. She wanted desperately to believe he cared about her and their life together, but she wasn't sure it was wise to believe he was capable of that.

"Well, do you accept it? I...haven't ever given jewelry to a woman before. I confess I'm rather nervous." He chuckled, but she saw the vulnerability in his eyes.

"Not even your mistresses?" She couldn't resist teasing him.

A wry smile curved his lips. "No. They were happy enough with rewards of flowers. Something befitting a temporary relationship."

Rosalind laughed. "Ah yes, the infamous Lennox technique—leave only pleasant memories behind. Even I have heard of that." But this had shown there was another side to him, one he hid from the entire world. A man of passions and desires that lay beneath that cool exterior. When he took her into his arms, she could taste that hunger for life upon his lips and feel it in the heat of his hands, held at bay through discipline and perhaps even fear.

"I suppose Emily has spilled all my secrets during one of your afternoon teas?"

"Certainly not. She sang only your praises. But other women *do* talk. And you are quite a topic of discussion for some of them."

His lips thinned in irritation. "I readily admit I'm not a natural wooer. I know what is expected of me, of course, but those are mere formalities. True wooing should come from somewhere more genuine, and in that regard my instincts are sorely lacking. But I have every intent to woo you as you should be."

"Well, in that case, I might let you." She stared at the necklace again and then reached for it. He lifted it out of her immediate reach.

"Allow me the honor."

Smiling, Rosalind turned her back to him and sat patiently, though her heart was hammering against her ribs.

Ashton laid the necklace against her throat and fastened the clasp. She touched the stones, and his hand covered hers.

"Thank you. It's beautiful."

His lips curved. "I'm sure you have lots of jewelry."

"True. But none that holds such importance," she assured him. "When my mother died, I wasn't allowed to keep anything of hers. My father sold everything, even her clothes." She admitted this painfully, each word hurting as she let herself remember the past. "Henry bought me a few jewels, but I never wished for him to spend money on them and asked him to stop. I had convinced myself I did not deserve them."

Ashton frowned. "You deserve whatever joys the world chooses to give you, as well as those you make for yourself."

"His greatest gift to me was helping me see that."

Ashton moved to sit beside her on the bench in front of his dressing table and cupped her face in his hands.

"This will be a new beginning for us, a chance to start over, as partners, not rivals."

He dipped his head and slanted his mouth over hers, the kiss full of tenderness and passion that left her muddleheaded. She could have kissed him like that forever, slow, sensual, and yet infinitely sweet as they explored each other.

When they finally parted, both were breathing a little heavily, and Rosalind's body ached for more of what that kiss had promised. Ashton continued to gaze almost dreamily at her mouth. It felt so wonderful to be the center of his focus and his hunger.

"Every time I kiss you I think it cannot be better than the last one, yet every time you surprise me." His soft words stirred heated longings inside her, not just for lovemaking but for other lost wishes as well.

She stared up into his eyes and bravely opened her heart. "When I was a young girl, I used to dream about this, a man who would say what you just said." She could feel the tears burning in her eyes, but they were happy tears. "Mayhap the dream is not as lost as I had feared."

Ashton cupped her chin and nodded. "Nor is mine."

She wondered what Ashton's dream was, but she was afraid he would not tell her. *Maybe someday he will tell me all that lies in his heart.*

Perhaps their marriage wouldn't be a disaster after all.

"Ashton?" she asked.

"Hmm?" His hand had moved to her neck and was gently stroking down her throat in a feathery caress.

"I don't suppose you'd let me invite my brothers to the

wedding?" She was only teasing, but Ashton seemed to consider it seriously.

"If you wish. Are you in contact with them?"

She shook her head. "Not since I left Scotland. Brock knew once I left I had to stay out of my father's sight and mind. Even if I married, my father might still wish to harm me or drag me back home. He is a wretched man. He never wanted me around, but he never wanted me to be free of him, either. To him, I was his property."

Ashton closed his eyes and rested his forehead against hers. "Now that you are mine, I'll protect you from the world if I have to. Don't let him cause you one more moment of fear."

She curled her fingers around his wrists. This time, being "his" did not sound like a possession of property, but a promise of something better. She felt safe, secure and even excited at the affection he was showing towards her. It was what she'd received from her first husband, and yet she had a feeling Ashton's affections ran even deeper. It made her think of an old Scottish ballad her mother used to sing. *"My laird's love is dark and deep, and 'ere he watches over me, this laird of the keep."*

"Thank you," she whispered.

He chuckled. "You need not thank me for that. It is my honor and privilege."

"If this is how you conduct your romantic gestures, I shall look forward to future ones. Shower me with more jewels, my lord, for this lady is worth it." Rosalind flashed an impish grin.

"Minx," he teased.

"Yes. And I believe you quite like it."

"I do." He smiled and stood. "Dinner?" He held out his hand. When she placed her palm in his, a heated spark flared between them, and she knew that deep down she was excited to see what being married to this man would be like. He was constantly changing her opinions about him and of marriage.

They were halfway to the dining room when they saw Charles in the hall patting his pockets and glancing about.

"Lost something?" Ashton asked.

Charles dug his fingers into the slender waistcoat pocket. "My watch. It's been gone all day." He spun around and headed back upstairs muttering.

A tiny giggle came from near the floor behind a potted plant a few feet from the dining room. Rosalind caught a glimpse of a dark-blue gown and little black booted feet disappearing from view. She squeezed Ashton's arm and nodded in the pot's direction. It was one of the farmers' children.

"Oh dear," she said with a raised voice. "Charles is always losing that watch. Wouldn't it be most amusing if it turned up on his bed while we are all at dinner?" She hoped Ashton would play along.

He grinned and they walked past the potted plant, doing their best not to laugh. "Most amusing indeed."

Before they reached the dining room, Rosalind tugged Ashton to a halt, studying his handsome face in the light from the wall sconces. His features were proud, aristocratic, even cold, but she was seeing him differently now. A lonely man with a family who did not understand the sacrifices he'd made to keep them secure all these years.

We are both survivors.

He gazed down at her, a tiny furrow between his brows. "What is it?"

"Would you... I mean..." She struggled for words. So many dreams had been abandoned when she was younger, but perhaps now...

"Children," she finally whispered. "That is to say, do you ever think you would want any?"

Ashton glanced down at the floor, then nodded. "I confess children have never been important to me, at least thoughts of having them. Obviously it is my duty to have an heir. Rafe has shown time and again that he cannot be allowed to take over the estate should something ever happen to me."

Rosalind noted something in how Ashton said the words and nodded. "I agree. You cannot have a *highwayman* inheriting the title and land. Lord knows he'd turn it into a thieves' den."

He stared down at her. "You know then that it was Rafe who stopped your coach?"

She nodded. "I was torn whether I should confess the matter to you, but I inferred from your tone just now that you already knew but did not know how to tell me."

"It is a delicate matter," Ashton agreed.

"I assume you'll have him return my coin purse?"

"I intend to settle matters, yes." He was silent a moment longer, and then that vulnerability was back in his eyes. "And what of you?" he asked, turning the subject away from Rafe. "Do you want children, I mean."

"Henry and I never had any. I fear I might be barren. Does that change anything?"

Ashton stared at her for a long moment. "No. If we are never blessed with children, that does not mean we aren't still blessed, even if Rafe does end up inheriting." Ashton's wry chuckle surprised her.

For some strange reason, his words about still being blessed struck her as sweet. *Too* sweet. Her eyes misted. If he kept doing this, she'd lose herself to him, and any ability she had to stop him from hurting her.

"I should like to try for children," she whispered.

Ashton gave her a courtly bow and a wicked teasing leer. "Then we shall try to make that desire come true, *several* times a day if need be, on every surface I can conceivably take you on, my dear."

The thought of them together, making love everywhere, had her blushing, even after everything they'd already done. Her blood burned with a fresh wave of lust.

"Perhaps we should start right now?" His voice was deliciously rough as he pulled her away from the dining room door.

She gasped as he shoved her behind a curtain away from a window seat alcove off the main hall. "What? Now?"

"Yes. Here. Right now." Ashton jerked the heavy baize curtain closed, sealing them in the small alcove. "Forget dinner. No one will miss us."

Her heart pounded as she struggled to think. What if someone came upon them? That thought only made her body spark to life even more.

"But—"

Ashton pressed a finger to her lips as he backed her up against the wall beside the window seat.

"Lift your skirts," he ordered, his eyes burning hot.

Grinning, she trailed her fingers up his chest. "Make me." She brushed her lips on his jaw, and he growled like a hungry wolf.

"Oh, I'll make you." He captured her wrists and held them above her head with one hand, using his other to bunch her skirts up. It was like that night at the opera so long ago, but this time, she wanted him to take her and be in control. He needed to win this battle, and she would let him, though after a bit of a struggle. One she'd enjoy. It was what made everything between them so exciting, because it felt so wicked.

Ashton's kisses seduced her into a state of bliss. She curled one leg around his hip, pressing closer as he unfastened his trousers.

"Don't make a sound," he murmured against her.

She clenched her trapped fists and held her breath as he kissed her neck and thrust into her. Her body welcomed him, squeezing around his shaft. She clutched the baize curtains as he released her hands, hanging on as Ashton possessed her in the hidden alcove. She couldn't think beyond what was happening between them.

The rhythmic sounds against the wooden wall, so close to where everyone else would be sitting down to dinner soon, made it that much more exciting. In that moment, Ashton owned her completely and she wanted him to. The climax hit her hard, and he silenced her cry with a kiss. He came seconds later, crushing her into the wall. Panting, they recovered slowly, bodies pressed together, enjoying the aftershocks of pleasure rolling through them. She nuzzled his cheek, her eyes closed, smiling faintly.

"Hellion," he said, smiling.

"Bastard," she kissed his lips.

"I'm *your* bastard." He touched his forehead to hers until their noses brushed. He seemed more than content, perhaps even happy. Seeing him like that filled her with a strange joy. As much as she loved to challenge him, there was an intensity to the moments when they seemed perfectly in tune with each other.

He nudged his hips against hers. "Hungry?"

Rosalind raked her nails lightly against his back. "Dinner will suffice, for now."

Ashton cupped her face, gazing at her as though they had each exposed parts of their souls. It was a secret sort of spell cast between them, two reluctant hearts starved for love and yet afraid to grasp at it. She saw that truth in his eyes and felt it in his hands as he held her.

Voices down the hall shattered the peaceful scene. With blushing smiles, they separated. She fixed her dress while he tended to his trousers. They held their breaths as Charles and Jonathan passed by their hidden spot.

"I don't know what Ash is thinking, marrying her," Charles grumbled. "Sure she's a lovely creature, but far from trustworthy."

Jonathan tried to cut in. "Charles, I don't think—"

"Really, Jon, think about it. He doesn't even like her. Sure, bedding a woman for lust is one thing, but *marrying* her? He's lost his bloody mind."

Rosalind stiffened, trying to block out the pain those words caused. Ashton gripped her by the shoulders as he waited for his friends to walk into the dining room and out of earshot.

"He's wrong. On my life, he is *wrong*," Ashton growled, softly enough for only her ears. "Do you understand me?"

Tears stung her eyes as she struggled to get free of him. "Let me go!"

Ashton shoved her back against the wall. "Not until you hear me out. However things may have started out between us, I want *you*, Rosalind. As a partner, as a wife, as a lover. Charles is a fool. He doesn't want the rest of the League to marry because he's afraid of being left alone."

She stopped struggling, but her heart still stung. He pulled her into his arms, holding her close. He rubbed his hands up and down her back, soothing her, but she despised the fact that it calmed her.

"Why should I believe you?" she asked, breathing in the scent of him, loving it and hating it at the same time.

Ashton slid a hand up to her neck, gently massaging the tense muscles there. It felt too good, Rosalind had to admit. But as Ashton had once admitted, such gestures were matters of technical finesse, not what was going on in one's soul.

"Believe me, Rosalind. We are cut from the same cloth. From the moment I met you, I could not get you out of my head. Even when you drive me mad, I still want you."

She gazed into his blue eyes. There were no shadows there, no hints of deception.

Rosalind finally nodded and wiped her eyes. "We ought to go to dinner before we are missed."

Ashton waited a moment longer before he pulled the curtain of the alcove back. "I never wish to see you cry, ever. Not because of something I've done."

She held her head high. "Then do not give me a reason to."

Ashton cupped her chin and brushed a thumb over her lower lip. "I won't."

She wanted so desperately to believe him. He took her hand,

and she let him lead her into the hall, her heart exposed and her soul shaking.

Can I stop myself from falling in love with him?

The fact that she did not know the answer right away scared her most of all.

CHAPTER 21

*A*shton glared at Charles over his glass of wine. His friend cocked a brow in silent question, which Ashton only answered with a dark scowl.

Regina cleared her throat, attempting to dispel the growing tension in the dining room. "The tenant farmhouses start construction in a few days, I hear."

Ashton set his wine down. "Yes, Higgins and Maple will be relieved. I've employed nearly every able-bodied man in the local villages to aid in the construction."

Joanna was in animated discussion with Jonathan. Rosalind was picking at her food while Rafe stared into the distance, quiet and a bit pale. Ashton worried that the bullet wound might be giving Rafe trouble. That was something he'd have to see to later tonight, after he'd boxed Charles's ears for being so free with his opinions.

"Well, that's wonderful news indeed," Regina said.

Rafe suddenly shoved his chair back from the table and stood.

"Rafe?" their mother asked.

"I'm sorry, Mother. I don't feel well and will retire for the evening. Please excuse me." He dropped his napkin upon the table and left the room.

Given the already unsalvageable awkwardness of the dinner, Ashton decided now was as good a time as any to deal with Rafe. He rose from the table.

"A thousand apologies. I need to speak with Rafe." He exited the dining room and chased after his brother, catching him by the stairs. Rafe was slowly climbing up, when he stopped and suddenly crumpled to the ground.

"Rafe?" He reached his brother seconds before the fall would have done him harm. "What's the matter? Have you had too much to drink again?" Ashton slung one of Rafe's arms over his shoulder.

"Ash, I'm sorry, I don't—" Rafe began, his voice oddly breathless. It was not at all how Rafe sounded when deep in his cups.

"Nonsense. Let me help you upstairs." He helped Rafe all the way to his chambers and settled him in his bed.

"I haven't been drinking. I swear." Rafe moaned and rolled over onto his side, his body trembling. Beads of sweat glistened on his brow.

Ashton sat down on the bed and placed the back of his hand on Rafe's brow. He was hot to the touch. A fever? Rafe's body twitched, and he clamped his jaw shut as his teeth began to rattle.

"I'm sending for the doctor." He pulled the blankets up to Rafe's chin and added more logs to the fire at the opposite end of the room.

When he glanced back at the bed, Ashton's fear began to climb into his throat. He'd never seen Rafe truly sick. None of his siblings had ever had more than a cold. Whatever was wrong now was more than that.

As he descended the stairs, Charles was waiting for him. "Everything all right?"

"No, I must send for a doctor. Rafe is unwell. Where are the others?"

"Finishing the last course," Charles said. "I thought Rafe looked a bit off. Shall I fetch the doctor? You could stay here and watch over him."

Ash seized at the offer. He'd feel much better if he could keep an eye on his brother.

"Who do you normally call for?" Charles ordered a footman to fetch him his coat and horse. The footman nodded and vanished.

"Dr. Finchley. He's about five miles south on the main road past the river. He has a little country house visible from the road."

"Right." Charles waved his hand at Ashton. "Go and see to Rafe."

"Thank you," Ashton called out as he ran back up the stairs. He'd admonish his friend for speaking about Rosalind when he was less worried about his brother.

He returned to Rafe's room again and pulled the bell cord to summon Rafe's valet. While he waited, he pulled up a chair beside his brother's bed and touched his forehead again. Half an hour passed in quiet silence as Ashton tended to his brother. Rafe lay still, his breathing slightly labored.

"Rafe," he said gently. "Charles has gone for the doctor."

Rafe's eyes opened and he stared at Ash, but his eyes were murky blue pools.

"Sorry, Ash." He coughed, his nose a little redder now. "I didn't want to ruin dinner. I'll be better tomorrow." Even as he said this, his teeth chattered.

"You'd better be. I cannot have you distressing Joanna or Mother. First you turn to robbery, and now you're ill." Ash rose from the chair and went over to the washbasin and dampened a cloth in the water. When he came back, he saw Rafe watching him.

"It was my first. I swear to you."

Ashton leaned over and placed the cool wet cloth across Rafe's brow. His younger brother shivered.

"Too cold," Rafe muttered. "Take it off."

"Rafe, you're burning up." He kept the cloth on. "And what did you mean, your first?"

"The coach, it was my first…robbery."

Ashton was torn between relief and frustration. He was relieved Rafe had only committed one such act, but he was frustrated that Rafe had thought it was wise to rob anyone at all.

"Why did you do it, you daft fool?" He kept the cloth on Rafe's head even when his brother shook and tried to brush it off.

Rafe exhaled, the sound slightly labored. "Because you remind me how much of a burden I am. Paying my debts, covering my mistakes and still managing to take care of Mother and Joanna. I thought if I could live on my own…"

Ashton growled. "I'd rather keep paying your debts than have you robbing coaches."

"I suppose I won't be doing much of that anymore, seeing as how your future wife shot me. Puts a man off his game when he fears he'll face bullets, especially from ladies." Rafe's smile was more of a wince.

"You're lucky the storm hindered her aim. She had every intention of killing you," Ashton chuckled, but he couldn't shake his fears for Rafe. His brother's body wouldn't stop trembling.

"Damned good choice in a wife. You had to find a bloodthirsty wench." Rafe licked his lips. "Could you fetch me some water?"

"Of course." Ashton stood and exited the room, nearly running into his brother's valet, who was accompanied by Charles and the doctor.

Ashton shook the older man's hand. "Thank you, Dr. Finchley. I apologize for the late hour."

Dr. Finchley pushed his spectacles up. "Seems your brother is having a difficult week."

Ashton grunted. "It would appear so. I'll fetch him some fresh water."

The doctor nodded. "Not a problem. I'll just take a look at him." He went inside, leaving Charles and Ashton outside.

"How is he?" Charles asked.

Ashton dragged his hands through his hair. "Not good. I've never seen him like this."

Charles reached out and put a hand on his shoulder. "What can I do to help?"

Ashton leaned against the wall. His body felt like it was weighted down with stones. "Thank you. I'm not sure what's to be done yet. You might as well get some sleep. We can talk in the morning once we know more."

"Wake me if you need anything."

Ashton patted Charles's back and headed for the kitchens, his mind racing. Now was not the time for him to be worried about his brother, but he was. Ever since they'd been boys, Ashton had always been watching out for him, protecting him from everything he could. But this...

"Ashton." His mother stood at the foot of the stairs, her eyes wide. "I saw Charles with Dr. Finchley. Is Rafe ill?"

"I think he has a fever. Finchley is examining him right now. I'm fetching Rafe some water."

"A fever?" His mother paled. "Let me get a glass. You must go and be with him and speak to the doctor." His mother headed for the kitchens.

With a sigh, he turned around and returned to Rafe's room. When he entered, Dr. Finchley was staring grimly at his pocket watch while holding two fingers to one of Rafe's wrists.

"How does he fare?"

Finchley released Rafe's wrist and slid the watch back into his pocket.

"I believe it's the grippe. He slipped into unconsciousness shortly after you left. I won't lie to you, Lord Lennox—I do not like the look of this. He's likely contagious, and you should keep his exposure to the rest of the house limited. Keep him warm and try to keep him drinking lots of water. Light broths for meals until his fever and nausea passes. If his conditions worsen, I might suggest bleeding him."

"The grippe?" Ashton murmured, his heart thumping hard against his rubs.

"Yes, a bad case it seems. I've come from visiting several people in the village. A man and a child have already died. If he's been to the village lately, he could have acquired it there. What concerns me most is that his earlier wound has already weakened him."

The world around Ashton shrunk, suffocating him. Two deaths? And Rafe carried the same illness? Normally a grown man could get through the grippe, but in his injured state, he might not withstand it.

There was a strange ringing in his ears. "Is there nothing to be done?" he asked.

"I'm afraid not. You must ride out the fever and hope he is strong enough to make it." Finchley patted Ashton's shoulder. "I'll come back tomorrow and check on him."

Ashton followed the doctor out. "Let me see you to the door."

After the doctor left, Ashton walked over to the stairs and sank to the floor, burying his face in his hands as a dozen emotions threatened to drown him.

"Ashton? What did the doctor say?" His mother's voice was tremulous. He looked up and blinked back the tears he'd been trying to hide. She was holding a pitcher of water, and when she met his gaze, her grip loosened on the pitcher. It fell from her hands and shattered upon the stone floor, the sound sharp and violent in the quiet night. The white china fragments glistened beneath the hall lamps.

"Just tell me," his mother whispered, her hands shaking so hard she clasped them in her skirts as though to hide them.

Ashton wiped at his eyes. "He has influenza. Finchley said he's seen cases in the village. In his weakened state this could be bad, Mother. We need to be prepared. The doctor believes he is contagious. We cannot risk exposing the others."

"Influenza." Regina clutched at the banister. "Ashton, you must not let him…" She swallowed the words, but he knew what she meant.

"You won't lose him," Ashton vowed.

"*We* won't lose him." Regina came over to him. Before he could protest, she bent and kissed his forehead. It had been years since his mother had done such a thing.

He reached up and grasped one of her hands, squeezing it. "Try to rest."

"I'll try. But it's a mother's duty to worry about her children. *All* of them." She gazed at him meaningfully before she left him alone.

He would not let her down. He would not let Rafe die.

~

CHARLES OPENED the door to his chamber and brushed the dust of the road off his clothing. Every muscle felt as coiled tight as a snake ready to spring. The grippe was normally not something to be worried about, but when he'd arrived on the doctor's doorstep the man's face had paled when he'd reported Rafe's symptoms.

"Is everything all right, my lord?" Linley was there in the shadows, polishing his shoes with a cloth as he sat in a chair.

"Mr. Lennox has fallen ill, and Ashton's damned worried about it. So am I." He scrubbed his face with a hand, trying to smooth the worry lines he felt forming there. "Linley, lad, did my watch ever turn up? Those rascals from the tenant farms filched it from my room, I'm sure of it."

"I haven't looked, my lord." Linley was studying the boots intently, rubbing far harder on them than was necessary. Charles came over and gripped the young man's hands to stop him.

"Easy, boy, you'll rub holes in the leather. Why don't you run downstairs and fetch something to eat? I know you forget most of the time. So off with you. I'm sure the cook will have leftover tarts from tonight's dinner." He patted Linley's shoulder, and with a reluctant smile, the boy stood and set the boots aside and left the room.

Charles scanned the room, then searched his drawers. Still no watch. It would be nice if at least one good thing happened to him today, but that didn't seem to be his fate. With a frustrated sigh, he threw himself down upon the bed. Something hard jabbed into his shoulder blades where he landed. He rolled over and moved the pillow back an inch to find a gleaming gold pocket watch.

At first he felt relief, but that soon changed. "This isn't mine. And it isn't working..." He was about to put it on the small table beside his bed when he froze. Something about this seemed familiar.

A memory of the night that he and Avery took Audrey Sheridan out on the town to start teaching her some of Avery's trade in spy work flashed through him like quicksilver. *Avery at the quiet little pub table where they wouldn't be disturbed, holding out a strange device that looked like a pocket watch...but it wasn't. Audrey's eyes gleaming with keen interest as she reached for it and opened it. A simple clock face was displayed until Avery pressed the latch a second time and a false bottom opened. Audrey turned the piece over and noticed the opposite side had a circular pattern of strange symbols and letters.*

"What is it?" she asked.

"A cipher decoder. A select few of us use them to decode letters. They are quite rare. The ring of symbols can be adjusted to match new letters. At the top of any correspondence we will match one letter and symbol in the top corner and once you have this you can mimic the matching pattern and decode the entire letter."

Charles pressed the latch and the false bottom appeared. "What in the blazes..." How had a cipher decoder ended up in his bedchamber? And more importantly, who had left it here? He hastily tucked the watch into his dresser drawer beneath some neatly folded shirts. That was a mystery he would have to solve once Rafe was better. Ashton would be too worried about his brother to focus on this new mystery.

Still…

Charles stared at the drawer, a sense of dread building inside him. Something didn't feel right about any of this.

~

SOMETHING WAS DEFINITELY NOT RIGHT.

Rosalind stood in the center of Ashton's empty bedchamber. It surprised her that she was bothered by his absence. She should have enjoyed the quiet, and yet she longed for his intense gaze and the way he made her feel as if she were the only person in the world.

That was one thing she hadn't realized she would enjoy, being the sole focus of a man's attention. Perhaps it was because he was genuinely interested in her and had no wish to hurt or use her— he just wanted her. With Ashton, the world seemed to halt and it was just the two of them, even when they were quarreling.

After his departure in the middle of dinner, she'd assumed he'd gone to see to his brother but would likely return. Then Charles had made his apologies, as had Lady Lennox shortly after dinner was over. Given their worried looks before they'd left, Rosalind had sensed something was wrong but wasn't in a position to pry. She'd refused to change out of her clothes and sent Claire to bed so that she might wait up for him. She jumped when the chamber door opened, but it was only Ashton's valet.

"My apologies, Your Ladyship."

"It's all right, Lowell. Where is Lord Lennox?"

The young valet's expression was somber. "Tending to his brother. He's taken ill with the grippe. The doctor told His Lordship we aren't to be in Mr. Rafe's room because of concerns the illness could spread. His Lordship is seeing to his brother himself.

I was told to bring him some clothes, but I am not supposed to open the door."

Lowell's hands shook as he collected a few items. It was obvious the young man was terrified. She straightened her shoulders, and with a little nod to herself she made a decision to help him.

Rosalind approached him and held out her hands. "Allow me to take them, Mr. Lowell."

"But—"

"It will be fine. Lord Lennox won't know you didn't leave them. I'm soft-footed when I need to be." She lifted her skirts and showed him a slippered foot. "Now, let me have those. Which way is Rafe's room?" She collected the clothes and received her directions before she left Lowell to tidy up the chamber.

Following the instructions from the valet, she found Rafe's room and set the clothes upon the floor outside the door. Then she knocked and rushed to the nearest alcove, hiding behind a marble statue of a half-naked nymph fleeing the arms of the god Zeus.

The door opened and Ashton appeared, his face pale as he collected the clothing and disappeared back inside. She was loath to admit it, but she was worried for him and for his brother, even if he was a damned highwayman. She knew enough of foolish brothers to know that when you loved one, you could not lose him without breaking your heart. And in some ways, she had lost three. She didn't wish that pain on Ashton.

Perhaps by the morning all would be well. She crept back down the hall, her heart sinking. Even though she despised what Rafe had done, she did not truly wish him ill. She had shot him, after all. Some might call the matter settled. And she certainly did not wish to see Ashton suffer by watching his brother endure such a harsh illness.

I wish there was more I could do.

"What are you doing, Lady Melbourne?" Lord Lonsdale's voice

made her jump. He stepped out of a doorway, holding a glass of brandy. His hair was tousled and his waistcoat was gone.

"I brought Ashton some clothes. He's taking care of his brother. Have you heard?" she asked.

Charles nodded. "Influenza. Can be a nasty business. Rafe's too stubborn to let himself get worse. I have faith that he'll pull through."

The words sounded hollow and forced, making the silence between them that much more uncomfortable.

"May I have a word with you? Privately?" He nodded at the doorway he was standing in.

"But it's private here. We are alone." She knew enough of men not to go anywhere too secluded with one who was intoxicated and didn't like her.

Charles shook his head. "In a house like this? No hallway is ever empty. Please." He stepped back, allowing her to pass by him. Thankfully it was not a bedchamber, but a parlor.

Rosalind took a seat at a lacquered card table and Charles joined her. He set his glass down and nodded at the brandy. "Would you care for some?"

"No, thank you."

She waited, unsure of what Charles wanted to say. Given what she'd overhead before dinner, she was unlikely to appreciate whatever would follow.

"I won't beat about the bush, Lady Melbourne. I've had far too much to drink this evening, and it's left me without my usual eloquence of speech. So I do beg your forgiveness." Even as he said this, she didn't miss the shrewd gleam in his eyes, something that told her he wasn't as foxed as he wished her to believe. He was one of Ashton's friends, after all. Ashton was a clever man and would only keep similar company.

"Please, speak what is on your mind, Lord Lonsdale."

"You and Ashton are..." He waved a hand. "Well, you are at odds, aren't you?" It wasn't so much a question as an observation.

Rosalind tilted her head to one side. "If we are, what business is it of yours?" She didn't ask this waspishly, but curiously, knowing what his answer would likely be.

"The man is more a brother to me than my own brother. I'd protect him with my life, from any threats. And *you* are posing a threat, Lady M. Quite a threat." His eyes flicked up and down her body.

She bristled. "I'm not a threat. He's a threat to me."

Charles chuckled. "Because he holds the reins, eh? But we both know what a wild creature you are. I'd rather have you free than risk my friend by letting you remain captured. A polecat bites when cornered."

He was comparing her to a polecat?

Rosalind met him with a level gaze. "Fortunate for you, my lord, that I'm able to maintain control of my temper and my claws. Now, what is it you wish to say?"

"You need funds to buy your freedom, do you not?" He folded his hands on the table, and despite the half-empty brandy bottle she noticed on the mantle behind him, she had a feeling his wits were quite sharp.

"Yes."

"What if you were able to receive those funds? Would you walk away from Ashton and his marriage bargain?"

If Rosalind hadn't been prepared, she would have let the sudden surprise flood through her. But thankfully she was able to bottle her reaction.

"Are you offering this out of charity? Or do you have some negotiations of your own in mind?" she asked.

"The only price for my buying your debts and seeing to your freedom would be that you never compete with him again. Walk away from any competing interests and bow out if he becomes involved in a bidding war with you. I want him to lose interest in the joy he finds in challenging you."

Her instinct was to tell Charles to go to blazes, because she never took anything from anyone that she did not earn. Yet the gift of her freedom back was tempting…too tempting. As much as she wanted to accept, she knew she could not. It would still be another form of servitude by playing to his tune of when to bow out and leave Lennox unchallenged. Still, it was worth seeing how determined Charles was to play this game.

"I suppose you want this to be kept a secret from him if I were to accept?"

"If Ash ever asked me, I would deny it until my dying breath."

"Why?" That was something she could not understand. "You know he means to control me and my property. Why would you, as one of his dearest friends, act in such a way as to prevent him from claiming what he desires?"

Charles reached for his glass and sipped, staring at her coolly. There was a hint of anger and a sliver of fear deep in his gray eyes. He didn't know he'd revealed that, but it was there.

"Because he is acting the fool. He has some silly notion that he'll be as happy as Godric, Lucien and Cedric, that he can buy you and in so doing buy your love. I know better than anyone that love is not a commodity that should be bought or sold."

Rosalind shifted restlessly as she felt his intense scrutiny settle on her once more.

"*Can* your love be bought?"

She stared at him. "It cannot. Love is something that is given. Sometimes it is earned, but it can never be bought. Affection, perhaps. Loyalty, certainly. But never love."

"I do not wish to see Ash hurt by this marriage scheme." He set the glass down and waited.

"As much as the man infuriates me, I do not wish to hurt him either. Especially not at the expense of my own happiness."

"Then you'll accept my offer?"

Rosalind weighed his offer against everything else that had happened in the last few days. The survivor in her wanted to leap at the chance to be free of Ashton's control. But she would also no longer have him in her life.

She was a woman of honor. She had promised to abide by the terms of their wager. If she walked away and later tried to resurrect the passion that was beginning to burn between them, it wouldn't happen. Pride and distrust would keep Ashton from opening himself up to her, and she would feel like a lowly cheat.

And if she was being entirely honest with herself, she didn't *want* to walk away. Ashton was proving to be a far better man than she'd assumed him to be. He could be sweet and playful, not simply dominating and seductive. Aside from her property, he had no desire to crush her or destroy who she was.

This might be my last chance at love.

Yes, he would own her, but if she in turn owned his heart, what would the rest matter? She, after all, could tell him no, could turn him away if she didn't wish to be with him. He'd made that clear, that he would never take anything from her that she wasn't willing to give. It was what made him so dangerously seductive. He promised to give her everything she desired, and it turned out what she wanted most of all was him.

"Well, what's it to be, Lady Melbourne?" Charles asked. A smug smile hovered about his lips.

She stood, walked up to him and took his glass of brandy, and with a confident smile, she tipped his glass back and finished the drink before setting it back in his startled hands. "I'm afraid I cannot accept. I'm honor bound by my promise. Unless he wishes to cry off, I'm to marry him at a date of our choosing."

Charles's hands curled into fists, his knuckles white as he got to his feet. "Are you certain? I could pay above your debts. Whatever else you desire. Name it and it shall be yours."

"I'm sorry, but there is nothing you could give me." The things she once wanted—love, a happy life, children—those had always been phantoms of the past, castles made of clouds. Yet if she stayed with Ashton, she may have one more chance to chase those dreams—and perhaps even catch them.

"You would condemn yourself to a loveless marriage?" Charles asked softly.

She nodded. "You seem so certain that love is impossible between us. I believe that we might come to love, if we are lucky." *And perhaps I have already.*

Charles frowned. "I won't let you go through with this. Ashton deserves someone better. A woman who loves him."

"Everyone deserves love," she agreed. "But he has made this choice, and we are bound by his decision. Goodnight, my lord." She brushed past him and exited the room, thankful when he didn't try to stop her.

Once outside, she clutched her stomach, trying to catch her breath. She had not realized that during the entire discussion her body had tensed, to the point where she now bordered on exhaustion.

There was something frightening about Charles. Not that she was afraid he'd harm her, but it was as though he was haunted by his past. That pain lingered in his eyes, secrets that drove a man to desperate ends. A man like that would do anything to protect the people he loved. Like a hungry wolf among sheep, he required constant watching.

I must tread carefully.

CHAPTER 22

*B*rock Kincade stood at the edge of the cemetery, staring out at the freshly upturned dirt of his father's grave. Moonlight washed the cemetery in pale cream and opalescent white. The carved headstones formed shadows almost as black as the night itself. But Brock was no longer afraid. The creature that had frightened him since he was a child was gone. Forever.

His horse gave an impatient huff and stamped his hooves, no doubt anxious to be back in the stables with a blanket on his back and fresh oats in his bucket.

"All right, you lazy beast," Brock muttered and stroked a palm over the animal's neck as he mounted up.

He departed the quiet churchyard and trotted back up the winding hill to Castle Kincade, the shallow moat filled with rainwater and the ancient wooden bridge lowered to allow passage into the keep.

It had been more than a hundred years since the castle had demanded defense, but like an old wolf, it was crouched and ready to do so at a moment's notice. Soon it would be a happy place again, one of joy and life. The crumbling towers would be restored, and Rosalind could come home.

As Brock trotted over the bridge, Aiden rushed out to meet him.

"Thank God! We've been waiting for you. You must come!" Aiden waved a groom over to take the horse.

"What's the matter?" He dismounted and followed Aiden inside the castle. His younger brother was paler than the night their father died.

"We have a visitor. Rosalind's in trouble—"

"Trouble?" Brock growled. They'd had enough trouble as it was and didn't need more, but he would do whatever was needed to help his sister.

"Aye, come inside." Aiden led the way to the one of the few rooms in the castle still suitable for guests. It was a parlor with outdated furnishings, but it had a working fireplace and windows that weren't broken. Their father hadn't seen much point in doing anything but the most minimal and necessary of repairs. He'd kept what small fortune they had locked tight, and it cost a lot to keep a castle in working order.

Brodie was waiting for them inside with two men. One was tall with russet-brown hair and brown eyes, eyes too sharp to miss anything despite the warmth in them. He was handsome, Brock supposed, but he might forget what the man looked like the moment he left the room.

The other was dark-haired and his eyes were almost black. There was something about him that gave Brock a prickling sense of unease. Both men exuded a powerful presence, but the dark-eyed man was clearly in charge. He was English, judging by his dress, which was enough to make Brock uneasy. Perhaps that was it, simply nerves putting him on edge.

"Lord Kincade." The dark-eyed man bowed to Brock. "I'm afraid I bear ill tidings."

"My brother mentioned our sister," Brock said.

"Yes. I am Sir Hugo Waverly, and this is Mr. Outis. I have been a business partner with Lady Melbourne for some time now. She had been engaging with a common rival of ours for the last several months in business dealings, and it seems the man has gone to extreme and ungentlemanly measures."

Brock continued to study the man. His fine but not extravagant clothes. His cultured voice that was smooth. Maybe he had misjudged the man. Distrust of the *Sassenach* was something every Scot was born with.

"What sort of measures?" Brodie stood behind the back of one of the chairs and leaned against it, his eyes narrowed.

"This other gentleman has every intention of gaining control of her money, her property *and* her life. He's a vile brute and will most likely kill her after he's married her and secured her fortune. She is at this moment trapped at his estate, waiting for him to arrange their marriage. Already he has procured a special license. I'm afraid the law is powerless to do anything to stop him, and as a friend of your sister, I knew I had to come and tell you at once."

"A man is holding Rosalind against her will?" Aiden glanced in Brock's direction.

The man named Hugo nodded. "He's a baron by the name of Lennox. I can tell you everything I know about him, but it's of the utmost importance that you rescue her before he does her any harm."

"Even if we are too late and they've married?" Brodie asked.

Hugo met each of the three brothers' stares. "Make no mistake. He *will* break her spirit as well as her body. You must do whatever is necessary to save her. You should bring her back here, where you can protect her. But I must warn you, he will come after her. And he won't be alone. He will bring his friends with him."

Brock and his brothers knew that the law could offer no protection to their sister, not from a husband and certainly not from a bloody noble. If she needed protection, they would have to be the ones to provide it.

"Thank you for coming to warn us." Brock held out a hand to the man.

Waverly accepted it. "Your sister is a lovely woman. My only desire is to help save her. I don't want that bastard Lennox doing her any harm." He exchanged glances with the man beside him. "I would advise you to hire some more men in the local villages to help protect your sister until cooler heads can prevail, or until he is suitably discouraged. Lennox and his men will be fast on your heels."

Brodie nudged Brock with his elbow. "I suppose we could use the help."

Brock considered it. "This Lennox fellow... He's truly a force to be reckoned with?"

Waverly bowed his head, visibly upset. "You have no idea. He's killed several men over the last few years. Men who got in the way of his plans."

"Brock, we have to save Rosalind," Aiden said.

Brock waved a hand. "Aye, we will." He faced Waverly. "Tell me where to find this baron and my sister."

Waverly nodded grimly. "I have a man stationed at his residence and will notify him to expect you."

Brock was puzzled. "You have someone working for him?"

"Fearing the worst, I've been keeping an eye on Lennox since your sister and I began to compete with him. My man will be able to assist you in gaining access to the house and your sister. I suggest you remove her under the cover of darkness and bring her back to Scotland."

"Thank you," Brodie said.

Waverly nodded. "Lennox must pay for what he's done, and I am willing to lend my services to bring him down."

～

ROSALIND BARELY SLEPT that night alone in Ashton's bed. She

missed the man, his warmth, his laugh, his touch. The scent of him clung to the sheets like a ghost lover. An empty bed had never bothered her before, but it did now because she knew what she was longing for. Her sweet and seductive baron.

As dawn peeped in through the windows, Rosalind crawled out of bed and pulled the cord for Claire. It was going to be a long day if she continued to feel this way. She jumped when the door opened, far too soon for it to have been Claire.

Ashton stood there, looking as bad as she felt.

"Rosalind?" He blinked, keeping his distance by remaining in the doorway. He was pale, his blue eyes heavy with shadows. "What are you doing here?"

"You said I was to stay in your chambers..." Had she done something wrong?

He walked a step farther into the room, dragging a hand through his hair. "I thought perhaps you'd take advantage and leave while I was seeing to Rafe."

She bristled. "I made a promise to you, my lord. I would not leave unless you broke our agreement first. Besides, someone has to look after you while you look after Rafe."

Ashton gave a half smile. "I'd kiss you for that, but I'm afraid you mustn't come any closer. I don't wish to endanger you..." His voice drifted off, and he braced himself against the wall with one hand.

"Ashton..."

"I'm fine. Just a lack of sleep. Please, just a moment." He drew in a deep breath. "Perhaps a...chair." He took another few steps forward, and Rosalind saw his body listing to one side.

She leapt toward him without thinking, catching him by the waist as he collapsed. They both toppled to the ground. Panicking, she rolled him over and gasped. He was unconscious.

"My lady!" Claire gasped from the doorway.

"Claire, please fetch Lady Lennox at once! He's ill!"

"What about you? You shouldn't be so close."

"Someone needs to tend to him. Can you help me lift him onto the bed?"

"Of course I can." But Rosalind didn't miss the concern in her voice as she aided Rosalind in lifting Ashton up onto the bed. This malady was striking fast enough to discourage anyone from getting too close.

"Fetch me a bowl of water, clean cloths and some clothes to wear. And have that doctor brought back to the house at once."

Rosalind was barely aware of her lady's maid running off; she was focused completely on Ashton. She perched on the edge of his bed and brushed his hair out of his eyes. His dark-gold lashes fluttered, and he shifted restlessly on the sheets.

"Rosalind…" He breathed her name in such a desperate tone that her heart ached.

She stroked his face with a gentle hand. "I'm here."

Ashton's eyes opened. He stared up at her through pain-fogged pupils. "Rafe. I need to—" He tried to sit up, but she gently pressed him down onto the bed again.

"You must rest, my lord. I will tend to Rafe."

Ashton chuckled, but it turned into a cough. "Why does the thought of that make me worried?"

Rosalind laughed, though she couldn't hide the strain in her voice. "Because I'll be tempted to prod his injured arm to pay him back for robbing my coach?" she suggested.

"Yes, that's it exactly." Ashton's lips formed a weary smile before his eyes closed once again.

Claire returned and set a washbasin on the table beside the bed and handed her a set of cloths.

"Thank you, Claire. Please tell Mr. Lowell I can tend to his master if he's worried about catching the grippe."

Ashton stirred again at the name. "Don't be too hard on Lowell. His mother died from influenza when he was a boy. He's frightened of it. You ought to be too, Rosalind. I don't want anyone else falling ill."

She dampened a cloth and laid it upon his brow. "It's too late to argue with me, my lord. You should know by now that I do as I please."

He sighed, his eyelids dropping again, and soon his breathing deepened with sleep.

Rosalind shifted her position so she could lean against the back of the bed and watch him. It would be so easy to run away back to London. But she couldn't abandon him, not when he needed her most. But it was more than that. She wanted to stay because, against her better judgment, she'd come to care for the bloody Englishman. All his arrogance, pride, stubbornness and pragmatism she'd despised were traits she possessed as well. They were cut from the same cloth.

She curled her fingers around his and gave his hand a squeeze.

"Be strong, Ashton," she said softly. "I wish for you to fulfill our wager. As silly as it is, I believe we just might find a measure of happiness together. When we aren't quarrelling, that is." Rosalind smiled and caressed his cheek. He turned his face into her touch. His lips moved but no words came out. His skin burned her to the touch. Such a fever…

"Please, Ashton. You must get through this." *You must.*

~

THE DREAMS BORN of a fever were always those of a nightmare. Ashton struggled to escape the clawing darkness, but the illness was too powerful. The fever swept him away, into memories that haunted him even when he was awake.

The haze of the cigar smoke in the gambling hell was thick enough that he could wave a hand through the air and disturb the clouds wafting about the men's heads. The sickly sweet scent was overpowering, and it made Ashton's eyes sting. They'd be red-rimmed by morning if he was forced to stay here much longer. But he had to find his father.

"Pardon me." He coughed as he tapped the nearest man playing faro. "Have you seen Lord Lennox? Tall man, light hair, narrow moustache."

The man shrugged off his hand but nodded at a distant door. "Aye, I know him. Through there, last I saw of him. But he's not alone."

Ashton expected that. The overdue notices and accounts his father owed had been piling up on his study desk at the townhouse for months.

"Thank you," he said, but the man was already focused on his game again.

A woman with hair too red to be natural sauntered up to him. "Should you be in here, boy?" Her gown, a clashing maroon, was cut low enough that very little of her figure was left to the imagination.

"Pardon?" Ashton tried to step away from the woman. He was but fifteen, a young man still, but old enough to know a lightskirt was trouble and costly.

"Still a babe," the woman cooed and brushed the edge of a lacy fan down his cheek.

He shoved the fan away. "Do not touch me like that again, madam," he warned. "I'm not a child."

For a moment the woman looked startled, and then she laughed. "A coy one. How charming. You like to be the master, dearie? That's a game I can play, for the right price." Her hand slid down to his hip, then attempted to move over to his groin.

Ashton caught her wrist. "My father, Lord Lennox, is with one of your women. I want to know where he is immediately."

The prostitute cleared her throat and snatched her wrist back.

"Oh, fine. He's in the farthest room on the left." She jerked her head at a distant door.

Ashton squared his shoulders and crossed the crowded gambling area to where the private chambers were. When he reached the darkened back room on the left, his hand trembled as he lifted it to knock.

There was no answer from within.

"Father? It's Ashton!" He hit the door again. He heard a groan as he tried the door handle. It opened and Ashton stared in agony at the scene.

There was no woman in the room. Only his father, lying on the bed, clutching his head in pain.

"Father!" He rushed over to the bed, but when he tried to help his father sit up, Ashton was struck hard across the face.

"Leave me, boy!" the man snapped.

Ashton put a hand to his face; the skin burning where the back of his father's hand had caught him off guard. His father had never hit him before.

"Father, please," he begged. "Come home. Mother needs you. We all need you."

Lord Lennox stumbled to his feet. "Damned whore took my coin purse." He patted his pockets. "Pocket watch, too."

"Father..."Ashton still touched his face where he'd been struck, but his father wasn't listening. He left the room, tripping over his feet into the hall. Ashton hurried after him, dodging the gaming tables. His father, although clearly inebriated, was still moving faster than Ashton.

Several other men shouted and cursed as Ashton's father bowled into them.

"Careful, man!" Someone shoved Lord Lennox toward the front door.

Ashton tripped and fell when a cane swung out and caught his boot tip. A young man with dark hair and black eyes laughed coldly. "Watch it, boy!"

"My apologies," Ashton muttered, scrambling to get back to his feet. His father vanished out the door.

"Father!" He reached the door in time to see his father lose his footing on the sidewalk and tumble into the street.

Time seemed to slow down. A carriage raced through the dark street and struck Lord Lennox. The horse screamed, and it drowned out the shouts of the man it trampled. Ashton's legs were rooted to the ground. The breath rushed out of his lungs. He was unable to move or speak as chaos erupted around him. Men rushed out to aid the distressed driver of the carriage.

"Dead! The man is dead!" Someone's cry cut through the fog of shock

and horror that held Ashton prisoner. He raced down the steps and skidded to a stop a few feet away from his father's crumpled body.

"Who is it?" the driver demanded.

Numb, Ashton stepped forward. "He's my father."

"He was your father," the dark-haired young man with the cane said. "Drunken fool." The man walked back into the club, leaving Ashton to stand there, lost, as his world crashed down around him.

"Ashton, please, be strong." A sweet voice danced around the corners of the pain flooding his head and his heart.

Tears stained his cheeks, but he felt too weak to lift his limbs. Darkness captured him again, dragging him down to where even fevered nightmares could not reach him.

CHAPTER 23

*S*weat coated Ashton's brow, and his fevered murmurs broke Rosalind's heart. She held her breath each time Ashton's chest rose and fell, fearing it would be his last.

The illness had claimed another three lives in the village since Ashton and Rafe had fallen ill three days ago. Terror had swept through Lennox House, but Rosalind had refused to leave Ashton's side. Her heart lodged in her throat whenever he lay too still in his sheets.

He had tossed about restlessly for the last hour before sinking into another frightening silence. His breathing had become shallow and his skin clammy to the touch. Every muscle in Rosalind's body tensed as she studied him, searching for any sign that he was slipping away from her.

You won't leave me, Lennox. Not like this. I demand a fair fight with you, you coward. I want... She prayed he could hear her thoughts. She was too afraid to utter them aloud. *I want to marry you.*

"How is he?" Regina stood by the doorway, her eyes red.

The two of them had become Rafe and Ashton's caretakers. Regina hadn't wanted anyone else to risk exposure, and Rosalind had agreed. They'd sent the younger servants away, and only the most stubborn had insisted upon staying. Rosalind was barely aware of anything happening outside of Ashton's bedroom.

There was some strange part of her that felt that if she were to lose focus on him for even one minute, she would lose him. She felt as though her strength was helping him to stay with her. It was foolish, but she wanted so desperately to believe she could do something to help him through this.

"He's sleeping again. I cannot tell if he's better when he's still or when he's restless." Her voice was a little shaky, the barest hint of the storm raging inside her heart. Rosalind's hands trembled as she removed the cloth on his brow and replaced it with a fresh one.

Regina came in and sat down next to Rosalind.

Rosalind leaned into Ashton's mother, needing just one minute to rest and recover. She and Regina had become close these past two days, like soldiers defending a fort entirely on their own. They had learned to read the evidence of tears in each other's eyes, the language of sorrow and grief, the flicker of hope and the glint of raw determination to see these dark days through.

She had always felt so alone after her mother had died, but now, facing losing Ashton, she'd longed for someone to take care of her in these rare moments of weakness. Regina had done just that, having seen to her care without a thought to herself. It was something she'd seen glimpses of in Ashton. That sense of self-lessness toward those he loved.

Ashton's mother touched the back of her hand to Rosalind's forehead, testing for a fever. "How are you?"

Rosalind sighed wearily. "I've survived much hardship in my life, but I've never felt so helpless as I do now."

When her father had been in a foul mood, he'd sometimes lock her in her room for days without food and only a pitcher of water. But those days paled in comparison to this battle, which she could not fight herself. It was up to Ashton to survive this on his own.

She could only watch and wait and do what little she could to make him comfortable.

"Your previous husband, was he…" Regina trailed off.

"No," Rosalind said. "Henry was a good man. My father was a brute. When at last I ran away, Henry rescued me from that life." She reached out and brushed a lock of Ashton's hair back from his face. "But this—this dreadful waiting—it's far worse."

"I know, my child. I know. We wish to fight the battles of the ones we love the most, but often we cannot." Regina curled an arm around her shoulders, giving her a sweet hug. Her mother used to do that, she remembered, many years ago, when life had not been so full of pain and shadows.

Ashton's lips moved, making Rosalind and Regina tense, but the words weren't comprehensible.

"He said something about his father earlier," Rosalind said.

Regina swallowed and nodded. "He was barely a young man when his father died. He doesn't talk about it, but I know he still suffers. He was there, you see, when it happened. It must haunt him beyond reason to have witnessed something so terrible at so young an age." Her eyes darkened with the weight of tears. "I see so much of my Malcolm in him, and it reminds me of what I lost. I have always been hard on him, and that is my sin to bear. I only wish I'd told him how much I do love him." Ashton's mother suddenly began to cry, and Rosalind hugged her back, offering the last bit of her own strength.

Rosalind stroked Ashton's arm. "He has a great heart. One he hides. He isn't cold. He can be insufferable and stubborn, but he's loving and warmhearted too. I misjudged him."

Regina sniffed. "It seems I have been a worse mother than I thought."

Rosalind shook her head. "No, I'm sure you've been a wonderful mother."

"I've spent years taking out my anger on him." She bowed her head. "I wish he knew how sorry I was for everything." She stood and walked over to her son to press a kiss to his forehead.

Rosalind rubbed her fingertips along his jaw. "If there's one thing I know about this man, he's too mule-headed to surrender to an illness."

Ashton's mother nodded but didn't speak.

Emotions whirled through Rosalind as she watched Ashton sleep. She'd hated his determination to own her and to win every battle before, but now she felt she was beginning to understand him. He was a man trying to take control of his life because he'd been so young when everything had spun out of control. He'd watched his father die, and his family responsibilities in the aftermath had weighed heavily upon him. It was no wonder that he was so set on having his way. It was the only way he felt secure.

Just like me...

When Ashton's hand suddenly twitched, Rosalind curled her fingers around his.

"I'm so happy he met you. You're the right woman for him."

Rosalind was moved by her words and the sentiment behind them. She wanted to be worthy of Ashton and wanted his family to welcome her as a worthy match for him.

"Thank you, Lady Lennox."

"Mother?" Ashton spoke, his voice hoarse.

Rosalind and Regina both turned to him. His eyes were open, but his gaze was still murky.

"I'm here, my boy, oh my darling boy." Regina brushed fresh tears from her eyes as she touched his forehead and smiled, her hands trembling.

Rosalind had trouble breathing. He'd asked for his mother, and she shouldn't have been jealous, but she had hoped for him to speak *her* name.

I should go. He doesn't want me here. She started to get up from the bed, but Ashton caught her wrist.

"Stay, *please*," he whispered. "I need you here." His blue eyes were filled with the echoes of his haunting dreams, but she saw his need for her as well.

He wants me to stay. But what she had really wanted to admit to herself was, *I am wanted.*

"See?" Rosalind said to Regina, a smile curving her lips despite her concern. "Stubborn man. I knew no illness would keep him abed for long."

Regina chuckled, and Ashton nearly smiled.

"I see you two have been bonding over my many flaws." It was a mere rasp of a reply, but she could see a glint of merriment in his tired eyes. He squeezed her wrist.

"Oh my sweet boy." Regina leaned over to kiss his forehead again. "I feared I might lose you." Regina's voice broke a little, and Ashton blinked slowly, a tear dripping down onto the pillow.

"Mother, please. I'd rather you be angry with me than to have you cry."

She sniffed but straightened herself. "I must tell you something, Ashton. It has weighed on me all these years, and you deserve to hear me say it. I've been a wretched creature, simply wretched toward you, my darling child. I..." She paused but waved a hand when Ashton tried to interrupt her. "You remind me so much of your father. You have his looks, his intelligence, his warm heart, but...but what I mistook for coldness all these years, it was strength. You are a good man, Ashton, and a good son." Regina had kept herself quite firm as she spoke, but at last a little sob choked her throat. "You are *my* son and I love you. Please forgive me for being so harsh on you all these years."

Rosalind leaned against the bedpost close to Ashton's head, and she saw him struggle for words. He still clutched her hand and was squeezing it hard now, as though what he was hearing was too good to be true. Had her father ever uttered such words it would have astonished her.

"There's nothing to forgive, Mother," Ashton promised, and after a quiet moment of simply gazing at his mother in a weary contentedness Rosalind suspected he hadn't felt since he was a child, he sighed and smiled. His eyes brightened, and he tried to sit up. "Rafe...how is he?"

"A little better than you. Sitting up in bed and taking food. I should get back to him now that you are awake."

"Mother, if you fall ill, I'll be most upset. I asked for no one else to tend to Rafe."

"Yes, well, someone had to." Regina sniffed. "Rosalind was quite insistent she wished to take care of you, and since we were the only two brave enough to risk tending to you both, I took charge of Rafe. No one else has fallen ill in the house. I believe we may be safe."

Ashton shook his head. "I won't feel safe until a week has passed with no one else falling ill."

"You may fret all you like, but for now you will do so from your bed." She leaned in again and kissed his cheek. "I must go see to your brother. Get well, my boy." She patted Rosalind's shoulder and exited the chambers.

Rosalind shifted her feet, which ached from standing so long. Now that Ashton had come around, she felt exhausted and oddly exposed.

"I..." Her voice trailed off, but when he smiled at her, it was a soft, dreamy expression, the sort a man might have after a long night of bliss between the sheets. Not unlike the one she had whenever she recalled being in his arms.

"Come here, sweetheart. You look ready to faint on your feet." He patted the other side of the bed where there was a place for her to sit down.

She walked around the bed and climbed up to sit beside him.

"Would you mind terribly if you helped me to sit up? My back is aching terribly after lying down so long," Ashton said.

She eyed him, his pale skin and glassy eyes. "Are you strong enough?"

He nodded. "I can lie back on the pillows. I need to be up. Feeling as weak as a kitten doesn't suit me," he growled.

She chuckled. "Considering a few minutes ago you were suffering fevered dreams, I think this is a vast improvement. You shouldn't rush your own healing."

"Fevered dreams?" He sighed heavily, and the sound twisted Rosalind's heart.

She gripped his arm and helped lift him up. "Yes, about your father."

"My father?" His expression darkened, but Rosalind didn't want to upset him, not after everything he'd endured. She leaned into him, kissing his cheek.

"I'm so relieved you are better. You gave me quite a fright." She tucked her head into his shoulder, careful not to lie too heavily against his side.

"Me too. The grippe is a damned nuisance." He glanced around the room and found the clock on the mantle. "Good Lord, is that the time?"

"Yes," Rosalind said. "You've been sick for three days."

"We still have a wedding to arrange, and the rest of the League will be descending upon this house at any minute."

"Oh? What for?" Rosalind's heart thudded against her ribs. The idea of them all coming here at once made her strangely nervous. What if they were like Charles and not at all pleased that she and Ashton were to be married? What if she never fit into their company the way the other wives had? Everyone seemed so at ease with one another, and those friendships ran deep. She was a stranger to them and couldn't ever see herself fitting in, not when Ashton wasn't marrying her for love.

Is my love for him enough for both of us?

"They wish to attend our wedding. It's tradition. I hope you don't mind."

She laughed even though her heart still ached. "I suppose keeping them all out of our business is impossible."

"It is," Ashton agreed. "You've met Emily, so you know that little woman always gets her way."

Rosalind giggled, remembering how well she and Emily had gotten along. "Yes, I quite believe she does." *At least I shall have one ally in the League of Rogues.*

Someone knocked at the door of the room.

"Who is it?" Rosalind asked.

"Charles."

"Don't let him in," Ashton warned. "I'm not yet well enough. I don't wish to make him ill."

Rosalind walked to the door and opened it a crack. Charles stared down at her from the crack in the doorway.

"He doesn't want to see you, my lord. He's afraid you'll become ill as well."

She started to close the door, but Charles shoved his arm through the slit and used his considerable strength to force it open.

"Charles, no!" Ashton coughed and tried to leave the bed.

"Bloody fool." Charles growled and rushed to catch him. He glared at Rosalind when she tried to help put Ashton back into bed. Charles's fine clothes were rumpled, and he seemed as exhausted as she felt, with dark circles under his eyes. While she had been tending to Ashton, he had helped keep the Lennox household running and had overseen the construction of the tenant farmer houses. Both he and Jonathan had been incredibly helpful.

"Make yourself useful, Lady Melbourne. Fetch some broth and bread from the kitchens. I need to speak to Ashton. *Alone.*"

"But—"

"It is League business and none of your affair," Charles said.

Rather than bow to Charles's insufferable attitude, Rosalind looked to Ashton. He met her gaze, his expression soft and understanding.

"I'm sorry, sweetheart, but I should speak with him. I promise I won't keep you out of my secrets forever." He winced, then added, "Broth does sound rather good. Would you mind?" Ashton's chagrined expression was the only reason she agreed to leave. League business or not, she would not have backed down to Charles unless Ashton asked her to.

Rosalind left the bedchamber but froze when she overheard Ashton speak.

"Why did you send her away, Charles?"

"Because she's our enemy. I just received a letter from London from the men you had looking into Rosalind's accounts. She and Waverly are more deeply connected than we suspected. They have more than one business venture together, and there were letters in her offices to him regarding reports of your interests in various investments and your companies. They were working together to spy on you, and through *you* to spy on *us*. I warned you that you weren't thinking clearly when it came to her, and I was right."

Waverly? They knew about him? He'd befriended her shortly before her husband had passed away. She'd been impressed with his knowledge of business and his keen eye for acquisitions. It had been he who had put her on the path to buying companies from under Ashton's nose. They'd communicated frequently regarding various interests, but among them had been Ashton's business strategies. They'd shared a laugh over sending him in circles and depriving him of companies he wanted to purchase.

A sick feeling turned Rosalind's stomach. Waverly had never given any indication he'd had a *personal* history with Ashton. It was just business…wasn't it? But now that she looked back, she could see that Ashton always managed to come up in their conversations. By her own intentions, she'd assumed, but she realized now Hugo had said things to make her think of Ashton, and that had prompted the discussions nearly every time they met at her offices.

I've been played—on both sides. The nausea only grew inside her.

"What do you mean they're working together?" Ashton demanded.

"Your future bride has been hiding things from you. This, and more," Charles said.

Rosalind knew she shouldn't eavesdrop, but they were talking about her. She pressed herself flat against the wall beside the door, ears straining to pick up the conversation.

"Explain."

"This goes beyond her companies," Charles said. "Her father and Waverly knew each other ten years ago in Scotland."

"What on earth would Waverly be doing up there?" Ashton's voice was soft but concerned.

"No idea, but it couldn't have been anything good. And his claws have never left that family. Your *sweet* Rosalind"—Charles sneered the word—"has been writing directly to Waverly for nearly six months. Did you know about that? For all we know she could be sharing his bed or telling him all our secrets. Ash, this is serious. You must send her back to London. Sever ties with her and rip up that blasted license. We must close ranks before she becomes privy to anything Hugo can use against us."

"Bloody hell," Ashton groaned. "Don't you see? This is exactly why I *must* marry her. I can play the puppet master just as well as he can. She's falling in love with me, assuming she hasn't already. It won't be hard to turn her against him. We can use her against Hugo just as easily as he is using her against us."

An icy chill shot clear through Rosalind, leaving her unable to think beyond the cutting words. *A puppet? That's all I am to him? And Sir Hugo knew my father but never told me?* That coincidence filled her with unease. She'd trusted Waverly, and yet it seemed he'd been manipulating her to act against Ashton. But why?

"You think she's so enamored with you?"

Rosalind held her breath. Her blood pounded in her ears so hard it nearly drowned out their voices.

"I *know* she is. She cannot resist me. You forget, I was seducing women years before you, pup. I still know a trick or two."

An invisible blade pierced her heart. Ashton was playing her like a fiddle, and what made it hurt more was that he was right. She *was* falling in love with him. She could not stay here, not when she was a pawn in this private game they were playing. She had warned him that was the one thing she would not stand for.

He'd stolen her heart and broken his promise.

Rosalind blinked away tears and hardened her heart. She would not be a victim. Not again. *I will not stay here, not when I'm neither wanted nor loved.*

She would need Claire to help her pack her things, and then she'd leave.

~

BROCK MOTIONED for his brothers to stay close behind him as they snuck up to the terrace at the back of Lennox House. After three days of hard riding with barely any sleep, they'd managed to find the home of the man who held their sister captive.

Brock checked the pistol he held, hoping he wouldn't have to use it, but if Lennox or his friends tried to stop them, he would. He glanced at his two younger brothers, both holding their own pistols, their faces grim as they studied the expansive country house. Thankfully there were a few lights by the windows, which helped conceal them in the darkness while they searched for a way in. Hugo's man was supposed to leave a terrace door unlocked for them.

"We ought to split up once inside. Search every room until we find her. Then we meet where we tied the horses. If you come across any servants or members of the household, restrain them so they cannot sound the alarm." They would not kill anyone, not unless it was absolutely necessary.

Like dark wraiths they slipped into the house through the

terrace doors, wearing dark clothes and black domino masks. If anyone saw them, they'd need to conceal their identities as much as possible. Brock was not foolish enough to think that Lennox would not figure out who had taken Rosalind, but the deception would buy them some time.

Lennox House was so very different from the stark and cold Castle Kincade. The halls were furnished with art, oriental rugs and statues. It was opulent compared to Brock's musty rooms and dreary gray stone walls. He couldn't help but despise Lennox that much more for it. A brute like him who hurt women and took advantage of them didn't deserve to live in such a state of luxury.

Brock and his brothers paused as they reached the middle of the house, ears straining for the sounds of servants. The hour was late, and likely the servants were downstairs seeing to their own meals.

Brodie slipped past Brock and Aiden. "I'll go upstairs."

Aiden nodded down the current hall. "I'll check these rooms." Brock left him behind as he trod on silent feet to the hall on the opposite end of the house.

I hope the bastard hasn't locked her away. He wasn't sure he could break down a door without being overheard. Moving from room to room, he tested the handles, and each time the doors would creak open. Many were empty, and sheets covered the unused furniture. But the closer he got to the main hall, the rooms changing from bedrooms to parlors and drawing rooms, even a music room.

The last door before the hall greeted him with the distinctive and not unpleasant smell of musty books. A library? Brock nudged the door open wide enough to slide inside. One peek among the books wouldn't hurt. He doubted Rosalind would be here, but he loved books.

A man's library reveals his soul. It was something his mother used to say. After her death, Father had sold all of her books and left the castle library barren, save for a few old novels he and his brothers had tucked away beneath their mattresses.

The Lennox library was impressive. The tall shelves brimmed with hundreds of volumes, which made a small part of Brock ache deep inside. What he wouldn't have given in that moment to settle in a chair and read one. Before Hugo's arrival he had been planning the restoration of their castle, and a new library had been high on his list of priorities.

There was a fireplace at the far end of the library away from the books. A pair of chairs faced the fire, and the flames played with shadows against the warm fabric of the chairs. It was clear this part of the library was used frequently. But if the fire was lit, then that might mean...

A hint of movement in one of the chairs caught Brock's eye and he froze. A feminine hand appeared around the edge of the chair and turned the page of a book that he now realized was resting on her lap.

The woman sighed, her soft sound full of longing. It called to him, and before he could stop himself, he was crossing the room toward the chair and its occupant, keeping to the shadows, hoping to perhaps steal a glance of her. The floor creaked beneath his boots, and the woman leaned forward, peering around the wing of the chair. He hastily pulled the domino mask off and tucked it into his coat, knowing it would be difficult to explain if he actually had to speak to the woman.

Blue eyes, like the waters of a loch beneath a midsummer sky. They struck him speechless, and for a moment he was lost in memories of sunlight and laughter. They reminded him of his mother's eyes, only a deeper blue.

"Who are you?" the woman asked.

"It doesn't matter who I am. Who are *you*?" he asked.

"I'm Joanna Lennox." She closed the book on her lap and slowly rose, setting the book and her blue tartan shawl aside.

Brock glanced at the shawl, instantly recognizing the tartan colors.

"I know that clan—MacCloud. Are you Scottish?" he asked.

"What? Oh no, my family has relatives who are, but not me." She laughed sweetly, and the sound filled his heart with a strange, delightful warmth.

Joanna walked closer to him, her lovely features a mask of puzzlement. "You didn't answer me. Who are you?"

Brock struggled to think of an excuse.

"I…" His mind blanked, and so he went with a truth that might at least aid him in his quest. "Is Lady Melbourne here?"

"Why yes, she's—wait a moment. Are you one of her brothers? Did you come down for the wedding?"

Wedding? That gave him an idea.

"Aye. I received a letter from my sister and came down to attend the wedding. I only just arrived and didn't wish to disturb the household." He widened his stance slightly, expecting her to try to get by him.

"Oh dear, you must be tired after such a long ride. Have the servants taken your things to your chambers?"

"Thank you, my lady, I've already been seen to. I was just looking for a room to warm up a bit in before going to bed." He watched her carefully, trying to find any trace of suspicion on her face that she didn't believe his story.

"Well then, come sit by this fire. I just finished my novel and was planning to retire soon. I'd be happy to lend it to you—if you enjoy novels, that is." She went over to the chair and handed him a book. "It's one of my favorites."

Brock stared at the title. *"Lady Jade's Wild Lord."* The author was L. R. Gloucester. He'd once adored novels, but his father had sold nearly all of them.

"Thank you," he said, holding the book reverently.

"I'm afraid I am still at a loss as to your name. Which one of

Rosalind's brothers are you?" Joanna came another step closer, almost within arm's reach.

"How do you know about us?" he asked, his eyes searching the room for something he could use to bind her hands together. The only thing he saw was the dark-blue ribbon in her hair and the lovely sash around her waist. But how to go about it…

"Oh, she's told me all about the three of you. Let me guess…" She tapped her chin, a playful smile upon her lips. "Are you Aiden, Brodie or Brock? I shall guess…Aiden."

"Like hell. Do I look like some young pup?"

"Brock then," Joanna said. "You look like a Brock. It's a very old name, Brock. I like learning about names and their meanings. Did you know Brock means badger?"

For an instant he was distracted by the way his name sounded on her sweet lips. It had been a long time since a woman had piqued his interest. He'd been busy of late dealing with his ailing father and the mountain of debts facing Castle Kincade. There was little time to tup a lass when he was plowing fields and working with stonemasons to repair parts of his home.

Bloody hell, what had he gotten himself into? There was no way he could avoid what he had to do now. If she alerted the rest of the house that Rosalind's brothers were here, it would risk everything. He had to neutralize the sweet lass in order to protect his sister.

"Badger?" he asked. "I didn't know that." He smiled at her, and she smiled back. A smart woman.

Inspiration struck when he saw her bite her lower lip and stare up at him through her dark lashes. He set the book back down on a nearby table, and then with a devil-may-care grin he closed the distance between them, catching her by the waist.

"It is a custom from my village to offer a kiss to those whose families are about to be joined." It was a complete lie, but he needed an excuse to distract her…and he wanted a reason to justify kissing her.

"Really? I've read about parts of Scotland, but I've never—"

"Shush, lass, and let me keep with tradition," he whispered, then bent his head and slanted his mouth over hers.

Her taste exploded upon his tongue, torturing him with her sweetness. She squeaked in surprise as he cupped her arse with one hand and fisted his other hand in the coils of her silken tresses.

She pushed herself away from him, a mix of shock and excitement in her eyes. "This is traditional where you're from?"

"Old as the bones in the hills."

She was about to free herself from him entirely, but something changed in that moment as she looked into his eyes. "And I suppose it would be rude of me to break with tradition."

Brock smirked. "Incredibly rude. You'd be insulting my entire clan."

"Well, Mother did raise me to respect other cultures." And with that she returned the kiss and tightened the embrace further.

She was a divine little creature, with curves perfect for his hands. The way she clung to him as they kissed erased almost everything around them. But he refused to let himself forget the task at hand. With deft fingers, he unfastened the sash at her waist, then loosened the pins from her hair and pulled the ribbon free. Brock couldn't resist indulging himself for a few more seconds before he pushed himself away and spun her around. She was too startled to resist at first.

"What are you doing?" she demanded, breathless out of a mixture of anger, fear and more than a little arousal. He caught her wrists and tied them with the sash. "This can't be traditional."

"I'm sorry about this, lass, but I can't have you calling for Lennox."

"Call for—" He lifted the slender ribbon and used it to gag her, just enough to muffle any sounds. Then he settled her back in the chair.

"Move from here in the next few minutes and I fear you will regret it," he warned.

Her blue eyes flashed with fire, but he fled the room before her body hampered his judgment further. He had to find his sister and escape. When he ducked out of the library, he caught sight of Brodie carrying someone over his shoulder at the far end of the hall.

Rosalind. Thank the heavens, they'd found her.

He rushed after his younger brother, trying to forget how hurt Joanna had looked when he gagged her and left her behind. There was something about that woman…a beautiful little bluestocking who kissed like a woman from a young man's dream but felt too real, too perfect in his arms.

You will be mine, sweet Joanna. It was a vow he carved into his soul. Once he was sure Rosalind was safe, he would come back and find a way to win Joanna's heart.

He'd focus on just how difficult that would be another time.

CHAPTER 24

$\mathcal{T}$he hour was late. The clock in the entryway chimed eerily in the silence. Rosalind replayed the hurtful words she'd heard Ashton and Charles say, her mind still reeling with the revelation of Ashton's betrayal. It was time to leave and return to London. She'd find a way to get her life back from Ashton's ironclad control some other way. There was no chance she would marry him now, the damned awful man.

Rosalind came down the main stairs, intending to fetch a glass of water from the kitchens without disturbing Claire, and suddenly froze when she heard cloth rustle. The hairs on the back of her neck stood on end. Someone was watching her. Doing her best to act unaware of the hidden eyes of servants, she started walking toward the servants' quarters to find Claire. The rustling of clothes was her only warning she wasn't alone.

Someone grabbed her from behind, covering her mouth tightly and lifting her by the waist off the ground. She struggled, trying to kick out, but when the man started to run, her body bounced hard against him and she couldn't get her limbs to cooperate in the right way to make the man drop her. She caught glimpses of the corridors, and then they burst out onto the back terrace. Warm night air kissed her skin as the man sprinted through the garden paths.

"Got her!" the man hissed. Rosalind wanted to believe she recognized the voice, but it was impossible.

Before she could get her bearings, she was being handed up into the empty saddle of a horse. Rosalind was about to scream for help, but a man's voice stopped her short.

"It's good to see you, little sister."

"Brodie?" she gasped. What was he doing here? She glanced down to see a second man, Aiden. How he'd grown up in the years she'd been away.

"Where's Brock?" she whispered. "And what are you doing here?"

"Brock should be here soon." Aiden nodded to the dark shape of the house behind them.

A figure leapt over the terrace railing, raced toward them and mounted his horse.

"Hurry! They'll soon discover we've been here."

"What? How? Neither Aiden nor I were seen," Brodie said.

"I stumbled upon a woman in the library," Brock admitted. "I had to restrain her so she couldn't cry out, but who knows how long before she frees herself and raises the alarm." He kicked the flanks of his beast, and the horse bolted forward.

The brothers followed him as they rode fast, leaving Lennox House far behind them and Rosalind in a state of confusion as she fought to keep up with them.

She didn't let herself stop to think about how her brothers had found her or why they were leading her away. Her heart had shattered into a thousand pieces, and she'd take any excuse to be as far away from that man as possible. He had betrayed her, was using her, just as she'd feared. The man she'd fallen in love with had let her down. His promises had turned to ash.

That damned bloody baron can rot for all I care! Even as the dark thought crossed her mind, it didn't ease the ache or guilt that she felt at abandoning him while he was ill. But his friends were coming, people he cared about more than her. He didn't need her—he never had. And more importantly, he didn't want her.

They rode for two hours before the horses showed signs of fatigue.

"We'll stop for an hour, let the horses rest," Brock announced. Rosalind followed her brothers as they urged their mounts to take cover behind a grove of trees. She delicately worked her hands, flexing stiff fingers, wishing she'd had her riding gloves. The leather straps had cut into her fingers and rubbed raw spots along her palms.

Aiden came over and took her hands, gently massaging them until the pain lessened. "Better?" he asked.

"Yes. Thank you." She felt strangely shy around her brothers. It had been years since she'd seen them, and they'd gone from young men who jumped at their father's shadow to tall, striking figures racing through the darkness.

Have I changed too? She knew she must have. The young woman in a brown woolen gown with loose hair and a nearly broken spirit was long gone. After she'd married Henry, she'd transformed into a lady she believed would make her mother proud. A woman in fine gowns, with dressed hair and manners to please all around her, as well as a woman who was intelligent and self-sufficient.

"Brock, what are you doing here?" Rosalind asked. At her question, all three brothers came to stand in ring around her, studying her grimly.

"She looks...fine," Aiden whispered.

"Aye, but he could have left bruises in places we cannae see." Brock's eyes raked over her body, scowling. His brogue had thickened in his concern.

"Bruises?" Rosalind snapped. "What are you on about?"

"The brute, Lennox," Brock explained. "We came so you dinnae have to marry him."

"It's a rescue," Aiden explained with pride, his chest puffing out a little.

"Rescue?" She bit back a laugh. But how had her brothers known she was marrying Lennox?

Brock was still scowling. "We had a visit from a friend of yours," Brock said. "Sir Hugo Waverly. He got your letter about Lennox ruining you financially, and he knew it would only get worse. He heard about the wedding and came to us for aid."

"Don't worry," said Brodie. "That man will never lay a hand on you again."

"But he—"

"It's all right, Rosalind." Brodie hugged her. "You dinnae need to tell us anything. You're safe now. We're going home."

She knew she'd have to explain to them that Ashton wasn't a brute at some point. A pompous arse who had betrayed her trust and broke her heart, yes, but not a brute. But that was the least of her concerns at the moment. They were taking her home—to the man she swore she'd never look upon again.

"*Home?* But I can't. Father—"

"Is dead." Brock's tone was flat. "He died a week ago. It's safe for you to return to Castle Kincade."

"Dead?" It took a long moment for that to sink in. The man who'd haunted her nightmares was *dead*.

A weight seemed to lift off her chest. Rosalind drew in a shaky but deep breath, as though she hadn't been able to breathe in years. The only person she feared in this world was gone forever. Her heart was hollow with the loss of a parent who had never been there for her. She knew she would never miss him, not after the ways he'd hurt her. If there was one thing she'd learned since she'd fled it was how to be strong and not let anyone make her feel guilty for being who she was.

He was a brute, and now he's dead. I shall not mourn him.

She looked to her brothers for confirmation. "Is it true?"

When the others nodded, only then did she dare to hope.

I can go home...

But home wasn't Castle Kincade anymore. It hadn't been for years.

"Do not worry, Rosalind," Brock said. "We shall take care of you now."

"But I don't need you to take care of me. I've been managing quite well on my own." She crossed her arms over her chest, scowling. If they only knew of the empire she'd built for herself. Granted, most of it was currently under Lennox's control, but...

"I'm sure you have," Brock said with a condescending smile. "But now you have us to do it for you."

She'd always hated being the baby after three brothers, and this was why. They'd never understand that she was a force to be reckoned with, not a damsel in distress.

"Besides," said Aiden, "Waverly told us what sort of man Lennox is. It doesn't sound like he'll take no for an answer."

There it was again. Waverly warning them about Ashton. Her business partner had pitted her own family against the League. Something didn't feel right. She ought to thank Waverly, especially since he'd sent her brothers to find her, and even more so since Ashton's confession to Charles. But now she trusted neither Ashton nor Waverly.

Was Ashton really the cold, dispassionate seducer he claimed to be? Or was he the man she'd hoped he was? She honestly didn't know, but she was never going to let her heart choose a man for her ever again. And she was definitely not going to trust any man as a business partner again.

I can play the puppet master just as well as he can.

Ashton's words were damning. A good man, the one she had started to fall for, would not have said that. He would have been honest with her about her involvement with Waverly and asked her about it. He would not have seduced her and manipulated her into marriage.

Dear God...

"What's the matter?" Aiden asked, stepping closer. "You've gone pale, sister."

"Ashton wanted my property because I had Waverly as an investor." She curled her hands into fists. "How could I be so bloody stupid? It was always about the companies. It was never about punishing *me*—it was about Waverly."

This realization hit her like a slap in the face. Even when she'd believed Ashton's motives were born out of revenge, he'd at least wanted her. But to ruin her and take everything she had simply to hurt another man...it was cold. Too cold.

I matter so little to him that I was not even the object of his vengeance, merely a pawn.

"Brock, I should like to go back to London—"

"No, we have to go to Kincade. At least for now. Waverly explained about Lennox and his League. They will come after you and try to take you back by force. London wouldn't be safe. We can protect you better in Scotland. You'll be among your own people again."

"But my life is here now. I can't leave it."

Brook shook his head. "You can and you will. Anything you want to bring home, one of us can return for."

"But my maid..." She couldn't leave Claire behind.

"She will be fine, I'm certain. Listen, Rosalind." Brock held her chin and forced her gaze his way. "We didn't just steal you away from him. I left Lennox's sister tied up and gagged in the library. That man will want to kill me after what I did to her."

She stared at him, remembering what he'd said before they left Lennox House. "What do you mean by that? Is Joanna all right?" When he didn't answer right away, she punched his shoulder hard. "What did you do to her?" Sometimes it was the only way to get a much bigger man to answer her.

"I may have…" He mumbled something, so she smacked him again. "Christ, woman, fine! I kissed her before I tied her up. The little bluestocking was sitting in a chair by the fire reading a book, and I may have gotten carried away."

"You idiot!" she groaned. "Poor Joanna. You compromised a perfectly lovely young woman? You're right, Ashton will want to kill you, and I wouldn't blame him!"

"Compromise? It was just a kiss. It's not like I tupped her."

Brodie shifted restlessly. "Maybe we should push the horses until we can reach an inn and trade them. I think Brock's actions have put us in harm's way more than we anticipated."

Rosalind had to agree with that. Brock had kissed Joanna and left her in a frightened state of being tied up and gagged. If Rosalind had learned anything about Ashton it was that he loved his family and would do anything to protect them. Or avenge them.

Rosalind sighed. "Brodie's right. We should keep moving. Ashton will be after us the moment Joanna tells him what happened."

She would have to leave Claire behind for now, but she could send for her once she reached Scotland.

What a bloody mess.

~

"Where has Rosalind gone off to?" Ashton grumbled as he climbed out of bed.

"Who cares? The woman is trouble." Charles tried to shove Ash back onto the bed when he swayed unsteadily.

There was a fuzziness in his head he couldn't shake. He needed to see Rosalind. Something in his gut clenched, a primal warning sign that something was wrong.

"Let me up. I need to find her." He struggled against the blankets and his friend's hands. He wasn't going to admit to his friend that he was worried she would leave. He'd begun to open his heart up to her, and if she decided to go back to London because he kept shutting her out, she would never trust him. He couldn't forget the hurt look in her eyes when he'd demanded that she leave him and Charles alone. He needed to find her and have a moment to explain everything.

"But—"

"No!" Ashton nearly fell out of bed, and Charles caught his left arm, holding him up.

"Help me with my boots. I *must* find her." He panted, trying to catch his breath as the room began to spin.

"Now that I won't do," Charles said with a scowl. "Because I'm *not* letting you leave the house."

Ashton didn't have the strength to fight him. "Fine. My slippers then. Help me find Rosalind. I have a strange feeling in my stomach." He laid a palm over his abdomen as the muscles there clenched and knotted.

"Not so strange," Charles said with a laugh. "You've barely eaten in days."

Ashton gripped his friend's shoulder. "This *isn't* a joke. The last time I felt like this was the night you were in the river. Do you understand me?" How could he explain it? His instincts, ones he'd honed over the years and never ignored, were telling him something was wrong.

All color drained from Charles's face. "I'll help you look for her."

"Thank you."

They exited the room, and Ashton glanced about. It was quiet. The house had long settled in for the night. Even the servants had gone to their quarters.

"Should we try the kitchens?" Charles suggested.

"Yes." They walked together in an awkward manner with Charles hovering close until Ashton regained some of his strength.

They were halfway down the stairs when they heard a muffled yelp from somewhere below.

"What was that?" Ashton asked.

"I'm not sure. Stay here." Charles helped Ashton brace himself against the banister and then rushed down the remaining stairs and vanished into the corridor it seemed the sound had come from.

Ashton panted, his breath still painfully shallow as he descended the remaining stairs. If something was wrong, he wasn't going to sit there and wait. Just as he reached the bottom, Charles returned with Joanna on his heels, holding a sash from her wrists.

"We have a problem," Charles said.

Ashton glanced between his friend and his sister. "What is it?"

"It's Rosalind. She's been kidnapped," Charles said. "By Scotsmen."

Joanna dropped the sash at her feet. "Her brothers. One of them caught me in the library. I think he was searching for her and didn't mean to find me. But she told me she *likes* her brothers. Why would they take her? Surely she's in no danger…"

"They'll take her back to her father." The thought chilled Ashton's blood.

"Is that bad?" Joanna asked, her eyes wide with concern.

Ashton rubbed his temples, suddenly even more weary. "It's very bad."

Charles stiffened. "How bad?"

Ashton met his gaze. "I wouldn't put it past him to kill her. He's a brutal man by all accounts. We must leave for Scotland tonight."

"But you're ill," Joanna added. "Charles can go, can't you?"

"No. I have to go." Ashton breathed. "I swore to Rosalind I'd never let anyone hurt her, including her father. The things he did to her…" He shuddered. "It doesn't matter if she's been helping Waverly. I have to save her." He stared at Charles. "*Please…*help me." He never begged anyone in his life for anything, but he was willing to now.

"The fact that you thought you had to *ask*…" Charles growled. "Treacherous or not, she's still a lady."

"We must leave at once." Ashton's legs shook, but he refused to let Charles and his sister see how weak he really was.

"Sit down before you fall down, you bloody fool," Charles snapped. "I'll handle this."

Ashton crumpled onto the stairs, relieved for once not to be in charge.

Charles turned to Joanna. "Have the coach pulled around and have the kitchens prepare food for travel. I'll get our clothes and wake Jonathan."

Joanna hurried off toward to the back door that would lead to the stables and Charles rushed up the stairs, leaving Ashton alone, feeling too weak and too damned lightheaded to be of any use. He was staring at the front door when he heard the rap of the knocker. Glancing at the grandfather clock against the wall, he realized how late it was in the evening. Too late for visitors.

Rap-rap.

He climbed to his feet and went to the door, leaning heavily against the solid wood as he opened it up.

"Good Lord, man, you look dreadful. Did we wake you?" Lucien asked, his face peeking through the opening. "Hope it's not too late."

"Not at all," Ashton said, out of reflex more than anything. He stumbled aside, allowing Lucien to come through. Cedric and Godric followed behind.

"We did wake him up," said Cedric. "I told you we should have stayed at the inn and come in the morning."

"Sorry about the hour, Ash." Godric slapped him on the shoulder. The gentle pat sent Ashton stumbling into the door as his body gave out.

Cedric caught him just before he could fall flat on his face. "Ash?"

"What's the matter?" Godric asked.

"Sorry, I can't—" His ears started ringing, and the world spun around him.

"Someone hold him…" The voice came through a distant fog, and he struggled hard but fell headlong into blackness.

CHAPTER 25

*L*ucien leaned over Ashton's body. "Good Lord. Is he dead?"

"Help him up, you fool." Charles hadn't gotten back in time to stop his friend's fall, and Lucien's joking tone was about as ill-timed as humanly possible. "It's the grippe. Rafe brought it home. They have both been sick the last few days." Lucien got down and helped Godric hoist Ashton up by his arms and legs.

"The grippe?" Godric paused. "What the devil was he doing out of bed?"

"It wasn't my intention, but we've had some problems," Charles explained as they carried Ashton back upstairs.

"Problems?" Lucien asked they followed Charles into Ashton's chambers.

"Yes." Charles walked over to the dresser where a basin with cool water was waiting for him. He wet a fresh cloth and placed it on Ashton's brow. "You see, Rosalind—"

Jonathan skidded into the room. "The coach is waiting in the front. We'll catch those Scot bastards!"

This only confused Godric more. "What the devil are you on about?"

Jonathan glanced at his brother then back at Charles. "You haven't told them?"

Charles shook his head. "I was about to."

"Then get on with it already," Lucien said.

"It's the bloody Scots," Jonathan blurted before Charles could say a word. "They tied up Joanna and kidnapped Rosalind and are heading back to Scotland. We were about to go after them."

Charles stared at Jonathan. "Thank you, Jon. Did I miss anything?"

"Hold on…" Godric paled. "The Scots. Rosalind's brothers?"

Charles checked the cloth on Ashton's brow. "We have to go after her."

"Tonight?" Lucien asked. "We only just arrived. The wives will be here tomorrow afternoon…"

Charles leaned against one of the bedposts, more weary than he'd felt in years. It was a bone-deep exhaustion that threatened to drag him down. But he had to stay on his feet, like his father had taught him. To do what's right, no matter the cost. Too bad the man had been a bloody hypocrite.

"We have to go," Charles said. "Rosalind is being taken back to her father. We can't let that happen. I swore to Ashton I would help bring her safely home."

"Why?" Lucien asked. "What about her father is so terrible?"

Charles opened his mouth to speak, but Ashton's exhausted voice came from the bed.

"He's a brutal man. Rosalind married the late Lord Melbourne to escape the man's tyranny."

Ashton was sitting up, his eyes still a bit glassy and his breathing shallow.

"Easy, old boy." Charles pressed him down into the bed. It scared the hell out of him when he saw Ashton collapse beneath the gentle pressure. It seemed the grippe was getting a second wind in him. He'd never seen his friend so weak, so helpless, with his gaunt face and pale skin. Ashton had always been the strongest of them all, the one with the most control. But now he seemed weak as a babe. It sent shivers down his spine to think that Ashton might not get better.

"So we need to catch up with three angry Scotsmen?" Cedric asked. "I guess I tempted fate this morning when I promised Anne a quiet week in the country."

"The coach?" Ashton asked Charles.

"Outside," Charles said.

"Have Lowell pack some clothes for me." Ashton lifted his body up again, and Charles and the others kept a close eye on him.

"Are you sure you're up for this?" Godric asked.

Ashton nodded. "She needs me."

Charles shared glances with the rest of the League. It wasn't going to be easy talking Ashton out of coming, not when a woman's safety was involved. Particularly a woman Ashton had feelings for.

"It wouldn't be the first time we rushed headlong into danger without proper rest or a decent plan of attack," Cedric mused.

"Our plan," Charles cut in, "is to catch up with those bastards on the road and beat them to a bloody pulp."

"Not much of a plan," said Godric.

"Well, I'm all for beating up bastards, but we won't catch up with them if we take the coach," Lucien pointed out. "And Ashton can't possibly sit a saddle."

Godric crossed his arms. "He has a point."

Charles knew that if Rosalind's father scared Ashton to the point where he was this desperate to get to her, it was bad. *Very* bad. Few things in the world frightened Ashton. If he was scared about something, then the rest of them should be terrified.

"A few of us could ride ahead," Jonathan suggested. "If we catch up, we could find a way to delay them."

"Yes." Charles nodded. "They have to close their eyes and sleep sometime." He rubbed his hands gleefully at the thought of matching his strength against them again in a fairer fight. "We also know which way they're headed."

"Go now," Ashton said, his voice hoarse as he coughed. "*Please.* We'll take the coach and follow you. I'm sure they'll take the Great North Road. It's the fastest. It leads straight to Kincade lands, about an hour north of Gretna Green."

"Jon." Charles grinned. "Up for a wild chase?"

Jonathan grinned back. "If I ever answer no to that, you have the liberty to strike me down."

"Then let's ride. These old maids"—Charles nodded at the others—"can catch up with us later."

"Ha-ha," Cedric snapped. "I can't wait for you to find a wife. Then I shall have the pleasure of mocking you for being an old maid."

"Then you will be waiting until Judgment Day." Charles was still snickering as he ducked out of Ashton's bedroom and into the corridor, with Jonathan on his heels. They had Scotsmen to chase and a lady to rescue.

~

FOR TWO DAYS Rosalind slept on the cold, hard ground. Even the sacks of grain had been better than this. Shivers racked her body beneath the thin blankets her brothers had packed. Mostly she just lay there, aching for someone she no longer had. Or, if she was brutally honest with herself, had never had. And every moment she despised herself for that weakness.

I shouldn't long for a man who viewed me as nothing more than a pawn.

When she closed her eyes and curled up in her blankets close by her brothers and listened to the wind whistle through the trees, she could feel the phantom press of Ashton's lips on hers. The memories, too vivid not to be real, made her body tremble with longing and her heart bleed all over again.

Damn that bloody Lennox to hell for making her long for him, for her body and soul to ache to be with him, even when he didn't care about her at all.

I'm a puppet to him, nothing more. So why does it hurt to leave him behind?

"Sleep, Rosalind." Brock's voice came from somewhere in front of her. "We'll reach home in a few hours after the horses have rested."

It irritated her that he was likely watching her sleep. Her brothers had split the nights and days into watches among the three of them. She'd volunteered to help, but they all scoffed at the idea that their sister should have to stand watch. From their stiffness that first night, she knew she'd wounded their male pride. Such fragile creatures, men. She nuzzled her face in the crook of her arm, trying to force herself to drift back to sleep.

When dawn arrived, Rosalind was fuzzyheaded with sleep and every muscle was stiff from lying on the ground. She climbed to her feet and stretched, trying to loosen up. It had been a long while since she'd had a cold, long night such as this.

"Here." Aiden handed her a slice of brown bread and some hard cheese, and she accepted them gratefully. She watched her brothers ready the horses while she nibbled on her breakfast.

Again she was overcome with the eerie sense she was traveling with three familiar strangers. They were taller and broader than she remembered. Their voices were lower and their laughter heartier. It was a curious thing to watch boys become grown men in the blink of an eye. It made her ache for the time she'd lost with them, even though it had been necessary for her own safety.

"Are you finished?" Brody asked when she licked her fingers clean.

"Yes." She accepted the flask of water he offered her and took a few gulps before she handed it back to him.

"We should go." Brock mounted up, and they all followed him.

The path they took to Kincade was not on the North Road, but a series of back roads, dusty trails and open fields. Brock had said that the North Road would be the route Ashton would most likely take if he pursued them. It was better if they could reach the castle without a confrontation and take shelter behind the walls before Ashton and his men arrived.

"Not far now," Aiden cheered as their horses trotted up a hill overlooking a vast loch.

Beyond the blue waters lay Castle Kincade, nestled in the midst of a vibrant green field. Rosalind's heart leapt as years of happy memories from before her mother's death came back. She had learned to swim in the shallows of that loch and learned to ride in the nearby forest.

I'm home.

And this time father wasn't there to blacken the castle or her life.

Her brothers rode past her, and for a long moment Rosalind stayed frozen upon the hill, fighting an internal battle. She could follow her brothers and return to a life in the Highlands, or she could return to London and face Ashton. She knew he wouldn't let her go if she came back to London. It wouldn't matter that she viewed their agreement as void after his breach of trust. But would he come after her in Scotland?

And some small part of her asked, Did she want him to?

"Rosalind!" Brock waved his arm from below on the sloping hill. With a sigh, she kicked her heels into her horse's flanks and followed her brothers.

The castle looked almost the same as when she'd left. How was that possible? Rosalind dismounted from her horse and let a groom lead it away before she followed her brothers into the front entrance. The craggy gray stones were like old friends, but part of her was also wary because darker memories still lingered in the shadows of the hall.

"You should rest. Would you like your old room? Or…" Aiden's cheeks turned a ruddy red. "Sorry. You should have another room, one of the nicer ones down here." He nodded to a hallway she'd never been allowed to visit when she'd lived here. An entire wing of sealed-off guest rooms.

"Brock had us open them after Father passed." Brodie curled an arm around her shoulders, giving her a gentle squeeze as they walked down the hall. Brock lingered by the stairs, watching the three of them, his gaze unreadable.

"How is he?" she asked as they both watched Brock over their shoulders. Her brother had taken the worst of the beatings intended for her before she'd fled and had always protected everyone from their father at his own expense. Worry ate away at Rosalind. What if her father's death had hardened Brock?

"He is..." Brodie struggled for words a moment. "Relieved. I think he feels guilty that he doesn't mourn our father, but none of us do."

"I understand," Rosalind said. She understood all too well the guilt of feeling so little grief at old Lord Kincade's passing.

"Why don't you take this room and sleep? We raced to get here. You could use a bath and a change of clothes. I'm sure I can find Mother's trunk in the attic."

"It wasn't destroyed?" She remembered all too clearly her father shouting that he'd sold the jewelry and burned the clothes mere weeks after her mother had died.

Aiden shook his head as he joined them outside her guest room. "Brock hauled the trunk up into the attic in the north tower and left it hidden beneath some old drapes."

Rosalind rested her hand on the door to the room. "You're right. I think I could use a bath and some rest." Her body felt heavy enough that if she took a swim in the loch, she would not stay afloat.

"Get some rest. We'll send someone to tend to your bath and bring you a change of clothes."

She hugged each of her brothers before they left. But within moments, there was a knock at the chamber door.

"Rosalind?" It was Brock.

"Come in." She was dragging a white sheet off a settee that backed up to a large feather bed with dark-blue drapes and faded gold tassels.

Her brother entered, his hands fisting around a packet of old letters.

When he did not immediately speak, she settled onto the couch, coughing slightly as dust wafted around her. Brock came over and slowly held out the packet. Thick twine bound the letters tightly, forming grooves in the old parchment.

"What are these?" she asked, taking the letters from him.

"I swore I would not give these to you, but it was father's dying wish. It is your choice whether you wish to have them or not." He backed up and nodded at the empty fireplace. "If they prove to be upsetting, you are free to burn them."

She plucked at the twine, unfastening them to retrieve the newest letter, one that wasn't faded like the others. "Do you know what they contain?"

"I do not. You may tell me after, if you wish, but I must see to the house. We have preparations to secure your safety. I've hired men from the village to assist us if anyone comes for you."

Rosalind nodded. "Thank you, Brock." When their eyes met, she was a child again, a girl of sixteen who was standing in a hall, her lip split and her face swelling from her father's fists, and he was the brother who'd stood between her and her father whenever he could. Her protector.

But I don't need to be protected. Not any longer. She could see in his eyes that he was realizing the same thing.

"Rest, little sister." He leaned down and kissed her forehead before he left her alone.

It seemed like ages before Rosalind worked up the courage to open the newest letter in the stack. She broke the wax seal upon the letter and unfolded the pages. It was a letter to her from her father.

. . .

ROSALIND,

I know you wish to burn this letter without reading past these first few words, but I beseech you not to do so. In years past, I was unkind because I knew I was among the damned, yet forced to walk among the living. And the hatred I had for myself I turned upon others, including you.

I am too proud to ask for your forgiveness before I am gone. But I beg you now to grant a dead man one last request. Before my death, I sent you a device which I was afraid to leave with these letters lest they fall into the wrong hands. It resembles a pocket watch when closed, but it can be used to decode the cipher in which these letters are written. I have trusted your brothers to guard these letters until you returned to Scotland with the decoder.

These letters, between myself and a man named Sir Hugo Waverly, detail how I aided him in crushing a Scottish rebellion against the Crown long ago, shortly after your mother died. He had the leaders secretly murdered, and I said nothing. I betrayed my people and my beliefs to fill the family coffers with gold.

So long as Hugo lives you are not safe. You must use these letters to destroy him, even at the cost of our family honor. A man like Waverly cannot be trusted. He must be destroyed. Your brothers would fear the repercussions, but you were always the bravest among my children. Be brave now.

Montgomery

ROSALIND'S KNUCKLES were white as she gripped the letter. The odd little watch she'd received before she left for Lennox House hadn't been a watch at all. Her father's words burned through her, striking fear in her after years of feeling safe. But now it was not him she feared.

Hugo. The man she'd thought she could trust, the man who'd sent her brothers to rescue her…had helped to kill Scotsmen who'd wanted to leave the Crown. And her father had been one of them. And then he had helped Waverly murder them.

My father was a traitor. The realization of that hit her hard, and she had to struggle to breathe. She had always felt that the anger he'd shown towards her had been meant for himself, and this answered many questions as to how the man had changed so quickly after her mother's passing.

Ashton was right. Hugo was a threat, and these letters were the key to his destruction. Her anger at Ashton wishing to use her to flush Hugo out into the open faded against the proof she held in her hands. The evidence that would destroy him.

With shaking hands, she folded her father's letter and tucked it beneath the other letters before she tied the bundle securely again with the twine. Then she slipped the letters into the folds of her skirt.

Tomorrow…tomorrow I can better decide how to use these to expose Waverly.

She would. There was no question what she had to do. She only wished Ashton were here to help her, though she hated herself for thinking that. He didn't love her, *would* never love her, but he would know how best to use those letters to ruin Hugo.

Then it occurred to her that Ashton would do anything for those letters. Anything. She considered writing to tell him what she'd found. What was it worth to him? Her property back, of course, and perhaps a company or two of his in exchange for the letters and the decoder? Some small measure of payback for using her as he had.

But she couldn't. It didn't feel right. As much as she wanted to strike out at Ashton for the pain he'd caused, she couldn't do it.

Rosalind was nothing but a mere pawn in a vast game between Waverly and Ashton. A game which she refused to play.

~

"A CASTLE. It would have to be a bloody castle," Ashton muttered as he knelt behind a large boulder bordering the lake facing Castle Kincade. Godric, Cedric and Lucien were with him on either side as they studied the massive edifice in the distance.

"So much for our plans of overtaking them on the road," Lucien grumbled.

Godric stared intently at the castle before glaring at Lucien. "Those Scots were devils when they fought us over bar wenches. I'd hate to see what they would do to protect their kin."

Ashton squinted at the castle. "It's not the brothers that worry me. It's her father. He's the real brute. Her brothers love her, but from what I gathered he's bad enough to scare them into obedience."

Godric and Lucien exchanged worried glances.

"We've never laid siege to a castle before." Lucien smiled grimly. "I suppose there's a first time for everything. But I'm afraid I left the family battering ram back at my estate."

Godric couldn't help but chuckle at that.

Ashton licked his lips, still feeling a little parched. They had ridden almost without stopping for two days, pausing only long enough to change horses at coaching inns. In that time Ashton had fought off the last bit of influenza, but it had left him weak and thirsty.

"Here." Lucien offered him a flask of water, which Ashton drank greedily.

Godric shifted in his crouched position and scanned the trees around them. "Charles and Jonathan should be back soon."

Ashton nodded at two figures who crept toward them, running in a crouch to avoid being seen by anyone watching from the distant castle. "There they are."

Once Charles and Jonathan reached them behind the rock, they all huddled close together.

"What did you see?" Ashton demanded.

"Men on the turrets," Jonathan said.

"Turrets? Lord…any crossbows?" Lucien muttered.

Cedric chuckled until Ashton glared at him. He cleared his throat and glanced away, as though trying very hard not to laugh. "Lucien, your sister should have been here. I imagine Lysandra could have built us a trebuchet."

Lucien laughed. "I dare say she could. But we'd need something capable of hurling more than snowballs at the enemy."

"Anyway…" Jonathan continued. "Those are just lookouts. There are more inside. I think they are expecting us to come after Rosalind with a small army."

Charles nodded. "Jon's right—there's something wrong about this, Ash. They've got men posted at the front gate and men on the rooftops in pairs. I don't have a clue how we will get inside. I can't guess the numbers we might face inside either."

"Well, Ash, what's your plan? We'll do whatever you ask, of course," Godric assured him.

Ashton's throat tightened. They had come all this way to face certain danger and poor odds.

"I…I appreciate that you all came with me. But I should go on alone. We didn't expect them to beat us back to their fortress. I cannot ask any of you to risk yourselves, not for Rosalind." For a long second his friends glared at him, their expressions hard.

Charles huffed as though offended. "You're a daft fool if you think we'll let you go on alone. That being said, I have a plan." A wicked grin spread across his face.

"Bloody hell, that's always a bad sign," Cedric muttered.

"Charge in and beat them soundly, I suppose?" said Godric.

"Ash," Charles continued, ignoring the others, "you take my horse and ride up to the gates. Demand an audience with Rosalind. Her father and brothers will refuse at first. Tell them you won't leave until you see her, and that once you have said your piece, you'll return to London. The rest of us will gain entrance to the castle by *any* means necessary."

"Notice how he leaves out the details on what those means are," Cedric whispered to Godric, who nodded.

"And then?" Ashton demanded. Any plan Charles concocted was bound to end up in trouble.

"Well...we'll need to find a way to distract her father and brothers while you whisk your lady love away to safety."

"Bravo!" said Cedric.

"Brilliant plan," said Godric.

"Best plan I've heard in ages." Ashton's voice dripped with sarcasm.

"Though there are a few flaws," Jonathan noted.

"Mostly flaws, really," Ashton agreed.

"Actually, it's a terrible plan," Cedric groaned.

"Utter rubbish," Godric concurred.

"We're doomed." Ashton sighed. At this point he was worried their position would be given away by Jonathan's laughter. "It's also the only plan we have," Ashton said. "Charles is right. They won't open their doors to all of us."

He turned his focus back to the castle. Rosalind was somewhere inside there. All alone and probably hurting if her father had exercised his temper upon her again. There was no choice but to risk everything to get to her.

"Jon, let me borrow your horse." He nodded in the direction of the woods where they'd hidden their coach and horses.

"Of course." Jon regained his composure and followed him, hunched over to keep out of sight. Once they were deep in the trees, they stood from their crouched positions.

"He's a good beast. Try not to let the Scots take him." Jonathan patted the black gelding's neck before he untied the reins and offered them to Ashton.

"I'll do my best. Tell the others I said thank you. For everything." Ashton couldn't put into words what the League meant to him or how he'd feel if he lost any of them.

"They know."

A sad smile curved upon Ashton's lips. "Take care of yourself, Jon." If things went poorly, he might not see any of them ever again.

"Be careful." Jonathan watched as Ashton mounted the horse and rode out of the woods toward the castle.

The sun beat down on Ashton's head, making his temples throb with an unwelcome headache. The fever from the influenza had gone but had left his skin flushed. If Rosalind's brothers did not let him inside, he very well might pass out and fall right off his horse.

Castle Kincade was a stout, craggy stone structure that had stood upon this hill for more than two centuries, weathering storms, armies and the winds of change. It was impenetrable. Not even Charles's wild schemes could find a way to break through.

"Halt!" a man somewhere above the battlements cried out in a thick brogue.

Ashton tugged the reins up and back, stopping his horse. It swung its head from side to side and pawed the dirt restlessly with one hoof. Ashton let his head fall back so he could stare up at the man on the ramparts watching him.

"State your business!" the man barked.

"I've come to request an audience with Lady Melbourne."

The man disappeared from view for several long moments and then finally reappeared.

"The lady says you can go and hang yourself!" He finished with a nod and a mocking salute.

"Rosalind!" Ashton bellowed. "I know you're up there! Give me one bloody minute and then you never have to see me again!"

The thought of never seeing her again was... No. He would not think about that. He had to see she was safe, and if she wasn't, he'd remove her immediately. Somehow.

He squinted up at the castle, and suddenly Rosalind's faced appeared. Her dark hair was pulled back at the nape of her neck, and she looked as tired as he felt.

"Please, Rosalind. Just give me a few minutes. That's all I ask."

Her gray eyes were stormy, and he couldn't miss the hurt in them, even as far below her as he was. She stared at him for a long moment, long enough that he feared she would simply leave him there at the gate.

"Very well," she finally said and disappeared.

He waited for a few minutes until sounds behind the tall wooden doors of the castle's entrance alerted him that they would open. At last the doors parted to reveal a darkened hallway. It was clear the castle had been remodeled long ago, and whatever was left of a courtyard had been walled in and floored and made part of the residence. Ashton slid off his horse, landing heavily upon the ground. He was barely able to catch his breath.

A man, heavyset and with a distrustful glare, walked up to Ashton and took the reins to his horse.

"*Sassenach*," the man muttered as he led Ashton's horse away.

Brushing dust off his trousers, Ashton entered the castle interior and abruptly halted. Several men stood there, three of whom he recognized as Rosalind's brothers, and every man was armed. He had seven pistols trained upon his chest. Two of the brothers parted to allow their sister to stand between them. But none of them in the room were old enough to be her father. Where was the eldest Kincade?

"Rosalind," he said gently as he studied her more closely. She seemed unharmed, no bruises, but Ashton knew from Godric's past that bruises could be easily hidden.

She turned to her brothers. "I will speak with him in the drawing room." When it was clear to her that her brothers intended to stay by her side, she added, "*Alone*."

"But—" the eldest protested.

"I'll be fine, Brock. I'll call if I need you." She waved a hand for Ashton to follow her. He did, but he nearly stopped when the men blocking his way didn't immediately move apart. Her brothers formed an impenetrable wall between Ashton and Rosalind.

"If you do even *one* thing that upsets her, we'll feed you to the dogs. Even if you are a nobleman," Brock warned in a low growl only Ashton and the two other brothers could hear.

"Understood." Ashton had no intention of upsetting Rosalind, and if he did, then surely he would deserve any fate that came his way. The three Scotsmen finally parted to allow him to pass so he could follow Rosalind.

They entered the drawing room, and Ashton noticed the furniture was coated with dust and the fabrics were faded and outdated. The Kincades clearly hadn't been able to keep their home in good condition. No doubt Lord Kincade saw Rosalind and her fortune as a way to restore their home to its former glory.

Rosalind stopped before the empty fireplace, her light-blue skirt stirring up dust as she turned to face him. He had a moment to admire the sloping grace of her neck and her lovely profile before she turned to him. A small ache that had been growing in his chest ever since she'd left had gotten even stronger now that he was close to her again. It never ceased to amaze him that this woman had captured his heart and dared him to dream about a better tomorrow.

"Rosalind, I'm here to rescue you." It seemed that he was at a loss for words yet again. He moved towards her, arms outstretched, desperate to hold her and reassure himself she was safe and well. He came within a foot of her, but then she held up a hand.

"Don't touch me. Don't you *dare* touch me."

He halted, his boots skidding on the rug, and he stared at her, confused. She should want to see him, shouldn't she? Before when she'd told him to go hang, he'd assumed her father had been issuing the orders and that once he was inside, she would be happy to see him.

"Rosalind, sweetheart…"

Her eyes glittered dangerously. "Sweetheart? *Sweetheart?* I'm no sweetheart of yours, you coldhearted, manipulative bastard."

The barb struck him hard. What had happened between when he'd woken up from his fevered dreams to now? They'd been so happy together...

He replayed the events, going over every detail in his mind from when he'd awoken to when she'd been taken. A pit dropped in his stomach.

Charles. She'd heard him speak to Charles when she'd gone to get him some broth.

Lord, he'd dug his own bloody grave, hadn't he? He'd said what he had to in order to appease Charles, but his words would have been damning to a woman who cared about him.

Her eyes shimmered as she spoke. "Say what you need to say and then leave."

"Are you all right?" he asked. "When I heard you been taken I feared the worst. Is your father here?" If he was, Ashton would throttle him.

"My father?" For a moment her brows drew together. She hastily shook her head. "He is dead. He died a short time ago. I am in no danger." Her voice softened, and he knew by the look in her eyes that she understood what he had feared.

I came for you. He silently begged that she could read his thoughts and trust him.

"Is that the only reason you came?" she asked.

It wasn't, but he wasn't going to make a fool out of himself over his bleeding heart.

"Or is it because you wanted these?" She pulled a stack of letters out from a secret pocket in her skirts.

He raised his brows. "What are those?"

"*These* are letters between my father and Sir Hugo Waverly. Ones that will prove he was a spy who helped destroy a Scottish uprising ten years ago." Rosalind stared down at the letters and then up at him. "You had no idea these existed, did you?" Her hesitation made him strangely relieved. She thought he'd come after her for some letters...and then the rest of what she'd said sank in.

These letters were proof of Hugo's actions that would sink the man's career as a spy and put a mark upon his back for the rest of his life. Ashton's hand twitched with the urge to reach for them, but he did not move. He sensed this was a trap, one in which he would not have both of his desires.

Choose one and I shall lose either way.

CHAPTER 26

*A*shton was here. He'd come for her. And yet all she could think was how angry she was with him.

He stood there looking down at her with those piercing blue eyes. Eyes that had widened with surprise when he'd realized just what she had in her possession. He hadn't known about these letters, but no doubt he suspected she had something on Waverly that he could use. That had been the whole point of his seduction, hadn't it?

He couldn't have come just for me. I'm a pawn to him, a piece to be moved about a chessboard.

The bundle of letters seemed to burn her skin, and she couldn't bear to hold the weight of them a moment longer.

Again she considered, for just an instant, that she ought to demand something in return, like his most profitable shipping company in addition to the return of all that was rightfully hers. A symbolic victory of sorts over him. But the truth was, she didn't want a reminder of him once he walked out of her life. If he wanted the letters, he could bloody well have them.

Even if it damns my family, I want nothing more to do with them —or him.

"Do what you will with them." She stepped forward and smashed the letters against his chest. She wanted to throw them in his face, make him feel how she felt right at that moment, her heart shattering. Yet she couldn't deny that part of her heart still betrayed her, begging to be close to him for just a moment longer.

Ashton grasped her wrist, not allowing her to retreat, the bundle of letters still clutched in her hand. The sudden move made her shiver, not out of fear, but desire. In the last few days without him, she had started to fade from within, and now his touch was setting fire to her senses all over again. A fire that threatened to turn her heart to ashes if she didn't protect herself.

He will always be like this for me. The man I want and can never have. The one who brought me to life and left me all alone.

She stared up into his eyes, hating him for how he made her feel, *loving* him for how he made her feel.

His other hand curled around her lower back. It reminded her of when they had waltzed at the country ball, the way they'd fit perfectly together. Bittersweet memories fluttered behind her eyes as she closed them tight, wishing she didn't have to be strong. But she had to. She jerked in his hold, trying to get free. But could she ever truly escape the man who had broken her heart?

~

"STOP." Ashton tried to calm his racing heart and focused on how good it felt to have her back in his arms, even if she was spitting like a wet polecat.

"No! Let me go!" She tried to tug loose, eyes full of that Scottish fire he'd come to love.

He held fast. "Not until you listen to me." Lord, he just needed to say it. So much for not being a bloody fool. If he said what he needed to say, it would take a weight off his shoulders if nothing else. And if she returned to London with him, he would be the luckiest fool in the world.

"I didn't come here for the letters. I didn't even know they existed until just now. I came here for *you*. Come back with me, Rosalind."

Whatever she'd expected him to say, that clearly hadn't been it. Her brows drew together and her lips parted. Her look of surprise and confusion was adorable. He wanted to kiss the tiny lines above her brow and ease the worry shadowing her eyes.

"What?"

"I want you, Rosalind. That has never changed. Everything I said and promised to you was all true. I want only you." He rubbed his fingers along her wrists as her hands still pressed the letters to his chest. He would let the letters go if it won her back. She was more important. *I can find another way to bring Hugo down, but I cannot lose her.*

Her long dark lashes fanned up, and she glared at him through stony eyes.

"All of it was true?" Her tone turned dangerously silky, and her brogue thickened slightly.

Hell and damnation, he was treading on dangerous ground. He recognized that tone. His hellion was furious with him. But he would not lie to her.

"Yes." He waited to hear the coffin lid snap shut on his fate.

She met his stare with a pulsing ferocity. "I will *never* be a puppet or a tool for any man. Do you understand me? There will be no more strings for you to pull, Lord Lennox."

His name upon her lips sounded like a curse, and he felt sick all over again. A puppet? The memory of the night he'd said those words was a bleak one. While he had intended to use Rosalind to destroy Waverly, he wouldn't have put her in harm's way or done anything without first telling her the truth. All of it.

He sighed, his shoulders heavy with the weight of his secrets.

"I was being manipulative, but not toward you. I needed Charles to be at ease. It was always my intention to tell you what I know about Waverly before we acted. I wanted to tell you everything, but I also had to know how you felt about me before I could." If he was ever going to win her back, he had to tell her the parts of his life that made his soul bleed, starting with the night in the river Cam.

She raised her chin. "I don't want any more pretty words from you, Lord Lennox."

"Woman, will you hear me out for one bloody minute?" If she said she wouldn't, he was tempted to kiss her—it was the only way he could silence that spirited creature into submission, at least for a few moments.

She narrowed her eyes, and he sighed.

"Please, Rosalind. I need to tell you. Hear me out, and then you can send me on my way."

Rosalind glanced away and then back at him. Her body's tension eased in his hold.

"Do you remember how I told you someone tried to drown Charles? That he was bound and gagged and carried to the river?"

Rosalind nodded.

"That man was Waverly, and he vowed revenge for that day for foiling his plans. For a long time we thought nothing of him—our titles and privileges saw to that. We became complacent, not realizing that Hugo, now Sir Hugo, had been biding his time. Waverly has been trying to kill us and those we love in one way or another for the last year. When I learned he was partnering with you, I thought I might learn something of his actions through you. The man's resources go far beyond those of a simple businessman, yet other than that we know little of what he's capable of. As he invested in your ventures, I saw an opportunity. I knew I could use your connection to him to draw him out and, with luck, learn things that could keep us safe from him. But then you bewitched me, and I became afraid to put you in harm's way."

She stiffened in his arms. "I bewitched you?"

"Yes, my little hellion. You were the perfect partner, the perfect woman, even the perfect enemy when you were so inclined. I didn't want to lose you, and I knew once I shared everything with you, you might walk away. That's why I waited so long to tell you." He didn't add how he would have chased her to the ends of the earth to convince her she was the only woman in the world for him.

He swallowed hard and spoke. "I was going to tell you the truth and let you decide whether you wished to help us. I would *never* have forced you on that matter."

"Of course you would have, you arrogant *Sassenach*," she muttered, trying to turn away from him, but he pulled her closer.

"Your safety as the woman I love will always come first," he said fiercely. "No schemes of revenge or business matters will ever be more important than that."

Her eyes widened, and he saw a glimmer of doubt in them that tugged at his heart. "Do not say things you don't mean. I have no illusions. I'm not the sort of woman that a man would feel that way about. I'm…" Her lip trembled. Did she not believe she could be loved or desired?

"I mean every word. I would protect you with my dying breath if you let me."

She shook her head. "I mean when you speak of love."

Everything inside Ashton went still, like a summer's day when there was no breeze and yet the sun wasn't too hot. He had said the words, hadn't he? They had come so easily. Not out of manipulation or word play or saying what one had to in order to gain some advantage. It had been a simple statement of fact. It was the purest realization he'd ever had. He did love her. So much that it had made him irrational.

"You speak of love when you mean duty or honor," Rosalind countered, not wanting to accept his words at face value.

Ashton smiled, and the exhaustion from the last two days lessened. He let go of her wrist and cupped her face in his hands.

"No. I speak of love because it is love that I feel. I love you, my little hellion."

Rosalind's gray eyes, once full of hate, and then doubt, were now filled with worry. "You cannot." She bit her lip, and he could barely hold his control over himself.

"Yet I do. So much so that I question every decision I make, asking myself if it's what's best for you. When you left"—his voice deepened—"I was half mad with fear."

She looked down at where the letters lay on the floor. "Only because I have what you need."

"Yes, you do."

Rosalind looked back at him in shock.

"You have my heart."

She peeked up at him through her lashes. "No man has ever gotten under my skin like you, Lennox." She stood up on tiptoes and curled her arms around his neck. Excitement flooded through him.

"*Please*. Tell me you love me." He closed his eyes for a brief instant, needing to hear those words more than he'd ever needed anything in his life.

"I do. God help me, I do love you, you stubborn man." She feathered her lips over his, and in that moment he swore if he had wings, he could fly.

Ashton returned the kiss, pulling her close, refusing to ever let his Scottish lass walk out of his life again. He teased her lips apart and tenderly ravished her mouth. He wanted to claim her right there, but with her brothers waiting outside it was hardly a wise course of action.

When he finally broke the kiss, Rosalind was leaning into him, her eyes dreamy, as if she too could barely keep her urges in check. That was what bewitched him, knowing that when they kissed it made them both become fools.

But we shall be fools together.

Ashton held on to Rosalind, and she curled into him, neither wanting to separate. He rubbed his hands along her back, trying not to think about all the worries that were building in his mind.

He needed to convince her to come home to London. Then, most importantly, he had to prepare all of her property, companies and debts to be freed from his control and given back to her, even after they married.

"Will you come back to London?" He made it a question, because this had to be her choice.

She gazed at him, pensive.

"I should add that if you do not, then I will move to the castle here. I'm not sure your brothers will be thrilled to have someone like me underfoot, but I'm not letting you go. Not again."

"You would move into a drafty old castle far away from your family and friends?" Hope filled her tone as though she was afraid and excited to believe what he was saying.

"For you I would." He would leave his entire world behind for her. Of course, he knew that keeping the League out of Scotland would be impossible. Within a fortnight they'd all have bought summer cottages nearby.

Rosalind brushed a fingertip down his cheek, her lips curving in a gentle smile. "My life has been in England for a long time now. London is my home. Now *you* are my home."

His heart skipped a beat. It simply couldn't handle the sudden surge of joy in his body.

"I suppose I ought to tell my brothers," she added. "They are ready to disembowel you."

"Because I want to marry you?" He supposed he couldn't blame them for being overprotective.

She wrinkled her nose and tried to hide a smile. "Waverly told them you were hurting me and forcing me into marriage. That's why they came to rescue me from your dastardly clutches."

Ashton shook his head. "That's ridiculous." But if that's what her brothers thought about him, no wonder they wanted to kill him. He would do the same to any man he thought would hurt his sister.

"I know it is." She leaned into him, embracing him once more before she bent down to pick up the letters. "You should take these. They are written in code, but my father sent me the cipher before he died. It should be in my chambers at Lennox House." She pressed the packet of letters into his free hand.

Ashton accepted them, his smile fading. "Rosalind, if these letters implicate your father as a traitor to his people and I use them to out Waverly, you and your family will be social pariahs. They might even be investigated by the Crown. I don't—"

She shook her head and pressed his lips shut with a fingertip. "Stopping a man like Waverly is more important. My family can weather the storm. Now, stop arguing with me." She turned and went to the drawing room door. Her skirts swirled at her ankles, and she looked every inch the fiery Scottish lass he knew her to be.

My *Scottish lass.*

When she opened the door, it struck something hard. Someone grunted out a Gaelic curse.

"Brodie!" Rosalind chastised her brother, and Ashton coughed to cover a laugh when he watched all three of Rosalind's brothers scrambling away from the door.

He couldn't blame them for eavesdropping. He and his friends had done the same thing once with Godric and Emily.

Ashton followed her out into the hall. All of the Scotsmen were waiting, hands on weapons, albeit loosely. But there was still an undeniable tension in the room. Brock was the first to notice them, and he glared at Ashton.

"So, did you tell him off?" he demanded.

"Shouldn't you already know?" she countered.

"We cannae hear a thing through those oak doors," said Brodie. "Just a bunch of spirited mutters."

Rosalind glanced at Ashton. "Then I should be the one to tell you. I'm going to marry Lord Lennox."

"But he's a damned woman beater!" Aiden shouted, raising his pistol at Ashton. "We should drown him in the loch!"

"Stop!" Rosalind snapped, stepping in front of him.

"Out of the way, woman," said Aiden. "He's filled your head with nonsense."

"Heads have been filled with nonsense, but not mine. Lord Lennox has never raised a hand to any woman. My first husband may have taken me in out of pity, but he taught me strength. I would not throw that strength away by running into the arms of a man no better than our father."

Rosalind's words gave the trio pause for thought, as they looked at one another as if asking what they should do next.

"Are you sure, Rosalind?" Brock asked. "Does he not have some hold over you? If he's forcing you in any way, we will drag him out of this house and dunk him in the loch."

Still weakened from his bout with influenza, Ashton knew he could fight, but he doubted very much he could stand against three very angry older brothers, or even one of them. He now understood Godric's hesitation whenever he spoke of these men. The eldest, Brock, was as tall as Ashton and with hands that could tear a tree trunk in half.

Rosalind leaned against Ashton, tucking her arm into his. "Yes. I'm sure. Our arrangement was a matter of honor before, but..." Her cheeks blossomed. "But I do love him. So much so it frightens me."

Aiden stared at her. "But does he love you back?" Ashton knew he had but one moment to convince Rosalind's brothers of his intentions.

"You have no reason to believe me, given what you were told by Waverly, but I love Rosalind with every breath in me. I would never force her to do anything she didn't want to do." He looked down into her face, startled by the love in her eyes. "She's *everything* to me."

Brodie tucked his pistol into his trousers. "This means you are returning to England, doesn't it?"

"Yes, it does. But once Ashton and I have settled some business there, we shall return here to visit, if you'll have us." She dropped her head a little, and the smile about her lips wilted.

Rosalind's brothers looked stricken at the news their sister was leaving them again, but Ashton had an idea.

He cleared his throat. "We should like you to attend the wedding. We shall set it for a week from now at my country estate in Hampshire. My home is yours so long as you'd like to stay."

Brodie and Aiden started to protest, but Brock held up a hand, silencing them.

"We'll come. And we thank you for your hospitality. We would like to attend the wedding and make sure you make our wee sister happy."

The two younger brothers stared at Brock in shock.

He glared back at them. "Close your mouths. We are going. End of discussion." His two younger brothers both stiffened their spines and nodded, as though agreeing to whatever silent command he'd just given them. "And you are more than welcome to come home, Rosalind, anytime. Even bring your Englishman if you wish." Brock smirked at Ashton, but there was no venom in it.

"Thank you, Brock," said Rosalind. "I couldn't imagine you all not being there. Not now that we've been reunited." Ashton couldn't miss the little catch in her voice. She recovered and sniffed. "Now, Ashton and I must make plans to return to his estate and then to London."

Ashton nodded, clutching the letters that would condemn Waverly, and he held on to Rosalind with his other hand.

The group of guards in the foyer started to shift as though ready to leave, but one man, half hidden in shadow, stepped more clearly into the light.

"I would offer congratulations, Lady Melbourne, but I'm afraid I have my orders. Where are the letters?" The man's Welsh accent was unfamiliar and put Ashton on edge.

Everyone tensed and no one else moved. The man was thin and muscular, with a face cut from stone and dark eyes.

"The letters. Give them to me." The man's voice was dispassionate, reminding Ashton of another man, one from his nightmares.

The letters were still in his hand, half hidden by his hip, but he knew if he dared to move, the man would sense it and spot them immediately.

"Letters? I don't know what you're talking about." Rosalind's tone was perfectly innocent, but she moved a step closer to Ashton.

The man raised his pistol, his dark hair threatening to fall into his eyes. In unison the other men in the hall raised their weapons, training them on Rosalind, her brothers and Ashton. This time it was Ashton's turn to stand in front of Rosalind.

"What the bloody hell is going on here?" Aiden growled. "You work for *us*. We hired you to protect us and our sister."

The leader of the men smiled, but it was one of cruel amusement. "And we'd have served you faithfully. But it seems she no longer wishes to be protected, and we have higher orders. Now, Lady Melbourne, the letters, if you please."

Ashton considered the odds, and they were not good. He was certain that more than a few would die if he and Rosalind's brothers chose to fight. Those were odds he was not interested in.

He held up the packet bound by twine. "I have the letters."

Rosalind stiffened beside him, her hand squeezing his.

The man grinned. "Well, hand them over, Lord Lennox."

"And let you shoot all of us afterward? I'm not a fool."

The man's smile turned into a sneer. "What's to stop me from shooting all of you and taking the letters?"

Ashton raised his chin, his voice taking on that commanding business tone that he was well known for. "Because you're a smart man. Hugo wouldn't have trusted such a task to a fool. Murdering Lord Kincade, his sister and brothers in their own hall, as well as myself, will bring forth such an outcry for justice that Hugo will abandon you to the law and let you all *hang*." He finished this last word with such force that no man in the room dared to breathe for a moment.

Hugo's man considered this, his eyes darting from Rosalind's brothers to Ashton and finally the letters. He nodded.

"What do you propose?"

It took much of Ashton's willpower not to sag with relief. Any sign of weakness could still get them all killed.

"I will walk with you outside. Once there, once I am assured of the lady's safety and that of her brothers, you may take the letters from me."

"Ashton, no!" Rosalind cried out, but he kept her behind him. He would do his best to stay between her and any pistols. He turned toward her, wishing he could steal one last kiss before he went outside to an unknown fate.

"Stay here. I need to know you're safe."

"We are in this together, remember?" Her sweet defiance warmed his heart.

"I remember. But you must learn to trust me. Now is one of those times." He stared meaningfully at her.

Rosalind narrowed her eyes, a hint of tears glinting in them. "Be careful. If you get hurt, I will wring your bloody neck."

Lord, he loved this woman.

"Understood, madam," he teased her before he turned back to Hugo's man, and all merriment vanished from him.

The man jerked the muzzle of his pistol from Ashton to the doorway. "This way."

The hired men formed a ring around Ashton as they headed for the door. As they backed out into the sunlight, Ashton raised a hand against the glaring sun. They were alone except for a wagon of hay and two goats that meandered past them grazing lightly on the grass leading up to the road. A pleasant day...and here he was facing a grim defeat. Not only would he lose the letters, but odds were his life as well.

The leader pointed at Ashton. "Hand the letters to me."

Ashton stared at the letters, sighed, then passed the packet to the man with a curse.

A shout from the wagon made Ashton jump. Jonathan and Charles leapt out of wagon, pistols raised.

"What were you doing?" Ashton said loudly enough so that only they could hear.

"The guards all disappeared once you went inside. We used the wagon as cover while we worked out how to get in. We were planning to gain entrance, but clearly you need us more here."

Cedric, Lucien and Godric came around the side of the castle at a brisk pace and flanked the hired men from behind. The other men glanced around, their fingers twitching on their pistols.

"Hand the letters back," Godric ordered.

Hugo's man shook his head. "Never."

"We will shoot you," Lucien warned.

"And we outnumber you," the man countered.

Ashton saw the determination in the other man's eyes. He knew the man would die to get the letters away.

"Whatever he's paying you, we'll triple it," Ashton said.

The man laughed. "If only it were that simple."

"Name your price then," Ashton offered, holding up a hand when the man took a step back.

"Not everything is about price, my lord. I have my orders."

He fired his pistol.

Ashton staggered back. At first he felt nothing; then he saw red blossom around his left shoulder. The pain soon hit as he clutched his now limp arm.

The world descended into chaos. Pistols fired and men shouted, calling for retreat, but his or theirs he couldn't tell. Ashton couldn't focus on any of that as he slumped to the ground. His head grew foggy, and the agony of his arm was a distraction he couldn't ignore.

"Ash!" Cedric's voice cut through the battle. Most of the pistols were on the ground as the men now attacked with swords and knives. But Ashton's mind still struggled to focus.

"Cedric?" he whispered, breathless.

Must get back inside... He struggled back up, his legs buckling before he fell again to his knees. The road rose up to meet him, hitting his knees and making him groan. *Must find...*

"Rosalind..." he said as the pain overtook him and blackness swallowed him whole.

CHAPTER 27

he sound of pistols made Rosalind jump. She clutched
her skirts and ran for the door, her brothers at her
heels.

"Rosalind, stay behind us!" Brock ordered, but she wasn't
listening. If Hugo's men were shooting out there, seven against
one...

"Ashton!" she cried out as she grasped the iron handle of the
wooden door that led outside. Her brothers all now held their
slender but lethal blades in one hand and pistols in the other.

Brodie helped her pull the door open, and a scene of wild
ferocity halted her in her tracks. Ashton's friends were fighting
men left and right. The clash of blades and fists made her sick. She
was a strong woman, but no one handled bloodshed well when it
was with those she'd come to care about. Her brothers dove into
the fray, bellowing out ancient battle cries that echoed off the
castle walls. Brock grabbed a man and swung him hard toward
the moat, the man shouting as he hit the water with a mighty
splash.

"Ashton!" she cried, looking around. It was then she saw

Cedric, holding a man on the ground. A crown of blond hair was all she could make out clearly.

No... No... No...

When she reached Cedric, he was pressing his hands into Ashton's shoulder. Blood oozed between Cedric's fingers as he struggled to keep hold of Ashton's shoulder. Ashton's eyes were wide open but unseeing, and his face white as marble. The battle seemed to have ended, and the men were collecting themselves and checking on one another.

"We need a doctor." Cedric gasped as he tried to lift Ashton up.

"Doctor?" Brock was suddenly kneeling beside her and Cedric. "I can fetch him. You have a horse?" he asked Cedric.

Cedric nodded toward the spot of woods a bit of the way down the road. "Behind the thicket."

Without another word, Brock sprinted toward the trees.

An unsettling hush overtook the dusty road. Godric and Cedric were hunched over, tying up two wounded men. Godric's leg was badly wounded, and he limped as he walked. Jonathan leaned over Lucien, who was resting against the castle wall, a slash from a sword deep across his chest, blood dripping down his stomach.

"Where's the one with the letters?" Charles asked, glancing around. His breath was heavy as he clutched at one arm, red seeping between his fingers. "He's not here."

"I count two others missing," said Godric.

Rosalind and Cedric shared glances. She couldn't erase the sight of Ashton's blood out of her mind.

Ride fast, Brock, she silently prayed. Every one of these men needed a doctor. Her brothers too were scraped and cut in places, the battle leaving no man unharmed.

"Let's lift him up," Godric said as he and Jonathan helped Cedric and Rosalind carry Ashton back inside. "He needs a bed."

Aiden rushed ahead of them. "There's an empty bedchamber this way." It was one of the many empty rooms that had been furnished years ago but left unoccupied. Aiden tore down the white sheets, and a cloud of dust billowed up, making everyone cough. They got Ashton settled, and Rosalind instructed her brother to fetch clean cloths and hot water.

"Was anyone else shot?" Rosalind glanced at the ragged group of men, bleeding and limping as they joined her in the bedroom.

"Just a few scrapes," Godric said, but Rosalind noticed his complexion was ashen. Pain lined his face as he shifted his weight off his injured leg. "Ashton was the only one who caught a bullet, luckily." The Duke of Essex's green eyes glinted with fury.

"Where is Brodie?" she asked. She tried to assess the rest of their injuries. A gash across Lucien's chest, Charles's pierced arm, Jonathan's brow was bleeding... They would all need seeing to.

Lucien cleared his throat. "He is securing the two men still alive. I'm afraid we're facing a bit of a situation."

"What do you mean?" She looked back at Ashton, brushing the hair out of his closed eyes. He didn't stir. Her heart beat as though each pulse cost her a second of Ashton's life, and she wished she could slow the pendulum of time so she wouldn't lose him.

"We will need to have a word with the local magistrate regarding the two who died," Lucien explained.

"Well, my brother Brock is the local magistrate."

Jonathan gave an obvious sigh of relief. "Well that's a small miracle. Explaining this to someone else would have been difficult."

Aidan returned then, carrying a stack of white cloths and a pail of hot water.

"Bring them here."

She dabbed the cloth in the water and pressed it to Ashton's shoulder. Ashton suddenly moaned softly. The blood was starting to thicken on his shirt. She'd never been a squeamish creature, but this... She swallowed down a wave of nausea and applied more pressure to the wound.

"Stay with me," she said, cupping Ashton's cheek.

His lips moved. "Rosalind…"

"I'm here." Her voice broke as she spoke. Charles bent over the bed beside her and took Ashton's hand, gripping it. Rosalind froze as she saw the tortured look in his eyes. If she had ever doubted the love between Ashton and his friends, the doubts were now long removed. She covered Charles's hand, which in turn held Ashton's.

"He's too stubborn," Cedric muttered. "Ash has been shot before. This isn't new to him." Cedric looked around the room as though seeking for the others to agree with him.

"That doesn't mean he should be making a habit of it," said Rosalind, frustrated with her inability to do more.

"Come on, old boy," said Lucien. "You can pull through this." He and the others formed a silent vigil around Ashton. Godric gave Rosalind a sympathetic gaze, as though he knew what it was like to sit at the bedside of someone he loved and fear they would never wake.

I suppose I am one of them now.

Charles laid his other hand over hers and gave her a gentle squeeze as they clung to Ashton. She silently prayed as she stared at Ashton's pale face. If only Brock would hurry and fetch the doctor…

～

ASHTON COULDN'T SEE, couldn't breathe. His body burned.

Flashes… Pieces of his life were scattered upon a fitful burst of wind, and his soul drifted away bit by bit.

His eyes flew open, and he gasped. Every muscle, every bone felt light, almost weightless. He was lying on a settee, light pouring through the bay windows of a room he recognized. He was in one of the old drawing rooms in his home in the country.

But things were *different*. The carpets were old, faded, the patterns more than twenty years old, and the draperies letting in sunlight were out of fashion.

I had those draperies changed ten years ago...

Ashton shook his head, trying to dislodge his confused, muddled stream of thoughts. Where was he? Home...but it was the home he'd had as a child.

The door to the drawing room suddenly opened, and he saw a younger form of himself walk inside. It was him as a boy of seven years, and he wasn't alone. Behind him came his father, a broad grin on his lips as he approached one of the cherry wood tables beside the fireplace, where a gleaming chess set waited to be played.

"If you win, Ashton, we will take breakfast up to your mother. And if I win, we shall go fishing, just the two of us, *after* we've given your mother her breakfast." Malcolm winked at the little boy.

Ashton stared at the scene in fascination, his heart aching. *I remember this day...*

It was one of a thousand such days he'd had as a child, full of warmth, sunlight and love. One that was full of endless possibilities and no urgency. The sort of day a fortunate child in a loving house would have.

How had he forgotten that? For so many years since his father had passed, he'd remembered only the man who'd gotten deep into his cups and visited gambling hells to waste their fortune. But he hadn't always been that way. He'd been kind once. Loving and playful. A man who'd spent hours fishing with his sons and teaching his daughter to ride. A man who loved and was loved.

Ashton's eyes burned, and he blinked rapidly.

"Father." He spoke the word, but neither the man nor the boy looked his way. They were intent on their game of chess. The boy crowed in triumph as he claimed the first pawn from his father.

"You were always talented at that game." A deep voice chuckled from behind Ashton, making him jump.

His father, looking like the man he'd watched die so long ago, stood behind him. But the haunted look he'd expected to find wasn't there. Only peace.

Confused, Ashton glanced between this vision of his father and the man who still played chess with his younger self.

"Father?" he whispered. How was it that he could feel like that seven-year-old boy all over again?

Malcolm came to stand behind him, watching their younger selves play chess. The squares upon the board were coated in lacquer, gleaming in the sunlight.

"Father, how...where...?" He was at a loss for words and blinked back a stinging sensation in his eyes.

"It's a place in between." His father watched as the young Ashton claimed another pawn, grinning at the younger Malcolm across from him.

Ashton looked around him. The sunlight heated his skin, and the smell of his mother's spring roses perfumed the air, their white petals blossoming outside the windows. Morning dew clung to the leaves, but there was no birdsong or breeze from the open windows.

"Between what?"

Malcolm's eyes were a mixture of peace and melancholy.

"Between your last breath and your first."

Ashton tried to understand what his father was saying. Splinters of memories formed inside his mind... Rosalind telling him she loved him, letters pressed to his chest, the crack of a pistol, blinding pain. Ashton clutched his shoulder, but it was a phantom pain. There was no blood on this shirt.

"I was shot." He strained to cling to those memories, but they were beginning to fade, like mist at dawn. Everything slipped into obscurity but Rosalind's face.

His father nodded at their distant selves still removing moving pieces around the board. "Do you remember that game?"

Ashton let go of his arm as the phantom pain subsided.

"I do." He could remember how the marble pieces had been cool against his fingertips, and the aroma of his father's pipe smoke clinging like a lover's perfume to the air. A scent he realized he still missed. Strange, he hadn't thought of those memories for years. He was always so focused on the future—and so afraid to look back.

"When I taught you to play it wasn't about victory or defeat. It was about how a man plays the game. The choices we make upon this earth. Not every decision has to be analyzed and thought out, but it should always *feel* right."

Malcolm placed a hand on Ashton's shoulder, and he felt all too young, like the boy he'd been all those years ago, the one who had crawled onto his father's lap after supper to study the maps of the world or talk about sailing to distant lands. It was why he loved his shipping companies—they were the last bit of that past he still embraced.

His father smile's was etched with lines of sorrow. "I failed you, my boy."

"You didn't—" Ashton protested, but his father shook his head.

"I did. But that is not your burden to bear. You must stop carrying the weight of my sins around your shoulders. You have so much left to do." He pointed to the chessboard. The room was empty now except for him and his father. No more ghosts of the past haunting them with memories of happier days.

As Ashton focused on the game of chess, and the pieces began to move on their own; pawns chased his knights, and bishops slid across the board. "What must I do?"

"Same as in the game. You must protect your queen, or the king is lost." His father's voice sounded distant, and when he turned to face him, he was gone.

Ashton choked down words he had left unsaid, knowing it no longer mattered. His father was gone.

My father's sins are not my own. He watched the battle unfold upon the chessboard until a ring of white pieces protected his queen.

Rosalind.

~

ROSALIND CURLED up on her side of the bed next to Ashton. It had been two long days since the doctor had extracted the bullet, sewn up the wound and seen to proper bandaging of Ashton's shoulder.

When she'd asked how soon Ashton would heal, he'd replied, "The rest lies with God." The doctor's parting words had left her ill and feeling hollow. She hadn't moved from Ashton's side except to tend to her personal needs.

"Ashton, come back to me," she begged for the hundredth time. Her fingers clutched his. She waited for a squeeze, a twitch, *any* sign that he was still there and she hadn't lost him.

She wiped at the tears that kept pooling in her eyes. She couldn't lose him, not when her heart had finally accepted him as her own.

"Please…" She would give anything in that moment for him to be all right. "I will never leave you again."

"I…will hold you to that…" Ashton's voice was rough, barely above a whisper.

"Ashton!" She felt his hand grip hers, squeezing weakly. She started to cry as she lifted his hand to her cheek and stared at his face. His dark-gold lashes fluttered, and she caught a glimpse of those blue depths she'd come to adore.

"There now." He removed his hand from her hold to brush tears away from her cheeks. A heavy sigh escaped him, and his gaze moved about the room. "What happened after…?" He didn't finish.

"My brothers and your friends fought off the hired men. Some died, others fled. Two were caught and will be facing punishment." She didn't want to talk about any of that. With him alive and awake, none of that mattered.

She just wanted him to get well so he could tease her and she could rile him up and tumble him into bed. There were a thousand things she wanted to do with him, and none of them involved dwelling on how she'd almost lost him.

"Ashton." She moved in closer.

His eyes settled on her face, and he smiled. "What's all this? Surely you didn't think I'd leave you? You still have a promise to keep."

He was trying to tease her, but she couldn't joke about this. Not when she'd almost lost him.

"Ashton, please." Damnation, she was going to blubber like a fool. "I need to apologize. I never should've left you."

Ashton shook his head. "*No*. Had our roles been reversed, I'd have done the same. You felt betrayed, and I gave you no reason to believe I wasn't speaking the truth." He paused, catching his breath. "The man you believed capable of those things is the man that I used to be. The man who used anyone and anything to achieve his goals. But from the moment I met you, I've wanted to be worthy of you. I don't want to be that heartless man any longer." He cupped her cheek as Rosalind gently grasped his wrist, stroking him in a desperate need to comfort him.

"Nonsense. You are the kindest man I've ever known," she insisted.

"I'm not. But if you let me, I shall endeavor to be worthy of that praise for every day of the rest of our lives together. You are *everything* to me, Rosalind." The simple word sent wild shivers of joy and fear through her.

"I've never been everything to someone before." She'd been a burden, a creature to be kicked about and shoved away, a thing to be pitied. Henry had cared for her in ways she'd never thought possible, but she hadn't been his world. She'd never been someone's *everything*.

"You are mine. I will show you what that means until my dying breath." There was a deep solemnity lightened only by love in his eyes as he held her gaze.

She sniffed and nodded. "You won't cry off then? About the wedding?" She'd been so afraid that he'd wake up from this wound only to realize she hadn't been worth any of this, certainly not almost dying over.

His eyes twinkled. "I walked alone into a castle with those brutes you call brothers to win you back. What do you think?"

A laugh escaped her. "I suppose that's true. You did face quite the odds." She knew he never took risks, not unless he'd secured his chances of winning first. But there had been no guarantee she would go back to London with him, or that her brothers would let him walk away with all his teeth.

The bedchamber door opened, and Cedric appeared. "I heard voices... Oh, thank heavens." He grinned at seeing them. Then he angled his head out to the hallway. "Wake up, you lot, Ash's come around."

Rosalind raised her brows as Cedric entered the room. The viscount shrugged. "We were in the hall, scattered about."

"But we have plenty of good beds..."

The rest of the League filed in behind Cedric, their fine clothes rumpled and hair mussed, each of them sporting bandages. They, like she, hadn't slept much the last two days, and it showed in their faces.

"We wanted to be within shouting distance in case you needed anything," Cedric explained.

Charles broke from the group and came over to Ashton's bed. "Glad to see you're awake." He looked between Rosalind and Ashton, smiling. She was no longer Charles's enemy, it seemed. The shy but welcoming smile reassured her of that.

"How's your shoulder?" Lucien inquired as he and the other rogues gathered around the bed.

"Like the devil himself is burning a hole through my body," said Ashton.

"I'll summon the doctor. He's sleeping upstairs." Godric departed, his limp still pronounced.

"Where are my brothers?" Rosalind asked, realizing she hadn't seen them in at least a day.

"Lord Kincade has been handling the inquiry regarding the deaths of the men, and he has also handled the investigation into the other men as well," Lucien said. "He advised us not to inquire further, and I'm more than happy to oblige. What occurs in Scotland should stay here. I've no interest in this trouble following us back to London."

"What about Brodie and Aiden?" she asked. "Did they find the ones who escaped?"

The others exchanged glances before Lucien continued. "Your brothers arrived back two hours ago, the horses exhausted."

A flicker of unease moved through her at Lucien's careful deflection. "Are they well?"

Lucien nodded. "They are, but they failed. The three men eluded them. The trail went cold a couple of miles away. They may have split up."

Ashton sighed wearily. "Then we failed."

Rosalind held her breath, wondering when the right time would be to bring this up. It seemed there would be no better time than now. She reached into the secret pocket in her skirt and pulled out a single letter.

"Here…" She held it out to Ashton, and he took the letter. Then he raised his stunned eyes to hers.

"Is this is what I think it is?" he asked.

"Yes." She blushed. "I kept one before I handed the packet to you. When we return to Lennox House, we can figure out how to decode it using the cipher."

"Good Lord." Lucien whistled softly. The others had all learned about the letters and what they represented. Even one might have the power to expose Hugo's dealings. But it would also blacken her family's name and possibly ruin it forever.

Ashton clutched the letter but made no move to open it. "Thank you, Rosalind," he said.

She only nodded, burying her fears. She knew what was at stake now. The weight of Hugo's sins far outweighed her family's name. If she wished to be Ashton's wife, she had to be prepared to help protect their families and one another from Waverly. They could in time perhaps repair their name if they shined a bright enough light on where the blame truly lay.

But what would that do to England and Scotland? she wondered.

"We'll let you rest, Ash," Cedric said. The men departed the bedchamber, but Ashton gripped Rosalind's hand as she returned to her seat.

"Come and rest beside me," he said. "I feel better when you are close."

She smiled. So did he. She needed him as much as he needed her.

She curled up by him again on the bed, careful not to lie near his wounded shoulder. Their hands remained linked, and she drifted to sleep deeply for the first time in two days, finally knowing Ashton would be all right.

CHAPTER 28

Hugo stood in front of the large fireplace in his study at his townhouse on South Audley Street. Waiting. His blood was roaring in his ears, and his head felt light.

He promised himself it would be over soon. The evidence of his foolish beginnings, evidence that could damage the country, let alone threaten his own life, would be back in his hands and could safely be destroyed. The League of Rogues would not learn how deep his interests went and could not unravel his carefully constructed web of lies and secrets.

The study door opened, and his butler nodded at him.

"Sir Hugo, Mr. Sheffield has arrived."

"Show him in. Is my wife still at home?"

"Yes, Sir Hugo. She was preparing to go out this evening. Should I tell her you wish to speak with her?"

"No. Send Sheffield in."

"Very good, sir."

Hugo turned back to the fireplace and only turned again once Daniel had entered. Daniel's coat was covered in dust from the road, but his face was bright with triumph.

"Did you get them?" Hugo asked, his heart pounding again.

Daniel slid a hand under the folds of his coat and pulled out a packet of letters. He handed them to Hugo. The parchment was yellow with age and the ink was a little faded, but the words were legible...words that would have outed him as the English spy who had orchestrated the destruction of a Scottish separatist rebellion by the murder of their monarchist leaders.

"Any problems?" Hugo asked as he ruffled the letters' edges in his hands.

Daniel hesitated before answering. "There was some loss of life in retrieving them, and two men were captured."

"Should we be concerned?"

Daniel shook his head. "Hired locals only. They know nothing."

"Good." Hugo smiled coolly. The League would never know about the content of these letters. He caught Daniel eyeing them.

"Do you have any further need of me this evening?" Daniel asked.

Hugo didn't bother to look at him. "No. You may go. Tomorrow we have plans to make."

"Sir?" Daniel waited, tapping his riding gloves delicately against his thigh, the only hint of his impatience.

"Avery Russell has been making use of Sheridan's youngest sister in his work here in London. I think it's time we escalate that. What would you say to seducing Miss Sheridan and involving her in a mission to France? I would very much like to have her disappear there. It would distract watchful eyes from our true mission. You know the one I mean."

"Yes, but..." Daniel's face reddened.

Hugo chuckled. "You're a genius spy, Daniel—don't tell me a little seduction frightens you off."

"It isn't that. I am involved with another, and—"

"Don't be naïve. Your loyalty is to the Crown. And in this

room, I represent the Crown and its interests. We'll talk more on this later. You may go."

Daniel bowed curtly and exited the room. Hugo's shoulders sagged as he held the stack of letters in his hands, weighing them.

His instinct was to burn them, but something gave him pause. After a moment's hesitation, he counted them, unfolded each one and checked the dates. One letter toward the end was missing.

He crunched the old sheets of parchment in his hand. The letters had been in Lennox's possession. If there was one man in the League who gave Hugo pause, it was him.

He was the only worthy adversary who played a game of chess with living pawns as well as Hugo did, and now Lennox had proved who would prevail.

He must have kept one before he handed them over to my agent. It was the only logical explanation. The late Lord Kincade would not have left one letter out. He was too methodical in their dealings to make such a mistake.

A sense of doom closed in around him, choking him like the river had when he'd tried to erase Charles from the world. The League had managed to outmaneuver him.

But hope still remained, however slim. They still needed to learn how to decode the message, and none of his agents had found the cipher that was sent to Rosalind. Perhaps it had been lost? And if the League were to discuss what they had found within earshot of his men... Well, at least then he would know what they knew, and he could prepare a defense accordingly. It was possible the fragments they possessed held nothing too damning. And with luck, his men might even be able to steal it from under their noses.

A sharp chill dug into the base of his spine. He held hope, but no illusions. The evidence they had could destroy the world he'd spent the last years building.

He leaned closer to the fire and let the packet drop on top of the logs. He watched the flames burn away at the letters.

And yet he was not safe. It was only a matter of time before a reckoning came.

~

IT WAS RAINING on his wedding day. Ashton stood at the front of the altar in the small cobblestone church only two miles from his ancestral home, listening to the rain whisper against the windows and the hum of it on the vaulted roof above.

"Even you cannot control the weather, old boy," Charles teased as he stood beside Ashton.

A rueful smile twisted his lips. "Indeed, I cannot." *Damn the rain. I will marry Rosalind today, no matter what.*

He waited, desperate to somehow distract himself from his nerves. What if she didn't show? No, she would. She'd promised him, and that promise held a greater weight than the most secure bank in England.

In front of him he saw Godric, Cedric and Lucien all in attendance with their wives, amused grins flashing his way.

"She'll come." Godric mouthed the words.

Ashton gave his friend the slightest nod of acknowledgement.

"Ash, I have to tell you something," Charles whispered in his ear.

Ashton glared at his friend. "Now? It had better be something to put me in a good mood."

"Oh, it is," Charles assured him. "Back at your home, when you were ill, I tried to lure Rosalind away from you by offering to buy her debts."

"You did *what?*" He did not look in Charles's direction again. If he did, he would strike the man down.

"Calm yourself. She refused the offer. Pointedly. That's a woman worth marrying. A woman worth betting a man's life upon." A hush crept through the church when everyone heard the sound of a carriage outside.

Ashton was shocked. Rosalind hadn't taken the opportunity to escape their marriage bargain? He knew now that she loved him, but before? She'd kept her promise even then. And she would keep it now.

The doors to the church opened and two figures entered, lit by a pale light from behind. A cloud of rain followed them, but the taller of the two lowered an umbrella he'd been holding to reveal the smaller woman beside him. Brock and Rosalind had arrived.

Three times Ashton had stood and watched his friends marry. He could scarcely believe it was now his turn.

I am a fool, but a happy fool. Ashton couldn't contain his joy at the sight of Rosalind, her cheeks flushed. Even across the room he could see the glint of a laugh in her eyes as she saw him waiting for her. Perhaps she had had the same moment of doubt about him being there, and the same moment of relief when she finally saw him.

The white gown on Rosalind's body was exquisite. The bodice had a pattern of intricate pearls sewn in, and the hem of the gown was layered with embroidered snowdrops. The silk of the dress shimmered as she walked down the aisle.

A true vision of beauty. A dream come true. Ashton's throat constricted as he struggled to retain what little control he had left. He worried now that he would not be able to speak when she reached him, and that would make the clergyman standing next to him very cross indeed.

When they finally reached him, Brock kissed Rosalind's cheek, then nodded to Ashton in a silent show of approval before stepping back.

Rosalind's mouth hinted at a smile when she saw how he watched her.

"You allowed it to rain?" she teased in a whisper only he could hear.

His lips twitched as he tried to hide his own smile.

"I'm not perfect, I'm afraid. But since when is rain a bad thing?"

She giggled, earning a disapproving eye from the man in the robes standing before them.

Ashton didn't hear a single word from the priest. No doubt someone would have to prod him when it came time to make his vows. All that mattered now was that he was here with the woman he loved more than his own life.

My cunning, darling, utterly wonderful rival.

He didn't need to own a woman to feel connected to her. Rosalind belonged to him in a way that transcended ownership. They were bound by invisible strands of love, affection and trust. She had been the only woman who'd ever tested his strength and made him stronger for it. Better for it. He had craved this for so long and yet not dared to hope he could ever have it.

I belong to her. For the first time in his life, he was smiling because someone had bested him...in the most wonderful way possible.

~

"HUSBAND..." Rosalind tested the word as she watched Ashton tweak his cravat. He cut a dashing figure in his blue waistcoat and buckskin breeches. At the word, Ashton raised his eyes to hers, and the slow curve of his lips making her flush.

"Wife."

Rosalind bit her lip. Had she truly been married today? It had been a blur of laughter, smiles and friendship that left her feeling wrapped in a cocoon of love. The League and their wives, as well as Ashton's family, had taken her into their lives openly and warmly. Even her brothers had been on their best behavior for once, despite being among so many Englishmen. Brock had promised her they would stay a few weeks while repairs were made to the castle.

Everything was perfect. She'd never known life could be so full of joy.

"Come and let me look at you." Ashton held out a hand, and she came to him. She had changed into one of her favorite gowns. A cream-colored gown with Belgian lace and red roses embroidered along the sleeves, the bodice and tracing up from the hem of the gown.

Ashton wrapped one arm around her waist. "An angel among the flowers."

She laughed. "I thought I was your Highland hellion?" She leaned into him, breathing in his warm scent, and then she noticed something missing. She frowned. "Aren't you supposed to be wearing your sling? The doctor said—"

"Hang the bloody doctor. I've been shot before. Slings are a nuisance. It's been two weeks. I'll be fine." He lowered his head and kissed her forehead. "I've been thinking, as a wedding gift, what if we...exchanged something other than rings?"

Her eyes widened with curiosity. "Oh?"

"Yes. I have a company, an old shipping line that I bought when I was a young man first restoring my family's fortune. I would like to give it to you as a sign of faith. I will tie it up in a trust that only you can control. It would be truly yours without any control from me."

"You would really do that for me?"

He nodded.

Her lips curved in a smile. "Then let me give you something in return. The little bank Henry left me. It's very dear to my heart, but I should like to give it to you. A true exchange."

Ashton's eyes softened and his touch on her tightened. "Lord, you make a man hungry for kisses when you talk of business." He lifted her chin with his hand and covered her mouth with his in a tender caress that soon burned straight through her.

"Ashton?" She had to fight to keep from giggling.

"Yes, sweetheart?" He trailed kisses down to her lips, and she opened her mouth, letting him deepen the kiss. Lord, the man was pure temptation.

"We have to go downstairs. Dinner will be waiting, and I know you still need to meet with your friends."

He exhaled, resting his forehead against hers, and she couldn't deny that she wanted to skip dinner too.

"You're right. Friends, dinner and then..." He nodded at his bed. *Their bed.* She felt a wave of heat in her, and her skin flushed.

With a wicked smile Ashton lifted her up and carried her to the bed.

"Put me down!" she gasped.

"Dinner can wait," he growled, the sound more sensual than dangerous.

He dropped her on the bed and climbed atop her, his hands sliding up her skirts so he could lie between her thighs. When he was determined to get her into bed, he didn't waste time.

"You're trouble." Rosalind laughed and then gasped as he did something to her underpinnings. Suddenly his hand had found its way between her thighs, stroking her folds. She tensed, startled at first, but then relaxed at his tender touch. A delicious fire spread through her whenever he caressed her. She moaned helplessly.

"Hush," he chided as he gently played with her, flicking one finger over her sensitive bud, then trailing his fingertips inside her. But it wasn't enough.

"If you don't—"

"Hush now, little hellion." He grinned at her.

He unfastened his breeches and nestled into her, thrusting into her with a hint of wildness that made her hungry for all the other things he could do to her. She came fast and hard, crying out her pleasure. Whenever they made love it was wildly exciting, yet it always ended with a perfect moment of tenderness. Ashton came apart above her, and his piercing blue eyes softened.

She could stay with him forever like this, their bodies

entwined. His hands held hers pinned into the bedding, their fingers interlaced. It was then that she suddenly looked up and realized there was a soft gleam above them. Something she hadn't noticed before.

"What is that?" she asked him, pointing upward. But she remembered the answer to her own question. It was the mirror, angled so that she could see herself and Ashton atop her. The image of their bodies together did something strange to her womb. It clenched and she felt herself needing him again. She tightened her legs around him, watching his body jerk in the mirror, and she clenched around his shaft in response.

Ashton panted as he began to harden inside her again. "The mirrors. They make things...*interesting...*" he finally finished before he leaned down to nip her bottom lip.

She agreed, captivated by the sight of them together. *My baron with his dark side.* She couldn't deny she loved it and him. "We should have more of them," she whispered in his ear. She nibbled his lobe, and he hissed a shallow breath as he thrust harder into her until they were falling off the steep cliff of passion once more.

"You are perfect," he whispered against her, his body trembling as she nuzzled his cheek.

"As are you," she chuckled. They were perhaps the two most perfection-minded individuals, and yet they had fallen for each other.

I can find no fault with him, at least none I don't possess myself. We are but two sides of the same coin.

"We should skip dinner." Ashton smiled and rocked his hips again, reminding her of their connection.

Rosalind bit her lip to keep from laughing. "I suppose we could rush dinner and then shoo everyone out. They would understand. It *is* our wedding night, after all."

"Indeed." Ashton lowered his head for one more lingering kiss. "I love you, my Scottish hellion. You were the answer to my silent prayers." His words made her throat tighten, and it took her a minute to compose herself.

"And you were the answer to dreams I had given up on long ago." She smiled through watery eyes. "I love you, baron mine."

No matter what came next, she and Ashton would face the future together, and the League would be by their side.

EPILOGUE

*A*shton stood in a private drawing room at his estate with the fire crackling in the hearth behind him. Before him stood his five closest friends. They had been through so much this past year, and yet in some ways it felt like only the beginning.

Godric leaned on a cane, his leg still giving him a bit of a limp. Lucien toyed with a slip of red silk. Cedric and Jonathan were pouring glasses of brandy for the others. Charles leaned against the wall by the door, his gaze pensive.

In his hand Charles held the small gold decoder device that he'd found in his room. Rosalind had confirmed that it was the one her father had sent. The key to unlocking Hugo's letters had been under their noses all along. Charles toyed with the device as he met Ashton's gaze, impatient to get started.

"What is with the cloak-and-dagger gathering?" Lucien asked. "Has there been a development regarding Waverly?"

Ashton removed a single letter from his waistcoat and held it up. Every man's eyes fixed on the few precious pieces of parchment. "We shall see."

"Is that…?" Godric's arms dropped to his sides as he came closer.

"It is," Ashton confirmed. He had informed his friends about the nature of the letters back in Scotland, but he had kept the existence of this surviving letter a secret until now.

"For so long we've wondered how Hugo had the resources and manpower to cause us so much grief this past year. And now it seems we have an answer. Sir Hugo Waverly is a spy. Of course, knowing this helps us little. Accusing him of such things openly would solve nothing. He is in service to the Crown."

"But if he had acted in ways the Crown could not officially condone…" Godric said.

Ashton nodded. "Exactly. Charles and I deciphered this message last night. This letter shows that Hugo was conducting his spy trade in Scotland and that he had the rebellion leaders murdered." Ashton paused. "Unfortunately, it also shows that Waverly worked with the previous Lord Kincade, who betrayed his own people."

"Ash, we know what we have to do," Charles said. "Outing that bastard and ruining whatever games he is playing could see him exiled from England, or worse. The Crown wouldn't defend him. If they did, it would be admitting that they sanctioned murder to keep Scotland part of Britain."

Ashton set the letter on the mantle above the fireplace and turned back to his friends, his throat tight as he spoke. "It also has the power to destroy my wife's happiness. This letter would blacken her family's name, paint her brothers as sons of a traitor. They would be outcasts among their own people in their own lands, simply because of the greedy actions of two men."

"Not to mention disrupt our entire nation," said Lucien. "Whether it was sanctioned or not, the appearance would be of England imposing its will on Scotland. That cannot end well."

"So what are you proposing?" Cedric asked. The tension in the room had thickened. Ashton knew this would be no easy thing to ask of them. No one man should make this decision.

"I suggest we put the fate of the letter to a vote. We either reveal its contents to all of England or we burn it here in this very fire." He waved at the dancing flames.

Jonathan cleared his throat. "You will need an odd number to ensure a majority. I shall withdraw, since I have no history with Hugo, unlike the rest of you."

"Fair enough," Lucien said. "I agree to a vote."

The other members murmured their assent.

"I vote to burn it, for Rosalind's sake," Ashton declared. The choice hadn't been an easy one, but in the end he realized it was the only way. Rosalind had offered her trust to him and had given him a weapon that she knew might ruin her family. But they had suffered enough from their father and did not deserve to be forever haunted by his ghost.

"I vote to reveal the letter," Cedric said. "He tried to kill Horatia and Anne. If we do not use this, he *will* try something again."

Ashton had expected that. Cedric, more than any other man, had suffered at the hands of Hugo's desire for revenge.

"I'm with Ash. We burn it." Lucien stroked his chin. "This isn't about victory. This is about moral character. Will the harm these letters cause outweigh the light they shed? We can find another way to stop Hugo. If he made a mistake in the past, he's bound to have made another."

Charles scowled as he stared at the letter above the mantle. "Hogwash. Even when his plans are foiled, Hugo is one step ahead of us. He has been the bane of my life far longer than he has been for any of you. We were *given* this opportunity. We would be fools not to use it, and not just for ourselves. We owe it to Peter."

Two to two.

Everyone turned toward Godric. He met their gazes before he sighed and cast his vote.

"As much as I want to reveal that letter," he said with a sigh, "I cannot bring myself to wreck your wife's reputation and happiness, and that of her family. But I also cannot allow this letter to divide England and Scotland more than they already are. I vote to burn the letter."

Ashton breathed a sigh of relief. His hands, which had been clenched into fists, slowly began to relax.

For a long moment no one said a word. Ashton turned to the mantle and picked up the letter. For one last moment he held the proof of Hugo's crimes in his palm. If only Hugo had known how close he'd come to ruin.

He glanced one more time at his closest friends. When no one said anything, he tossed the letter on the fire. The flames licked along the edges of the letter. The wax seal melted, pooling like drops of blood. Ashton and the others waited until the letter had turned to ash.

Cedric frowned at the sight, and Charles's lips twisted in a silent half snarl. But the vote had been made, and there would be no going back.

"It is done," Ashton said.

"But the battle is far from over." Charles joined him by the fire and used the poker to stoke the flames. Fire shot up around the ashes, dancing angrily. The rest of the League flanked him and Charles, watching the letter burn.

"Hugo," Ashton said to himself, "we are coming for you."

~

HUGO WAVERLY SAT in his study, head in his hands as he clutched a bottle of brandy. For nearly two days he had been drinking, ever since he'd heard of Lennox's marriage to Rosalind Melbourne.

At any moment, he expected his life as he knew it to be over. His past would be revealed, his career would be ruined, and he would be a marked man.

He rubbed at his eyes and put the bottle to his lips just as he heard a knock on the door.

"What is it?" He expected to hear his butler, but instead Daniel Sheffield stood there, with a slip of paper in his hands.

"An urgent letter from your man in Lonsdale's employ." He walked over without preamble and set the letter in front of Hugo.

He growled and started to lift the bottle up, uninterested in hearing what he already knew, but Sheffield stopped him.

"Read it." He tapped the letter, and it was then that Hugo realized it had been opened. Sheffield had read it.

Scowling, Hugo snatched up the letter and read it. Tom Linley stated that the Rogues had held a private meeting at Lennox House and burned a single letter after taking a vote. The vote had passed three to two, calling for the letter to be destroyed for the sake of England's relations with Scotland and for freeing Rosalind's family from the cloud of its treasonous past.

It took a moment for the truth to fully settle in his mind.

He wasn't going to be exposed. He was safe.

He held no illusions as to the reasons why. They had done this for sentimental reasons, nothing more. And that would be their undoing. He picked up the letter from Linley and turned to toss it into the fire behind his desk.

"We are so close, Peter. So very close," he said absently as he let himself drift into the past, to a much darker time when he had lost his friend forever, and a time beyond that, when he had lost even more.

"I will find justice." He carved the vow upon his heart and watched the parchment blacken to ash. "Both for you...and my father."

Thanks for reading *Wicked Rivals*. I hope you enjoyed it! Check out this fun art by Joanne Renaud of Ashton and Rosalind for Christmas!

Want three free romance novels? Fill out the form at the bottom of this link and you'll get an email from me with details to collect your free read! The free books are Wicked Designs (Historical romance), Legally Charming (contemporary romance) and The Bite of Winter (paranormal romance)

CLAIM your free books now at: http://laurensmithbooks.com/free-books-and-newsletter/, follow me on twitter at @LSmithAuthor, or like my Facebook page at https://www.facebook.com/LaurenDianaSmith. I share upcoming book news, snippets and cover reveals plus PRIZES!

REVIEWS HELP other readers find books. I appreciate all reviews, whether positive or negative. If one of my books spoke to you, please share!

YOU'VE JUST READ the 4th book in the League of Rogues series. The other books in the series are *Wicked Designs, His Wicked Seduction, Her Wicked Proposal,* and *Her Wicked Longing.* I hope you enjoy them all! There are more League adventures on the way!

Read the first chapter of *Her Wicked Longing* now by turning the page!

THE
LEAGUE OF
ROGUES

TWO NEW SHORT STORIES

Her Wicked

Longing

LAUREN SMITH

CHAPTER 1

*G*illian Beaumont knew the day was bound to be full of trouble. As she worked to tame the curls of her mistress's hair, she fretted over the wicked gleam in Audrey Sheridan's eyes. Gillian was used to this mischievous glint, but today it seemed doubly intense, and the way her lips curled at the ends in a little smile added to Gillian's worry even more. The last time she had looked that way, Audrey had been chasing a rogue around a sofa, demanding to be kissed.

"There you are, my lady." Gillian finished putting the last pin in her mistress's hair.

Audrey's brown eyes twinkled as she met Gillian's gaze in the mirror. "Perfect. I have to look my best today. The League is coming over for tea in an hour and…" A delicate blush bloomed in her cheeks.

"And Mr. St. Laurent will be there?"

"Er… I suppose so," Audrey replied vaguely.

Gillian was all too aware of how her mistress felt about that particular gentleman. He was a fine man with green eyes and sun-kissed blond hair. Gillian supposed he was attractive, but he never made her feel the way she'd heard women ought to feel around a man they fancied.

Gillian glanced at her own face in the mirror as she tidied up the vanity. Perhaps she was different from other ladies. She placed the ivory-handled brushes next to a set of exquisite tortoiseshell combs. Unlike Audrey's dark chestnut hair, Gillian's hair was an unremarkable brown and her eyes a soft heather gray. She'd never stood out as a beauty, but she wasn't unattractive, either. She was, in short, the perfect sort of plain woman who worked best as a lady's maid or a companion.

As the bastard daughter of an earl, Gillian had been taught not to expect much of her circumstances, though her father had provided enough for her and her mother. They had lived comfortable if unassuming lives in a little townhouse near Mayfair. When she was fifteen, her father died and she'd been forced into service to support her ailing mother. She'd had no real experience as a companion, but she'd heard from a friend of her mother's that Viscount Sheridan was searching for a lady's maid for his youngest sister, someone close to her in age.

It was unusual to have a lady's maid so young, but Audrey had insisted her maid be close in age. And that was how Gillian, almost sixteen by then, had become Audrey's maid and loyal, protective shadow. A year later, Gillian's mother had passed away.

Now Mama is gone, and I'm all alone.

She frowned. That wasn't true. In many ways, being lady's maid to Audrey was a bit like being Audrey's friend. They shared secrets and went on far too many adventures for Gillian to feel comfortable about. There was a familiarity between them that certainly wasn't normal for a maid and a lady. Audrey had a large heart and a spirit that could not be caged.

"Gillian, could you run a few errands for me today? I believe we have a few articles to post in the *Quizzing Glass Gazette* that will need to run in the next few weeks. Would you mind seeing to that for me?" Audrey was plucking at the waist of her blue cambric muslin gown, where it was fitted perfectly to her trim waist. The dress had ornamented designs on the bodice. Her dress's style and its high waist made Audrey's tiny body look longer. The full skirt was trimmed with lavender gauze that made it look light and almost feathery at the hem.

Audrey had exquisite taste, something she'd insisted her maid cultivate as well. Gillian wore a lavender muslin gown with more flair than a usual lady's maid would wear. It was close in style to the gowns she'd worn when her father was alive.

"Well? Do you mind very much?" Audrey's voice pulled Gillian out of her thoughts.

"Of course, my apologies, my lady. I was woolgathering. Yes, leave me the articles, and I will see them placed in the proper hands."

"Excellent." Audrey walked over to her escritoire and withdrew three carefully packed articles and handed them to Gillian.

"Do you need anything else, my lady?" Gillian asked.

"Not at the moment. Oh, and remember, tonight we will be going to that hellfire club."

Gillian froze midstep, her spine stiffening. The hellfire club, how had she forgotten?

"My lady, I really don't think we should—"

Audrey tapped a dainty foot and crossed her arms over her chest. "Gillian, you know that awful Gerald Langley belongs to that club. What was it called?" Audrey tilted her head, looking up as she seemed to search her memory. "Sinners and Sadists, no... Wait!" She lifted a finger in the air. "The Unholy Sinners of Hell."

Gillian flinched. "Must we go tonight? The men could be dangerous." It wasn't as though their lives were free of gossip and trouble, what with Audrey's elder brother, Cedric, being a member of the infamous League of Rogues. Cedric and his friends had been in life-threatening situations more than once and caused scandals at least every other week. The last thing Audrey needed was to run off and find more trouble—at least that was Gillian's opinion.

"Nonsense. We should be perfectly fine. They allow ladies to attend their unholy festivities, and if we bring along Charles and his valet as escorts, we shall be quite safe."

"Lord Lonsdale? He's not exactly a man of sterling reputation. You remember the swans. Everyone was so scandalized."

Audrey giggled. "Of course I do. I was there. Charles isn't so bad. I had a bloody hard time trying to kiss him, you remember. He's more of a gentleman than he lets on."

With a little hum that wasn't exactly agreement, Gillian headed for the door, but Audrey stopped her.

"The dresses! I completely forgot. You must go to Madame Ella's and retrieve the gowns. Try them on to make sure they fit," Audrey said.

Gillian sighed and nodded. It wasn't the first time she had been asked to try on one of Audrey's gowns. They were almost identical in stature, both short and full-figured. She suspected her mistress was trying to give her a little thrill of pleasure, but Gillian feared longing for things she could never have.

From the moment she'd grown old enough to understand her place as an illegitimate child to a member of the peerage, she'd stopped oohing over the prettiest gowns and had given up dreams of finding a nice gentleman to marry. The acceptance of her fate as a domestic servant had been wearying, and while she adored working for Audrey, even when they were knee-deep in trouble, it didn't stop her from wishing for a quiet life in a little cottage somewhere.

"Thank you." Audrey gently shoved her into the hall, and Gillian headed down the stairs to find her bonnet and coin purse. By the time she finished her errands, the League of Rogues and their wives would have arrived for tea, and Audrey would have little chance of getting into trouble.

Gillian smiled at Sean Hartley, the handsome young Irish footman, as he handed her a small coin purse.

"And what errands does our lady have you running today?" Sean asked, his Irish lilt and fine looks a temptation to all the upstairs maids in the Sheridan residence.

"I'm to collect a few dresses and a few items need to be posted. Could you have the carriage brought around for me?"

Sean grinned. "More dresses. One would think she has enough," he teased and winked at Gillian.

Gillian smiled back. "One would think." She liked Sean. He was like an older brother, playful and kind.

He left her alone in the hall as he summoned a coach. She clutched her purse and the *Gazette* articles to her chest, making sure she wouldn't drop either by accident. No one was around to see, which was good because Sean knew the truth of Audrey's double life. He could be trusted, but neither Audrey nor Gillian wanted to risk anyone else knowing.

It was her lady's best-kept secret. The infamous, sometimes overly critical pen of Lady Society, the anonymous social columnist for the *Quizzing Glass Gazette*, was none other than Audrey Sheridan. Gillian's mistress had written articles for years now, challenging gentlemen to fall in love and publicly exposing those in society who sought to harm others, but her favorite pastime was matchmaking for the rogues she held dear.

Her latest victory had been exposing the betting book at White's, where a man named Gerald Langley had offered five thousand pounds to have a woman publicly ruined. But Audrey wasn't finished with him yet; she had every intention of exposing Langley's involvement in the hellfire club.

And I must go along with it, or else she will get herself into real trouble. Gillian shook her head, tempted to laugh. Was she always to be the voice of reason? It was exhausting keeping her mistress out of trouble time and again. What Audrey truly needed was a man to chase after her and keep her out of harm's way while she led her life of adventures. A man like Jonathan St. Laurent. Once Audrey was married, Gillian would have an ally in her mistress's husband, and she could finally relax.

Sean returned and opened the front door of the townhouse for her.

"Don't worry—I'll keep an eye on her," Sean promised.

"Thank you." Gillian meant it. She worried, as did all the servants, that Audrey would get into a scrape she could not get out of if they did not look after her. Gillian climbed into the coach, settled back, and closed her eyes briefly. She would be facing a long night ahead if they were to infiltrate the hellfire club after midnight.

By the time she reached Madame Ella's modiste shop, she had rested and successfully dropped off the Lady Society articles to their publisher. She felt refreshed and ready to deal with the dress fittings for Audrey. Knowing her lady, it could take a while if the gowns were elaborate, and they were always elaborate.

She had the driver wait for her while she entered the shop. A matronly woman with silver-gray hair was kneeling by a young woman who was wearing a rose-silk gown. The young woman seemed to be around Audrey and Gillian's age of nineteen. She had light-brown hair, professionally styled, and smiled pleasantly at Gillian, assuming by her clothes that she was likely a young woman in a similar social circle.

Madame Ella glanced up and smiled. "Miss Beaumont! What a treat. I have the dresses, but you will need to try them both to be sure." The dressmaker knew Gillian would try on gowns when Audrey could not come herself.

"Of course." Gillian crossed the shop and set her things down in a small curtained area, then took the two gowns from Madame Ella. She quickly removed her own walking dress and tried on her simply tailored evening gown first. It had buttons up the front and was easily examined in the narrow mirror of the small fitting area. But Audrey's evening gown required assistance to be laced up in the back.

"Madame Ella?" she called out. "I need assistance with the laces."

The curtain moved, and she turned halfway, glanced over her shoulder, and gasped. A handsome man with dark hair and soft brown eyes was staring at her, his lips parted. He held a pair of fawn gloves in his hands but didn't move. Her partially unlaced back was exposed to his view. His eyes traced the length of her bared spine, and she could almost feel his gaze, like invisible fingers tiptoeing down her skin.

It made her feel dizzy to know he was seeing her like this, exposed and vulnerable in such a sensual way. His lips curved, just showing a hint of what he must be thinking about as he swept her again from head to toe. Gazing into his brown eyes, she felt like she was falling into an abyss of dark, erotic thoughts. A small voice in the back of her mind warned her she was in dangerous territory. If she'd been a lady like Audrey, she could have been compromised by this.

"My apologies." The man recovered and averted his gaze, his cheeks turning a ruddy red. Gillian's face flushed as well. Yet she still couldn't find her voice to speak. When she stared up at the tall, dark-haired stranger, she simply couldn't *think*. Her heart fluttered wildly, and her stays were suddenly too tight.

"James?" A feminine voice called out. "Where are you? I would like to see if the gloves match this gown."

James, her handsome stranger, half smiled at her and then slowly lowered the hand holding up the curtain. Right before his face vanished from view, his eyes locked on hers, and with a cocky grin he whispered, "Never be ashamed to show such lovely skin."

The curtain fell back into place, and it was as though Gillian could suddenly breathe again. She clutched her arms to her chest, her breasts heaving. She tried to calm down. Who was he? Why had hadn't he dropped the curtain at once? Surely he knew how scandalous he'd been.

"Miss Beaumont? Are you ready for me to help with the lacing of the gown?" Madame Ella called outside of the curtain.

"Yes, please come in," she replied, her tone breathless. The dressmaker came inside and made quick work of the laces.

"Well, how does it fit?" Madame Ella asked. Gillian hastily studied the gown and nodded at the dressmaker.

"This will do. Thank you, Madame Ella." She tried desperately to collect her thoughts. Would she see him in the shop again? If he had been assisting a woman buying gloves, they were likely already gone, since she had taken her time finishing trying on Audrey's gown. She hoped he was gone so she wouldn't have to face him, yet she also didn't want him to be gone. The two feelings pulled her in opposite directions. She redressed in her lavender gown and left the dressing room. Her slipper caught on the carpet, and she stumbled.

"Oh!" Gillian gasped, bracing herself for a fall, but instead she fell right into a hard masculine chest. Gentle hands curled around her waist, holding her. The man grasped her more firmly and she was lifted slightly up and into his arms, so that she pressed fully against him. The enticing scent of sandalwood and pine filled her nose, and she raised her head to stare up at the man.

Him.

The handsome mystery man named James. His brown eyes were warm and bright. Her stomach gave a fluttery flip.

"My apologies again." James chuckled and hesitated a moment before he released her waist.

"James? What are you doing?" It was the pretty brunette woman Gillian had seen when she first entered the shop.

"Letty." James greeted her warmly and stepped away from Gillian, but only enough to allow the other woman to come closer to them both.

"Hello." Letty smiled at Gillian. "Don't tell me my older brother was bothering you? He swore to be on his best behavior today. Not that I believed him for a minute. He's a bit of a rogue, you see. Trouble follows him about." Letty's eyes were the same enchanting brown as her brother's. Gillian hated to admit she was relieved they were siblings and not…

It shouldn't matter, but it does.

"No, he's fine. I mean, he was behaving…" A fresh wave of heat and embarrassment swept through her. She usually didn't speak to ladies, not like this.

"I seem to be disrupting the day of Miss…" James looked expectantly to Gillian, clearly hoping she would give him her name. It wasn't proper, this sort of introduction, but at this point *nothing* between them had been proper.

"Beaumont. Gillian Beaumont." The late Earl of Rutherford

had been Richard Beaumont, but though she bore her father's surname, one would not make the connection or guess that she had been born on the wrong side of the blanket. There were plenty of Beaumonts in London who had no relation to the Rutherford title.

"It is a pleasure to meet you, Miss Beaumont. I'm Leticia Fordyce, and this is my brother James, Lord Pembroke."

Gillian nearly swallowed her tongue. *The Earl of Pembroke.* She'd heard the whispers of Audrey's friends over tea, speaking of this man with a wicked smile and gentle brown eyes. He was a mixture of roguish fantasy and perfect gentleman. An enigma the ladies of the *ton* couldn't puzzle out. And yet no one had won his heart. He was just the sort of man she would have longed to dance with at a ball, a man she might have had a chance with if her mother had been married to the Earl of Rutherford and not a mistress. But that life would never be hers, and she had to stop thinking about what might have been.

Gillian struggled to think. "It's lovely to meet you both," she managed finally.

What would Audrey Sheridan do? Gillian knew exactly what Audrey would do, and it was not what she would do.

"So, my brother is disrupting your day?" Letty grinned, a little impish smile curling her cupid's bow mouth as she glanced between them.

James stared down at his boots before he glanced up at Gillian, a sheepish grin drawing her focus to his lips. The man had such kissable-looking lips. She jolted. She rarely allowed herself to think of men like that. Her life had always been focused on work and keeping busy. Surviving in London meant abandoning thoughts of marriage. No man would take a penniless illegitimate woman to wife, at least no one above her station.

"I believe Lord Pembroke was looking for you, and I stumbled into him," Gillian replied, trying not to let her nerves show. She wasn't accustomed to speaking directly with members of the peerage.

"Ah." Letty giggled. "We are finished with Madame Ella. Are you as well? I thought we might go to Gunter's for some ices. Would you care to join us?"

Letty's expression was so full of hope that Gillian's heart twinged with guilt. She had to say no. She couldn't go to Gunter's, not with the earl and his sister. It simply wasn't done. They had mistaken her for a gentle-born lady like Audrey.

She struggled for an excuse. "I regret I must go to a bookshop and pick up a few novels."

"Oh…" Letty's face fell, but James's brown eyes gleamed as he stared at Gillian.

"We are in need of novels too, aren't we, Letty? We shall accompany you, and once we have satisfied our literary thirst, we can quench our physical thirst at Gunter's with tea and ices." The earl declared his plan with such determination that Gillian could not see how she could refuse him.

"I suppose that would be fine…" Living a small lie for a few hours couldn't hurt, could it?

"Wonderful! Did you bring a coach, Miss Beaumont? We have one and would be delighted to take you home after Gunter's if you wish to spare your driver the time," Letty offered.

"Oh no, that's all right. I will have him go to Gunter's and wait for me," Gillian said. If they were to drop her off at the Sheridan townhouse on Curzon Street, it would not take him long to figure out who she really was. She couldn't bring herself to face them should they discover her deception. If she could keep up the pretense for a short while, all would be well.

I should not be doing this…but Audrey doesn't need me this afternoon, and it will be nice to pretend for a few hours. This might have been my life under different circumstances. It was quite selfish to say yes to this madness, she knew, but she was fascinated by James and liked

s sister. Surely one visit to a bookshop and Gunter's wouldn't
o her any harm. Surely...

GRAB GILLIAN **and James's story now HERE!**
To see what other steamy books I've written, turn the page!

OTHER TITLES BY LAUREN SMITH

Contemporary
The Surrender Series
The Gilded Cuff
The Gilded Cage
The Gilded Chain
Her British Stepbrother
Forbidden: Her British Stepbrother
Seduction: Her British Stepbrother
Climax: Her British Stepbrother

Paranormal
Dark Seductions Series
The Shadows of Stormclyffe Hall
The Love Bites Series
The Bite of Winter
Brotherhood of the Blood Moon Series
Blood Moon on the Rise (coming soon)
Brothers of Ash and Fire
Grigori: A Royal Dragon Romance
Mikhail: A Royal Dragon Romance (coming soon)
Rurik: A Royal Dragon Romance (coming soon)

Sci-Fi Romance
Cyborg Genesis Series
Across the Stars (coming soon)

Lauren
SMITH
TIMELESS ROMANCE

ABOUT THE AUTHOR

Lauren Smith is an Oklahoma attorney by day, author by night who pens adventurous and edgy romance stories by the light of her smart phone flashlight app. She knew she was destined to be a romance writer when she attempted to re-write the entire *Titanic* movie just to save Jack from drowning. Connecting with readers by writing emotionally moving, realistic and sexy romances no matter what time period is her passion. She's won multiple awards in several romance subgenres including: New England Reader's Choice Awards, Greater Detroit BookSeller's Best Awards, and a Semi-Finalist award for the Mary Wollstonecraft Shelley Award.

To connect with Lauren, visit her at:
www.laurensmithbooks.com
lauren@Laurensmithbooks.com

ABOUT THE ILLUSTRATOR

*J*oanne Renaud, who earned a BFA in illustration from Art Center College of Design, has been writing, drawing and painting as long as she can remember. She went to college in a variety of places, including Northern Ireland and Southern California, and enjoys history, comics, children's books, and cheesy fantasy movies from the '80s. She currently works as both an author and a freelance illustrator in the Los Angeles area. Her novel "Doors" was released from Champagne Books in 2016, and her illustration clients include Simon & Schuster, Random House, Houghton Mifflin, Macmillan-McGraw Hill, Harcourt Inc., Scholastic, and Compass Media.

WEBSITE: http://www.joannerenaud.com/
DeviantArt: http://suburbanbeatnik.deviantart.com/
Tumblr: http://suburbanbeatnik.tumblr.com/
Facebook: http://www.facebook.com/joanne.renaud.7
Twitter: http://twitter.com/suburbanbeatnik

Made in the USA
Monee, IL
18 June 2022